Also by Alafair Burke

Judgment Calls

MISSING JUSTICE

MISSING
JUSTICE

A SAMANTHA KINCAID MYSTERY

ALAFAIR BURKE

HENRY HOLT AND COMPANY ▪ NEW YORK

Henry Holt and Company, LLC
Publishers since 1866
115 West 18th Street
New York, New York 10011

Henry Holt® is a registered trademark of
Henry Holt and Company, LLC.

Library of Congress Cataloging-in-Publication Data
Burke, Alafair.
  Missing justice : a Samantha Kincaid mystery / Alafair Burke.—1st ed.
    p.   cm.
  ISBN 0-8050-7392-2
  1. Public prosecutors—Fiction.   2. Women judges—Crimes against—
Fiction.   3. Missing persons—Fiction.   4. Women lawyers—Fiction.
5. Portland (Or.)—Fiction.   I. Title.
PS3602.U755M57   2004
813'.6—dc22   2003067767

Henry Holt books are available for special promotions
and premiums. For details contact: Director, Special Markets.

First Edition 2004

Designed by Victoria Hartman

Printed in the United States of America
10 9 8 7 6 5 4 3 2 1

For Jim, Andree, and Pamala

MISSING JUSTICE

1

IF IT'S TRUE that dreams come from the id, then my id is not particularly creative.

The dream that makes its way into my bed tonight is the same one that has troubled my sleep almost every night for the past month. Once again, I relive the events that led to the deaths of three men.

The walls of the stairway pass as a man follows me upstairs. I force myself to focus on my own movements, trying to block out thoughts of the other man downstairs, armed and determined to kill me when I return.

Time slows as I duck beside my bed, reach for the pistol hidden in my nightstand, and rise up to surprise him. The .25 caliber automatic breaks the silence; more shots follow downstairs. Glass shatters. Heavy footsteps thunder through the house. In the dream, I see bullets rip through flesh and muscle, the scene tinted red like blood smeared across my retinas.

I usually wake during the chaos. Tonight, though, the silence returns, and I walk past the dead bodies to my kitchen. I open the pantry door and find a woman whose face I know only from photographs and a brief introduction two years ago. She is crouched on the floor with her head between her knees. When she looks up at me and reaches for my hand, the phone rings, and I'm back in my bedroom.

It is four o'clock in the morning, and as usual I wake up chilly, having kicked my comforter deep into the crevice between my mattress and the footboard of my maple sleigh bed. I fumble for the phone on my nightstand, still ringing in the dark.

"This better be worth it," I say.

It's Detective Raymond Johnson of the Portland Police Bureau's Major Crimes Team. A member of the search team has found a woman's size-seven black Cole Haan loafer in the gutter, but Clarissa Easterbrook is still missing.

The call came only eight hours after my boss, District Attorney Duncan Griffith, had first summoned me to the Easterbrook home. It was my first call-out after a month-long hiatus and a new promotion from the Drug and Vice Division into Major Crimes. I was told it would just be some quick PR work to transition me back into the office.

So far, the transition had been rough.

When I pulled into the Easterbrook driveway that first evening, I cut the engine and sat for a few last quiet moments in my Jetta. Noticing Detective Johnson waiting for me at the front window, I took a deep breath, released the steering wheel, and climbed out of the car, grabbing my briefcase from the passenger seat as I exhaled.

I climbed a series of steep slate steps, a trek made necessary by the home's impressive hillside location. Despite the spring mist, I was able to take in the exterior. Dr. Townsend Easterbrook was clearly no slouch. I wasn't sure which was bigger, the double-door entranceway or the Expedition I'd parked next to.

Johnson opened one of the doors before I'd had a chance to use either of the square pewter knockers. I could make out voices at the back of the house; Johnson kept his own down. "Sat in that car so long, Kincaid, thought something might be wrong with your feet."

At least my first case back on the job brought some familiar faces. I had met Raymond Johnson and his partner, Jack Walker, only two months ago, when I was a mere drug and vice deputy. But given the history, however recent, I felt a bond with these guys—the gunky kind that threatens to stick around for good.

"You must not have given up all hope, Johnson. You were waiting at the door."

"I was beginning to wonder, but then you tripped something off walking up the path, and I heard a voice somewhere announcing a visitor. George fucking Jetson house. Gives me the creeps."

The Easterbrook home wasn't exactly cozy, but I'd take it. Neutral colors, steel, and low sleek furniture—the place was a twenty-first century update on 1960s kitsch.

With any luck, Clarissa Easterbrook would turn up soon, and there'd be no need to disrupt all this coolness.

Johnson caught my eye as I studied the house. "Look at you, girl. You're almost as dark as I am." He grabbed my hand and held it next to the back of his. Not even close. Johnson's beautiful skin is about as dark as it comes.

"Yeah, but you're *still* better looking."

He laughed but it was true. He also dressed better than me—more Hollywood red carpet than police precinct lineoleum. "Griffith dragged you back from Maui just for this?"

"I flew in last night. I sort of assumed I'd have Sunday to myself before I headed back in tomorrow, but the boss must have thought it would do me good to get some hand-holding practice while we wait for Easterbrook to turn up. You know, ease me out of drug cases into the new gig."

"They usually do," Johnson said. "Turn up, I mean. She probably went shopping and lost track of time or went out for a drink with the girls."

"Right, because, of course, that's all women do in their spare time: shopping and girl talk."

"This is going to take some getting used to, Kincaid, after seven years of MCT work with O'Donnell."

I didn't react to the mention of my predecessor. "Just doing my part to lead you down the path of enlightenment, Ray. Clarissa Easterbrook's an administrative law judge, not some bored housewife."

"Oh, so it's only women lawyers who excel beyond malls and gossip. Got it. Note to all detectives," he said, as if he were speaking into a dictation recorder, "the new Major Crimes Unit DA says it's still OK to diss housewives." He dropped the routine and cocked a finger at me. "Busted!"

There was no arguing it, so I laughed instead. "Who's in the back?" I asked, leaning my head toward the ongoing murmurs.

"Walker's back there with the husband and the sister. We got here about half an hour ago, and the sister showed up right after. We haven't been able to do much more than try to calm them down. We need to start working on the timeline, though. I stayed out here to wait for you. I suspect Dr. Easterbrook's still getting used to having a brother in the house."

It was unusual to have MCT involved so early in a missing persons case, but Walker and Johnson were here from the bureau's Major Crimes Team for the same reason I was: to make sure that our offices looked responsive and concerned when the missing judge showed up and to triple-check that the investigation was perfect, just in case she didn't.

"Sounds good. I'll do my part for the family and any press, but for now you guys take the lead on interviews."

"Music to my ears, Kincaid."

He began walking toward the back of the house, but I stopped him with a hand on his elbow. "I assume you're keeping things gentle for now, just in case. And absolutely no searches, not even with consent." If Clarissa Easterbrook had encountered anything criminal, everyone close to her would become a suspect, especially her husband. We couldn't do anything now that might jeopardize our investigation down the road.

"I should've known it was too good to be true. All DAs just got to have their say. It's in the blood." I could tell from his smile that he wasn't annoyed. "No worries, now."

We made our way to the kitchen, walking past a built-in rock fountain that served as a room divider. The Easterbrooks had sprung for marble countertops and stainless steel, Sub-Zero everything, but it looked like no one ever cooked here. In fact, as far as I could tell, no one even *lived* here. The only hint of disorder was in a corner of the kitchen, where the contents of a canvas book bag were spread out on the counter next to a frazzled-looking brunette. She had a cell phone to one ear and an index finger in the other.

Jack Walker greeted us. With his short sleeves, striped tie, and bald head, he had enough of the cop look going to make up for his partner. "Welcome back. You look great," he said into my ear as he shook my hand with a friendly squeeze. "Dr. Easterbrook, this is Deputy District Attorney Samantha Kincaid."

There are women who would describe Townsend Easterbrook as good-looking. His brown hair was worn just long enough and with just enough gray at the temples to suggest a lack of attention to appearance, but the Brooks Brothers clothes told another story. On the spectrum between sloppy apathetic and sloppy preppy, there was no question where this man fell.

He seemed alarmed by the introduction. At first I assumed he was nervous. I quickly realized it was something else entirely.

"Please, call me Townsend. Gosh, I apologize if I was staring. I recognized you from the news, but it took me a moment to draw the connection."

It hadn't dawned on me that, at least for the foreseeable future, former strangers would know me as the local Annie Oakley. One more daily annoyance. Terrific.

"I'm sorry to meet you under these circumstances, Dr. Easterbrook. Duncan had to be in Salem tonight, but he wanted me to assure you that our office will do everything within our power to help find your wife."

When Griffith called, he had insisted that I use his first name with the family and assure Dr. Easterbrook that he would have been here personally if he weren't locked in legislative hearings. Other missing people might disappear with little or no official response, but Dr. Easterbrook's phone call to 911 had ripped like a lightning bolt through the power echelon. The wife was sure to turn up, but this was Griffith's chance to say *I feel your pain.*

And Easterbrook clearly *was* in pain. "Thank you for coming so quickly," he said, his voice shaking. "I feel foolish now that you're all here, but we weren't sure what we should be doing. Clarissa's sister and I have been calling everyone we can possibly think of."

"That's your sister-in-law?" I asked, looking toward the woman in the corner, still clutching the phone.

"Yes. Tara. She came in from The Dalles. I called her earlier to see if she'd heard from Clarissa today. Then I called her again when I saw that our dog, Griffey, was gone, too."

Walker tapped the pocket-size notebook he held in his hand with a dainty gold pen that didn't suit him. Most likely a gift from one of his six daughters, it looked tiny between his sausage fingers. "Dr. Easterbrook was just telling me he got home from the hospital at six-thirty tonight. His wife was home when he left this morning at six."

A twelve-hour day probably wasn't unusual for the attending surgeon at Oregon Health Sciences University's teaching hospital, even on a Sunday. Looking at him now, though, it was hard to imagine him steadying a scalpel just four hours ago.

Easterbrook continued where he must have left off. "She was still in bed when I left. Sort of awake but still asleep." He was staring blankly in front of him, probably remembering how cute his wife is when she is sleepy. "She hadn't mentioned any plans, so when I got home and she wasn't here, I assumed she went out to the market. We usually have dinner in on Sundays, as long as I'm home."

"You've checked for her car," Walker said. It was more of a statement than a question.

"Right. That was the first thing I did once I was out of my scrubs: I changed clothes and walked down to the garage. When I saw the Lexus, I thought she must have walked somewhere. I tried her cell, but I kept getting her voice mail. Finally, around eight, I thought to look out back for Griffey. When I saw he was gone too, I drove around the neighborhood for what must have been an hour. I finally got so worried I called the police."

In the corner, Clarissa's sister snapped her cell phone shut and blew her bangs from her eyes. "That's it. I've called everyone," she said, looking up. "Oh, sorry. I didn't realize anyone else was here."

"From the District Attorney's office," Townsend explained. "Ms.—Kincaid, this is Clarissa's sister, Tara Carney."

It was hard to see the resemblance. My guess is they were both pushing forty, Tara perhaps a little harder, but they had been different kinds of years. Clarissa was a thin frosted blonde who favored pastel suits and high heels. Tara's dark brown pageboy framed a round face, and she looked at ease—at least physically—in her dark green sweat suit and sneakers.

She acknowledged me with a nod. "I called everyone I can think of, and no one's heard from her today. This just isn't like her."

"She's never gone out for the day without telling someone?" Walker asked.

They both shook their heads in frustration. "Nothing like this at all," Townsend said. "She often runs late at work during the week, we both do. But she wouldn't just leave the house like this on the weekend. With the dog, for hours? Something must be wrong."

We asked all the other obvious questions, but Tara and Townsend had covered the bases before dialing 911. They had knocked on doors, but the neighbors hadn't noticed anything. Clarissa hadn't left a note. They didn't even know what she was wearing, because when Townsend left that morning she was still in her pajamas.

Her purse and keys were missing along with Griffey, but Townsend doubted she was walking the dog. She always walked him in the morning, and sometimes they walked him together after dinner if they were both home. But she didn't take Griffey out alone after dark. Anyway, we were talking about ten-minute potty trips, not all-night strolls.

Walker was rising from his chair. "Finding out how she's dressed is a priority." He was shifting into action mode. "If we go through some of her things, do you think you might be able to figure out what she's wearing?"

"*You* would be the one to go through your wife's belongings," I corrected. We had to keep this by the book. "I think what Detective Walker's suggesting is that you might be able to tell what clothes are missing if you look at what's here."

"Right," Walker agreed. "And it would help to get a detailed description out as fast as possible." It would also help us determine if we were all wasting our time. Maybe Clarissa had packed a suitcase and her dog to run off voluntarily with a new man—or simply to a new life without this one.

"You either overestimate my familiarity with clothing or underestimate Clarissa's wardrobe. Tara, can you help? I doubt I can be of any use."

I suggested that we all go upstairs together while Tara looked through Clarissa's closet. Johnson offered to stay downstairs in case anyone knocked, but Easterbrook assured him that the house's "smart system" would alert us if anyone approached the door. Of course, Johnson already knew that, so I gave him a warning look over my shoulder to join me as I followed Townsend and Tara up the hammered-steel staircase. No way was he sneaking around down here while the family was upstairs, especially in a house with its own intelligence system.

The Easterbrook master suite was the size of my entire second floor, a thousand square feet of spa-style opulence. Townsend led us through a large sitting area, past the king-size bed, and around the back of a partial wall that served as the bed's headboard. I couldn't help but notice that the lip balm on the nightstand was the same brand as my own, the paperback novel one I'd read last year.

The back of the suite contained a marble-rich bathroom adjoining a dressing area roughly the size of Memphis. Townsend wasn't kidding about his wife's wardrobe.

Tara started flipping through the piles of folded clothes stacked neatly into maple cubes. The hanging items looked work-related.

After she'd gone through the top two rows, Tara blew her bangs out of her face again. "She tends to wear the same few things when she's around the house, but the ones I can remember are all here. I just don't know."

Townsend stood in the corner of the closet, seemingly distracted by a pair of Animal Cracker print pajamas that hung from a hook. Tara was unfazed by the moment's poignancy, or at least she did not let it halt her determination. She was examining rows of shoes stacked neatly on a rack built into the side of the closet. "Well, it looks like her favorite black loafers are gone. Cole Haans, I think. But I can't tell what clothes are missing; she's just got too much stuff."

She walked over to a Nordstrom shopping bag on the floor next to the dressing table. She pulled out a red sweater, set it on the table, and then reached back in and removed some loose price tags and a receipt. "These are from yesterday," she said, looking at the receipt. "Town, these are Clarissa's, right?"

She had to repeat the question before he responded. "Oh, right, she did mention something about that last night, I think."

"Can you tell anything from the tags?" Walker asked.

"No," Tara said. "Well, the brand name, but then it's just those meaningless style names and numbers."

"Did anyone go shopping with her? We could find out what she bought from them," I suggested. I knew I told Johnson I'd leave the questions to them, but I couldn't help myself.

Townsend seemed to wake up for a moment. "I believe she went with Susan, but—"

"I'm sorry." Walker interrupted, holding up his pen and pad. "What's Susan's last name?"

Tara looked disappointed. "Susan Kerr, a friend of my sister. I've already tried calling her, and all I got was the machine."

A store clerk would be able to determine from the item numbers what clothes Clarissa purchased Saturday. It wouldn't be easy to get that information at eleven o'clock on a Sunday night, but it was worth trying.

"We'll track someone down from the store," I suggested, looking toward Ray and Jack. "Can't we pull a number for someone at Nordstrom out of PPDS?" The Portland Police Data System compiled information from every city police report and was the handiest source for accessing an individual's contact information.

Within a few minutes, Walker had the home telephone number of a store manager mentioned in a recent theft case. A manager would not be involved in your average shoplifting case, but this one had been unusual. An employee at one of the local thrift stores had bilked Nordstrom out of thousands of dollars in cash by taking advantage of its famously tolerant return policy. The bureau estimated that every Nordstrom brand dress shirt donated to the thrift store during the last two years had been returned to Nordstrom stores for cash by either the employee or one of her friends.

Hopefully the manager would be sufficiently grateful to the bureau for cracking the case that he'd forgive us for calling him after ten o'clock at night. Walker made the call on his cell to leave the Easterbrooks' line open, just in case.

As it turned out, the Easterbrook phone rang just a few minutes later. I found myself watching Townsend to see how he responded. Did he really expect the caller to be Clarissa? Or did he act like a man who already knew we wouldn't be hearing from her? So far he seemed legit, if dazed. He hadn't made any of the obvious slipups, the ones you see on *Court TV*: using the past tense, buying diamonds for another woman, selling the wife's stuff, things like that.

Whoever was calling, it wasn't Clarissa. Listening to one side of the conversation was frustrating. "I see. . . . Where was he? . . . No, in fact, she's . . . missing"—Townsend's voice cracked on that one. "The police are here now. . . . Yes, that's terribly kind of you, if you don't mind." Some more earnest thank-yous and a good-bye, and Townsend set the phone back on its base.

"That was a fellow who lives a few streets down. He works with me at the hospital. He and his wife were leaving the Chart House and found a dog running in the parking lot with its leash on. It's Griffey."

Walker had reached the Nordstrom manager, who generously offered to meet him at the store to track down what Clarissa Easterbrook had purchased yesterday and was—we hoped—still wearing.

About fifteen minutes after Walker left, a voice similar to the one that announces my e-mails at home declared, "Good evening. You have a visitor." Ray was right. Creepy George Jetson house.

I looked out the living room window to see a man in his fifties struggling to keep up with an excited yellow Lab dashing up the slope to the front door, straining against the leash. A woman of roughly the same age followed.

When Easterbrook opened the door, the Lab finally pulled free from his temporary handler, dragging his leash behind him. He leaped on Easterbrook's chest, nearly knocking him over. He was a sticky mess from the drizzle, but you could tell he was a well-cared-for dog. Townsend absently convinced Griffey to lie down by the fountain, though the panting and tail thumping revealed that he was still excited to be home.

A dog like Griffey probably had an advanced degree from obedience school, unlike my dropout, Vinnie. Vinnie was actually expelled. Or, more accurately, I was. When it became clear to the teacher that, despite her instructions, I caved to Vinnie's every demand to avoid his strategic peeing episodes, she suggested that I re-enroll my French bulldog when I felt more committed to the process. Two years later, Vinnie and I have come to mutually agreeable terms. He has a doggie door to the backyard, an automatic feeder, and a rubber Gumby doll that he treats like his baby, but if I don't come home in time to cuddle him and hear about his day, there's hell to pay. Griffey, on the other hand, appeared to do whatever Easterbrook told him.

Easterbrook introduced Griffey's new friends as Dr. and Mrs. Jonathon Fletcher. I guess you have to give up both your first and last names when you marry a physician. Dr. Fletcher's looks said *doctor* more than Townsend Easterbrook's. In contrast with the flashy Expedition and high-tech house, I noticed that the Fletchers pulled up in a Volvo station wagon.

Mrs. Dr. Fletcher did her best to provide comfort. "I'm certain Clarissa's just fine, Townsend. A misunderstanding, is all. We just have to find her, and that's that. Now, when's the last time you saw her?"

She made it sound like we were trying to track down a lost set of keys.

"This morning," Townsend said. "She was still in bed. I had back-to-back surgeries, and when I got home she was gone."

"Well, dear, I'm surprised you even get a chance to operate anymore. Jonathon tells me how busy you are, developing the new transplant unit. Sounds like that's going extremely well."

Apparently Mrs. Dr. Fletcher was so used to her job as conversationalist to her husband's colleagues that she was slipping into autopilot. Understandably, Townsend cut her off.

"Who knows? Still so much to do," he said. Translation: Who the fuck cares about the hospital right now? "I didn't even realize Griffey was gone until a couple of hours ago. When did you find him?"

"Right around ten," Dr. Fletcher said. "A group of us were leaving our function at the Chart House, and this feisty fellow was running around in the parking lot. Initially, everyone assumed he escaped from one of the neighborhood yards or something. But then someone noticed he was dragging a leash. Our friend went after him, figuring someone had lost hold of him. When he checked the tag, what do you know? Our own Griffey Easterbrook."

The Chart House sat just a couple of steep miles down from the Easterbrook home. The elegant restaurant was located on the winding, wooded section of Taylor's Ferry Road that ran from the modest Burlingame neighborhood in southwest Portland, up about two miles to OHSU, and then back down again into downtown Portland. Spectacular views of the city made the route one of the most popular spots in the area for walks, runs, and bike rides.

It was not, however, the safest place for a woman alone at night. About a year earlier, two guys from the DA's office were taking a run there after work. They heard what they thought was a couple goofing around behind the bushes, a man wrestling his squealing girlfriend to the grass. Fortunately, the woman heard them talking as they ran past and yelled, "Help, I don't know him."

The bad guy got away, but the ensuing publicity had called the city's attention to the potential dangers of the area. It was no longer common to find women alone on the path after dark.

The Fletchers' discovery of Griffey there was not a good sign.

Johnson must've been thinking the same thing, because he decided to revisit what I thought had been our mutual decision not to search the Easterbrook/Jetson home. He pulled me aside while Townsend continued the conversation with the Fletchers.

"I know we're playing it safe, but finding the dog changes the picture. We need to go through the place now while he's still playing victim. If we wait until a body shows, he might lawyer up."

I shook my head. "I still don't like it," I said. "Look at him—he's a basket case. Later on, his state of mind might kill any consent we get from him. If, God forbid, her body does surface, we can easily get a warrant, since this is her house. We won't need to have probable cause against the husband."

"And what do we do about the fact that our doctor can move whatever he wants and start dumping evidence the minute we're out of here?"

Johnson's point was well taken, but it wasn't enough to justify a thorough search this early in the case. Not only could Townsend try to throw out the search down the road, we'd pretty much be killing any chance we had of continued cooperation from him. In any event, if Townsend was involved in his wife's disappearance, he certainly could have disposed of any incriminating evidence before calling the police.

I explained my thinking to Johnson and proposed a compromise. "Why don't you offer to take a look around to make sure there's no sign of a break-in? I don't have a problem with you doing a general walk-through; I just don't want a detailed search yet. If you check for broken windows and the like, we can at least look for the obvious and avoid any major fuckups."

"Okay with you if I ask him about it in front of his buddies?"

I gave a quick nod. If Townsend felt pressured to consent to a search because his friends were around, so be it. Courts only care about claims of involuntariness if the supposed coercion comes from law enforcement.

Before Johnson walked away, I added, "We should also get people searching up on Taylor's Ferry. Hopefully, by the time the department has a search plan together, Walker can tell us what she might have been wearing."

Griffey perked up when Tara came down the stairs, apparently satisfied that nothing helpful was going to come from foraging through her sister's closet. I'd already been positively disposed toward her based on her obvious concern for her sister, and I warmed to her even more when she found the energy to get down on the floor with her sister's dog and comfort him with a bear hug.

After a few minutes spent on introductions to the Fletchers and the inevitable words of comfort, Tara grew antsy again. "Griffey, up," she commanded, pointing him toward the stairs. "Sorry, I can't sit still. You mind if I throw him into the tub real quick, Town? He's a little crunchy, and it'll give me something to do."

It was clear that Tara's nervous energy was grating on her brother-in-law; he seemed more at ease once she'd followed Griffey to the second floor and he could turn his attention back to the Fletchers.

"I keep expecting the phone to ring, but I'm not sure exactly what kind of call it would be; maybe a ransom demand or something. Obviously, I want it to be Clarissa explaining that this is all a misunderstanding, that she went with a friend somewhere and forgot to leave a note, and Griffey just happened to get out . . ." He was just rambling. I didn't point out that the leash suggested Griffey had not simply escaped from the yard, but that someone had been walking him. Townsend would come to the realization in his own time.

I was beginning to think that a ransom demand would be good news at this point. At least it might indicate that Clarissa was alive.

"This lifestyle of ours," Townsend said, looking around. "Why does any of it really matter? Maybe it just invites problems."

Johnson used the moment as his in to ask permission for the walk-through. Consistent with everything else about the man, his transition was smooth.

He started by asking Dr. Easterbrook if he'd ever noticed

anything that might suggest that someone was scoping out the house or following them, perhaps planning a way to get to Clarissa by herself.

"No, nothing at all like that," Easterbrook replied. "This neighborhood is so isolated up here. We hardly see anyone on our street who doesn't live here."

"Can you think of anyone who has a conflict with you of some kind? Someone who might be motivated to do something to scare you or retaliate against you?"

"Why would someone hurt Clarissa to get to *me*, detective?"

"Just exploring all possibilities, doctor. Maybe a disgruntled patient from the hospital? A former employee?"

"No," Townsend said, slowly shaking his head. "Clarissa would occasionally get some threats about her cases, but she always assumed they were only blowing off steam. Never anything we considered seriously. No one would want to hurt her. She's such a good person."

"I was just exploring all the possibilities," Johnson repeated. "Come to think of it, we should probably take a look around and make sure there's no signs of a break-in, just in case. Do you mind?"

"Of course not, but I'm sure I would have noticed something earlier. Given the security system, I don't see how anyone could have gotten in."

"As long as you don't mind, I'll go ahead and check it out. No harm, right?"

Johnson sidled off before anyone might want to stop him, and the Fletchers seized the opportunity to extricate themselves from a situation where they knew they couldn't be of much help. As they launched into their goodbyes, feeding Townsend more premature assurances that everything would be okay, I caught up with Ray. Truth was, I didn't want to be alone with Townsend, struggling like the Fletchers to avoid all those lame clichés—this will all work out, only a silly misunderstanding, and other completely useless pronouncements suggesting the speaker had any clue as to how the night would end.

We hit the basement first. My basement is a dark, damp, dusty wreck of concrete and cinder block that my imagination has populated with thousands of spiders and their cobwebs. The Easterbrooks' had been finished into a laundry room and a home gym that had better equipment than my health club. Not only did we not find any bodies, blood, or guts, there weren't even any windows to check. In place of the flimsy things that are so often kicked in for basement break-ins, the Easterbrooks had glass bricks.

Climbing back up the stairs, we could hear Townsend letting the Fletchers out the front door, so we headed up to the second floor, where Tara had Griffey in a bathroom off the main hallway. She was fighting to get a dog brush through the hair on his hind leg. Predictably, Griffey stood compliantly while Tara tried to avoid pulling his entire coat off by the roots.

She looked up at us from the tile floor, removing her hand from the brush to push her bangs from her forehead. The brush stayed entangled in poor Griffey's coat. "I was just wondering whether I should show this to you. I thought he felt a little crusty downstairs when I was petting him, but it looks like he's actually got something dried on his coat back here."

Johnson knelt down and looked more closely at the side of Griffey's hip. Then he reached into an interior pocket of his suit jacket, removed a latex glove, and slipped it over his right hand.

"Do you mind giving us a second, Ms. Carney?"

Tara seemed surprised by the request but left the bathroom, closing the door behind her.

"Looks like clay or something," Johnson explained, "like he brushed up against it here on his side."

"Shit. We should have gotten the crime lab over here imme-diately when the Fletchers called."

I was beginning to panic. Why the hell hadn't Johnson been on top of this? "Wasn't obvious," he said, responding to the unspoken question. "Until you're certain what you're dealing with, it's hard to decide what kind of resources to put into it. Considering the small chance of any evidence off the dog, plus the likelihood that we're dealing with a runaway wife, and it's a tough call."

It made sense, but it didn't excuse the fact that we nearly allowed Tara Carney to take the source of what might be our best piece of evidence so far and soak him in a bathtub.

Johnson flaked some of the beige paste from Griffey's coat into an evidence bag, then marked it with his name and the date using a Sharpie pen.

Shit. What else had we missed? "I think we should go ahead and get the crime lab out here and search around Taylor's Ferry. Everything about this feels bad."

"Your call," he said, pulling out his cell phone.

This new gig was going to take some getting used to.

2

By 7 A.M. the next morning, I was watching my first Major Crimes Unit case unfold on television. Nothing like an attractive, professional, missing white woman to satisfy the hunger of the viewing masses.

I sat in the eighth-floor conference room of the Multnomah County District Attorney's Office, location of the office's only TV set, flipping channels in a futile attempt to track the coverage. Out of principle, I boycotted the Fox affiliate for running the tagline CASE OF A REAL-LIFE CINDERELLA? in a graphic beneath the talking head. I finally gave up and settled on the local morning show, which seemed to be covering the story in the most detail.

Cut to some guy named Jake Spottiswoode, so-called field correspondent, also known as the kid right out of college who gets sent with his Columbia Gore-Tex jacket into the rain.

"Good morning, Gloria. Behind me in southwest Portland is the home of Dr. Townsend Easterbrook and his missing wife,

Administrative Law Judge Clarissa Easterbrook. Dr. Easterbrook reported the mysterious disappearance yesterday evening, shortly after returning from a day of surgery at OHSU.

"Residents of this quiet neighborhood are fearing the worst," Gore-Tex continued, "since learning that one of Judge Easterbrook's shoes was discovered in the street on Taylor's Ferry Road last night. That discovery was particularly ominous given that the shoe was found only half a mile from where her dog was found earlier in the night, alone but still on his leash. The community is helping police in the search effort and say they still hold out hope that Judge Easterbrook will be found safe and unharmed. We've been told that the family will be coming outside any minute to make a statement."

"Jake, what can you tell us about what Clarissa Easterbrook might have been doing before she disappeared? Was she walking the dog?" Watching Gloria Flick lean forward and dramatically furrow her brow, I remembered why I never watch this show. Gloria Flick was annoying as hell.

While Flick continued to feign concern, Gore-Tex explained that the police had refused to rule out any possibilities. Although this was formally a missing persons case, they were moving forward on the assumption that foul play might be involved. Trying to fill air time before the press conference, the rain-soaked rookie correspondent touched upon Clarissa's position with the city. "We're hearing, Gloria, that Clarissa Easterbrook, as an administrative law judge, is not the kind of judge that many of us would envision, in a courthouse, presiding over trials. Rather, she hears appeals from the administrative decisions of city agencies. Because many of those matters are considered routine and, in fact, somewhat bureaucratic, police are discouraging the media from speculating that Judge Easterbrook's disappearance could be related to her official position."

The viewing public was spared any further attempt to explain the boring work of an administrative law judge when Clarissa Easterbrook's family assumed its place behind a podium that had been set up in the Easterbrook driveway.

Joining Tara and Townsend were an older couple I imagined were Clarissa's parents, along with a woman I didn't recognize. Townsend tentatively approached the mike. Make that about ten mikes. Unlike Tara, he had changed clothes, but the bags under his eyes were every bit as pronounced.

As the attending surgeon at the state's teaching hospital, Townsend was probably used to speaking to a crowd. But today he seemed focused on merely making it through the notes he carried to the podium. His voice lacked affect, and he didn't look up once from his reading:

"My wife, Clarissa Easterbrook, has not been seen since six o'clock yesterday morning. She disappeared somewhere between then and last night at approximately six-thirty P.M., when I returned home. We believe she was wearing a pink silk turtleneck sweater, charcoal-gray pants, and black loafers, one of which was found on Taylor's Ferry Drive early this morning. Our dog was discovered last night in the same area, near the Chart House restaurant. We are asking anyone who may have seen her, or seen anything in that vicinity that might be related to her disappearance, to please call the police immediately. Clarissa, we love you and we miss you, and we want you to come home to us safe.

"Behind me are Clarissa's sister, Tara Carney; her parents, Mel and Alice Carney; and her dearest friend, Susan Kerr. On behalf of all of us, I'd like to thank everyone who is helping in this search effort. Members of the Portland Police Bureau and the Multnomah County District Attorney's Office were here late last night, and the media have been great about getting Clarissa's picture out there and asking for information. We're very grateful for all the support and concern that has been shown for Clarissa and our family. Thank you again."

Whoever wrote the script was savvy enough to know how to play the game of political institutions. Appear supportive of the police department and the DA's office early on, and you'll have all the more leverage down the road if you threaten to turn. Reporters were shouting out questions now, but there wasn't much for Townsend to add. Yes, it was certainly possible that something might have happened to her while she was walking the dog, but the police were not ruling out other possibilities. No, there hadn't been any ransom demands or other communications about the disappearance.

Once the family retreated into the house, the station ran more pictures of Clarissa and repeated the description of her clothing. Nordstrom had come through. From the montage of photographs—at a picnic with Townsend, at Cannon Beach with Griffey, on the lap of a shopping-mall Santa Claus with Tara—I began to feel I knew this woman. She was aging gracefully, keeping her hair blond but neatly bobbed, allowing the wrinkles to show beneath a light dusting of makeup. And in every picture she had the same big, generous smile that had greeted me the one time I had met her at a women's bar conference a couple of years ago. I couldn't bear to watch.

As I was clicking the TV off, Russell Frist stuck his perfectly salt-and-peppered head into the conference room. "Welcome back, Kincaid, and welcome to the Unit. The boss tells me you're in the thick of things already."

The District Attorney must have called Frist first thing this morning. Recently appointed supervisor of the Major Crimes Unit, my new boss had a reputation for screaming at other lawyers and making them cry, but also for being a good prosecutor. I had vowed to keep an open mind about him, but sitting there beneath his gaze, I found myself intimidated. At six foot three and a good two-twenty, Frist put in enough time at the gym to test the seams of his well-cut suit.

It wasn't surprising that Frist referred to the trial unit that prosecuted all person felonies as "the Unit." He'd been handling major crimes for at least fifteen years, so other kinds of cases had no doubt stopped mattering to him long ago.

"Looks like it," I said. "When he sent me out to the Easterbrooks' last night for some hand-holding, I don't think either one of us thought it was going to turn into something like this, literally overnight."

"Well, we should talk. Give me about fifteen minutes, then meet in my office?"

Fifteen minutes wasn't enough time to get any actual work done, so I continued making my way through the pile of mail that had accumulated over the past month. As unpampered county employees, we usually have to take care of our own office moves when we change rotations, but someone had been nice enough to relocate my things from my old office down the hall at the Drug and Vice Division to what used to be Frist's office in major crimes.

Everything, that was, except for my black leather, high-backed swivel chair. A good office chair is nearly impossible to come by when you work for the government. Most of the chairs around here had ceased being adjustable years ago and had funky-smelling upholstery fit for the county's HAZMAT team. About a year ago, I had spent four full months sucking up to the facilities manager, begging for a decent chair. The campaign was not my proudest moment; let's just say it involved me, a lunchtime knitting class, and a decade's supply of ugly booties for the woman's baby.

Now someone had taken my vacation as an opportunity to run off with the spoils of my labor. The culprit clearly lacked two essential pieces of information. First, I would stop at absolutely nothing to get that chair back. And second, I'd have no problem proving ownership. The day I got—no, make that *earned*—my chair, I committed vandalism against county property by scratching my initials in a secret spot and vowing we'd be together forever.

But for now, I was stuck with a sorry-looking lump of stinky blue tweed on casters.

Otherwise, the new office was a step up. In my old office, I had an L-shaped yellow metal desk with a corkboard hutch. Now I had an L-shaped gray metal desk with a corkboard hutch, plus a matching gray file cabinet all to myself. Whoever had done the move had replicated my old office (minus my special chair) to a T, all the way down to the two pictures stuck in the corner of my corkboard: one of Vinnie gnawing on his rubber Gumby doll, the other of my parents in front of their tree on my mom's last Christmas.

I met Frist as requested in his new corner office, legal pad and pen in hand, ready for a fresh start in a new unit, with a promotion I had wanted since I joined the office. It took most attorneys five to seven years of good work and shameless ass kissing to get into MCU, and I'd done it in less than three with my pride largely intact. Given my Stanford law degree and three years in the Southern District of New York at the nation's most prestigious U.S. Attorney's Office, some would say I was actually running behind.

I took a seat across from Frist, trying not to think about the last time I was there with the office's previous tenant.

True to his reputation, my new boss skipped the small talk and got down to business. "I thought we should touch base since you're new to the Unit and I'm still getting used to this supervision gig. You know the deal: we handle all nondomestic person felonies, basically murders, rapes, and aggravated assaults. Robberies we treat like property crimes and send down to the general felony unit. You can decide whether you want to bring any files over from your old DVD caseload, but I'd recommend against it. You'll have your hands full enough here without having to juggle Drug and Vice."

It took some concentration to focus on the substance of what Frist was saying. He had one of those deep voices you have to tuck your chin into your chest to impersonate, a common practice around the DA's office. He sounded like that anti-war governor from Vermont who ran for president, but this proud conservative ex-marine would never oppose a war, let alone go to Vermont. Frist was booming something at me, but his eyes kept darting alternately between my breasts and somewhere just above my forehead.

"You're starting out with something less than a regular load. Usually we'd give you the cases of whoever left, but O'Donnell obviously had some doozies that'd be hard to start out with. So I took over his caseload, kept about a quarter of mine, and gave you the rest. As the new person, you'll be on screening duty."

MCU's screening assignment is a notorious time-waster. Paralegals dole out the incoming police reports among the various trial units: major crimes, gangs, drugs and vice, general felonies, domestic violence, and misdemeanors. But to make sure that no one misses a heavy charge and issues it as a throwaway, any report that even arguably establishes probable cause for a major person felony goes to MCU for screening. The problem is, cautious paralegals end up finding potential felonies in every run-of-the-mill assault. Now I'd be the one to waste hours separating the wheat from the chaff. So much for my big impressive step up in the prosecutorial food chain.

Frist covered a handful of issues he thought I should be aware of on the cases I'd inherited from him, then changed the subject. "Now, as for this Easterbrook matter, I talked to the boss. I don't think he intended to throw you into the middle of things so quickly. You know, he figured the judge'd turn up in a couple of hours, and he wanted to make sure we did what we could in the meantime. But now this thing's looking like it's got real potential."

When I first started in the DA's office, I was sickened by how excited the career prosecutors seemed to get over a juicy incoming murder case. I swore I'd never treat human tragedy as career fodder. But it had since become clear to me that attorneys who have stuck with this job for any amount of time handle it one of two ways: They either get off on the adrenaline of their files or they become apathetic. Compassion is a straight path to burnout. I wasn't yet to the point where I looked at a person's murder simply as a trial challenge, but, when I did, I'd rather approach my cases as a passionate competitor like Frist than yet another of the lazy plea-bargaining bureaucrats we keep around here.

But precisely because Frist was competitive, he wanted in on this one. "Go ahead and ride the case solo while she's missing, but if a body turns up, you don't want this as your first murder."

I opened my mouth, but Frist was all over me. "Zip it, Kincaid. I know you're hungry, but you can forget about running this on your own. And don't think I'm picking on you for being new. Or because you're a woman."

Out the window went the staples of my reliable boss-fighting arsenal. Clearly I'd need to be more creative.

"We always have two attorneys on any death penalty case," he explained, "which this may very well be, if it's a kidnap gone wrong. And Clarissa Easterbrook isn't exactly your typical murder victim. Every person out there who thinks he can benefit will be crawling up our asses to scrutinize every aspect of this investigation and prosecution."

"Is it still my case, or should I go ahead and tell MCT to call *you* the next time they find a shoe in the gutter at four o'clock in the morning?"

"Nice try," Frist said, shaking his head and smiling. "But

whereas some people who held this job in the past were lazy fucks who'd rather play golf than practice law, I want to make sure we do things right around here, even if we all have to work our asses off. Including me. So keep your MCT phone calls, and we'll talk later about how to split the work if the need should arise. I never said who'd be first chair, now, did I?"

I said "fine" but couldn't resist being a little pouty about it.

As I was leaving his office, Frist dropped a closing comment to my back. "Besides, Kincaid, from what I hear, MCT's got an inside line to you in the middle of the night."

"Yeah, my pager number," I said, pretending not to recognize his not-so-subtle allusion to Detective Chuck Forbes. Despite my every attempt to be discreet, the whole world seemed to know we had something going on.

"Sorry. That was probably what human resources would call 'inappropriate.' Color me repentant." He placed his hand dramatically over his heart. "Seriously, when you're ready, we'll need to talk about how you want to handle that. We can keep you off his cases or not, whatever you think is . . . appropriate."

I knew he was being fair, but inside I cringed. I pride myself on not letting my personal life interfere with my job. In the two years since my divorce, I had complied with my self-imposed prohibition against dating cops and DAs. It's hard enough for a woman barely out of her twenties to be taken seriously as a prosecutor. If cops and colleagues start to look at you as dating prey, you're toast.

I headed straight to Alice Gerstein's desk to pick up some of the weekend custodies. As the senior paralegal in the unit and possibly the most competent member of the DA's office, Alice had already entered today's new cases into our internal data system. We only had until two o'clock this afternoon to present probable cause affidavits to the court on anyone arrested over the weekend without a warrant, so issuing custodies was always the first priority of the day.

Alice welcomed me with a fat Redweld file marked MCU SCREENING. I struggled to hold it in one hand, my coffee in the other. Judging by its weight, the file held close to thirty cases. "Could you give me a few of the regular unit custodies too? You know, so I can use them to break up the monotony a little?"

Alice was no pushover. "Sorry. Frist has got me under strict orders. The newbie doesn't get any real cases until the screens are finished. I know for sure that at least Luke is absolutely delighted by your addition to the unit. All last week, he was counting down the days."

I usually resent it when the all-female staff tries to enforce the office's rules against me, because it's common knowledge that most of them let the rules slide with their favorite male attorneys. But Alice is a soldier in what she sees as the daily war of keeping this place running, so I sucked it up and headed back to my office with the dregs. If Luke Grossman had stuck it out, so would I.

About an hour later, I was reading my nineteenth police report, the closest one yet to a major crime. Alas, it turned out to be another no complaint to be shipped off to the Domestic Violence Unit. The victim called 911 to report that he was walking down the street, minding his own business, when a woman shot an arrow at him from a balcony overhead. That's right, an arrow. What we call in this business a weapon, triggering major crime jurisdiction.

Bad news for me, the 911 call turned out to be woefully incomplete. For example, he left out the fact that the archer was his ex-girlfriend—who, by the way, was on Portland State's archery team and had a restraining order against her ex. He also forgot to mention that the weapon—to wit, one arrow—

had a pink rubber Power Puff Girl eraser popped onto the tip. No wonder the patrol officer's only arrest was of Newman himself, for violating the restraining order. At the arrestee's insistence, his complaint was written up, even as he was transported to and booked at the county detention center.

I scrawled my initials next to a big fat red MCU DECLINED stamp in the file's log notes and then went ahead and no complainted the potential misdemeanor charges as well. No use making someone in DV waste their time with Newman's whining.

My phone rang just as I was tossing the file into my out box.

"Kincaid." The butch phone answer is one of the small but very cool perks of being a prosecutor.

"How you doing there, Kincaid? I was afraid your extension might not have moved with you."

I recognized Ray Johnson's voice. How could he be so chipper when he'd undoubtedly been at the Easterbrook house most of the night?

"Pretty amazing. The county somehow manages to keep all the phones straight, but I still have to share a copy of the evidence code with the entire unit. What's up? Don't tell me. Judge Easterbrook turned up alive and well, rambling about a probe from little green men?"

"Nope. My instinct tells me that's not going to happen, not even that first part. One good sign, though, is that the husband's schedule checks out at OHSU. Three back-to-back surgeries. He's accounted for from seven A.M. to six P.M. No strange behavior."

"You mean it's a good sign for *him*."

"And a good sign for our vic. If the husband didn't do her, she's less likely to be dead." The bizarre mathematics of murder in a world where most violence against women is inflicted by husbands and lovers.

But Johnson wasn't ready to clear Townsend Easterbrook. "On the other hand, maybe it happened in the morning, and the guy goes off to work like it's nothing. Wouldn't be the first time. And, of course, the alibi's meaningless if he hired someone.

"I also got some preliminary info from the crime lab. They picked up some unidentified latents around the house, but the one match they got in AFIS was with the one Walker left on the door knocker. Other than that, the only thing they've got is on our boy, Griffey. Remember that gnarly-looking scum the sister found on the dog?"

"Sure, clay or something." My hopes were up. Cases had been solved before by the unique composition of dirt left behind at a scene. Or, in this instance, on a dog.

"Nope, not clay. Paint."

Interesting. Dogs out walking in the rain don't usually come home with body paint.

"And how are we going to find out where that paint might've come from?" I asked.

"One of the lab guys is getting together with some paint geek from Home Depot. They've got a color-match computer. It's a long shot, but they might be able to tell us the brand name if there's a perfect match. From there, we could check the stores for any recent orders. In any event, they'll make us up a paint chip, so if we ever do have something to match it against, we won't have to use the dog hair. In the meantime, the PIO's going to put a call out in the next press briefing for tips. Hopefully, we'll get some reports of a neighbor who was painting in the area. Even if we don't get our bad guy, it might at least help us figure out where the dog has been."

Better the bureau's Public Information Office than me. I try to stay away from the media.

"Any other news?"

"Nothing of any use. Looks like Griffey's the only mutt with anything to contribute. We called a K-9 unit out there this morning to see if one of their dogs could pick up a scent on

Clarissa. No luck. The handler told me the scent was long gone. Probably the rain."

"Any luck getting in touch with Susan Kerr?" It would be helpful to see if Clarissa's friend had noticed anything unusual when they went shopping on Saturday.

"Haven't managed to reach her yet."

"She's around," I said. "She was with the family at the press conference this morning."

"I know. She called my desk this morning; probably got my name from Tara. I missed her when I called her back, though. When I catch up with her, you want to go out on the interview with me?"

"Any reason to figure she's a suspect?" DAs don't usually tag along on witness interviews.

"Yeah, guilty of being a rich muckety-muck. I did a little recon on our girl. She makes the Easterbrooks look like Jerry Springer trailer trash."

"Careful, Ray. Not all of us can afford those Hugo Boss suits you strut around in."

"The point is, she's loaded. I thought we might cut through some of the predictable bullshit if you talked to her."

"No problem. It's my first day cooped up in the office, so the sooner the better." As usual, Johnson was right: Lots of rich people find speaking to the police beneath them. Depending on who Susan Kerr turned out to be, she might expect a personal call from District Attorney Duncan Griffith or even from the mayor herself.

I hung up, pleased that I hadn't given in to the urge to ask Ray if he'd seen Chuck this morning. I was surprised I hadn't heard from him yet.

I'd managed to reject only another three cases before my thoughts drifted back to Clarissa Easterbrook. If she was still alive, what was she doing right now?

I paged Johnson, and he returned the call right away. "Didn't I just talk to you?" he asked.

"Have you thought about searching Easterbrook's office?"

"I thought you wanted to play things cool with him for now," he said.

I realized that he thought I was talking about Townsend. "No, Clarissa's office. Maybe there's something there that would at least give us some leads."

"It's looking like she was snatched from the neighborhood, so we've been working from that area out. The office has been less of a priority, but, yeah, you're right, we should at least check it out. I'll get someone on it."

"Don't worry about it. I'll do it and call you when it's okay to go in."

"Really, Kincaid, it's all right. I know you're new to this, but DAs don't usually do any of the runaround work. One of the perks of the job, right? Bossing cops around?"

"Trust me, there will come a time when you rue the day you encouraged me to be bossier. I'm not doing this to take the load off you; I'm doing it because I'm going stir crazy in this new rotation. Plus, I have a feeling that if you guys storm into a judge's office with a search warrant, the chief judge will be on the phone to Duncan demanding my head."

"We're talking about me, Kincaid. I don't storm. I slide." He dragged out the vowel in his last word.

"You get the drift."

"That I do. Go to it, then. Call me when you need me."

I buzzed through the rest of my screens, the promise of doing some real work motivating me like a crème brûlée waiting at the end of a bad meal.

When I was done, I called the mayor's office. Although Clarissa's position entitled her to be called Judge, hearings officers are actually part of city administration. Anyone who disagrees with a city agency's decision has to take an administrative appeal to a city hearings officer before he can sue before a "real" judge. In short, when it comes to city bureaucracy, a judge like Clarissa Easterbrook is the last stop before the courthouse.

I explained the situation to the mayor's administrative assistant, who referred me to Clarence Loutrell, the chief administrative hearings officer.

Hanging up the phone, I swiveled my chair around to look out the window. Okay, it was more of a cranking than a swivel with this particular chair, but it was enough for me to see that there wasn't a break from the rain yet. I generally prefer to handle this kind of thing face-to-face. It's harder for someone to reject a request in person than to say no to a faceless voice on the telephone.

Fuck it. The walk in the humidity was sure to leave me with a puffy head of cotton-ball hair for the rest of the day, but four hours at a desk after two weeks on the beach had me yearning to get out. Besides, I could put my hair through a wind tunnel, and it wouldn't matter. Clean clothes and a lack of BO is about all you need to meet minimum standards for the courthouse crowd.

I signed myself out on the MCU whiteboard without explanation, following my practice of staking out ground early in a new job the way Vinnie pees everywhere he goes to mark territory. No way was I going to join the kiss-ups who leave notes on the board detailing their precise location. That's what pagers were for.

I kicked off my black Ferragamo slingbacks and threw them in my briefcase while I shoved my stockinged feet into my New Balances. I'd lost enough of my good shoes to Portland's damp streets.

On my way out, I swung by my old office in DVD. Kirsten

Holloway, newly promoted from the misdemeanor unit, had already covered the place with her wedding photos and stuffed animals. She would learn her lesson quickly. By the end of the week, anonymous pranksters would be sure to have her cute little animals posed in backbreaking positions violating the laws of thirty-six states. I didn't even want to think about the Post-it notes she'd find stuck around the bride and groom.

In the meantime, no sign of my beloved chair.

I entered City Hall from its new Fourth Avenue entrance. The city had completed what seemed like endless remodeling about a year ago. What used to be a dingy back entrance through a metal door was now the main entrance, hugged by pink pillars and a rose garden.

The refurbished City Hall beat the hell out of my rundown courthouse. The renovation had exposed the building's original marble tile and woodwork. To the extent that there was any natural light on this crummy day, it flooded into the lobby through the atrium skylights. The tiled staircases that had once been enclosed in a stairwell were now open, exposing five floors of original copper handrails and plating.

I took the stairs to the third floor, then ducked into the corner to switch my shoes. Judge Loutrell's office was in the suite at the end of the hall.

I was in luck, or so it seemed. After a short call, Loutrell's secretary told me he was in and willing to see me. Even though I should have made an appointment, of course.

Loutrell rose from his desk to greet me. He was tall and thin, balding but trying hard to conceal it with his last few wisps of white hair. I shook his hand and introduced myself as a Deputy District Attorney. "I'm sure you already know that Clarissa Easterbrook has been reported missing."

"Yes. I was shocked when I heard it on the news this morning. It's just not like Clarissa to be gone like this."

"That's what others have been telling us as well, so the police are investigating every possibility. For now, they're focusing primarily on Judge Easterbrook's neighborhood, but since I work at the courthouse and was in the area, I thought I'd see if anyone she works with might have any theories about where she could be or people the police should be talking to."

"Gosh, not offhand. I wish I could help, but I didn't talk to Clarissa much and I don't know much about her personal life."

"What about her professional life? Has there been anything unusual lately for her at work?"

"Not that I can think of. Like I said, we didn't talk much, and all of us work pretty independently. I'm the chief administrative officer, but that doesn't mean much other than filling out some forms and whatnot."

Now came the tricky part. "I'm sure it's a long shot that her disappearance would have anything to do with work, but we want to make sure we cover all the bases early on. What would be really helpful to the investigation is to take a look in Judge Easterbrook's office. You know, just to make sure nothing seems out of the ordinary."

I was about halfway through the request when Loutrell began to finger the pen resting on his leather desk pad. By the time I was finished, he had picked it up and was twisting the cap around in circles.

"Well, yes, I can see why that would be an important part of what you're trying to do. But I'm sure you understand that I can't just open up one of our hearing officers' offices for you."

"Judge Loutrell, one of your coworkers is missing. From everything I've heard, including what you just told me, this is not a woman who would run off without some explanation. One of her shoes was found in a gutter. All I'm asking for is the chance to rule out the possibility that this had anything to do with her work so the police can focus on more likely possibilities."

"I understand all that, Ms. Kincaid, but I'm sure you understand that there are privacy issues at stake."

"Clarissa Easterbrook is not a private attorney. She doesn't have any clients, so we're not talking about privileged material. The only privacy rights at issue are Clarissa Easterbrook's, and I think it's safe to say that she'd want us to take a look under these circumstances."

"I just don't know." He was still twisting the pen cap.

"I can have the police apply for a search warrant if you think that's a more appropriate procedure." I managed to make it sound like an offer to be helpful instead of a threat.

"I just don't think this is something I should be handling."

"The mayor's office pointed me to you. You're the chief administrative hearings officer."

"And I told you that title means little in this context. I think you should talk to the City Attorney's Office."

I thought about arguing but decided it was a waste of time. Loutrell was a timid bureaucrat who was more concerned about straying beyond his authority than finding Clarissa Easterbrook. He had also said the magic attorney word: The City Attorney represented all city agencies, including the hearings officers. If Loutrell told me to go to his attorney, I didn't have much choice.

Luckily, the City Attorney's Office was just one floor up. When I explained to the receptionist what I needed, however, she told me I'd need to talk to the City Attorney himself, Dennis Coakley, who wasn't going to be back until the end of the day. I left my name and number and did my best to encourage her to get the message to him as soon as possible.

On my way back down, I noticed the listing for Clarissa

Easterbrook's office on a sign at the third-floor landing. I followed the arrow to the left, away from Loutrell's office, and found the suite number I was looking for.

A receptionist with a pierced nose and red pixie haircut was busy juggling calls, repeating, "City hearings department, please hold." After three times she exhaled loudly and looked up. "Welcome to my world. How can I help you?"

At least she had a sense of humor about it. I gave her my best empathetic smile and introduced myself. She made the connection to Clarissa's disappearance on her own. "Oh my God. I have been going crazy in here this morning. I didn't listen to the news this morning and came in early, before anyone else was around. The calls started around seven-thirty, and I was, like, What do you mean she's missing? I had to go out to my car and listen to the news on the radio. Finally, someone came in this morning at nine to explain the situation to me. The phone's been ringing off the hook."

"What kind of calls?" I asked.

"Reporters, mostly. I don't know what they expect me to tell them. I've been reading the prepared statement I was given. Hold on a sec, okay?" She jumped back to juggle the phones, telling each caller, "Clarissa Easterbrook is an important member of the city community. We hope for her speedy return, and our thoughts and prayers are with her family at this critical time." As she repeated the line, she handed me a memo from Clarence Loutrell with the typed-out statement.

Once she'd gotten through the on-hold callers, she let the phone ring unanswered while we spoke.

"Seems like a small office. You must be pretty close to her."

"I guess. I started here last fall. I work for her and one of the other hearings officers, Dave Olick. I'm pretty much their entire staff. I do the phones, the secretarial work, any legal research that comes up. I graduated last spring from Lewis and Clark.

It wasn't exactly my dream job after law school, but it's a job, at least. I'm Nelly by the way. Nelly Giacoma."

The Portland legal market, like legal markets everywhere, was getting tight. I wasn't surprised that a recent law graduate might have to clerk for an administrative law judge for a while. This one's nose ring, lollipop hair, and what I now saw was a yin-yang symbol tattooed on her ankle probably didn't help.

"Since I'm across the street at the courthouse, I just dropped by to see if the people who worked with Clarissa had any thoughts on where she might be, that kind of thing."

Nelly shook her head slowly while she spoke. "No, I just have no idea. Everything was fine last week. She was working when I left at five Friday, and she said she'd see me on Monday."

"You can't think of anything unusual that's happened lately? Something that might be connected somehow?"

"Well, about a month ago, some guy on one of her cases sort of blew up at her."

"Do you know anything about the case?" I asked.

"Not really. The guy was getting evicted, but I don't know what the issue was."

"If you could pull the file, I can go through it while you get some of those calls." I tilted my head toward her phone, which was still ringing.

"Gee, I don't think I can just let you go through the file."

"At least parts of it are public record."

"But I don't think the whole thing is, especially when the case is still pending. Besides, I don't even know what case it is. I'd have to go through all the files and try to find it. I better check with Judge Loutrell and get back to you."

I picked her brain for more about the ticked-off evicted guy or for any other cases of note, but didn't get any further. "What about stuff outside of work? Did you talk to Clarissa enough to know anything about her personal life?"

"Well, I know she's married."

Oh, yeah, they were best friends, all right.

"And how did that seem to be going?" I asked.

"Good, I guess. Clarissa's pretty private, though. Or she is with me, at least. We're pretty much employer–employee. But she's really, really nice. I hope she's all right. I'm sure she is, isn't she?"

I nodded and smiled, doing my best to appear unworried. When I said goodbye, Nelly apologized that she couldn't be more helpful but assured me she'd talk to Loutrell about going through the files. I handed her my card, but I knew she wouldn't get back to me. Loutrell would forward the request to Dennis Coakley, leaving me in the same spot I was already in.

All I had to show for my out-of-court venture was a head full of frizz and a few extra calories burned on the stairs. So much for making a difference in the world.

While I was waiting at the crosswalk back to the courthouse, my pager vibrated at my waist. I recognized the number as the Major Crimes Team desk and called back on my cell.

After half a ring I heard, "MCT. Johnson."

"Hey, Ray. It's Samantha. I got a page."

"I know. It was from me. We finally got hold of Susan Kerr. I'm headed out with Walker to her house now. Can you meet us?"

"Where's the house?"

"Up in the west hills," he said.

"Can you swing by the courthouse and get me? I took the bus in today." Schlepping across downtown to check out a car from the county lot would take longer than the short ride from the courthouse up into the hills.

"Damn, Kincaid. What are you doing riding the bus? We got to get you livin' a little larger."

"I ride the bus because I'm a good citizen, Raymond. I recycle too."

"You are definitely a different kind of DA, girl. Riding the damn city bus with the rest of the citizens. I'll swing in front on Fourth in about ten minutes. Cool?"

"Yep. See you then."

I used the ten minutes to make sure nothing urgent was waiting for me back in the office and to put something called *mud* in my moisture-crazed hair for the trip. My best friend, Grace, is a hairdresser. She cut my dark brown locks (the bottle says coffee, to be exact) into a wispy little do a few months back, and to her chagrin I was in the ugly process of growing it back into my boring reliable shoulder-length bob. According to her, all I needed was the right product to see my hair through its growing pangs. I must have been doing something wrong with the mud, because by the time my fingers were done crimping and twisting, I looked like Neil Young in drag.

I left the courthouse just as Johnson and Walker pulled up in a white unmarked bureau Crown Vic.

Lunch-hour traffic had begun to accumulate downtown, but the drive was quick once we crossed I-405 and got out of the downtown business district. As Johnson maneuvered the tight curves up the west hills, I asked Walker what they knew so far about Susan Kerr.

"Not too much. Her PPDS printout's right there," he said, reaching back to hand me a sheet of green computer paper from the Portland Police Data System. "Nothing to see. She's forty-two, no criminal history, drives a Mercedes."

"The big one," Johnson cut in. "I told you, the woman's got some cash."

"We don't know much more than that. One criminal complaint four years ago for a smash-and-grab," Walker explained.

Portland has low violent crime and high property crime, driven primarily by a large population of street kids and drug addicts. Almost everyone with a car has at some point been a smash-and-grab victim. My poor Jetta's windows have been smashed on three occasions, once for my stereo, once for the gym bag I stupidly left in the backseat, and once for nothing but a new Lyle Lovett CD. That one really pissed me off.

Walker pulled his spiral notebook from the breast pocket of his shirt to refresh his memory. "The co-complainant on the smash-and-grab was Herbert Kerr at the same address. Presumably the husband, but he's got a 1932 date of birth. He died two years ago."

"Hey, some women go for the old guys. Look at you. You've got a woman." Johnson was laughing at his joke, but Walker gave his partner a look to show he wasn't amused.

"Yeah, and she's been stuck with me for thirty-two years. Somehow I suspect I'm not Susan Kerr's type."

"Well, I *know* I'm not."

"Excuse me, fellas, but could we get back to talking about the case? For the record, I think any woman would be lucky to have either of you."

"Sorry, Sam," Walker said. "Lack of sleep gets to you. Truth is, we're not getting anywhere. Media coverage is usually good on a missing persons case, but this one's out of control. Calls have been flooding into the hotline we set up, but it's a bunch of stuff that's either wrong, contradictory, or totally irrelevant."

"Like what?" I asked.

I could tell he didn't know where to begin. "Well, we've got people in the neighborhood telling us they saw her walking her dog on Sunday at eight A.M., eleven A.M., three P.M., and seven P.M. We've got people all over town calling us about possible sightings today. Then we've got the callers who need us to know everything they ever happened to notice about the Easterbrooks—that their landscapers were out on Tuesday, that UPS left something on the porch on Friday, that the windows were open overnight on Saturday. You don't want to tell people to stop calling, but you'd think these people would have the good sense to know they're not being helpful."

"Don't forget the psychics, Jack."

"Ah, Jesus. The psychics. One lady called up crying that Clarissa was at the bottom of the Willamette and couldn't cross over to heaven until we recovered her body from the river. Fucking ghoulish. There's just way too many nut jobs out there for us to keep up with the leads."

"Well, I think I might have something worth pursuing," I said. I gave them the limited information I'd gotten from Nelly Giacoma about the ticked-off evicted guy.

"Hard to look into it without knowing who we're talking about," Johnson said. "Want us to get a warrant for the office?"

"I'm working on it. I think it'll be faster to go through the City Attorney, but I'll let you know what I hear. What about the husband?" I asked. "He still acting like what you'd expect?"

Walker answered. "Yeah, seems all right. I was over there this morning. You know, shook up but not overwrought. He's definitely in no shape to be cutting anyone open; he was doing what he could to get his hospital rounds covered. But he's out there on the news, being cooperative. I'm not getting a vibe from this one."

"Me neither," Johnson said, "but you never can tell."

I assumed when the car stopped in front of one of the nicer Portland Heights spreads that we had arrived at Susan Kerr's. As deluxe as the place was, however, it must not have been good enough because she was making some improvements. There was a dumpster in the driveway and a construction truck across the street.

I opened my door, but Johnson wasn't ready to drop the subject of Townsend Easterbrook. "I know you got your boss to think about, Kincaid, but I think we need to at least consider whether we should ask the guy to take a poly. Far as I'm concerned, the husband's always a suspect. I don't care who he is."

"OK, we'll talk about it after we're done here." I stepped into the rain, making my way to the house as quickly as I could.

3

I WAS SURPRISED when a maid answered Susan Kerr's front door. Definitely not a Portland thing. This woman had real money.

The maid led us through three rooms and told us to sit in the fourth. Big on color-coordinated stripes, dots, and paisleys, Susan Kerr's taste was the decorating equivalent of a Laura Ashley orgy. And, as far as I could tell, every room we passed was what most would consider a formal sitting room and what I would consider useless: no bed, no TV, no snacks. Maybe that was the purpose of the home improvements; I could hear construction noises coming from somewhere deep inside the house.

I recognized Susan Kerr from the press briefing. As I took in her powder-blue suit, French twist, and full face of makeup, a few bars of that Stephen Sondheim song about ladies who lunch came to mind. She had that great dewy skin I always envy, beautiful dark hair and eyes, and had probably even had some work done, but she looked seriously uptight.

Before we'd even completed the introductions, the maid was

back with a tray of coffee and tea. "Thanks, Rosie. You heading out to yoga?"

Rosie nodded.

"Go ahead and take my car. I'm not going anywhere." When Rosie left, Susan explained. "I've turned her on to yoga for some back spasms she's been having, but her sunroof's leaking, and the shop can't fix it until next week. Poor thing showed up this morning soaking wet. "

Maybe I had judged Susan Kerr prematurely.

"Sorry about all this banging," she said, gesturing in the air the way people do when they try to point to a sound. She pulled a clip from her hair and shook her head slightly. Loose brown waves tumbled past her shoulders. "I've got this creepy basement fit for Freddy Krueger, and I finally broke down to have it refinished. Anyway, I'm sorry I wasn't at Clarissa's last night. I was at a fund-raiser for the museum and didn't get Tara's message until nearly midnight. She told me to call her, but I can't believe she didn't tell me why. When I woke up this morning, Clarissa's disappearance was all over the news. Of course, I called Tara at once to find out who I could talk to. She's the one who gave me your number, Detective Johnson."

"Tara and Townsend tell us you're probably Clarissa's closest friend," Johnson said. His gentle comment called for a response but didn't steer the conversation in a particular direction.

"Better than friends, detective." Kerr leaned forward and touched Johnson's forearm as she spoke, a gesture that was somehow more reassuring than flirtatious. She must have sensed that Ray had arrived at her home with some preconceived notions. "With my parents gone, I've known Clarissa longer than anyone else in my entire life. She's the closest thing to a sister I've got. We've been through it all together."

We stayed silent during her pause. For Johnson and Walker,

the silence was probably part of the strategy. I was quiet because I couldn't help but think of Grace and how lost I'd be if anything ever happened to her.

"I want to believe that there's an explanation," Susan said, "but I keep coming back to what I know is true. This is totally unlike Clarissa. She's so . . . responsible. Predictable. She'd never go off like this without telling someone: Tara, Townsend, me, her parents. She's surrounded by people who are close to her. She'd never let us worry this way. Something terrible must have happened."

This time, the silence that followed wasn't enough to prod Susan into speaking, so Johnson gave a gentle nudge. "Everything we've learned about the case so far leads us to think that we're investigating a crime here, not just a missing person. Part of what we're doing now is putting together a timeline for the last few days. Maybe you can start by telling us about the last time you talked to Clarissa."

"Sure. It was just Saturday. Townsend was working at the hospital—nothing new there—so Clarissa had the whole day free. We had a late lunch, then went to the Nordstrom anniversary sale."

"How was her mood?" Johnson asked.

"Same old Clarissa. Fun, talkative, sweet. Afraid to spend money." Susan paused and smiled. "Sorry. If you knew Clarissa . . . well, you'd know what I mean. Best sale of the year, and I had to talk her into buying a couple of sweaters. She's very practical."

Susan and Clarissa clearly lived in a different world from most of us. I'd seen Clarissa's closet, after all. I couldn't imagine what Susan's must be packed with.

"Any financial problems that you know of?" Johnson asked.

Susan laughed. "Oh, God, no. She and Townsend do fine. It's just Clarissa's way. We grew up in southeast Portland, you know. About half a step up from the trailer parks. Well, *she* was half a step up. I was basically right in there. She worked her way out by studying hard and putting herself through school."

"Did you go to school together?" I asked.

She laughed again. "Sure—through high school. If you're asking how *I* dealt with my generational income challenge, I won't waste your time by making it sound heroic. I was lucky enough to be the prettiest aerobics instructor at the Multno-mah Athletic Club when my husband Herbie decided to settle down. We were married for ten years before he passed away. I've always felt a little guilty for having at least as much as Clarissa when I can barely balance a checkbook."

I had to hand it to her. Susan Kerr had a hell of a personality. There's something reassuring about a person who is so comfortable about who and what she is.

"So when exactly was she with you on Saturday?" Walker asked.

"I picked her up at her house around one. We had a long lunch, probably until three, then shopped at Lloyd Center until I dropped her off around seven."

"Can you think of anything unusual that came up?" Walker was quicker to move to narrow questions than I would have been.

"Like what?" she asked.

"Anything," he said. "Someone following her, a run-in with someone, something she seemed worried about. Things like that."

"Anything at all that you think possibly could be helpful," I added.

She shook her head. "No. We certainly didn't notice it if someone was following us. I mean, who would follow us?" Susan's comment seemed to trigger her own memory. "Well, actually, about a month ago, she did mention some guy in her caseload who was getting a little creepy. She usually writes off the stuff people say to her as nothing, but this guy had her a bit unnerved. I told her to call the police if she was really worried, but I don't think she ever did. She told me a few days ago that she hadn't heard anything else from him; I forgot to ask her about it on Saturday." She was no doubt wondering whether she'd ever have another chance.

"Her assistant at the office mentioned something similar to me, but she couldn't give me the file. Do you remember anything else about the case?" I asked.

"I don't recall whether she ever used his name. The irony is that Clarissa actually felt sorry for the guy, but there wasn't anything she could do for him. He was getting evicted from public housing under some policy that lets them kick you out if someone visits you with drugs?"

I could tell she wasn't sure if she had it right, so I nodded to let her know that I was familiar with the policy.

"Anyway, it was a big mess. Clarissa didn't think she could stop the city from doing it, but the guy said he'd lose custody of his kids if he didn't have a place for them to live. She was worried that if she called the police about the letters and it turned out that he was only blowing off some steam, she'd make it even harder for him to keep his kids."

"Do you know what he did that had her on edge?" I asked.

"Just a couple of letters, I think. Ranting and raving the way a lot of people do, but something about how she should have to know his pain someday. I know I agreed with her at the time that it sounded a little threatening."

"And you don't know whether she did anything in response?"

"No. It alarmed her at first, which was why I suggested she call the police. I asked her about it a few times after that, but she seemed to have gotten over it."

I'd had similar experiences. A defendant gets in your face,

and it feels like a conflict that could rip your guts out. By the end of the week, it's just another story to share at a cocktail party to distinguish yourself from all the other boring lawyers.

"Is that enough for you to be able to find the file?" she asked.

"Should be," Johnson said. "We'll be sure to follow up on it. What about Clarissa's personal life? She seem happy in her marriage?"

Susan Kerr leaned back in her chair, took in a deep breath, and smiled politely. "I was wondering when you'd get to that. Classic, right? Whenever something goes wrong, it's got to be the spouse. Hell, poor Herbie died of a heart attack, but don't think I didn't know what some of his friends were whispering behind my back."

Johnson had clearly dealt with this kind of response before, because he handled it like a pro. "I know this is upsetting for you, but, as Clarissa's best friend, you're the one who can be most helpful in pointing us in the right direction."

"Well, thank you for that, but whatever the right direction is, that ain't it. If I thought for a second that Townsend had anything to do with this, I'd be leading the charge. Shit, I love the man, but I'd probably kill him myself."

"This early in the case, we have to consider every scenario."

"Well, you're on the wrong track. Townsend and Clarissa are a great team. To the extent she ever complains, it's the stuff every couple deals with—finding enough time for each other, who does the dishes, boring shit like that. I doubt Townsend's ever raised his voice to her, let alone what you're thinking. It's just not in him."

Johnson and Walker were polite enough not to roll their eyes. They'd been around long enough to know what ordinary citizens don't want to believe—you can never tell who has it in them to kill.

It was almost two by the time Johnson and Walker dropped me off downtown, and I was starving. The rain had finally stopped, so I walked the two blocks to Pioneer Courthouse Square, got a small *radiatore* with pesto from the pasta cart on Sixth and Yamhill, and headed back to eat at my desk. When I went to erase my sign-out on the whiteboard, I found that anonymous coworkers had written, *Shoe shopping, Back to Hawaii,* and *Does Kincaid still work here?* next to my original OUT. The graffiti made me laugh, but I went ahead and erased it while I was at it.

I hit the speakerphone to check my voice mail but was interrupted by the rap of fingers against my open door. I swung my chair around to find Jessica Walters, the only female supervisor in the office and someone who I was pretty sure had never spoken a word to me during my tenure as a DDA. As usual, she wore a tailored pantsuit and oxford-cloth shirt, her trademark pencil tucked neatly behind her ear.

"Jessica. Hi." My surprise to see her, combined with the more than mild intimidation she inspired in me, ruined any chance I might have had at witty repartee. Walters had been a prosecutor for nearly two decades, put more men on death row than any other DA in the state, and, as far as I could tell, never had cause to doubt that she was smarter and quicker than anyone else in a room. She was currently in charge of the gang unit.

"Welcome to the club, Kincaid. You're the first of your kind up here. Congratulations."

"Thanks, but I thought you were the first. Weren't you in MCU before you got your own unit?"

"Yep, was up here for almost ten years. So was Sally Herrington, before she jumped ship to join the dark side. But you're the first hetero—a role model for all the straight women in the office who said it couldn't be done."

51

There was a crowd of paranoid younger women in the office who were convinced that the boss created the appearance of gender fairness in the office by promoting lesbians who were perceived to be less likely to rock the cultural boat captained by his buddies. The truth was sadder. The atmosphere here was so rough, both for women and for dedicated parents, that the lawyers who were (or intended someday to be) both of those things requested other "opportunities" in the office. So-called voluntary transfers to nontrial units like appeals, child support, and parental terminations became their own kind of self-imposed mommy track.

If anything was going to kill the conspiracy theory and the office culture, it was the increasingly rampant rumor that Jessica and her drop-dead gorgeous partner of nine years were trying to get pregnant. I couldn't wait to watch a tough guy like Frist wiggle in his seat while "Nail Them to the Wall" Walters breast-fed her kid during a homicide call-out. Payback for every time I've had to listen to colleagues bemoan uniquely masculine complaints like jock itch and beer-goggle bangs.

"To tell you the truth, I was beginning to wonder what was going on with you in that department. Now all the support staff can talk about is you and Forbes. After all the ninnies in this office that guy has bagged, he's stepping up in the world."

Given my general anxiety about dating a cop, the last thing I needed was a reminder of the many brief relationships this particular one has had over the years. If ours turned out to be as fleeting, I might be known as yet another Forbes conquest.

Jessica must have realized that I didn't take the comment as she intended it. "I was saying you're a good catch, Kincaid, but I should probably keep my mouth shut and stick to work. It's a well-deserved shot you've got here. You're gonna be great."

"Thanks, Jessica. That's really nice of you to say."

"No problem. Just remember, don't let these fuckers give you too much shit. You'll need to pay your dues at first, but then it's about carrying your fair share of the load. Don't be afraid to get in their faces if you need to."

I thanked her for her advice before she left, mentally crossing my fingers that there wouldn't be a need for me to demonstrate that I already knew how to push at least as hard as she did.

Among my many waiting voice mails was one from the City Attorney, Dennis Coakley. He'd chosen to leave me a message at my desk even though I'd given the receptionist my cell phone number. I'd intentionally phone-tagged people before and knew there was only one way to win this game.

I called the number he'd left for me, which, of course, led to his assistant. She told me he was in a meeting but assured me she'd tell him I called.

"He *is* back in the office?" I asked. "I just want to make sure he's going to get the message."

"Yes, he's back. I'll let him know you called just as soon as he's out of his meeting."

With that, I threw my running shoes back on, signed out, and trekked over to City Hall. I gave the receptionist at the City Attorney's Office my name and explained that I wanted to see Dennis Coakley.

She seemed confused. "Didn't we just speak on the phone?"

"Yep, that was me."

"Um—did he call you back or something? I haven't given him the message, because he's still occupied."

"That's OK, I'll wait," I said, as I settled into a chair near the front door. Nonresponsive answers might be objectionable in court, but they work wonders in the real world. Ten minutes later, Dennis Coakley himself came to the front desk and called my name. Faster than a doctor's office.

Coakley's office was conservative but well furnished, and I took a seat at the small conference table he led me to. I'd seen him around town before, and he looked no different now than he always did: wheat-colored bowl cut, glasses thick as microwave doors, bad suit.

Before I had a chance to say anything, he took the lead. "Given your presence here, Ms. Kincaid, I feel I need to say something that I shouldn't have to. I know your line of work requires you to deal with some people who—well, let's just call them uncooperative. But I hope you didn't feel you needed to come over here personally to exert pressure on me. Frankly, I find it a little insulting. I happen to know Clarissa Easterbrook and would like to do whatever I can to help find her."

"It's nothing like that. In fact, I appreciate your calling me back so quickly. It's just that this is my first day back in the office for a while, and I needed the air. Your assistant mentioned you were in, so . . ." A lie, to be sure, but much better than admitting my tendencies to be an untrusting freak.

If Coakley sensed the fib, he was kind enough to gloss over it. "Good. No misunderstandings, then. Tell me what you need from us to help."

"At this point, we don't know. Officially, it's still a missing person case, but so far nothing suggests that Clarissa took off on her own, and the police don't have any leads. You probably heard that they found her dog and her shoe by Taylor's Ferry Road." He nodded sadly. "You can imagine the scenario that brings to mind. But we haven't ruled out the chance that this could have something to do with her work. We just want to go through her office to see if anything there leaps out at us."

He scratched his chin as if I had just asked him to calculate the circumference of his coffee cup using only the diameter. "This has never come up before. I'm not sure I can let you do that. Let me look into it, and I'll get back to you tomorrow. As long as there are no legal hurdles, it shouldn't be a problem." He started to get up to walk me out.

I stayed in my seat. "I assumed we'd be able to get in today. The sooner the better."

"I'd like to be able to do that, but I don't see how I can."

"Unlock the door, and I can have an officer here within the hour."

"I can't just let the police roam through a judge's files, Ms. Kincaid."

"Call me Samantha. And of course you can. She's not an actual judge; she's a hearings officer. I assume if any other city employee was missing, this wouldn't be an issue."

"But the fact that she's a city employee makes Clarissa my client. I just need enough time to make sure there's no privileged information in her office. If there is, I'll let you know I've withheld something, and we can go over to the courthouse and figure it out from there."

"Look, this isn't tobacco litigation. What kind of privileged information are you worried about? We're just trying to find out where she is."

"I know, and that's why I'm probably going to stay here all night doing document review in her office, so you can get in as soon as possible. But our hearings officers call for legal advice and might keep memos of those conversations. If something like that exists, and I turn it over to you, it waives privilege. I can't do that."

"I'm sorry, Dennis, but that makes absolutely no sense. How can the judges call you for advice when the city's a party to the disputes they're handling?"

"Well, obviously we don't give advice on how to resolve individual cases as hearings officers, but we are their attorneys in their status as city employees. It's a complicated relationship. All the more reason for me to make sure we dot our *i*'s and cross our *t*'s, which I assure you I will do by tomorrow."

"I'll do the search myself, if that helps. I'm an attorney too, and I won't disclose anything that shouldn't be disclosed."

Unfortunately, Coakley knew that's not how attorney-client privilege works. "But you don't represent the city, so I can't let you fish around in the files without reviewing them first. If you knew specifically what you wanted, I could look for it right now and give it to you, assuming nothing needed to be redacted. I got the impression, though, that you won't know what you're looking for until you find it."

"I think that's probably right. I know she was having a problem with one of the appellants in a public housing eviction case. Both her clerk and her friend mentioned that he'd written letters to Clarissa that she found threatening, but they didn't know his name. Is there some way you could track that down, short of doing an entire review of her office?"

"Should be."

I told him everything I knew so far about the case.

"Let me see what I can find out. You want to wait here, or should I call you?"

"I'll wait. Thanks." He seemed to find my choice insulting.

Five minutes later, I felt my pager go off. The MCT number again.

I took the liberty of using the phone on Coakley's desk to return the call. This time, I was expecting Johnson to pick up, but the voice that answered "MCT" belonged to someone I'd known for fifteen years: Chuck Forbes.

The first time I saw Chuck screech his yellow Karmann Ghia into the lot at Grant High and then step out in his washed-out 501s, I was hooked. As much as I didn't want to be, I had to admit I still was.

I hesitated a moment too long. "Hi, it's Samantha Kincaid. I think Detective Johnson might have paged me?"

"You need to shake the salt water out of your ears, Kincaid. It's Chuck."

"Oh, hey. What's going on?"

"Two weeks in Hawaii, and that's all I get? *What's going on?* Bad news is going on, but Raymond's standing over my shoulder waiting to break it to you. Everything all right?"

"Sure," I said. "Why wouldn't it be?"

"Ray's glaring at me," he said, "so I'm going to hand you off. But call me later, OK? I want to hear about your trip."

I had tried to play it cool, but Chuck and I were way past new-relationship head games. "And I want to tell you all about it. I missed you, Chuck."

"Yeah. Me too," he said sweetly, before handing the phone to Johnson.

"They found a body in Glenville. I'm heading out there now."

"Is it Clarissa?" I asked.

"We don't have an official ID yet, but, yeah, looks like it's going to be her."

What I felt at the moment couldn't have been about any meaningful personal attachment to Clarissa Easterbrook. But I nevertheless felt myself go empty at the confirmation of what I'd already been suspecting, and I wondered how I was going to handle a job that would make this feeling routine.

"Kincaid, you still there? I got to bounce."

"Sorry, yeah, I'm here. Tell me where it is, and I'll meet you there," I said, fishing a legal pad from my bag. The lead detectives needed to arrive at the crime scene as soon as possible, so it was mutually understood that I'd have to fend for myself. I scribbled down a street address that Johnson told me corresponded to a construction site at the outer edge of the suburb of Glenville.

"I need to take care of a couple things and pick up a county car, but I'll meet you guys out there as soon as I can. Call me if you need anything."

I walked out of Coakley's office, telling his assistant that something had come up and I needed to leave.

"He went down to Judge Easterbrook's office, if you want to try to catch him," she offered.

Dennis Coakley was leaving Clarissa Easterbrook's chambers as I was walking down the hall. He carried a legal-sized manila file folder and a small stack of documents.

"You really crack the whip, don't you? Here I thought I'd worked pretty fast."

I tried to muster a smile. "I'm sorry. Something came up at the office and I need to head back. I thought I'd try to catch you on my way out."

"Good timing, because I think I found what you were looking for. Looks like this is it," he said, holding up a file labeled *Housing Authority of Portland v. Melvin Jackson.* "No privileged information there, so I had Clarissa's assistant make copies if you want to just take them with you."

He handed me about twenty pages of paper that had been clipped together.

"I'm sorry I can't do more for you right now, but, like I said, I'll do the review as fast as I can."

I let him think I was satisfied leaving it at that. For now.

I started to head directly to the county lot by the Morrison Bridge to pick up a car, then remembered Russell Frist's admonition not to run the case solo if it turned into a murder.

I stopped in the office, hoping Frist would be in an afternoon court appearance. My plan was to leave him an e-mail so he'd know how hard I tried to follow his advice. Unfortunately, he was at his desk shooting the shit with Jessica Walters. I rapped on the door to interrupt.

"Good to see you, Kincaid. I was beginning to wonder whether this morning's screening duty was enough to chase you out of here," he said.

"I'm not so easily chased."

"There you go. Don't let this guy push you around." Jessica was getting up from her chair. "I'm out of here. VQ after work?"

The Veritable Quandary was a veritable institution of downtown drinking and a longtime hangout for the big boys at the DA's office. Russ told Jessica he'd stop by for a quick beer, then asked me if I wanted to join them.

"I doubt I can make it. Something's come up and I'm actually on my way out to Glenville."

"Anything having to do with Glenville is my cue to leave," Jessica said. "Russ, I'll catch you later. Sam, if I can't get you a beer tonight, we'll do it next time."

"So," Russ asked, "what in suburbia could possibly be more important than a Monday-night drink?"

"Ray Johnson just called. I don't have the details, but someone found a body near a construction site out there. The unofficial ID suggests it's Easterbrook."

To my surprise, Russ made the sign of the cross. "Damn it. Just once, I'd like to see a happy ending on one of these cases."

I was tempted to ask whether he was sure what ending was happier: closure for the living left behind or the hope that remained in a missing person's absence? I kept the thought to myself.

"I told the MCT guys I'd meet them out there," I said. "Are you coming with me?"

"You think you're ready for this, Kincaid?"

"Look, Russ, I appreciate the concern, but if I didn't think I was ready, I wouldn't have accepted the rotation. You told me this morning you thought I was in over my head, so I'm asking if you want to go. Make up your mind, because I'm leaving."

"You've been on a call-out before?"

I flashed my best sarcastic smile. "You know I have, Dad." All new DDAs tag along on a homicide call-out when they first start in the office. If you counted the scene at my house a few weeks ago, I guess I'd been to two.

"Fine, then. I'm switching into good-boss mode. If you don't think you need me, go on your own. But page me if you need me, promise?"

I gave him my most earnest assurances while he wrote down his pager number.

"I'm sure I'll be fine," I said.

"I'll limit myself to two beers at VQ just in case. Call me later, just to let me know what's up?"

It was fair enough, so I told him I would.

I made a brief computer stop to check out Melvin Jackson and get directions to the address Johnson had given me.

I ran Jackson for both local and out-of-jurisdiction convictions. Nothing but a two-year-old DUI and a pop for cocaine residue a year before that. Maybe the second one sounds major, but a stop with some burnt rock in your crack pipe translates into a violation and a fine in Portland, Oregon. What did I expect to find on his record? Repeated offenses for stalking and kidnapping? Despite common perceptions, a remarkable number of murder defendants have no prior involvement with law enforcement.

Next stop: Mapquest. Glenville's one of those new suburbs. You know the kind: stores in big boxes, houses with four-car garages on quarter-acre lots, plenty of Olive Gardens for family dining. I'd watched it grow over the past five years, passing it on the freeway each time I drove to the coast. But I'd never be able to find my way around it without a little virtual help.

I clicked on the option for DRIVING DIRECTIONS and then entered the addresses for the courthouse and the construction site. Two seconds later, voilà—turn-by-turn directions with accompanying map. Whenever I try to figure out how a computer can provide driving directions between any two points in this enormous country of ours, it starts to hurt my head. I choose to chalk it up to magic.

I hoofed it to the county lot, checked out a blue Taurus from the fleet, and did my best to follow the painfully detailed directions.

Around mile four on Highway 26, my cell rang. MCT again. They should have been using my DA pager to reach me. I was careful not to give my cell number out for work.

The call turned out to straddle the line between the personal and professional, a differentiation I'd successfully maintained until a couple of months ago. It was Chuck.

"Where are you?" he asked.

"Just past the zoo. I'm on my way to Glenville."

"Good, I was hoping to catch you in the car. Sorry to bug you on a call-out, but I wanted to make sure you knew that Mike and I are working on this thing too. It didn't sound like Johnson got a chance to tell you."

No, he hadn't. This was great. A relationship with Chuck broke not only my no-cop rule but also the completely independent, profession-neutral rule against dating Chuck. He makes me, in a word, crazy. He is stubborn, headstrong, mule-minded, and every other synonym for a particular characteristic that does not blend well with what I like to call, in contrast, my well-established personality. Dating him would be hard enough; working with him would only make matters worse.

"Russ Frist is running MCU now, and we haven't talked yet

about how to handle this. Hell, Chuck, you and I haven't even talked about it. Given that we haven't spoken to each other in two weeks, maybe this is a nonissue. But right now my mind is on this case, not our relationship. Your working on this investigation is going to force the issue."

Chuck, of course, had no problem talking about "us" just minutes after learning about a murder. He had been in MCT for nearly two years now, which translates into roughly forty homicide cases. Work in this business long enough, and you see death as a detached professional, the way a plumber must view a burst pipe.

"Whoa, back it up, Kincaid. I haven't talked to you for two weeks because you said you needed time away with Grace."

"And I did. All I was saying, Chuck, is that things were all hot and lusty for a while there, and now you haven't talked to me in two weeks. More importantly, I'm in the middle of my first murder case and just can't deal with this right now."

"Hot and lusty, huh?"

Damn him. "Shut up and answer the question."

"I didn't hear a question, counselor."

Crazy. That's what he makes me. Two minutes on the phone with him, and I already had visions of running my Jetta off the road. I hung up instead.

The phone rang immediately.

"I think we got disconnected," he said.

"You know these pesky west hills," I replied.

"Cut you off every time. Look, I'm sorry I pissed you off. All I was trying to say was that you went to Maui because you needed some space. The funny thing about space is that you only get it if the people close to you step back and give it to you."

"I needed to get away from work and from my house, where really bad things happened, Chuck. I didn't need distance from you."

"OK, I understand that. I was there for the aftermath, re-member?"

I passed a sign announcing the approaching exit for Glen-ville and realized I needed to wrap this up. "Look, I'm sorry we didn't talk earlier," I said. "It doesn't matter whose fault it is."

"Sure it does. Let's say it's my fault."

That's my boy. "The point is, we still don't know if it's a good idea to work together. I'll tell Frist to call your lieutenant and take care of it."

"What, like your father called Griffith? You know what kind of shit I'd take down here for that?"

Yes, that had been a bit embarrassing. Dad's a retired forest ranger and former Oregon State Police officer. He can be a little protective. After the recent festivities at my house, Martin Kin-caid had called the District Attorney to make sure that no further coworkers would be getting shot in my living room or other-wise endangering his little girl.

"All right," I conceded, "no calls to the lieutenant."

"It'll be fine. The LT knows about the situation so he's got Mike and me doing the grunt work. No confessions, no searches, strictly backup. The priority right now is to hurry up those phone records Johnson's been waiting on. As other things come up that need to be run down, we'll take care of it while Johnson and Walker work lead. Glamorous, huh?"

"When you say it that way."

"Can you live with it, Kincaid, or do I need to turn in my badge and gun? Your choice."

"You'd do that for me, Chuck Forbes?"

"You bet. But then I wouldn't have a job. Might hang out at your house all day and night, unshaved and overfed. What do you think?"

"I think you better get off the damn phone and find me some phone records."

"Ooh, baby, that's *very* hot and lusty."

"No more of that," I said. "Call me later, OK?"

"Ball's back in my court?"

"For now," I said, and hung up.

When I finally got to the point where I was supposed to go .18 miles and then turn right for .07 miles, I nearly ran into the yellow crime scene tape.

PPB had used the tape to close off the entirety of what the sign declared was a state-of-the-art office park, COMING SOON. A young officer stood at the foot of a gravel road leading to the construction area. I flashed my District Attorney ID, and he described the several turns I'd need to make around the various office buildings.

The day was beginning to lose its light, and the bureau's crime scene technicians were erecting floods at the edge of a wooded area that surrounded the new development. I could see Johnson and Walker were already here, talking to some of the techs. I parked behind one of the bureau's vans and prepared myself for Clarissa Easterbrook's corpse.

I'd seen four dead bodies in my life. One was my mother's, two were in my living room last month, and one was on my first and only homicide call-out. On that one, I'd been lucky enough to draw a fresh OD. Depending on how the events leading to her death unfolded, Clarissa Easterbrook could have been dead up to 35 hours.

Johnson met me at the car and we walked toward the woods. I could tell from the surrounding area that the developer had clear-cut the old growth that must have previously covered these hundred acres or so. When we reached the end of the clearing, Johnson turned sideways and stepped carefully through the trees. I followed and, just a few feet later, saw what used to be

Clarissa Easterbrook, still in her pink turtleneck and gray pants. A lot of good that piece of investigative work had done.

In novels, there's often something beautiful or at least touching about the dead. A victim's arms extended like the wings of an angel, her face at peace, her hand reaching for justice. This was nothing like that. Clarissa Easterbrook's body was laid on the dirt, face up. The right side of her head was gone, and I could find nothing poetic about it.

The only worthwhile observations to be made about the corpse were scientific. I initially focused on the disfigurement of her head, but Johnson pointed out the discoloration on what remained of her face. Purple streaks stained the left edge of her face and neck, like bruising against skin that otherwise looked like silly putty. "Looks like someone moved her."

When blood is no longer pumped by a beating heart, it settles with gravity to the parts of the body closest to the ground. Clarissa Easterbrook was on her back now, but immediately after her death she had almost certainly been lying on her left side.

I watched as crime scene technicians methodically photographed and bagged every item that might potentially become relevant to our investigation. A candy wrapper, several cigarette butts, a rock that looked like it might have blood on it. These items meant nothing now, but any one of them could prove critical down the road. I looked at Clarissa's body again, surrounded now by all this construction and police work, and swore I'd find whoever did this to her.

I gave Johnson and Walker the file on Melvin Jackson's case that Dennis Coakley had copied for me at City Hall. I also gave them approval to file the standard search warrant application used after a homicide to search the victim's house. We agreed, though, that they'd continue to take it easy on Townsend unless the evidence started to point to him.

The police would be working the crime scene for the rest of

the night, but I signed out after a couple of hours, when Johnson and Walker left to deliver the news to Clarissa's family. I don't envy the work of a cop.

It's not as if prosecutors don't have bad days. Our files are filled with desperation and degradation. Even the so-called victimless cases involve acts that could be committed only by pathetic, miserable people who've lost all hope. Compare that to fighting over money for a banking client, and it looks like we're doing the heavy lifting.

But, in the end, I'm still just a lawyer. I issue indictments, plead out cases, and go to trial. When it comes to the investigation, I might make some calls on procedure, but it's the police who do the real work. They're the ones who kick in a door when a search needs to be executed. They're the ones who climb through the dumpster when a gun gets tossed.

And Johnson and Walker would be the ones to visit Clarissa Easterbrook's family members tonight to tell them that their lives would never be the same again. These days, that concept is overused, as we all say that the crumbling of two towers changed the world forever. The kind of change I'm talking about can be claimed only by the families of the three thousand people trapped inside. It's the kind of change that causes every other second of life—the birth of a child, a broken leg, the car breaking down at the side of the road—to be cataloged in the memory in one of two ways: before or after that defining moment in time.

From what I knew of it, everyone deals with the grief of a murder in his own way. There is shock, then rage, then depression, and ultimately some level of acceptance. But then the differences emerge. What kind of survivors would Townsend, Tara, and Mr. and Mrs. Carney become? The ones who die inside themselves and walk around each day wondering when their body will catch up to their soul? The ones seeking numbness in a bottle, the neighbors whispering about how things used to be different? The ones who run the Web sites and help lines and victims' rights groups? Clarissa's family still had options for the future, just not the ones they thought they had when they woke up yesterday.

4

By the time I returned the county's car and caught the bus home, it was after nine o'clock and there were three messages from my father on the machine. The gist of each, respectively? How was the first day of work? I hope you're not working late already. And, finally, You're not working on that case with the missing judge, are you?

I promised myself I'd call my father back before bed, but not just yet. A normal person might want to veg out, watch a little TV, and hit the hay. I wanted to run.

Running is my therapy. My ex-husband called it my escape. No matter what the problem, a run always helps me see life in perspective. Plus, I still felt like I needed to sweat out the rum and mint from the sixty-seven mojitos I must have ingested poolside in Maui.

Even tonight's short three-miler did the trick. After one mile, images of Clarissa Easterbrook's misshapen head and discolored flesh began to slip away. After two, I stopped thinking about work entirely. By the time I got home, I was ready to call my father.

"Sammy?" he said immediately. Dad had recently discovered the wonders of caller ID as part of his constant effort to stay busy. After thirty-plus years of marriage, two years as a widower hadn't been enough for my father to feel relaxed at home alone.

"Yeah, Dad. It's me."

"Late night at work. I was wondering if you were OK."

"Everything's fine. Just a lot to catch up on since I've been out—and with the new unit assignment."

"I bet. So how are the people at the new gig? A step up from the bozos in the drug unit?"

As pleased as my father is that I've used my law degree to follow him into law enforcement, he gets frustrated by the personalities I've had to deal with over the years. The colorful language he uses to discuss my office is his way of showing he's on my side.

"I guess so. The new supervisor's this guy named Russ Frist. Seems pretty decent so far."

"Any cases look interesting yet?"

"You know, they're interesting, but a little depressing. I'd rather hear about what you've been up to. We've hardly talked since I got back."

"You know me. Typical retiree stuff: a couple of movies, some gardening, a trip to the shooting range. Exciting, I know."

"I noticed that my lawn was mowed while I was gone. Thanks."

"No problem. It's not like anyone else needs me. So what kept you so late at the office?"

He was trying to be subtle, but he obviously wanted to know if I was involved in what he was still following as a missing persons case.

"You probably saw the coverage on the administrative law judge. I was wrapped up in that most of the day. Actually, I started working on it last night."

"Jeez, Sam. The minute I saw the news this morning, I knew it. Do you really need to be on a case like this one right off the bat?"

"Those are the kinds of cases I'm working on now, Dad. Major crimes tend to come with the territory in the Major Crimes Unit."

"Very clever, wiseacre. But you know this isn't the usual territory. You're going to be right in the middle of the firestorm, cameras all over you. Nothing will bring out the crazies faster. Did you ask your office to put you on something else until you get used to the new rotation?"

"No, Dad, and I don't plan to. This is my job; you should be proud of me for getting promoted. I didn't become a prosecutor to handle drug cases the rest of my life."

My first excursion from my standard drug and vice caseload had finally come last month when I had prosecuted a psychopath for the rape and attempted murder of a teenage prostitute. By the time the case was closed, a couple of nut jobs had broken into my house, bashed me on the head, and killed the former supervisor of the Major Crimes Unit. I'd avoided a similar fate only because I'd forced myself to become a good shot years ago when my ex-husband insisted on keeping a gun in our apartment. My father may have been a lawman himself, but he hadn't gotten used to the idea of his little girl shooting her way out of trouble.

"I *am* proud of you, Sam," he said, "but maybe you should hold off on something so big. You're finally out of the spotlight after the Derringer case. This one's going to put you right back out there. For all you know, this judge has run off on a lark. She'll be home safe and sound, and you'll end up the target of some obsessed freak who saw your picture one too many times in the paper."

"Well, this is what I want, OK? And, anyway, she didn't run off, as you say. They found her body today. She's dead. It's a murder case. Does that make you feel better about me handling it?"

I should've stopped then. I'd already gone too far. But I was tired, stressed out, and angry for reasons I couldn't even understand.

"There's no way I'm walking away from a case like this," I said. "Maybe you hung up OSP and ran off to the forest service, but I'm sticking it out."

I apologized immediately, but the words were still out there. I was too young to remember the switch, but I knew Dad had quit the Oregon State Police to become a forest ranger when I was still a kid. My mother had never been particularly comfortable as a cop's wife. You never knew when that expired tag you pulled over on highway patrol was going to belong to a guy running from a warrant, thinking to himself, *I'm never going back.*

I had vague recollections of my parents' hushed arguments behind their bedroom door about Dad's job. At the time, I had no idea what they were all about, but in retrospect, and in light of the timing, I gathered that Mom had put the screws to him.

And so Dad had let go of his law enforcement dreams to patrol Oregon's national forests until his retirement just last year. He enjoyed the steady outdoor hours and his federal pension, but I knew he sometimes wondered what he'd missed out on in the career he left behind for his family.

"I just want you to be proud of me, Dad. When you treat me like a little girl, I feel like I'm not in control of anything in my life."

"You know I'm *proud* of you, Sammy. Of course I'm proud of you, not just for your work but for everything you've accomplished. I'm sorry I even brought this up. This isn't about you, it's about me; I forget sometimes how strong you are. But you're my only family left, kid. I don't want anything bad to happen to you."

Why hadn't I seen it that way before? "Nothing's going to happen. Hey, a couple psychopaths came after me, and I still turned out OK." We both laughed. "Seriously, Dad, I am so sorry for what I said. I snapped at you because, honestly, I've got some doubts myself about how I'm going to learn to get through days like this one. I went out to the crime scene this afternoon, and seeing her body—I can't stop thinking about it. But I really want this assignment. I'll probably do more than my fair share of whining about it," I added, "but I want to feel like it's OK to do that around you without you telling me to take myself off the case, all right?"

"In other words, the old man needs to lay off."

"Dad—"

"I'm kidding," he said, cutting me off. "Get some sleep now, OK? You must need it after the day you've had."

I was still feeling guilty about my little tirade. "Can I come over for dinner tomorrow night?"

"You know you don't need to ask. You can even bring the runt."

He was referring, of course, to Vinnie. Dad had taken him in while I was gone, saving me from a choice between the kennel and sneaking Vinnie into the hotel.

When I hung up, Vinnie turned away from me, still pissed off about the temporary abandonment. He caved when I headed up the stairs, though. By the time I hit the sheets, he had grabbed his Gumby doll and jumped in with me.

No matter how important the missing person, an investigation moves more quickly once the body is found.

Dennis Coakley, who had been dragging his heels yesterday, had hurried to a slow crawl. I got his message first thing Tuesday morning: "I heard the terrible news about Clarissa and wanted you to know I'm still working away here, the highest possible priority. I'll call you when I'm done."

We'd see about that.

I also had a message from Susan Kerr, who clearly moved at a much faster clip. "Hi, this is Susan Kerr. Obviously, I've heard the news, and I won't even bother trying to tell you how horrible the night was for everyone. I think the reality is still setting in for all of us. Anyway, I wanted you to know that I'll be helping Clarissa's family with arrangements—they're obviously not in the best state right now to pay attention to all the details. Tara's doing OK, definitely a help to her parents. Townsend, on the other hand—well, quite frankly, I'm worried about him. In any event, I'm doing what I can, so, if you need anything from anyone, please feel free to call me. Anything at all." Before she hung up, she left every possible number where she might be located.

Susan was dealing with death by taking charge. My mother had been the same way. The few times she'd lost anyone—and I mean anyone: a neighbor, a cousin, her father—she went straight to work. Call the funeral director, the insurance companies, the creditors. Prepare frozen casseroles and lasagnas to store for the family. It was like she had a death checklist, full of tasks to keep her busy until the body was in the ground.

Watching my mother in action, I had never understood her motivation. Did she need to stay distracted from the death itself? Was it a means of obtaining control over a world that felt unpredictable? Or was it just an earnest desire to help those who weren't as strong as she was? Whatever Susan Kerr's motivation, I was glad someone close to Clarissa could play that role. Having seen Townsend attempt to deal with the mere possibility of his wife's death, I couldn't imagine what the confirmation of his worst fears had done to him.

I replayed the message to scribble down her phone numbers, then went on to the next voice mail. "Hi, Samantha, Susan Kerr again. Just wanted to let you know I think I'll go ahead and call Duncan, just to make sure you've got all the support you feel you need, OK? Thanks, Samantha. I appreciate having someone devote her personal attention to my friend."

I wasn't surprised that someone with Susan Kerr's resources already knew my boss. If she wanted to make sure he was giving me all the support I deserved, I was all for it.

With the voice mails out of the way, I called Johnson to check in.

"We broke the news to the family last night. The parents and sister first, then the husband. Nothing unusual. The sister gave us the official ID while we were working on the search."

"The husband didn't have a problem with it?"

"No. We explained that a search of the vic's house is standard and that we had a warrant. He said he understood that the investigation needed to proceed."

"Did you find anything?"

"Nothing that means anything yet. We took bank records, credit card statements—the usual stuff that sometimes means something down the road. But we already knew from the walkthrough the other night that we weren't going to find any obvious signs that she'd been done in the house.

"Chuck and Mike came through on getting records for the recent credit card charges and cell calls. We're still working on getting the toll records for the home phone.

"We've got a charge at Nordstrom on Saturday. Adds up to the items we found in the shopping bag, plus the pants and sweater she was wearing on Sunday. The only charge after that was on Sunday, right after noon, at the Pasta Company."

I knew the place. Or places, I should say. The Pasta Company is a popular local chain.

"Which one?" I asked, since I could think of six or seven locations off the top of my head.

"Terwilliger and Barbur." Made sense. Only a mile or so from the Easterbrooks'.

"I sent a patrol officer over there with her picture. A couple of employees said they recognized her because she's in there a lot, but no one could place her there for sure on Sunday."

"There's no way to know if she was alone?" I asked.

"No, but she probably was. One order of linguine in browned butter, no tip. A carry-out order, it turns out. Walker drew short straw and got trash duty. Duly noted beneath the sink: one empty Styrofoam container from the Pasta Company."

"So she picked up lunch on Sunday and ate at home by herself. Great. All that work, and the credit card records don't get us any closer than we were the other night."

"Did I say I was finished, Kincaid? Damn, girl, anyone ever tell you you're a glass-half-empty kind of woman? I haven't told you about the autopsy yet."

"The ME's done already?" It usually took a couple of days.

"It's been a light week so there's no backup. He made the cuts first thing this morning. Report should be finished tomorrow, but I just got off the phone with him a minute ago. You want to continue to interrupt me, or do you want to get to the good stuff?"

"Consider me quiet."

"Yeah, right. I'll get in what I can. Anyway, cause of death is what we assumed: blunt force trauma to the right side of the head. He was having some difficulties with time of death, though. He couldn't use some of the factors that help when the body's fresh. It had clearly been awhile, because she was cold."

"How long does that take?" I asked.

"That puts us back to yesterday. But things get tricky past that window. And they were even trickier in this case, because we were right about her being moved. I'll spare you the details, but the ME's got a problem interpreting things like bloating and bugs when he doesn't know what kind of environment the body was in. We couldn't tell him if she was inside, outside, wet, dry, in a heater, whatever."

"So—"

"Patience, woman. See, you were about to say, 'So he can't tell us the time of death,' right?"

"Maybe." *Definitely.*

"See, now, that'd be an inaccurate statement. ME calls and tells me he might have to give us a wide window for time of death unless I know when she ate last. At the time he called me, I didn't, but, you see, now I do. And the ME tells me she died within one to three hours of eating noodles, which he found in the stomach contents. Assuming she ate the food around twelve-thirty, she died between one-thirty and three-thirty."

"Broad daylight."

"You got it. Makes an abduction off the street less likely but still possible."

My phone beeped, indicating that another call was coming through. The name of the DA's secretary flashed on the caller ID screen. I let the line go to voice mail.

"What else?" I asked Johnson. "Was she raped?"

"Unclear. Looks like she was naked when she was hit. The ME says there was no spatter on the clothes, either low or high velocity, which he'd expect to find. But there was brain matter and blood transfer—like smears—inside the sweater, as if it was pulled on afterward. Also, he found spermicidal jelly in the vaginal canal, but no boy juice and no substantial tearing. No skin under the nails, no sign of a fight."

"What's all that mean?"

"Means she probably had sex, but it might or might not have been rape. The stuff he found was the spermicide nonoxynol-9, which comes on most condoms. There was a time when that would've ruled out a rape, but things have changed since the bad guys learned about the DNA databank. And if she was just trying to get through it alive, she might not have fought back."

"On the other hand," I said, "maybe it's not a sex crime at all, and the coroner found something left over from consensual sex."

"Right. So I need to follow up with the husband and see what he has to say."

"How much are you going to tell him?" I asked.

"Nothing. If it's about to go public for some reason, we'll get to them first. Other than that, it's on a need to know basis. I'll ask him the last time they had sex and what kind of birth control they use. He'll no doubt draw some inferences about that and ask me if she was raped, but I'll tell him what I'm going to tell the rest of the family, which is the truth: We don't know."

"How about Melvin Jackson? Have you had a chance to talk to him yet?"

"Who's that again?"

"The evicted guy? Wrote mean, threatening letters? I gave you the file yesterday."

"Right. Sorry, we've been juggling a lot here. When we broke the news to the family last night, I asked them if the name sounded familiar, but they didn't think Clarissa ever mentioned him by name. We haven't followed up yet with Jackson, but it'll happen."

"Very good. Anything else?"

"You know, we're also checking on everyone close to the vic. I even checked out our girl Susan Kerr. At the museum all day setting up for a fund-raising auction, then schmoozing all night, just like she said. So we're working from the victim out, but Jack and I agree we also need to take the location into account."

These were standard investigative approaches. On the assumption that the crime isn't random—since they rarely are—police look to the aspects of the offense that are unique. That usually means investigating everything there is to know about the victim. Victim's a working girl? Most likely killed by a trick or her pimp. Dealer? Probably a transaction gone bad or a robbery.

But crimes have also been solved by focusing on location. Who, for example, would know the layout of the home from which the sleeping child was kidnapped? A neighbor. Maybe a handyman. And here Johnson made a good point. The Columbia Gorge and Forest Park were the locals' favorite body-dumping destinations. Who would find their way to the edge of a previously nonexistent office park?

"Do we know who the future tenant is?"

"There isn't one. It's one of those 'if you build it, they will come' things." In recent years, Portland's suburbs have enticed out-of-town firms to relocate operations to this area with the promise of tax subsidies, an educated workforce, and ready-to-go infrastructure. "We're going over lists of the usual suspects within a two-mile radius of the crime scene and the Easterbrooks'. Jack's working on getting a list of workers at the construction site. There's a couple different unions and subcontractors involved, so it's taking a little longer than we'd like. We're also looking at old police reports involving any incidents along Taylor's Ferry Road. It's mostly car prowls and a few robberies."

"Page me if you need anything," I said. "As soon as I'm done screening custodies, I'm going to review Clarissa's files." Unfortunately, no one at City Hall knew that yet.

"We can send someone over for that," he offered, assuming I had permission to go in.

"No, I better do it. I'll be able to get through them faster."

"I'll try not to take that personally, Kincaid."

"Hey, law school's got to be good for something, right?"

A decent morning at work never lasted long. When Johnson and I were done, I retrieved the message from Duncan's secretary. The boss wanted to see me.

Duncan was tan as ever, despite the rain. He had to be closing in on fifty, but in appearance the guy was strangely age-ambiguous: a full head of white hair, the kind of wrinkles that are "distinguished," and a movie star smile that in my presence has left his face only once.

"How was Salem?"

"Useless as always. Legislators just don't get what we're trying to accomplish. I was down testifying yesterday about drug courts. The liberals don't want to see anyone go to prison on a drug case, and the law-and-order types want to lock 'em all up, whether it works or not. But you're done with drug cases now, aren't you?"

"Looks like it," I said. "Thank you again, Duncan, for giving me a chance in Major Crimes."

"Well, I know it's what you wanted. You might not remember this, Samantha, but you told me that the first time I met you. It's the only time a job candidate has ever admitted wanting to prosecute murder trials. Most people try to hide that kind of ambition."

"You asked me what appealed to me about being a state prosecutor after having served as an AUSA, and I told you the truth. The feds rarely get a murder case."

"Still, it showed you had balls, if you can excuse the phrase."

"You might not believe this, sir, but that's not the first time I've heard that particular compliment. Some day we might even get a gender-neutral word that captures the same gravitas."

"See, that's a perfect example of what I'm talking about. You showed that same personality during your initial interview. When you choose to, you can say what you mean and still be very charming."

When I choose to. For now, I chose to ignore the backhanded part of the compliment. But if he didn't get to the point soon, that voluntary charm of mine was going on strike.

"I asked you to go with the police to the Easterbrook home on Sunday for a reason. You've proven that you've got a real compassion for victims, and I know you've got the ability to be diplomatic and to show this office in its very best light. I also thought it was a chance for you to ease into the new rotation with an MCT call-out.

"But I assumed at the time that Clarissa Easterbrook would turn up. Obviously, she did not, and as a result of my decision you're now on one of the highest profile murder cases we've had in a long time. If we're going to take you off it, we should do it sooner rather than later. Less disruption for the family and for MCT."

"I don't want to be pulled off," I said. "I've already talked to Russ about this, and he's going to oversee as necessary."

"My concern isn't with your experience or your skills. You're a terrific attorney."

"But you have a concern?"

"Susan Kerr called me today," he said, sitting back into his chair and steepling his fingers.

"She told me she was going to. I take it you know her?"

"It's hard not to know her when you've got a public life in Portland. Bert Kerr had his hand in everything, a big fund-raiser for progressive causes. I remember when I first ran for this office, he bought me an eighteen-year-old whiskey at Huber's and asked me what I was going to do as district attorney. He wasn't happy with the typical sound bites; he pressed me on everything: standing up to the police about reverse drug buys, the death penalty, improving the quality of life for neighborhoods. When we were done—and I'll never forget it—he said, 'You're about as good a man as we're gonna get for a job that puts human beings in cages.' A month later, he raised $40,000 for my campaign on a single night.

"Susan—don't call her Sue or Susie—was his new wife back then, and you can bet the tongues were wagging. She was probably about your age, and, my God, she was wild. Everyone assumed she was in it for the money and would be banging the pool boy on the side. But once people talked to her, they just fell in love. She never tried to act like something she wasn't. And she came through for Bert in the end. He was a mess his last couple of years, and she worked her tail off to make sure no one knew it. A good friend of mine told me that by his last days she was basically running the show, signing his name, doing whatever she needed to create the appearance that Bert was still going strong. So, yeah, she can throw her weight around with the best of them, but I have a lot of respect for her."

"What did she say about the case?"

"She said she appreciated the police coming to her home for her convenience. She was also pleased to have an attorney on the case so early. Less likely to have any problems that way. She wanted assurances you'd be free to oversee things, which I, of course, gave her."

"But?"

He chuckled. "Always jumping to the bad news, aren't you? As far as *buts* go, this one was minor. Let me ask you: Where is this investigation heading? Is the husband a suspect?"

"Not at this point. He hasn't set off anyone's hunch bells yet, and he's alibied at OHSU all day Sunday. But he's not cleared, either, so it's natural that the police are still keeping him in mind."

"Susan was concerned about the tone of the questions about the victim's marriage. She got the impression that the police might be looking in only one direction."

I tried to assure him that the police, if anything, were leaning against the husband as a suspect. I told him about Melvin Jackson and the search for any sex offenders near the crime scene.

"Why did the police ask Dr. Easterbrook to take a polygraph last night?"

"They didn't. They've mentioned the possibility, but we haven't made a decision about whether that's the right way to go yet."

"Maybe you've got some mixed signals. Susan Kerr tells me that the police, in addition to being very curious about the state of the Easterbrooks' marriage, asked the husband for a poly last night, just minutes after telling him that his wife's body had been found. That's why she was upset enough to call me."

"Shit. Well, she didn't mention it to me, and she just left me a message this morning."

"She thought it would be best not to put you in an awkward position between her and your detectives, so she brought her concerns to me."

"I don't know what to say, Duncan. I'll ask the MCT guys about it."

"Good. I need you to be the woman you're being today on this, Samantha, the person who came in here for your interview; not the hothead who puts a line of attorneys outside my door complaining about bad behavior."

It has never been a *line:* a slow dribble, maybe. "I only know how to be one person, sir."

"Dammit, Sam. You know what I mean. I'm just warning you, you're dealing with some very influential people on this one who don't look kindly on mistakes. In addition to Mrs. Kerr, you've got Townsend Easterbrook. Let me be clear: If he's the guy, you crush him. But not until there's good reason to. He's not your typical perp who's used to being thrown against the car and frisked for looking the wrong way. He's the chief administrative surgeon at OHSU. For Christ's sake, the man singlehandedly got the hospital's pediatric transplant wing off the ground again after everyone wrote the project off as dead. He's Mother Teresa with a penis."

"So you're asking me to give these people special treatment." It wasn't a question.

"If you could even begin to think like a realist, you'd know I was asking you to give them the expected treatment."

There was no use putting up a fight over this, since I'd already been treating Townsend and Susan "as expected." I assured him I got the message, loud and clear.

Back at my desk, I put in a page to Johnson. Why hadn't he told me about the polygraph? My phone sat silent, though, as I finished screening duty with just a few more strokes of the pen. I couldn't wait here all day for him to call—it was time to get my hands on Clarissa's files.

I got lucky. My first choice judge, David Lesh, had just finished a plea and was working in his chambers. Lesh was a former prosecutor. He was also a former employee of the City Attorney's Office, but his job there was to advise the police. He wouldn't look kindly on Dennis Coakley's obstructionism.

He gave me a warm welcome. "Get in here, Kincaid. I haven't seen you since all hell broke loose. How are you holding up? You look great."

"Thanks, Judge." Lesh was a regular fixture on the happy-hour circuit and an absolute nut, but his position required certain formalities. "I'm doing surprisingly well. I took some time off, and now I'm in the Major Crimes Unit."

"Well, good for you. You deserve it. If it means anything, I think you did a great job in the Derringer trial."

His delivery, without an iota of irony, evoked a sharp laugh from me. An actual guffaw. "Oh, yeah, ended beautifully," I said.

"At least you've got a sense of humor about it. So what are you here for?"

"I'm working on the Clarissa Easterbrook case."

His tone changed markedly, as was Lesh's way. Irreverence always took a backseat to the things that mattered. "I heard about that this morning. The saddest thing. She was such a nice woman. Did you know her?"

"No, but I did meet her once. I guess you knew her from the City Attorney's Office."

"Not from work so much as just being around City Hall together. She was a really great gal, the kind of person who genuinely wanted to hear the answer when she'd ask how you were doing. Are you guys getting anywhere on nailing whoever did this to her?"

"Bureau's working on it," I said, shaking my head, "but nothing yet. That's actually why I stopped by. We want to look at her files to see if someone might have had a grudge, but we're having some problems getting in. I don't want to get too far into an explanation since it would be ex parte, but I'd like to get someone over here from the City Attorney's Office, if you don't mind."

Judges weren't supposed to talk about a case with only one of the lawyers present.

"I take it Coakley's not letting you in?" he asked.

"Well, he hasn't said one way or the other, but I wanted to do the file review yesterday. I even walked over there and was ready to do it."

"Let's see what he's got to say about it."

He picked up his phone and punched in a number from memory. After Lesh was a prosecutor and before he was a judge, Coakley was Lesh's Duncan Griffith. Some bad blood was rumored, so this might be fun.

"Dennis Coakley, please. This is Circuit Court Judge David Lesh."

Lesh was too much of a pro to drop his poker face, but I'd heard him make calls before. He's usually just plain old David Lesh.

"Mr. Coakley, how are you? . . . I've got Samantha Kincaid in my chambers. Do you have a second to walk over here for a quick discussion? . . . Well, she doesn't seem to agree. . . . Unless you tell me she can get in there right now to see what she wants to see, I think you do have a disagreement. . . . I *know* it's unconventional, but it's also the easiest way to do it. Do you really want to formalize this? I could have her apply for a warrant, in which case you wouldn't even be here for my decision. . . . All right, I'll see you in a few."

A pissed-off Coakley walked in a few short minutes later. If we'd been in Toon Town, his face would have been red, his ears smoking, and he would have been storming in at a forty-five degree lean. In the real world, his neck vein was pulsing. Not nearly as cute.

"All right," Lesh said, once Dennis was settled, "any need for a court reporter?" We both declined. "Just so you know,

Ms. Kincaid was careful not to tell me too much about the nature of the dispute until you were here. I know she wants to look in Clarissa Easterbrook's files, and you told me you didn't feel you were able to accommodate that, at least not on the DA's timeline. Is that about right?"

I nodded, but Coakley had come ready for a fight. "Honestly, Judge, I can't even believe we're here. Ms. Kincaid showed up at my office yesterday, unannounced. I gave her the one and only file she described as being of interest, and I've been working ever since to view the remaining files for privileged information. I'm nearly done, and pulling me away from that process only slows things down. I feel ambushed."

Lesh asked me if I wanted to respond.

"I was not trying to ambush anyone, your honor. The problem is that Mr. Coakley assumes he has the singular right to decide when and where and under what terms those files can be reviewed as part of a pressing homicide investigation. The fact of the matter is I could have applied for a search warrant and shown up at City Hall with police to execute it. I thought having a judge mediate the discussion might facilitate an agreement about the matter."

"Right," Coakley scoffed, "and you just happened to pick a judge who used to work for me."

Lesh made a T with his hands. "Whoa, that judge is still in the room, thank you very much. As you know, Dennis, I made a decision when I became a judge not to remove myself from all cases involving the city or the DA's office, just the ones that were pending while I worked for those offices. That said, if you think I'm biased, you are welcome to ask me to recuse myself, and I won't fight it. We'll get another judge for you. Just say the word."

Local custom holds that judges will remove themselves from a case based solely on an attorney's request. But local practice holds that no lawyer ever actually makes such a request lest it burn them down the road, either with the challenged judge or the one unlucky enough to pick up the extra work.

"That's not necessary, your honor."

"Then let's get down to business. You know why the DA wants to get into those files: There's always the possibility that someone on a case had it out for Clarissa. Tell me precisely what your concern is about letting her have a look." Lesh gestured at me. "You'd be doing the review, right? Not your officers?"

"That's correct, your honor."

Coakley repeated the same line he'd given me the day before.

And Lesh had the same response. "Wait a second. I don't understand why her files would contain any communications with you. The city's a party, for Christ's sake."

"We don't know what kind of internal memoranda she made about other privileged matters in an employment context, though, your honor, or how she maintained those memoranda. I just want a chance to peruse each file and ensure that it contains only case information. It's standard practice in document production."

Lesh made my argument for me. "Maybe in a civil suit, but this is a murder investigation. You're talking about a theoretical possibility that Clarissa Easterbrook—who is now dead, by the way—not only had a conversation with someone in your office but that she recorded it in some form and then placed it in a case file where Ms. Kincaid might stumble upon it unwittingly. And you think this possibility warrants a delay in a murder investigation?"

"Not a substantial one, your honor. As I said, I'm almost done."

Lesh shook his head. He had worked both the civil and criminal sides of the bar, but even he was incredulous at this particular civil litigator's priorities. "How far have you gotten, Dennis?"

Coakley pursed his lips and thought a second. "Probably eighty percent."

"And was there anything in that eighty percent that you needed to redact?"

"No, there wasn't."

"Of course not," Lesh said. "OK, here's what we're doing, kids. Dennis, get the files that you've completed ready for Ms. Kincaid to review at City Hall. Where should she go?"

Coakley clearly thought about arguing, but hedged his bets that things could get worse and relented. "Clarissa's office would probably be best."

"Good. While she reviews those, you're free to continue working on the remaining twenty percent. But if she gets done before you do, too bad. The two of you can race to the finish."

We both said thank you and started to leave. Before I walked out, Lesh called me back. "Samantha, do you have a minute?"

"Of course, your honor."

Once the door was closed, he asked me to sit down. "What was that all about?"

"I'm not sure what you mean."

"I certainly hope that's not the case, or you're going to have a very rough career ahead of you. Did you really need me for that?"

"We were at an impasse, your honor. I thought you'd help us reach a compromise, and you did."

"It's my job, Kincaid, and I haven't turned into one of those lazy sacks who's complaining about more work—yet," he said, knocking on his wood desk. "But you didn't even talk to Coakley about this before coming to me, did you?"

"Not since yesterday," I said.

"Before Clarissa's body was found," he said, shaking his

head. "The guy was eighty percent done, so he meant it when he said he'd been working on it. The fact is, you could have come to the same solution with a phone call. But he probably gave you a hard time yesterday, so you decided you'd teach him a lesson. And don't think for a minute that I'm not aware why you handpicked me as your weapon."

I didn't say anything.

"It's not my business, but—just some friendly advice. I know Coakley, and I'd bet money that word of this will get back to Griffith." That would be terrific, given the meeting we'd just had. "Don't forget, I've worked for that office too. You've got to stop butting heads, or you're in for a world of hurt."

People feel perfectly free to lecture me about butting heads, but who scolds the buttheads? Maybe Lesh could bend the will of jerks like Coakley through charm and personality, but I've found those kind of people will run me over if I don't stand up for myself. I still loved Lesh, but until he walked a mile in my Ferragamos, he didn't have a clue as to what my job was like.

I thanked him again for his help and headed back to my office.

5

WHILE I WAS packing up what I needed for the file review, I heard a tap on my open door and turned to find Russ Frist wheeling my long-lost leather chair into the office.

"Lucy," I said in my best Desi impersonation, "you got some 'splaining to do."

He flicked a manila envelope onto my desk in front of me.

"Good shot." I looked at the envelope but didn't open it.

"What can I say? Too much ultimate Frisbee in the Corps."

"I wouldn't have guessed that about you, Frist. When I was in college, the ultimate Frisbee guys were big dope smokers."

"Right, but they probably never inhaled. Let's just agree that you probably shouldn't extrapolate too much from your Harvard experience, Kincaid."

"Nor you from the Marine Corps."

"Touché."

"Now shut up, soldier, and tell me why you have my beloved chair."

"Open the envelope," he said.

Inside, I found two Polaroids of my chair and a series of ransom notes written with letters cut from magazines.

"A couple of the guys heard about your unhealthy relationship with the office furniture and thought it would be a funny way to welcome you to the Unit. I put the kibosh on it after Duncan called you out on the Easterbrook case. Seemed like it would be in poor taste."

"Gee. You think?"

"Just take the chair, Kincaid. You have been spared the usual rites of passage."

"Spared, or is this simply a reprieve?"

"You're a smart woman."

"Great. I'll keep my back up."

"Like you wouldn't anyway?"

As he turned to leave, I said, "Don't you want to know about the Easterbrook case?"

"Of course I do. I was just waiting to see if you'd tell me on your own."

I was starting to like this guy. I filled him in on what I'd learned so far from the investigation. "I was just about to head over to review the victim's files." I left out the part where I hauled the City Attorney into court to speed access. "You want to come with?"

"The joys of document review. No thanks. If I liked scouring through boxes of files on the off chance of finding a little nugget, I'd be over at Dunn Simon making a shitload of money."

It's helpful as a prosecutor to remind yourself occasionally of the things (other than lots of money) that go along with civil practice at the big prestigious firms. I was a summer associate at Dunn Simon after my first year in law school. I got paid twice what I make in my current position for what amounted to a two-month job interview. But I knew I'd never want to work there after a young partner explained to me why he loved the peculiar formatting that the firm insisted on for each and every document: "It's just the Dunn Simon way." Yuck.

"I don't know, Russ. Might have to pull a Little Red Hen on your ass."

"I'm afraid I'm not familiar with your literary reference. I tend to read material for adults."

"Yeah, right. The kind with pictures that fold out in the middle. I mean that you don't eat the bread unless you help plant the grain. I'm picturing myself in the first and only chair in *State v. Yet to Be Determined* for the murder of Clarissa Easterbrook."

"You keep dreaming, Kincaid, because it's not gonna happen. Besides, I've got a good excuse, not that I need to give you one. Judge Maurer sent a case out for trial this afternoon that I was sure would settle, so I need to get ready. Have fun with those administrative law files, though. Sounds like a blast."

I welcomed my chair back into its new home and scooted old blue crusty into the hallway with a piece of paper pinned to its back that read HAZARDOUS WASTE. Given the state of the budget around here, it still might be a step up for someone.

Nelly Giacoma remembered me from the day before. She tried to sound chipper when she welcomed me into the office, but I could tell from her puffy eyes and congested voice that she'd been crying. I asked if I could see Clarissa's files.

"Dennis Coakley told me you'd be coming by. I needed to keep busy, so I helped make sure we had all the pending cases. He's got everything in piles for you in the conference room at the end of the hall."

The conference room turned out to be little more than a storage space that held the water cooler and a bulletin board posting the required equal employment disclosures. There were four boxes of files stacked in the corner and a small table I could use for work space.

"Do you need anything?" Nelly asked.

"No, I should be fine. Thanks."

"You sure? Because I think I'm going to head out. Judge Olick told me to take the rest of the day off. I was going to try to finish some things up, but I'm pretty useless right now."

"You should definitely go. I'll be fine."

"Thanks. Just let yourself out."

I thanked her again and turned to the files. I began by spreading the boxes side by side on the floor, quickly scanning the file headings to see if anything jumped out. Nope. No IN THE EVENT SOMETHING BAD HAPPENS or LITIGANTS WHO HATE ME files, just case names.

I started at the beginning, dictating the names of the parties and the nature of the dispute for each file into the hand-sized recorder I still owned from my days at the U.S. Attorney's Office. The machine served more as a paperweight in my current position, since the District Attorney staff refuses to type for the deputies. But considering I didn't even know what I was looking for, taped notes would be good enough for now.

Case after case, nothing seemed relevant. One thing was for certain: There would be no problems finding things of interest in *my* files. In fact, the problem would be too *many* defendants who were angry, mean, or outright psycho enough to go after me. On a weekly basis in the drug unit, some dealer who blamed me for the sentencing guidelines would throw me a devil eye, his thrusted chest, or—the very worst—the blood-boiling c-word. Hell, I could fill one side of a tape with the spitters alone. Experienced prosecutors know always to sit at the end of the table farthest from the defendant.

Clarissa Easterbrook's caseload, on the other hand, was a major snooze. How disgruntled can a person be about a citation for unmowed grass, an unkempt vacant house, or a toilet left on the front porch? Although a few of them huffed and puffed in their appeal papers, the tough talk was generally reserved for the nosy neighbors who had sicced the city on them or the unfeeling civil servants who responded, and even those were rare. More typically, the appellants tried hard—embarrassingly so—to be lawyerlike in their prose. Lots of henceforths, herewiths, and theretofores.

When I got to the *J*s, I came across the Melvin Jackson file. Now *this* one stood out. At least two letters a week for the past six weeks, filed in reverse chronological order under CORRESPON-DENCE. They began as pleas for compassion about his recent past, which I learned went like this:

Melvin Jackson was the father of three children, ages two to six. He and his wife, Sharon, had always struggled with their shared addictions, but when their youngest son, Jared, was born addicted to crack cocaine, Melvin entered the rehabilitation program offered by the office for Services to Children and Families as an alternative to losing Jared. Through the program, Melvin had gotten clean. Sharon hadn't. One afternoon, Melvin came home from his part-time job as a Portland State janitor to find another man leaving his apartment and Sharon inside naked, smoking up with Jared in her arms, the other two children curled together on the sofa. He told her to choose between the drugs and her children. The next morning, Sharon went to SCF and signed a voluntary termination of parental rights.

Melvin had been taking care of the kids ever since. He saved enough money for a used van and was getting by through public housing, public assistance, and occasional work as a landscaper and handyman.

Melvin was about to lose his public housing because of his unemployed cousin, who moved in with him a year ago in exchange for watching Melvin's kids when he worked. One night four months ago, a community policing officer assigned to the Housing Authority of Portland caught the cousin and her friends smoking pot on the apartment complex swing set. The officer found less than an ounce, decriminalized in Oregon, so the only repercussion for the cousin was a ticket for possession, no more than a traffic matter. But federal regulations authorize public housing agencies to evict tenants who have drugs on the property. The problem for Melvin was that public housing evictions aren't by the tenant; they're by the unit. Two days after the swing set smokeout, HAP served Melvin with a notice of eviction. Then an SCF caseworker told him his kids would be placed in foster care if he became homeless.

I knew a little bit about these kinds of evictions. A few years ago, the United States Supreme Court upheld the federal housing policy nine-zip, permitting the eviction of a law-abiding grandmother whose grandson smoked pot on public housing property. Never mind that she'd taken in her grandson to save him from a drug-addicted mother. The only option for someone in Melvin's place was to hope for leniency, but it would have to come from the housing authority; a court could do nothing about it.

Clarissa's notes in the file suggested that, at least initially, Melvin had earned her sympathy. One entry during the second week she'd had the case noted:

> Called Cathy Wexler @ HAP: zero tolerance policy/won't budge. Called SCF info line: No knowledge/can't discuss ind'l case, but 'very possible' take kids if lose housing.

She had even run some computerized searches on Westlaw looking for authority to support the argument that HAP was prohibited from adopting a zero-tolerance policy on eviction.

Unfortunately for Melvin, however, he chose a course of conduct that had probably obliterated that sympathy before

Clarissa had found any law to back up the creative argument she was trying to craft on his behalf. By the fifth letter, his tone had changed. All caps and exclamation points don't go over well with judges. More recently, Melvin's letters became aggressive:

> *Do you have children of your OWN, Judge Easterbrook? What kind of person would allow this to happen? Maybe someday you will know just how UNFAIR life can be. Are you trying to BREAK me?*

I could see why Clarissa wrote them off as the desperate words of a desperate man. But the benefit of hindsight made me wonder if Clarissa might still be alive if someone had been able to help Melvin Jackson or at least deflect his anger from a judge who was on his side but powerless to do anything about it.

As I was starting in on the *N*s, Dennis Coakley walked in with another box of files. If I was counting right, that made me a hell of a lot faster than he was.

"Not very exciting, is it?" he said.

"Not particularly."

"So was it worth that little scene you scripted this morning?"

"Won't know until I finish the files," I said. If I had boy parts, he never would have called my power move a *little scene*. It would be a *fast ball*, a *line drive*, an *outside shot*, or some other ridiculous sports analogy that I don't understand.

"Just like I couldn't know if I had something important to deal with until I took a look," he said, stomping off.

By the time noon came around, I had finished reviewing the very last file. Nothing. Two hours of work and all I had to show for it was my monotone summary of Clarissa Easterbrook's pending caseload. The drone of my own voice, combined with the steady hum of the water cooler, had been enough to make me nod off a few times.

My legal pad was hardly used, but to keep myself from sleeping I had made three lists. One was a list of cases where Clarissa said something at the hearing to indicate she'd be ruling for the city, but where she hadn't yet issued a formal ruling. Maybe someone decided to ensure a rehearing with a different judge. Possible, but not probable.

The second list was even shorter. I jotted down a few names to run in PPDS when I got back to the office, but each seemed an unlikely suspect. Sheldon Smithers found a lock on his front tire, courtesy of the city, after one too many unpaid parking tickets. He made my list for sending a rant about the hypocrisy of reserving parking spaces for the administrative law judges in the city lot. That, and the serial-killerish name.

Then there was Ronald Nathan Wilson. A month ago, Ronald punched the glass out on the hearing room door after Clarissa denied his challenge to the city's seizure of his car. It's a long way from vandalism to murder, I know, but the seizure was for picking up a decoy in a prostitution sting, sinking Ronald deeper into the creep pile. And, again, the name didn't help. Six letters each: first, middle, and last. Everyone knows 6–6–6 is the sign of the devil.

I wasn't sure what to do with my third list. These were cases from which Clarissa had recused herself. A restaurant manager whose application for a sidewalk café license had been rejected. A homeowner whose third-floor addition was enjoined under the nuisance code. A contractor complaining that his requests to rehabilitate buildings in the Pearl District had been declined unfairly.

Maybe one of them had complained that Clarissa had a grudge against him but hadn't gotten word yet that she was recusing herself. I knew it was a stretch, but I had to leave that room with *something*.

I used my cell phone to check my work voice mail. As long as there were no new fires to put out, I was actually going to make my lunch date with Grace. Only three new messages: one from Dad reminding me about dinner, one from Frist about a grand jury hearing at the end of the week that I had already calendared, and one from Jessica Walters asking me to try her later. Still nothing from Johnson.

I considered returning Dad's call but wasn't up for another conversation like we'd had the night before. Instead, I flipped my phone shut and considered myself on a well-deserved lunch break.

Grace and I have a handful of regular lunchtime meeting places located roughly halfway between the courthouse and her salon, Lockworks. Today's pick was the Greek Cusina on Fourth, which I always spot by the gigantic purple octopus protruding above the door. Don't ask me what the connection is.

Grace was waiting for me in our favorite corner booth, great for people-watching. We could peek out, but a potted rubber tree plant made it unlikely we'd be seen from the street.

She looked terrific, as always. Physically, Grace and I are yin and yang. I've got dark-brown straight hair; her color changes by the day, but I know those cute little curls are naturally blond. She's trendy; my clothes (unless bought by Grace) come in black, gray, charcoal, slate, and ebony. I'm five-feet-eight, she's five-three. She eats all she wants, never works out, and can wear stuff from the kids' department. I eat half of what I want and run at least twenty-five miles a week, just to maintain a size in the single digits. She's put together; I'm a mess. Set aside those differences, and we're twins.

"Hey, woman," she said, standing up to kiss my cheek. "I've missed you. I sort of liked being roommates. Maybe we should try it here at home."

"Might not be the same without the beach."

"Or the rum," she added.

"Don't sell the condo just yet; we could wind up killing each other. Did you order already?"

"Yeah, I figured it was safe."

Grace knows I always get the Greek platter: a gyro, a side of spanikopita, and a little Greek salad. That converts into roughly six miles.

Once I'd settled in across from her, Grace asked me to tell her all about my new life in the Major Crimes Unit.

"I promise I will get to it, but, please, not just yet. I need a break from thinking about the horrible things people do to each other. Tell me a little bit about your homecoming. Anything good at the salon?"

Grace opened Lockworks, a two-story full-service salon-slash-spa, in the haute Pearl District a few years ago. Never mind that back then she was a marketing executive without a beautician's license. What Grace had was business sense. She managed to swing a loan for an entire warehouse, which she converted into the first of what are now many upscale salons targeting the hordes of trendy young professionals flocking to Portland. Today the building alone is worth millions, and clients wait weeks to pay Grace a small fortune for a haircut or highlight.

"I've been swamped. The first vacation I've taken since I opened that place, but it doesn't keep people from getting pissed off. I've been on my feet for the last forty-eight hours, comping cuts for clients who refused appointments with the girls who were subbing for me."

"I guess they know you're the best."

"One way to look at it," she said.

"Or they're just pricks."

She clinked her water glass against mine.

For the next fifteen minutes, I sat back and listened to Grace's stories about beautiful people who aren't as beautiful as they want to be. The whining, the temper tantrums, the unrepentant displays of vanity. I had packed away half of my chicken gyro by the time she finished telling me her latest Hollywood story. Grace has become the preferred stylist for the film productions that increasingly choose to go on location in Portland. Apparently, someone with too much money offered Grace a big wad of dough to do body waxing for an eye-candy movie being shot in the Columbia Gorge about windsurfers. Fortunately, Grace had enough money to take a pass.

"In addition to the obvious yuck factor, most of the half-naked unknowns are teenagers," she explained.

"I would've thought that was right up your alley, Grace. You're ripening pretty well into a dirty old woman." I had teased Grace endlessly in Hawaii each time her gaze predictably and shamelessly followed whatever young stud crossed our field of vision. I plowed through the entire Jack Reacher series during our poolside time; Grace was still working on the same novel on our flight back to Oregon.

"As tempting as that sounds, there's a little too much Oedipal potential there. Better stay put in the city for now. Check out men my own age." She gave me that cute little wink she somehow manages to pull off when she's being cheeky. "Now can we please knock off the chitchat and get down to business? What have you been working on? I want every last detail."

Because of my job, Grace's skin has thickened to violence through osmosis. When I first started handling compelling prostitution cases in DVD, she saw me through more than a few long nights.

My ex-husband once told me I shouldn't talk about my cases while people were eating; it wasn't polite dinner conversation, whatever the hell that is. Down the road, I returned the favor by telling him it wasn't exactly polite dinner behavior to use our dining room table to screw the professional volleyball player he picked up at his new job at Nike. Now, Shoe Boy was a distant memory, and Grace listened to my stories whether we were eating or not.

I brought her up to speed on the Easterbrook case, then told her about my unproductive morning reviewing files. She wanted to know how the police could begin to tackle a case with no weapon, no witnesses, and no physical evidence. I explained MCT's strategy of following up on facts that make the case unique.

She was bothered. "I understand what you're saying about the statistical odds that the murder has something to do with whatever the victim might have been involved in, but there's still something about it that rubs me the wrong way. It's like you're investigating the victim, blaming her for getting killed."

"Right, but would you feel that way if it wasn't someone like Clarissa Easterbrook? Someone who looks like us and has a good job and does the kinds of things we do? When the victim's a doped-out street person, wouldn't you automatically assume that the lifestyle had something to do with the fact that she happened to show up dead?"

"But then you're talking about someone who you know was involved in activities that can be dangerous. There's no reason to believe that this woman was a drug addict or a prostitute or sleeping with someone else's husband."

"So the police snoop around to find out whether she was. Despite what people think, the odds of getting swiped off the street by a total stranger are so slim it would be irresponsible for the police to assume that scenario without at least looking into the possibility that something about the victim got her killed."

"Well, do me a favor. If I show up dead, don't let anyone snoop through my life."

"How about you do *me* a favor and don't show up dead?"

"OK, but if I do, I'll try to make it somewhere interesting. Then you could bypass the personal stuff and follow up on the location as the angle. Maybe some abandoned castle in the Swiss Alps."

"A little outside my jurisdiction," I said. "And stop being so morbid."

"Said the proverbial kettle."

"We can't *both* be dark. I need my Grace to balance me out a little."

"Fine, but I want to go back to your case. What's so interesting about the location?"

I did my best to describe the place where Clarissa had been found and told her Johnson's theory that it may have been someone familiar with the construction site. She was conspicuously quiet. "What?" I asked.

"Nothing. I'm just trying to catch up with you. Your food's nearly gone and I still have my entire lunch to eat."

"Thanks for pointing that out, skinny girl."

"Don't mention it."

"Seriously, what were you thinking about?"

"I think there are probably a lot more people who know about that location than you might assume."

"Grace, it's all the way out on the edge of Glenville."

"Right, where lots and lots of people live and work. Sam, you've only lived in northeast Portland and never ventured beyond the city center. Where do your cops live?"

"Johnson lives up by the University of Portland. I think Walker lives in Gresham." That put Ray in north Portland, not far from my own Alameda neighborhood, and Jack out in the county's east suburbs.

"And Glenville's all the way on the southwest edge of the county, which is why the three of you think the fastest growing city in the State of Oregon is the boonies. You guys might see it as Timbuktu, but a hundred thousand people know the land out there as well as you know Alameda."

"When did you become such a Glenvillean? Grace Hannigan, are you shopping at Burlington Coat Factory without telling me? Or maybe a new man—one with a minivan and a cul-de-sac?"

"Perish the thought," she said. "If you must know, I was looking into opening another Lockworks out there. There's a boom right now, and most of it from people with money who need haircuts."

"So are you doing it?"

"Nah. Too big a risk. When I bought the warehouse, I knew in my gut that the Pearl was going up. I didn't know just how far up—I hit the lottery in that sense—but I knew I was ahead of the market. With Glenville, the market's already full of people gambling that the growth's going to continue. It didn't make sense to get in this late in the game."

"So no Lockworks for Glenville."

"Right. Anyway, getting a second shop off the ground would have been a major pain in the ass. Who needs it?"

"All that work might get in the way of hanging out with me," I said.

"Couldn't let that happen."

The waitress stopped to clear our plates. I left a token morsel on the plate, so I could tell myself I didn't eat the whole platter. Grace took great pleasure in telling the waitress she was still working on it.

"And how's the rest of the new job? Are you going to share your toys with the other kids this time around?"

"My problems, Grace, are never with the other kids. They're with the supposed grown-ups watching over us."

Grace knew about some of the run-ins I'd had with cowork-ers in the office, all of whom happened to be my superiors. She says I have a problem with authority. I say my only problem is that the assholes are the ones who get promoted.

"And what lucky soul gets to put up with you now?" she asked.

"It's hard to believe, but he seems pretty decent so far. Sup-posedly he makes people cry, but I've never actually heard that from anyone firsthand."

"Does the new boss have a name?" she asked.

"That would be one Senior Deputy District Attorney Russell Frist," I said, deepening my voice into the best Frist boom I could muster. "Resident weight-lifting crew-cut-wearing stud muffin."

Grace was smirking.

"What?"

"I can't decide whether to tell you," she said.

"Well, you have to now. You can't announce that there's something to be said and then hold out on me."

After the requisite symbolic pause, she said, "Fine," as if I'd dragged it out of her. "I don't repeat the things clients tell me, but I suppose there's no harm in telling you that someone's a client. I know Russell Frist from the salon."

"Big bad butch Russ Frist goes to Lockworks? For a crew-cut?"

"Nope, not the hair. No point paying sixty bucks for that."

"Oh, please tell me that you wax his back," I pleaded.

"Not that good. But he does get a monthly no-polish mani-cure and pays extra for the paraffin wrap."

When I got back to the office, I was still in a good mood from my big food and small secret. The rest of the office might think of Frist as a mister scary, but I knew he had soft hands. I like people who are hard to sum up. They make life interesting.

My first stop was to see Jessica Walters.

She was leaning back in her chair with her stocking feet on the desk, one hand holding the phone to her ear, the other tapping her trademark pencil on her armrest. The person on the other end of the line was having a bad day that was getting worse as the conversation continued.

"You're smoking crack if you think I'll agree to probation. . . . I don't care if your guy's in denial, Conaughton. As far as I'm concerned, the most important part of your job is to smack him out of it. I'm not the one who needs a talking to, but you'd rather waste my time from the comfort of your office than haul yourself to county for a much-needed sit-down. . . . I'm hanging up now, because it's not going to happen. Either take the forty months or confirm the trial date. Call me back with anything else and I'll stop talking to you."

She set the handpiece in its cradle as gently as if she'd been checking the weather.

"Close case?" I asked.

"Typical plea-bargaining bullshit. They're never as close as the defense wants you to think."

"I got your message earlier. What's up?"

"You believe in coincidences, Kincaid?"

One of my favorite crime writers says there's no such thing, but I'd never thought much about it. "Sure," I said, "when I need to."

"Honest answer. Well, I do too. They happen all the time, or at least that's what I'm telling myself on this one. Your vic called me Friday."

"On what case?"

"The city judge, Clarissa Easterbrook. She called me Friday and left a message."

"About what?"

"I have no idea. I was in trial all last week. I took the message down with the rest of them and have been working my way through the list. The name meant nothing at the time I wrote it down, but when I got to it this morning it gave me the heebie-jeebies."

"What exactly did she say?"

"All I wrote in my call book was her name and number. If she had said what she was calling about, I would have noted it."

"You didn't realize this until today?"

"Watch it, Kincaid. That sanctimony's better spent on the rest of the fuckups around here. All I had was a name and number. I don't think she even said she was calling from the city hearings department."

I could see how that could happen. "Can you think of any reason she might have been calling? Are you in any groups together? The Women's Bar Association, maybe?"

"Sure, along with forty-three percent of all the other attorneys in this town. Did she call *you*?"

"Good point. Whatever it means, thanks for telling me. I'll pass it on to MCT and see if it connects up with anything else. Do you have the number she left?"

On the way back to my office, Alice Gerstein stopped me in the hall and announced that Clarissa Easterbrook's sister was waiting for me in the corner we call the reception area.

"When did she get here?"

"Right before noon."

I had checked my voice mail around then, but no one had left a message about the pop-in.

"Did she say what she wanted?" I whispered.

"Just to talk to you about the case. I offered to have you call her to set an appointment, but she insisted on waiting."

Tara Carney had finished the crossword during her wait and moved on to the jumble. I apologized for making her wait and explained that I was out of the office and didn't know she was planning to come in.

"I really didn't mind. I've been running out of things that make me feel useful, so waiting here to talk to you . . . well, at least it was something."

Apparently Susan Kerr wasn't the only one who was trying to stay busy. I offered Tara the best we had around here, a Dixie cup of water. Don't knock it. Until a few of us pooled our own funds for a cooler, the only water we had was brown.

Once we were in my office with the door closed, I asked her why she'd come in.

"There's something I haven't told the police yet, and it's been weighing on me. If I tell you, can it remain confidential?"

People hear about the sacred attorney-client privilege on TV and assume it's going to apply to me. It doesn't. I did my best to explain to Tara that I represented the State, not her. I'd do my best to be discreet, but if she told me something that related to the case, I'd almost certainly tell the police, and I might have to disclose it eventually to a defendant.

"That's the thing," she said. "I don't know if it relates to the case."

"If you have any reason to think it might, you really do need to tell me, Tara. I can't promise to keep it confidential, but I will treat the information with respect. We'll use it for the investigation, but it's not like I'm going to issue a press release or gossip about your sister."

She looked into my face and must have decided to trust me. "I think Clarissa was cheating on Townsend."

I couldn't hide my frustration. How could she not have mentioned this before? I'd let Grace make me feel bad about the police poking around in Clarissa's life, and it turns out there was something to discover after all.

"I didn't know what to say earlier. That first night, he was standing right there and was so upset; I couldn't mention it. Then when the police told us they found Clarissa's body, I was with my parents. I know the police were asking about her marriage, but I didn't want to say anything in front of them."

"So whom was she seeing?" I asked.

"That's the thing. I don't even know. She never told me. But she told me a few weeks ago—and she made me swear up and down I would never tell anyone—that she had fallen in love with someone else. She said she wanted to leave Townsend. I was shocked."

"Do you know if she actually started the process of leaving him? Did she tell Townsend or go to a lawyer?"

"I don't know. I think I made her angry. She wanted me to support her and be happy for her, and I was crummy."

"How so?" I asked.

"'What about your marriage? How could you cheat on Townsend? Why don't you try counseling?' That kind of stuff. I felt really bad when she said she only told me because she thought she could depend on me. I tried to stop being judgmental after that, but I think the damage was already done."

"She didn't tell you anything more?"

"No. I tried to get her to tell me who he was, but she refused. She wouldn't even tell me where she met him. We mostly talked about how she was afraid to be alone. She wanted to leave Townsend to be with this other person, but she wasn't sure he was prepared to be with her. I got the impression he might have been married too, like he wasn't necessarily in a position to live happily ever after with her. But she didn't want to keep living with Townsend when she was in love with someone else, so we talked about how she felt about being on her own."

"And did she come to any decision?"

"I think her mind was already made up; it was just a matter of when. We talked about how I adjusted after my husband left me. That was different, though. I have two kids, so my hands were too full to permit a meltdown. She was picturing herself alone at night with nothing to do and wondering how she'd get through it. Clarissa's one of those women who's always been with someone."

I knew that feeling. I had been one of those people before my divorce. Now I don't know what ever made me feel like I could live with anyone but Vinnie.

I poked and prodded with more questions, but Tara didn't know anything else about Clarissa's extramarital activities.

"Do you think she told Susan? I got the impression they were like this," I said, crossing my fingers, "but Susan hasn't mentioned this either."

"They are—I mean, they were." She was still getting used to the past tense. "In some ways they were more like real sisters than Clarissa and I were. If anything, they were almost too close, if that makes any sense. I think Clarissa came to me because I was less likely to challenge her. Clarissa always felt she owed it to Susan to live up to her expectations. Family's supposed to love you unconditionally, right?"

I could tell she was wondering whether she'd lived up to that obligation. "I'm sure she knew you did, Tara." It was my best effort, but it sounded no better than the shallow things people said to me when my mother died.

"I hope so."

"What do you mean about Clarissa living up to Susan's expectations?"

"That's a bit of an overstatement. I don't always choose my words very well. I think Clarissa wanted to be more like Susan.

It's been that way since they met in sixth grade. Some girl threw gum in Clarissa's hair on the bus, and Clarissa was afraid to stick up for herself. Susan was the new kid in school from California, and everyone else was avoiding her. But when this girl threw gum at Clarissa, Susan—without saying a word to Clarissa—followed her off the bus and told her she'd kick her butt if she ever messed with Clarissa again. From that point on, they were friends, but Susan was always looking out for Clarissa. I don't think that dynamic ever went away."

"But if Susan took care of Clarissa, why wouldn't Clarissa confide in her about something like leaving Townsend?"

"I don't think I'm explaining it well. Susan wouldn't have just listened to Clarissa, which I think is what Clarissa wanted from me. She would've gone to Townsend and told him to pay more attention to his marriage or something. Who knows? She might even have tracked this other guy down and told him to shape up and be with Clarissa if that's what she wanted. That's the way Susan is."

I'd just met Susan, but I could already picture it. "I'm sorry, Tara, but I think I need at least to talk to Susan and see if maybe she knew who the other guy was."

"But I thought she already said there weren't any problems in the marriage. In fact, I got the impression she was upset that the police even asked about it."

"If she doesn't think it has anything to do with her death, she might just be trying to protect Clarissa's reputation—like you were."

She didn't say anything.

"If it matters, I don't see the harm in talking to Susan about your concerns."

"I'm mostly worried about Townsend. You don't know him. The way he was Sunday night? He's usually nothing like that, and things have only gotten worse since then. He's an absolute wreck. I don't think he can take any more. My parents and I are having a hard enough time on our own, but now we're worried about Townsend too. If he finds out, I don't know what he'd do."

"I'll be as discreet as possible," I promised, "but I can't ignore what you've told me."

By the time Tara left the office, she understood that she could no longer control what became of the secret her sister had confided in her.

I needed to tell Johnson about Clarissa's phone call to Jessica Walters and what I'd learned from Tara. And I still needed to follow up on what Duncan had told me this morning: Had Johnson really asked Townsend for a polygraph?

No one picked up at MCT, so I paged him again. He returned the call fifteen minutes later from a crime scene. I could barely hear him over a chorus of angry voices in the background.

"Sorry about the delay, but today's been a bitch. I got a home invasion gone bad here right now. Two guys dead and a front yard full of gangbangers taking sides. We're meeting back at Central at four to go over where we are on Easterbrook. Can it wait till then? We can patch you in on speaker."

"It can wait, but I'll meet you over there." I knew from experience that attending a meeting by conference call is a guaranteed way to be confused and ignored, two areas where I didn't need help.

"Sounds good. We should have the bad guys separated from the less bad guys by then."

I turned my attention back to the task of reviewing the files I had inherited from Frist. With only a partial caseload, I had thirty-two pending cases and thirteen waiting to be reviewed for prosecution decisions. Far fewer files than in DVD, where I'd celebrate if I fell into the double digits, but homicides, sex offenses, and felony assaults would require more of me than the drug cases I had learned to prosecute on autopilot.

By midafternoon, I had finished compiling a calendar of all scheduled appearances and a list of motions, responses, phone calls, and other follow-up projects that needed to be done. If only I could learn to get the actual work completed as efficiently and neatly as I could list it.

MCT was housed in the downtown Justice Center, just a quick diagonal across the Plaza Blocks from the courthouse. I took the stairs to the fourth floor. When I got to MCT's large suite of cubicles, Chuck threw me a Diet Coke from the mini fridge and a look from deep down in a naughty place. I missed the soda by a mile, but I definitely caught the look. As usual, Chuck Forbes didn't miss a thing.

"Nice catch, Kincaid. Something distract you?"

"Just your piss-poor aim. Mike, don't ever rely on your partner in a gunfight."

Chuck's partner, Mike Calabrese, was finishing off the second and, for him, final bite of a Krispy Kreme glazed. Licking his fingers, he said, "That boy there doesn't need his gun. He disarms the world with his rapier wit."

He disguised the New York accent, giving the impression he was mimicking something Chuck said recently, most likely after their annual shooting re-quals. Seven times out of ten, I could outshoot Chuck at the range.

Johnson took control of the meeting once everyone was settled around the table. "Thanks for coming back in. As it turns out, the LT OK'd us for overtime on this, but I appreciate that everyone was willing to show anyway. I know it was a bad day out there today. Before I let you in on what Walker and I have been working, where are you guys on the paperwork?"

Chuck and Mike knew the question was aimed at them. Chuck took charge.

"We got everything we were asking for. Nothing on the credit cards other than corroboration for what the wits have been telling us. We got charges at Nordstrom on Saturday for the clothes she was wearing and the stuff the sister found in the shopping bag. Then Sunday we've got the lunch at the Pasta Company. We checked the bills for the last twelve months, and nothing's jumping out. Same with the bank records.

"The vic's cell phone gets a little more interesting. The general pattern is slow: a few calls to the house, office voice mail, that sort of thing. Very few incoming calls. The last two calls were one Sunday afternoon to the Pasta Company and one Saturday afternoon to her house. I figured I'd let one of you guys check that one out with the family, since you're the contacts."

I saw Johnson jot it down in his notebook. "That it?" he asked.

Chuck and Mike exchanged glances. "My partner here has been saving the best for last," Mike said. "We get a break in the pattern about three months ago. Suddenly our victim starts using all those minutes she's prepaid for, and it's almost all calls back and forth between her phone and one belonging to Metro Council member Terrence James Caffrey."

T. J. Caffrey was a well-known liberal lawmaker. He had previously been a member of the county legislature but recently ran for and won a seat on the Metro Council, whose sole purpose was to enforce Oregon's unique restrictions against urban sprawl. In the 1970s, the legislature essentially drew a big circle around the Portland area's existing development and established that line as a boundary between urban and rural land. Since then, as the region's population had grown, the urban center had exploded with new development. The result was a much denser metropolitan area, but the open space beyond it had remained just that. Only the Metro Council had the authority to redraw the line that separated urban from rural.

Johnson reached his hands toward Calabrese like he wanted to squeeze his cheeks and kiss the top of his head. "Now *that* is what I'm talking about. Feels like we're swimming through maple syrup and suddenly something breaks. Too many phone calls to a married man; it might boil down to old-fashioned lust after all."

"That fits in with something I got this afternoon," I said. I told them about my visit from Tara. T. J. Caffrey's own marriage would explain why Clarissa thought that leaving Townsend wouldn't be enough to make her happy.

The guys were predictably ticked.

"Happens in every case, don't it?" Calabrese spoke for them all. "These people don't tell us what they know; then they bitch and moan when we can't find the bad guy fast enough."

Before I had a chance to voice Tara's reservations, Johnson was back on track. "It's all right. Now we got some pieces coming together. I've got something that might fit in with the Caffrey angle too, but let's hold off on that for now. You got anything else?"

"Only a one-minute phone call on Friday to the Multnomah County District Attorney's Office. We figured Kincaid could track down the details."

"I've already got them. Jessica Walters paid me a visit this morning." I explained to them that Jessica had been in trial last week, only made the connection today between the voice mail and our case, and had no idea why our victim had been calling her.

"Raises some interesting questions, doesn't it?" Walker asked. "We've got an assertive, good-looking woman calling Nail 'em to the Wall Walters. Maybe she was a closet muncher and got involved in something over her head."

Walker was a good man, so I tried to write off his "deduction" as generational. As for his choice of words, it was nothing I hadn't heard before in the DA's office.

"Seems unlikely. I talked to Jessica about it today, and Clarissa Easterbrook's name meant nothing to her until Monday."

Johnson jumped in. "Right now, it's just a phone call; nothing we can do with it. Mike and Chuck gave us Councilman T. J. Caffrey to follow up on; Kincaid got us Melvin Jackson to talk to. And Jack and I have a couple guys we're going to be picking up when we break. Can you run it down for them, Jack? My voice is toast."

Jack Walker flipped through various computer printouts as he spoke. "We cross-referenced prior sex arrests with address records from the surrounding area. Based on that, we got twenty-seven guys within a couple of miles."

If the public had any clue what was walking around out there with the rest of us, they'd lose any remaining faith in the criminal justice system's sentencing priorities.

"But that includes any sex offense," Walker explained, "even the wienie wavers and stepdads. Of the twenty-seven, we've got a couple who are more interesting. One's got a forcible rape and sodomy, lives with his mother about five blocks from the construction site. Name's John Peltzkelszvich, or however you pronounce that. I mean, buy a freakin' vowel, for Christ's sake. Anyway, he's on parole, so we should be able to get access to him through the PO.

"The guy we like best right now, though, is Gregory Banas. He's farther out, almost two miles from the site. Only prior conviction is a misdemeanor sex abuse for grabbing a woman's crotch in a mall parking lot. But, get this: Banas's name comes up twice. Remember the attempted rape a couple years ago on Taylor's Ferry that Bradley and Rees from the DA's office broke up?"

We all nodded.

"The woman's name was Vicki Vasquez," Walker explained.

"No arrest, but Bob Milling from East Precinct called this afternoon. He was working the case when he was still at Central. Good guy. Vasquez was never able to make a solid ID, but when she was flipping through mugs, she pulled out four who could've been the bad guy. Her favorite?"

"Greg Banas?" Calabrese asked.

"Correctamundo," Walker said. "Milling wanted to put him in a lineup, but Vasquez moved back to California. Said she wanted to put the whole thing behind her. At the time, Banas lived in one of those big apartment complexes on Barbur Boulevard." I knew the location, not far from the running trail along Taylor's Ferry. "About a year ago, he moved to one off Highway Twenty-six in Glenville, so we've got potential familiarity with both the crime scene and the presumed pickup spot."

Ray Johnson nodded. "And location's going to matter on this one. Heidi Chung called from the crime lab. The paint geek from Home Depot says that the paint on the dog matches paint going up on the exterior of the office park. Mocha cream, to be exact."

"Would the paint have been wet on Sunday?" Walker asked.

Johnson had apparently asked the same question already. "They were painting Friday and Saturday; on Sundays the work is shut down. But they leave the scaffolding and paint out."

"This doesn't make sense," Chuck said. "We've been assuming the bad guy swiped the victim from the street, leaving the dog and the leash behind. Now we're saying bad guy takes victim and her big strong dog? Does the bad guy—location to be determined—then dump her in Glenville and drop the dog near home? No way."

"I'm with you," Johnson agreed. "But let's try it this way, going back to our old-fashioned lust theory. Husband's off at the hospital all day, so vic meets her phone pal for a day of romance. Maybe he picks her up for a drive to the coast, and they take the dog with them. They fight about the things people fight about when they're screwing each other but married to other people. He hits her in the head a little too hard. Dumps her in Glenville on the way back—Griffey jumps out for a tinkle, comes back with paint—then leaves the dog and the shoe on Taylor's Ferry to get us thinking abduction."

Chuck was nodding with every sentence. "That could be it."

"Or it could still be an abduction," Walker added, "but the paint comes from the bad guy, not the building. There's Peltzkelszvich and Banas, but we've also got a couple of site workers with problems. Maybe the paint goes from the site to them to the dog."

Johnson thought about it. "It's possible. I didn't like any of the work guys for it, though."

Walker filled the rest of us in. "We found a bunch of dirtbags working up there, mostly through one union. There were a couple of rapes, some robberies, and a mess of DV assaults. But the robberies were all commercial, and the rapes weren't strangers—one was an ex-girlfriend, one was the guy's step-daughter. Nothing that seemed in line with our scenario."

"I hate to be the party pooper—" The four detectives' shared chuckle cut me off. "OK, playing my usual role of party pooper," I revised, "maybe it's just paint. Plain, generic taupe-colored paint. I mean, how precise can the paint geek get it? The stuff's not DNA, right? Griffey still could've come across it wandering around the neighborhood."

It was too soon to begin connecting all the dots. Walker and Johnson needed to get out there and talk to the men whose names had come up and see if anything shook out.

"One last thing," Johnson said. "I called the husband today about the condom, and it wasn't his."

"Did you tell him the ME found spermicide?" I asked.

"No way. I just told him we were still running some tests, and it would help if we knew the last time they had intercourse and whether they'd used any kind of barrier method of birth control. Turns out the doctor had his tubes tied. They hadn't had sex since the Tuesday before she disappeared, though, which explains why the autopsy didn't find anything."

"Was he all right with the questions?" I asked. I still needed to talk to Johnson about the polygraph request.

"Actually, he seemed pretty thrown off by the whole thing. He was sort of out of it in general, though. I guess no one wants to think about something like that happening to their wife. Anyway, when I found out the condom wasn't his, I was thinking sex offense. But it fits with what Chuck and Mike got, too. Maybe the vic was using condoms on the side with Caffrey."

"Doesn't mean Caffrey did it, though," I said. "It would just explain the spermicide."

We were stuck again.

As we broke up, Chuck tried to get my attention. I raised a finger in his direction as I ran to catch Johnson alone.

"Griffith got a call today from Susan Kerr," I said. He looked at me but didn't say anything. "Did one of you ask Townsend Easterbrook to take a polygraph last night?"

The look on his face said *So that's what this is about.* "Yes. As a matter of fact, I did."

"I thought we were going to talk before you did anything on that."

"You weren't there, Sam. Am I supposed to stop everything and call you before I make any kind of decision on one of my investigations?"

I ignored the rhetorical question because, like most rhetorical questions, it was stupid. "If this was just another procedure, why didn't you mention it to me this morning?"

"If you want me to say I'm sorry so you can tell your boss

you did what you needed to, then I'll do it, Sam. I know how your thing works over there at the courthouse. But the guy had just gotten the news and was being cooperative; the moment was right to ask him to help us eliminate him. If I turn that into a DA decision—and I mean any DA—it gets political and never would've happened. No offense against you personally, but I just needed to do it."

"So you admit you intentionally went behind my back." I'd nearly gotten killed going out on a limb on one of Johnson's cases. I couldn't help but sound indignant.

He closed his eyes and shook his head. "No, it wasn't like that."

My stare must have told him I wasn't buying it.

"OK," he said. "Maybe I could have brought it up with you at the crime scene yesterday. But I could tell when we were riding up to Kerr's house that the subject made you nervous, so I decided to play it by ear. Honestly, last night at the house, it seemed like the right move to make."

"Well, it wasn't," I said. "From everything I've heard, this guy's on the verge of losing it. I don't need you pushing him over the edge by asking for a poly the minute after he learns his wife was murdered. And don't tell me you would've done it with another DA, because that's bullshit and we both know it."

He bit his lower lip and avoided my gaze. Maybe we didn't know each other as well as we'd assumed.

I finally broke the silence. "What's your problem with the guy anyway? If he didn't do it—and I don't think any of us really thinks he did—how could you put him through that?"

"It's not about suspecting him, Kincaid, it's about doing the investigation right. He was being so cooperative, I thought, if I asked, he'd say Sure, let's do it right now, whatever I can do to help. As it turned out, that's not how it went, so it probably wasn't worth getting you so fired up."

"He won't take it?" I asked. I had assumed from the conversation with Duncan that Townsend was put off by the request but would nevertheless humor the police.

"I overstated that."

"What exactly did he say?"

"The question seemed to catch him off guard—not like he was threatened by it, but more like his feelings were hurt. You saw how out of it he was that first night at the house. It was the same thing. Then he finally said he didn't see a problem but would let me know today."

"And what did he say today?" I asked.

"Nothing. I had to call him about the nonoxynol. He didn't mention the poly, and I held off on pressing him. See, now that *really* would've pissed you off."

"Don't push it, Ray."

"Look, I'm sorry I went around you, but I know what it's all about with you guys and Duncan Griffith. I didn't want to put you in a bad spot."

I wanted to be able to say that I was different from all the other MCU deputies he'd seen over the years, impervious to hierarchical pressures, but I couldn't begin to articulate the subtle distinctions that I found so important.

"No, you didn't want me to tell you to back off. And, in the process, you made me look like an idiot in front of my boss when I defended you. Do anything like that again, and I'll forget you're my friend and start acting like all the other MCU deputies you never would have pulled this on."

"Yep, friends. Got it."

"Ray, I meant that, but I also need to do my job."

He was biting his lip again, but at least now he was looking me in the eyes. He finally smiled and shook his head. "Yeah, we'll be all right. Go wait for your bus or whatever it is you do after work."

"I drove today, as a matter of fact, but, sorry, we're not quite done yet. When do you plan to talk to the councilman?" If Griffith gave me a sit-down based on Susan Kerr's concerns about etiquette, I'd really be in the doghouse if Johnson accused an elected official like T. J. Caffrey of murder under my watch.

"I figured I'd go by his house tonight and ask him whether he's been keeping a little piece on the side. I'll make sure the wife's nearby when I get to the Trojans. Kids, too, if he has any." He placed his hand on my shoulder to make sure I knew he was kidding. "Don't worry, Kincaid, this is me we're talking about. Tough stuff won't work on a guy like that anyway."

True, and tact *was* right up Johnson's alley. As long as he agreed that some diplomacy was called for, I couldn't be in better hands.

With work wrapped up, I was more interested in getting into the hands of another detective. I stopped by Chuck's desk just long enough to tell him to meet me at my house. I was going to my father's for dinner, but I could spare an hour or so if he wanted to catch up.

"Catch up" is precisely what I meant when I said it, but his expression when he said, "Leaving right now. An hour might be enough," had me scrambling out the door, sucking down Altoids as fast as I could take them. Damn that Greek Cusina. By the time I got to the Jetta, I had broken into a full sprint and was sweating garlic. Very attractive.

I used the wonder of cell technology to multitask in the car, calling Griffith with the update while I maneuvered various body parts in front of the air vents in an attempt to cool off. The commute was remarkably quick. Drivers in front of me would look in their rearview mirrors and immediately yield the lane. Apparently jerking around like a strung-out freak pays off when others practice defensive driving,

When I rolled past Chuck's '67 Jag to pull into the driveway,

I gave him my best come-hither look. I placed both feet on the ground before stepping out of the car. Slinkier than my normal spread-eagle hoist.

I bent purposefully and ever so seductively at the waist to reach my suit jacket in the passenger seat and then flicked it over my shoulder, one New Balance thrusting to the side with a determined hip. I parted my lips and let my tongue linger at the break before I spoke. "You coming in with me or not?"

He returned my blistering gaze. Then he started laughing. A full-on, eyes shut, hands-to-the-face bust-up.

I fought competing urges to run away and cry, or to punch him in the head and then run away. "That wasn't the response I was looking for."

He tried to regain his composure but couldn't help himself. "I'm sorry. But I just left you fifteen minutes ago at the precinct. What the hell happened to you?"

I caught a glimpse of my reflection in the driver's window. The combination of the air vents, my sweaty head, and that damn mud Grace had given me had left my hair in a state of Rocky Horror. Throw in the white Altoid powder sprinkled across my clothing, and I was totally pathetic. I draped my jacket over my arm, pulled in my thrusted hip, and tried to explain.

"I was running to my car and got a little warm and—"

What was this? Maybe Grace was right when she said I didn't understand men, because this one was racing up my walkway steps, straight toward me, and he wasn't laughing.

I ran ahead of him into the house and let him catch me at the end of my upstairs hallway. Just outside the bedroom.

If there is a mathematical formula to calculate sex—maybe intensity times duration—then the next hour could very well have brought us back to par despite the two-week break.

6

I SEE CLARISSA Easterbrook in a pink silk sweater on Taylor's Ferry Road, holding Griffey by his leash. A man in an ankle-length duster and brown leather hat has stopped to pet the dog. The man asks if she has seen the view of Mount Hood and begins to lead her to a crest through a clearing in the trees.

He reaches his hand out behind him to guide her, but now it's my hand he grasps. When he turns his head to smile down at my trusting face, I recognize Tim O'Donnell. My expression changes from confusion to shock, as I open my mouth to scream for help.

"Babe, wake up, what's wrong?"

My right elbow flew out instinctively, and Chuck bolted upright, holding his ribs where I jabbed him.

"Oh, God, are you OK?"

"Yeah, I'm fine," he said. "You just took me by surprise."

"I guess we fell asleep."

"You fell asleep. I watched."

"That's more than a little disturbing."

"Tell me about it. Your hair's even worse than it was when we started; you snore; and a spindle of drool was working its way from your lip to the mattress."

"I'm really going to hurt you this time," I said, reaching over and poking my fingers into his side.

With one swift move, he had my hands above my head. "Stop it, I was kidding. You weren't drooling, you don't snore, and your hair—well, you're cute as hell, Kincaid." He gave me a kiss and let me go. "I woke you up because you looked like you were having another one of those dreams. I've seen cops after a shooting, and it can take a long time to get over."

"I'm over it. Just one of those weird naked-in-front-of-the-classroom dreams."

"Was I there?"

"No, that'd be one of *your* dreams. I hate to kick you out of bed, stud, but I really need to get a move on. I promised Dad that Vinnie and I would come over for dinner tonight, and I can't show up with bed head."

"That poor impersonation of a dog over there is invited, but I'm not?"

Vinnie was spread out like a bear rug in the hall, still looking annoyed that he'd been locked out of the bedroom during play-time. Vinnie's got bug eyes, bat ears, and a face that looks like it was flattened by a steel plate. I couldn't tell if the snort he emitted was in response to Chuck's comment or just one of his everyday snorts.

"When your date's a French bulldog, you can talk about boring family stuff without being rude," I said.

"I don't mind if you talk about your boring family. I just want to be fed."

I did feel guilty running out on him, and Dad would enjoy

seeing Chuck. "Fine. But I need some time alone with Dad. Give me an hour's head start, and we'll have dinner on the table right when you get there."

The last thing I needed post-vacation was one of the bricks of beef my father feeds me whenever he cooks, so I had e-mailed a list of ingredients in the morning and promised to cook if he'd pick them up. New to computers, he was still so impressed by the technology that he didn't even complain about the menu.

"You look great," I said, adjusting the collar on the blue shirt I'd given him for his most recent birthday. He had complained that it was too young for him, but it brought out the blue in his eyes and the silver of his hair. "You didn't have any problems printing out the shopping list?"

"I've turned into a real computer whiz since you left." I had helped him hook up his Dell right before my trip. "It's so easy I was even thinking of telling Al to get one."

Al Fontana is my dad's ninety-year-old neighbor and checker partner. He's also a dirty old man.

"Dad, you put that man on the Internet, and he'll be dead in a month from Viagra and porn."

Point taken.

It wasn't long before Dad got to the heart of things. Apparently I wasn't the only one who spent the day uncomfortable with where we left things the night before. "I know we talked about this, but I want to tell you in person that I'm sorry I got you so upset last night."

"You're making me feel worse. I was a total jerk."

"Fine, let's put last night behind us, and I won't make any apologies. What I'm trying to say is that I'll try not to let my own hang-ups get in the way—"

"Dad, you don't have any hang-ups—"

"Please, Sammy, let me finish. All I was saying was that this woman was surrounded by powerful people. I may not have stuck it out as a cop, but I saw enough to know you'll be looking long and hard at everything she was involved in. If you wind up stumbling onto something, they'll make your life a living hell."

So that's what this had been about. Dad wasn't afraid I'd get chased around the city again by a wingnut; he was worried some cabal of "powerful people" would target me for annihilation. As long as I've known him, Dad has had an almost delusional distrust of those who find themselves at the top of the hierarchy of influence. I typically find this characteristic endearing, but occasionally it makes me crazy. Like at my rehearsal dinner in Manhattan, when he was so cold to my now ex-husband's "blue-blood" parents that I was afraid Roger was going to call off the wedding. OK, in retrospect, that wouldn't have been so bad. But now he was letting his paranoia get in the way of his pride in my career.

I shook my head in disbelief. Part of me wanted to unleash—to tell him how much I resented the guilt I'd felt all day about last night, to tell him he could keep his supposed apology. It only served to raise the issue again in a whole new light. But I didn't want to say anything that I'd regret.

Instead, I kept a measured voice. "Dad, I told you before that the MCU is where I want to be. That means I'll be dealing with bad guys, and if some of them happen to be important and influential, so be it. In fact, I would think that you'd prefer me to prosecute the privileged."

"I obviously didn't do very well getting my point across. I was trying to explain what my worries had been, but that I know that you're going to be better than I was at handling the pressures that might come with a case like this."

"Oh, come on, Dad. You know that's not true."

"No," he said, "you said it last night—I hung up OSP."

"You were in a different situation. You had a wife, a child." He shook his head, and I could tell he wanted me to drop the pep talk. "I was old enough to remember what it was like. Mom was pressuring you—"

I stopped midsentence when I saw the look on his face. It was clear I'd said something wrong.

"I'm not sure what you think you remember, sweetheart, but your mother never pressured me."

"Dad, it's OK. It doesn't make me think any less of her. She was worried about you getting hurt."

"Sam, just stop it. You don't know what you're talking about."

"Then why *did* you leave OSP?" I asked. Once again, this conversation was getting us nowhere.

"I don't want to talk about it. Let's get dinner started."

Everyone close to me—Grace, Chuck, Roger (back in the day)—has always complained that I change the subject when the going gets rough. I guess it runs in the family.

"Not yet. I want to know what this is about. You're upset, and it apparently has something to do with why you moved over to the forest service."

"I promised I would support you in your job, and I'm going to keep my promise. Let's just leave it at that."

"Dad, I remember you and Mom arguing right around when you changed jobs. It was the only time you *did* argue, in fact. You tried to keep it from me, but I'd hear you in your room—"

He laughed. "If you think we didn't argue over the years, we kept it from you better than we thought."

"Thick walls," I said, knocking on the one behind me. He was changing the subject again, and not very convincingly either. My parents' marriage had been as solid as they come. Even before I made the mistake of walking down the aisle of doom with Roger, I'd known that we'd never come close.

Whatever was going on now, I could prod Dad all night and he would still never budge. So I grabbed a bag of vegetables from the counter and began chopping.

By the time Chuck arrived, the salad was tossed and the salmon was broiled. After pumping palms, slapping backs, and a few other male welcoming rituals, he found me in the kitchen, took one look at the pink fish, and whispered in my ear, "If I swear you're not fat, can we please have some steak?"

The man knew me so well. "I'm in no condition to run after this evening, so the least we can do is eat something healthy."

"What was this evening?" Dad called out from the living room. "Must have been big to keep you from running."

Chuck winked and mouthed the word *big* at me.

I rolled my eyes. "No more work talk tonight." I put dinner on the table, and for the next two hours we talked about Hawaii, my dad's computer, movies, and politics. We made it through the conversation with no shootings, no bodies, no demons from the past—just three normal people sharing a meal.

As ten o'clock approached, Dad clicked on the local news, and I moved to the kitchen to take on the dishes.

As the familiar staccato theme song faded out, I heard an anchor report: "In our top story tonight, new developments in the investigation into the death of Judge Clarissa Easterbrook. Find out why her husband is railing against the Portland Police Bureau." I ran into the living room just in time to catch: "But first, Morley Rutherford's going to tell us what we can expect in the way of weather tomorrow. Morley?"

I resisted the urge to throw my sudsy sponge at Morley Rutherford's fat freckled head while he droned on with his entirely predictable springtime weather report. Why not kick off the news with an announcement that the earth's going to rotate tomorrow?

Once Morley wrapped up with his seven-day graphic of clouds and showers, the camera finally cut back to the anchor. "At a surprise news conference held just moments ago, the husband of slain judge Clarissa Easterbrook accused the Portland Police Bureau of focusing the investigation on him rather than looking for the real killer."

The footage cut to Townsend at a podium in front of his house. "When I learned yesterday that some monster had killed my beloved Clarissa"—his voice broke and his hands trembled, but he continued to read from the statement in front of him— "I thought that nothing in the world could ever be worse than at that moment. But the course of the Portland Police Bureau's investigation has convinced me that there is a more horrific possibility, and that would be if the person or people responsible for her death were not brought to justice. The police tell me they have no suspects in my wife's death, but they spent hours in our home with a search warrant, interrogated our friends looking for problems that did not exist in our marriage, and asked me to take a polygraph examination, suggesting that they would not be able to investigate other suspects fully until I proved my innocence. So that is why I am standing here tonight.

"I have not even buried my wife"—he wiped away a tear and swallowed but kept his eyes on his notes—"and I am here in front of cameras, forced to deny something that is inconceivable to me. I did not—and could not ever—hurt Clarissa."

The words themselves were no different from the typical denials always issued in these cases, some truthful, some not. A bet placed at this point in the game would reflect nothing but hunch. That Townsend was seeking to tip those odds became clear when a familiar face replaced his at the podium.

I shushed Chuck and my father. Their outraged comments were drowning out the voice I had hoped never to hear again. "Good evening. My name is Roger Kirkpatrick."

My ex-husband hadn't aged. It was probably a deal with the devil. He had the same short preppy haircut he'd worn in New York, before his commitment to a "freer" lifestyle in Oregon had caused him to grow his brown curls into what I had called the Doogie Howser look.

He proceeded to announce that he and his firm, Dunn Simon, had been retained by Townsend Easterbrook to oversee a team of private investigators and to help ensure that the police sought out the real killers instead of harassing the victim's family and friends. Then he went for broke.

"To satisfy the police department's baseless suspicions, Dr. Easterbrook submitted voluntarily this afternoon to a polygraph examination administered by retired FBI agent Jim Thornton, a recognized expert in the field. Agent Thornton has certified," he said, holding up a paper I assumed was an affidavit from Thornton, "that Dr. Easterbrook's answers were truthful. He had nothing whatsoever to do with his wife's death, and the police have wasted precious time by doubting him. No one should have to prove his own innocence, but Dr. Easterbrook has. Now it's time for the Portland Police Bureau to join the search for justice by finding whoever is responsible for this terrible loss."

Just as abruptly as he'd appeared, Roger was gone, replaced by the anchor. "Dr. Easterbrook's attorney concluded his remarks by saying that his firm had begun its own investigation and would share its work with law enforcement."

"The only thing he knows how to share is his di—" As furious as I was, the natural instinct to behave in front of my father silenced me. I couldn't even hit the MUTE button, thanks to my ridiculous yellow rubber gloves. I gave up, threw the remote on the sofa, and headed into the kitchen to exchange the gloves for something more helpful.

By the time I had sucked down half a pint of Cherry Garcia ice cream, I was ready to talk again, but Chuck and my father had already covered all the bases: Why hadn't Townsend gone through the police? A surprise press conference only creates more conflict. Just how legit was this polygraph? Depends on the questions, the equipment, and the administrator. And, the doozy of the night, why the hell had Townsend hired Shoe Boy? He doesn't even practice criminal law. Did Townsend know his new attorney was my ex-husband? Surely Roger would have told him.

I figured since they'd finished all the objective analysis, I could jump to the part that was anything but. "You know what? He wins. I'm off the case. I'm telling Frist tomorrow."

My father said nothing. Neither did Chuck.

Fine, I'd do the pep talk myself. *No, self,* I said in my head, *you need to finish what you started. Don't let him get the best of you. Act like a professional.* Then the coach in me found a winning theme, one that deserved to be spoken aloud: "You know, what if Townsend actually did it? Imagine Roger and me in trial together."

Chuck put his hand on my shoulder. "Maybe it's best if you did recuse yourself."

"Forget it. I'm not letting him chase me off my own case." When I beat Roger during our first-year moot trial competition at Stanford, he attributed the win to the side slit in my skirt. I should have known to stay away. Handing him his ass in trial (and in pants) would be sweet satisfaction.

My dad was noticeably quiet. As Chuck carried his coffee mug into the kitchen, I looked at him and raised my eyebrows. "So?"

"It's up to you, Sam. I'll support you either way."

"But, what about—"

"Unh-unh. Don't use this to revisit what we put to rest earlier. This is about you and your case, not me." When he turned the television back on, I knew I wasn't getting any further with him, so I tried my luck in the kitchen with Chuck.

As I hugged him from behind, my pager buzzed. He felt it too.

"Duty calls, counselor."

I recognized the number as MCT's. No doubt it was Johnson breaking the news about the press conference. He could wait a few minutes.

"What's going on with you? You got awfully quiet in there."

"Nothing's going on." He kept his back to me.

"What are you upset about?"

"It's fine, Samantha. Don't worry about it."

Samantha? Chuck's got plenty of names for me: Kincaid, Sam, Sammy, babe, the list goes on. But Samantha? Things were not fine. "Is this about Roger? You can't possibly be jealous."

"See, I knew you'd turn it into that, Sam. That's why I wasn't going to say anything. Suddenly I'm an overbearing jealous pig with testosterone poisoning."

"Not quite that bad. More like a piglet." He didn't laugh. "Seriously, Chuck, what's going on?"

"Johnson and Walker are doing all the legwork on this case, and Mike and I are stuck on the sidelines because of what I've got going with you. Don't get me wrong; I don't have a problem with that. But now that Roger's involved, maybe you should at least consider the possibility that *you* should be the one to step aside."

My pager buzzed again. Johnson was probably waiting for my call before leaving the precinct.

"I did. You were sitting right there. The first thing I said was *I'm off the case.* Now I think I should stay on it. There will be plenty of cases you work that will go to another DA. Who knows? Maybe we'll even decide it's all right to work together."

"Why do you say it that way: Who knows? Like it's so crazy

132

for us both to work a case? How come you trust your judgment going against your ex-husband, but you can't be on the same team with me?"

More buzzing. "Honestly? Because my ex-husband's an asshole, and dealing with assholes is pretty much what I do for a living. You, my dear, are dangerous for a whole different reason," I said, leaning close. "I don't always think straight when it comes to you."

He placed his hands on my shoulders and smiled, then pushed a strand of hair behind my right ear. "Consider me assuaged, Kincaid," he said, kissing my earlobe. "Now call whoever the hell's been paging you. You think I haven't notice you staring down at that thing?"

Johnson picked up on the first ring. "I got a call from the husband's lawyer. We fucked up big-time. I need you to sign a warrant on Melvin Jackson."

Portland's one of those towns that shuts down at 10 P.M. My Jetta was one of the few cars on the Morrison Bridge, and I walked into MCT ten minutes after I left my father's.

Johnson was standing at the printer, proofreading pages as they spooled. "This is just about done. The search is for his apartment, and he's also got a Dodge Caravan registered to him."

"Back up. What the hell's going on?"

"The husband's people dug up something we missed. They're back there," he said, gesturing to an interview room down the hall.

"They're here?"

Then, with his usual spot-on timing, my ex-husband walked into the room. "Detective, I—oh, sorry, I didn't mean to interrupt. You're looking well, Samantha."

"I know." My worn-out Harvard T-shirt and jeans didn't

make the best ensemble for our first post-divorce face-to-face, but confidence is the ultimate accessory.

He, on the other hand, hadn't changed out of the suit he'd worn for the press conference. And, sure enough, close up, I was able to confirm it: the red power tie was the one I'd placed in his stocking on our last Christmas together.

"No introductions necessary, I see," Johnson said.

"Samantha and I went to law school together—"

"And were briefly in the same marriage," I added.

Johnson looked amused, and Roger seemed uncomfortable. Score.

"I'm at Dunn Simon now, Samantha. I wasn't sure if you'd heard."

"Saw it on the news, in fact, about half an hour ago." I couldn't stomach letting him know I'd read about his move from Nike to the Portland powerhouse firm in the Oregon State Bar bulletin a year ago.

"The firm made me an offer I couldn't refuse," he boasted.

"From what I remember, Roger, there weren't a lot of offers you could refuse."

"Nice to see you haven't changed."

"Nope, but apparently you have," I shot back. I just couldn't help myself. "I wasn't aware that Dunn Simon was in the criminal law business."

"It's not, but Townsend Easterbrook's not a criminal. He's the attending surgeon at OHSU, another one of our clients. He doesn't need a defense attorney. He needs someone to dig for evidence, and no one does that better than a civil litigator."

Johnson saved us from what was about to turn into a Dunn Simon marketing speech. "Well, alright-y, then. Glad the two of you could catch up. I was just telling Samantha that you preferred to wait until the DA had signed off on the warrant."

"I'm sure you understand, Detective, that given the course

of the investigation, my client would feel better knowing for certain that the warrant has been approved. I'll wait until it's finished."

I knew from experience that there was no point arguing with Roger. What he lacks in personality he makes up for in tenacity. I was surprised he didn't insist on reading the document over my shoulder. Instead, he retreated back to the interview room.

Johnson's affidavit was nothing pretty, but it was a rush job and contained what it needed: Melvin Jackson's pending appeal, his letters to Clarissa Easterbrook, and—this was the biggie— the documents confirming his recent employment as a part-time landscaper at the Glenville office park.

"Jesus, Johnson," I said, signing the cover form on the DA review line.

"I know. It's bad."

I didn't care if he knew. This was unbelievable. "How in the world could we have possibly missed this? You have the employee lists; you have Jackson's file. You're tracking down a crotch grabber, but you need the husband to hire a fucking lawyer to find Melvin Jackson's name sitting right there?"

"We were stupid, but we weren't that stupid. Remember I told you that we got the list of workers from the unions?" I nodded. "Well, we did it through the unions because when we asked the site's foreman for a list, he told us which unions were doing the work. Apparently, though, the contractor for the build is allowed to use some nonunion labor, which he didn't exactly advertise at the site. Melvin Jackson was one of the nonunion guys. Landscaping."

"So how did a bunch of Dunn Simon pencil-necks figure it out?"

"Luck." Johnson didn't know me well enough yet to know that I think luck is for whiners. He did know me well enough not to leave it at that. "When I talked to Townsend last night,

I told him we'd look into people who worked at the site as part of the investigation. He probably mentioned that to his lawyer, but the lawyer didn't start with the foreman to get a list of employees; he started with the company that owns the property. Turns out Dunn Simon represents them too. One big happy family."

"Well, it's signed now, so you can send them all home for the night. I hope you'll understand if I don't stick around for the goodbyes. What judges are on call duty tonight?"

"Maurer and Lesh."

"You should be all right with either one of them. Maurer's got kids, but Lesh is probably still up. Loves the *Daily Show*. Call me if you have any problems."

"Sure thing."

He stopped me as I was walking out. "Hey, Kincaid. Thanks for understanding. We'll make up for it tonight."

"Sounds like it could've happened to anyone." In truth, I wasn't convinced there hadn't been some sloppiness, but he was beating himself up enough as it stood. Laying off felt like the right thing to do, given our afternoon confrontation. "I'm just glad someone caught it."

"Well, between me and you, considering the someone? That shows real class. And, just to prove I know I got some time out in the doghouse, that's all I'm gonna say about your old law school friend back there. That could've been hours of material."

More like days, but he didn't know the half of it. "Much appreciated, Ray. You be careful on that search. Jackson's desperate."

When I finally got home, it was too late to call my father. I checked the machine; no messages.

Vinnie was waiting for me in bed with a note tied to his collar.

I recognized Chuck's scribble. "I couldn't fit through Vinnie's doggy door so I guess it's another night alone. Sweet dreams."

The best I could do was no dreams, which was as good as it was getting these days. Unfortunately, the slumber didn't last long. Five hours in, Jack Walker called to fill me in on the search.

"You guys find anything?" I asked, groping for the lamp.

"You could say that. This thing's ready to go."

I asked him to walk me through it from the start.

"Lesh agreed to sign the warrant as a no-knock," he explained, meaning they could enter the house without knocking first. "So we call out the emergency response team just in case the entry goes bad. Never know with the kids and all.

"We kicked the door. Jackson's asleep on the couch. His three kids are sacked out in the bedrooms. We took them out into the hallway to secure the apartment and get the scene under control."

"Handcuffs?" I asked.

"Just for Jackson. He was one unhappy camper about us waking the kids, and we didn't want him going mental on us." Under the circumstances, a court would go with that.

"Then what?"

"Once we secured the apartment, our first priority was placing the kids. We had SCF on-site with a foster placement ready, but Jackson wigged when he saw them coming. He was a complete wreck, pretty much offered to confess if we'd call his mom."

"He *admitted* it?"

"Hold on. I wrote it down verbatim." I heard him flip some pages. "Here it is. 'You're here for me. This don't involve my kids. I'll show you what you came for; now just let them stay with their nana. These kids been through enough.'"

"Holy shit."

"It gets better. SCF calls the mom—did it right there in front of Jackson so he'd know we weren't jamming him. We tell him she's on the way and even let the kids lay down in the apartment next door while they're waiting. So then Raymond goes, 'All right, Melvin. We're all stand-up here. Now what were you saying about showing us what we came for?' Melvin says, 'It's in the van. Keys are on the table.'

"We leave backup watching Melvin and the apartment while we head out to the parking lot with the keys. We slide open the door, step in, and find six gallons of mocha cream paint."

"Anything else?" I asked.

"Not in the van. So we go back up to the apartment and say to Jackson, 'I guess you've been watching the news, Melvin.' He must've lost his desperation by then, knowing that his mom's on the way for the kids. He tries to play it cool and is all, 'The news? Man, I don't know what you're talking about, the news.' And I said, 'You must've known we were looking for the paint, Melvin. You just told us where to find it.' And so then he admits that he knew we'd been looking for the paint."

"Anything in the apartment?"

"Oh, yeah. Melvin keeps a great big fat file on his eviction case, including copies of all the letters he sent the vic. We also found some drafts of letters he must not have sent, and those were even worse. We bagged 'em up already, but I wrote down here that one of them said, *Maybe someone should show you what it's like to lose everything, bitch.* Guess he decided that wasn't likely to get him anywhere."

Neither would her death, but murder is rarely rational.

"Then Melvin's mom shows up. And let me tell you, Mama Jackson is a major piece of work. Came damn close to waking up the entire floor. Kept screaming at us to get her boy out of those handcuffs. We were trying to calm her down. Then

Raymond walks out of the back of the apartment with a hammer looped over his pen."

"What hammer?"

"I'm getting there. I thought I was supposed to give you the facts in the order they happened."

Cops love to fuck with lawyers, even when they're prosecutors, and, as much as Walker loves me, I am still a prosecutor.

"Ray found a hammer stashed on the top shelf of the bedroom closet. Looked like it had been wiped down, but you could still see a little blood. The crime lab's checking for sure. We should have an answer by morning."

"So what happened when Jackson saw that you found the hammer?"

"That's what was fucked up. It wasn't so much what Jackson did; it was what the mother did. She went absolutely nuts. Hands on the hips, doing the sassy head thing: 'I *knew* this wasn't no routine search. This here's about that white judge. I been trying to tell this fool the po-lice gonna be knockin' on his do', but, no, Melvin, you got yo'self too busy to listen.' Then she starts homing in on Johnson, going off about how he planted the weapon and how could he turn his back on his own people, that kind of shit."

"Can't be the first time you guys had to deal with a pissed-off mother."

"Sure, you get used to it, but she took our attention away from Jackson. No one got a chance to see his reaction when he realized Johnson found the hammer. There's something about that first look, that expression on their face when they realize you've got 'em. It's too bad you can't get that look into evidence, right there for the jury. Because the minute you see it, you know. You know it in your gut, This is the guy. And we missed it."

"Oh, come on, you know it's your guy anyway. You got the

weapon, the paint, the letters. You said yourself that Jackson practically confessed."

"I didn't say he was getting off. Shit, the guy's toast. But it's the look, Kincaid, and the mom kept us from seeing it. You've got no clue what I'm talking about, do you?"

I did, actually. There's a thrill—no, it's nothing short of a high—when you've got the defendant on the stand, you're building a rhythm with him on cross, and then you ask the karate chop question, the one you've been headed for from the very start. But you sneak up to it through the back roads, taking every possible detour, so no one knows it's coming, least of all the defendant. And when he realizes there's no good way to answer it, he gets that look. He flashes back to his attorney warning him to stay off the stand. Then to him telling the attorney, 'That bitch ain't got nothing on me.' And then he pictures what you both know is coming, the jury reading that verdict. It's a look of panic and utter hatred.

An arrest without the look was like hitting it out of the park without the crack of the bat. Or a perfect drive off the tee without feeling the ping of the ball against the sweet spot of your club. For Walker, this case clearance was purely utilitarian.

"Maybe it's not too late for you to get the look," I told him. "Is Jackson talking?"

"Doesn't look like it. He's the type who would have, but once the mom was done giving Johnson the black-pride trip, she started in on Melvin about a lawyer." Walker slipped back into his Mama Jackson routine. "'Don't you be talkin' to that Uncle Tom and his cracker-ass po-lice buddies. You get yo'self a public defender.' Before you know it, Melvin's lawyering up."

"How clear was it?" I asked. Thanks to the Supreme Court, the police are allowed to ignore a suspect's reference to an attorney if it's ambiguous.

"Couldn't get any fucking clearer: 'I want a lawyer.'"

The four magic words. We couldn't touch him. If we were going to get anything else out of him, it would have to be through his court-appointed lawyer.

"It's all right," I said. "We don't need it. The statements he made before he invoked will come in, and they look bad, especially with the threats. Assuming the crime lab finds the vic's blood on the hammer, he's done."

"I got to say, given our fuckup earlier, it felt good to nail the bastard. Johnson's down there now booking him at MCDC, and I'm writing up the reports." Jackson would spend the night in the Multnomah County Detention Center so he could be arraigned tomorrow morning. "We're both running on empty right now and have a back load of comp time. Call us tomorrow if you need follow-up, but I don't think either of us will be at the precinct. My wife's gonna leave me if I don't eat a meal with her and the girls soon."

"She'd rather have you at the house than the OT? Must be true love, Walker." And it was, too. Take a look around a detective squad, and the cubicles are filled with comically enhanced mug shots, doctored rap sheets, and the occasional pinup. Walker's is filled with photographs of his wife, Sandy, and their houseful of daughters. I'd never met them, but I'd followed their lives through pictures from the wedding day to their Six Flags vacation last August.

"Still don't know how I got so lucky." I was touched that Walker would express that kind of sentiment to me. Then came the follow-up. "From what I hear, I could've wound up with a prick like Roger Kirkpatrick."

"Just for that, Walker, I'm starting a list of tomorrow's follow-up work. Some for you for saying that, and some for Johnson for telling you about it."

We both got a laugh out of it. "See?" he said. "I wouldn't have said it if I didn't think you could handle it."

"Sure you would." These guys think I don't know what they put some of my coworkers through. "Now get some sleep and enjoy your day off. We've got more than enough for arraignment tomorrow. Just tell the crime lab to call Chuck or Mike with the lab results, OK?"

"Done. You're going Agg Murder, right?"

With what we had, proving Jackson killed Clarissa wouldn't be hard. But to get an aggravated murder conviction, I'd need to prove that the murder occurred under one or more special circumstances.

I knew what Walker was really asking, but answered the question narrowly to avoid the discussion. "I'll plead it tomorrow as an agg, probably based on the vic's status as a judge."

Walker wasn't interested in legal theories. He knew you could file aggravated murder charges without seeking the ultimate sanction. "But will your office go for the death penalty?"

"I'm sure that will be discussed. Whatever happens, it won't be my decision."

It was the same cop-out I used whenever I wondered what would happen if I ever got a death penalty case, and I tried to find comfort in it as I hung up the phone. As opinionated as I am, this issue is one of the few that leaves me scurrying up the nearest fence.

When I finally fell back asleep, it was only because I convinced myself that Jackson's sad circumstances and lack of a prior criminal record would limit the stakes of the case to a life sentence.

7

It was there in the pile of custodies the next morning. My first Major Crimes Unit call-out had been cleared and was ready for issuing. Unit rules be damned; I grabbed the file off Alice Gerstein's desk so I could prep the complaint against Melvin Jackson before turning to my screening cases.

For now, I kept the complaint simple, one count of aggravated murder and one alternative count of plain old garden-variety murder. Pleading the case as an agg murder requires a special circumstance. If Jackson killed Clarissa during the commission of either a kidnapping or rape, that would qualify. But there were problems with both theories. We had the condom and the ME's opinion that Clarissa's clothes were put back on her after she was killed, but we didn't have the traditional indications of rape. Clarissa's shoe and the paint provided circumstantial indications that Jackson pulled Clarissa into the van before he killed her, but if he killed her during the struggle and then put her in the van, it wasn't a kidnapping.

I avoided both possibilities and instead used Clarissa's

employment as an administrative law judge as the special circumstance. As long as the jury believed that Melvin killed Clarissa because of her official judicial duties, that was enough.

I passed Frist in the hallway as I was walking to the printer to pick up the complaint.

"We need to talk about that cluster fuck of a press conference last night on the Easterbrook case. The guy was nice enough to confine his bitching to the bureau, but Griffith's still gonna want a briefing."

"I think we're OK from that end. The husband's attorneys turned over some information last night, and the police arrested Melvin Jackson a few hours ago." I left out the part about one of the attorneys being my ex-husband. Although people in the office knew I was divorced, only a handful of them knew who the ex was. One of the advantages of keeping your own name. "When I left MCT last night, the husband's people were playing nice. I think the press conference was a wake-up call."

"Looks like it worked. Jackson's the disgruntled tenant?"

I nodded.

"What did they find on him?"

I told him about Dunn Simon's list of nonunion labor at the office park and the evidence the police found when they executed the search warrant. "I was just doing the complaint. Do you want to see the file before arraignment?"

"You know you should have called me, Kincaid."

"I thought you told me to run with it until we got to proceedings."

He looked at me skeptically.

"There's nothing to worry about, Russ. Everything's under control."

In light of how things had come together, he couldn't argue with that. "All right, let me see the complaint." He took a quick look. "Good call. If you add in a rape charge, it might cloud the motive. Most newbies would've thrown in every theory they could think of."

"You only need one when it's good," I said. "I'm going to head over at two for the arraignment. I assume you don't need to come with me."

"The DA at the Justice Center can handle it, Kincaid."

"Nope. It's my first arraignment on an agg murder. I'm doing it myself."

"Are the screens done?"

"They will be soon."

"All right. Don't forget to call Duncan."

I didn't need to. When I got back to my office, I had a voice mail from Duncan's secretary asking me to come down to his office. Terrific.

He had seen the press conference. Even worse, he had gotten a phone call from Dennis Coakley. Dennis must have slept on it and woken up even angrier.

I tried to calm him down by telling him about the Jackson arrest, but the distraction proved temporary.

"What exactly did we talk about in here yesterday?" he demanded.

"Duncan, I know you're upset, but please don't talk to me like I'm in kindergarten."

"When you act like a child, Samantha, you get treated like a child."

I couldn't help it. I exhaled in a way that might have sounded like a scoff. "I can't believe you actually just said that. Does anyone really say that?"

"Watch it, Sam. You're a good attorney, but I won't have my people talk to me that way."

Threatening to fire me was the typical trump card around

here, but now I had one of my own. "Or what, Duncan? You're going to fire the woman who almost got killed last month on the job because she ruffled some feathers trying to find the madman who's snatching women off the street?"

"Don't even think about playing that game with me. Next thing you know, you'll be the talented young attorney who was never the same after that shooting."

The entire time I'd worked here, I'd always caved when it came down to the last shove. If I was going to stick around, it was time to set some boundaries. I couldn't spend the rest of my career being lectured on a daily basis.

"I guess what it comes down to is how bad you want me to apologize. I refuse to suck up to Dennis Coakley."

"You are so off base. This is not about Coakley, it's about your respect for me and the authority of this office. I asked Dennis what time you hauled him over for the pissing match. You went straight from here to Lesh's. You didn't listen to me at all yesterday."

"You're forgetting the part where I went off on my detective about the polygraph request and then called you to make sure everything was fine."

"See, only you could turn that phone call into something that helps you here. You didn't mention anything about Coakley, did you? It's always bits and pieces of information from you, Sam, and it's getting old."

"OK, so maybe I could have mentioned it to you then while we were talking," I conceded, "but I won't apologize for what I did to get those files. It was important, and Coakley was being an ass."

"Well, at least you recognize that it wasn't exactly masterfully executed internally." We were finding just enough common ground for our egos to cling to as we brought the conversation down to a calmer level. "I don't know, Sam, maybe I put you into this a little too quickly. I called Lesh. He did his best to cover for you, but I could tell he was worried about you too. And we haven't even talked about this press conference. Wasn't that your ex-husband?"

I nodded. Duncan's memory ran deep.

"I think I should pull you off," he said. "Maybe out of MCU entirely, but definitely off this case."

"I can't believe I'm saying this, Duncan, but if you do either of those things, I won't want to work here anymore. And I won't go quietly."

Whether it was because he valued my work or feared what I could do to him in the media, the threat actually worked.

"Then here's the deal. This is the last time we have one of these talks. You start thinking about the ramifications of what you do, or you're going to have to go your own way."

"Deal," I said, with a salute. It was as much as either of us could hope for right now, but at least we were talking instead of yelling.

"Christ, your *ex-husband*? There's stubborn, Sam, and then there's just plain masochistic."

"Think of it this way. I guarantee you: No way does Roger Kirkpatrick call you to complain about this case. It would take all the fun out of torturing me."

"I'll take some comfort in that, then. All right, if you're staying on this thing, we'll need to schedule a conference with the death penalty committee to talk about what sentence to seek."

That's right. We've got a death penalty committee. It's not as bad as it sounds. When Duncan ran for district attorney in this liberal county, he acknowledged that he was personally opposed to the death penalty but nevertheless promised to administer it since it was Oregon law. The purpose of the committee is to have the same group of attorneys—all experienced career prosecutors—evaluate every aggravated murder case in comparison to previous ones and try to achieve the impossible: the even-handed application of the death penalty.

"I'll send out an e-mail looking for times," I said.

"They usually take about ninety minutes. And invite the family to come an hour after we start. I guess we'll need to go through the husband's lawyers now that he's represented. And, remember, I don't care what your ex did to piss you off. Be civil."

I worked like a fiend all morning so I could run off some of my resentment at noon. I changed into my workout clothes in the eighth-floor locker room and was warmed up by the time I got to the river. I decided to bump it up from my usual flat three-mile loop along the Willamette and did a five-miler around the west hills instead.

I slowed to a jog after a brutal half mile up a steep incline. I was out of breath and wishing I'd brought a water bottle when I realized I was just a couple of miles from Susan Kerr's house. I decided I had time for a short detour.

I recognized the Expedition in the driveway with the OHSU parking permit. My immediate reaction was to wonder what Townsend was doing at Susan Kerr's in the middle of a workday. Then I realized he wouldn't be back to work this soon after his wife's murder. So how suspicious was it for him to be here? The two of them did, after all, have a friendship through Clarissa and were both stomaching the same loss. Maybe they were talking about Jackson's arrest.

Remembering Duncan's ultimatum, I held off on interrupting them and decided to add Townsend's visit to the list of things I needed to discuss with Susan Kerr.

By the time I made it down the hill, into the courthouse, and out of the locker room shower, I had just enough time to tuck my damp hair into a clip and walk across the Plaza Blocks to Jackson's arraignment.

The Plaza Blocks' official designation as a park is a bit of an overstatement. They're nothing more than two city blocks of grass with a few trees and some benches. In the mid-1800s, the two blocks epitomized a quaint vision of city life, providing a forum for citizen oration and assembly. The south block, Lownsdale Square, was the gentlemen's gathering place, while women congregated safely in the northside Chapman Square.

These days, the one thing that distinguishes the Plaza Blocks from some of the more remarkable downtown parks is their location beneath the seventh floor of the Justice Center, otherwise known as the Multnomah County Detention Center. Once word got out that MCDC inmates had a view of the park, the plaza blocks became home to more than their fair share of singing, sign holding, and breast flashing.

Although it was just after lunch, it was still pretty early in the day for your average criminal's loved ones, but one young devotee was already out. She was probably in her twenties but looked older. Several years of chain smoking, combined with regular methamphetamine use, is hell on the skin. She wore skin-tight dark-blue Wrangler jeans, a thick brown belt with a heavy gold buckle, and patent-leather stilettos. A spaghetti-strapped red lace camisole revealed a multicolored tattoo of a large eagle in the cleavage of her impressive bosom. She was yelling, "I got this for you, Darryl! It stands for freedom, baby! Can you see it?" The refined gentlemen of Lownsdale Square would not have been pleased, but I decided I liked her.

I took the stairs to JC-2, the courtroom for the two o'clock arraignments. There was a stir when Judge Levinson called for Melvin Jackson. Given the continuous news coverage on the case, even the courthouse regulars were curious. Jackson's orange jail uniform was accompanied by handcuffs and leg shackles. Apparently he hadn't been on good behavior since his booking.

It showed. His hair was matted, and his eyes were blearier than the usual first-morning bloodshot. I suspected pepper spray.

Jackson qualified for court-appointed counsel. Because this was an aggravated murder case, the attorney was sure to be good, a member of Oregon's capital defense bar.

This afternoon's lucky winner? Graham Szlipkowsky, public defense veteran and colorful courthouse regular. Graham is probably fifty and tries cases in corduroys and tennis shoes. With salt-and-pepper hair cut like a mop and a matching beard, he looks more like a Muppet than one of the city's most experienced trial attorneys. He told me once that his mother insisted on the waspy first name to even out his Polish father's last name. As a result, neither of his names quite suits him, and everyone calls him Slip instead.

Slip's a straight shooter, perfect for this case. He didn't need the glory of a high-profile trial and would be smart enough to know the situation was hopeless. After some unsuccessful motions to suppress the critical evidence, he'd be looking for a plea to avoid a death sentence.

The appearance should have been perfunctory. A quick waiver of speedy trial rights from Jackson, a token request for bail from Slip, and Judge Marty Levinson would order the defendant remanded until trial. Any other result at an agg murder arraignment was largely theoretical.

On the other hand, there's something about me and theoretical possibilities that seems to click. After the usual brief conference with his client, Slip asked Levinson for additional time in light of "some unusual circumstances." A rookie defense attorney would've been torn a new one, but Slip had enough earned credibility that the judge deferred.

Great. For my own satisfaction, I'd walked over for a routine hearing that was technically the responsibility of the JC-2 DDA. Now that I knew "unusual circumstances" had arisen, I had to stay. You don't know from waiting until you've spent time in a courthouse. Doctors? Mechanics? The DMV? Forget about it. I settled into a seat at the front of the galley while the assigned arraignment deputy moved through more routine matters.

Seven arraignments and forty minutes later, Slip informed the clerk he was ready to go back on the record in *Jackson*. I took my place again at counsel table, called the case, and asked the judge to hold the defendant without bail.

As expected, Slip contested the request.

"May it please the court, Graham Szlipkowsky for the defendant, Mr. Jackson. Your honor, my client respectfully requests that the court consider alternatives to remand without bail. We recognize that the charge of aggravated murder triggers a presumption of no bail, but it is, after all, merely a presumption. Mr. Jackson has no prior criminal record and is the single father of three young children who require his care."

So far, so routine. And so hopeless. It was the next part of Slip's request that must have reflected the forty-minute recess.

"Regardless of defendant's custody status pending trial, Mr. Jackson does not waive his right to a prompt hearing of probable cause. We request that a preliminary hearing be scheduled at the earliest possible date so that my client can contest the charges immediately. He sees no need to await a trial date."

Levinson was neither impressed nor amused. He took off his glasses, scratched his bald head, and said, "You're kidding me, right?"

Most people have heard of prelims from the high-profile California cases. They're mini-trials to determine whether there's sufficient evidence to hold the defendant over for trial. The federal system and just about every state uses the less burdensome, more secretive grand jury process instead. Oregon, as usual, had forged a third way: a theoretical procedure for conducting preliminary hearings that never actually took place. As a result of confusing court decisions and years of local practice, indictment by grand jury was the routine.

Jackson did not, however, want to do this the routine way.

"I would never kid, your honor." Slip was good at handling cantankerous judges.

"You've explained to your client that the State's burden at a preliminary hearing is considerably lower than at trial?" Levinson asked. The question was more for Jackson's sake than Slip's. "That all the State has to do is show probable cause? And that the Court is required to draw every possible inference in favor of the State?"

"I've explained that all to him, your honor. Mr. Jackson's highest priority is to be with his children. He is afraid he'll lose his kids if he doesn't nip these charges in the bud. He knows it's an uphill battle, but he wants at least to have that chance. As your honor well knows, the grand jury process is even more lopsided."

The prosecutor runs the show with the grand jury. No judge, no defense counsel, no defendant.

"Your honor," I said, "I already have this case scheduled for grand jury. He has no right to a preliminary hearing."

"But he's not indicted yet, is he? And now he's asking for a prelim."

I tried to explain that wasn't how it worked, but Levinson wanted to keep his docket moving.

"I don't see the harm, Ms. Kincaid, and I don't want to leave all these people waiting here while the two of you argue about it. Friday, JC-Three, at nine o'clock. I assume you can make it, Ms. Kincaid?"

"Of course," I said, since that was the only acceptable answer to a question that had used *you* in the collective sense. Judges assume prosecutors are fungible. If I had open-heart surgery scheduled for that morning, I'd have to find someone else. Fortunately, I did not.

Neither did Slip. "I can clear my calendar, your honor."

"Very good. As for bail, nice try, Mr. Szlipkowsky, but, unh-unh, I don't think so. Remanded."

I told myself there was nothing to worry about. Beating charges at a prelim is unheard of.

I passed Russ on the way back to my office. I was beginning to think the man lived in the hallway.

He looked at his watch when he saw me. "You spent an hour and a half over there to do one arraignment. I need to find you some more work, Kincaid."

I told him about Jackson's request for a prelim and the Friday hearing date.

"You've got to be fucking kidding me. We don't do prelims."

"Try telling that to Levinson while he's behind on his docket."

"Well, we can't be ready to put on evidence by Friday morning. Did you ask for more time?"

"No."

He looked frustrated.

"It would've been pointless, Russ, and it's just a prelim. Weapon, threats, paint, statements. Done. It'll take two hours."

"Let's see," he said, ticking my points off on his fingers. "Hammer: no blood tests yet; threat: every judge gets them, including whoever you draw for the prelim on Friday; paint: you need an expert or else Jackson's just a laborer with a can of beige paint; and statements: you better hope they come in. I know your guys were out there just for the warrant, but a lot of judges will say Jackson was under arrest the minute the cuffs came out."

Jackson hadn't yet been Mirandized when he admitted knowing that the police were there about the paint. His statements would be admissible only if the court believed that the police had handcuffed Jackson to restrain him temporarily during the search rather than to arrest him.

"You worry too much," I said. "The threats are motive, and I'll line up a paint expert. That's enough for probable cause right there, and I guarantee you the crime lab will find a blood match on the hammer. The only problem is I'm supposed to have discovery to Slip by the end of the day. There's some evidence suggesting the victim was having an affair, and I think we need to turn it over."

I had been hoping to have more time to mull over Tara's revelation, but Jackson's request for the quick prelim forced the issue. The failure to turn over exculpatory information could lead to a reversal down the road.

"Christ." Frist rubbed his temples. "Exactly what kind of evidence are we talking about?"

I told him about Tara's visit. It was more than mere rumors; according to her sister, Clarissa admitted she was contemplating divorce because she was in love with someone else.

"You don't know who the someone else was?" he asked.

"Not with any certainty, but we've got a theory." I told him about the calls to T. J. Caffrey.

He started shaking his head before I had even finished. "I'm not sure I'd tell the defense about any of that. Even if she was having an affair, there's nothing concrete tying it to the murder, and you don't know for certain who the guy was. A few phone calls don't mean anything."

I understood his argument. The rules on disclosure allow the prosecution to hold back just about anything that's arguably innocuous. But with the growing numbers of innocent men being freed from prison in cases where the prosecutor sat on information, I tend to fall on the side of broader disclosure.

I explained my analysis to Frist. There was both physical and testimonial evidence suggesting that the victim may have been having an affair, and the phone records showed that the calls between Clarissa and Caffrey made up the bulk of her cell phone usage. I wouldn't turn Caffrey's name over to Slip directly, but I'd give him the phone records and a report about Tara's statement so he could decide for himself if they were relevant.

"Suit yourself," Frist said, "but if this case goes to trial, and he tries to turn your victim's supposed boyfriend into his one-armed man, you'll regret it."

"You're dating yourself. Satanic cults are the 'other guys' of late."

"You're pushing your luck, Kincaid, but I'll go along with you anyway. Duncan's going to want to call Caffrey as a courtesy," he said resignedly. "I'll tell Duncan; you take care of the husband. We don't want him learning about this at the prelim."

Great. Getting information to Townsend meant a phone call to Roger. In the hierarchy of pleasantries, I ranked it just beneath walking a plank of nails into a shark tank.

"And, speaking of the prelim," I said, "tell me I can do it without you."

"I'm afraid I've got no choice, Kincaid."

I started in on my spiel about how wasteful it was to use two attorneys on a prelim, but he interrupted. "No. I meant I don't have any choice but to let you go solo. I've got thirteen victims coming in on a sex-abuse grand jury. Some chick who ran a home day care didn't notice her boyfriend diddling all the kids."

I never wanted to get used to these cases.

"I'll do it by myself, then. Don't worry. It will be fine." I started to walk away, then realized I'd forgotten something.

"Oh, can you do a death penalty meeting tomorrow at two? Duncan told me to get everyone together."

"Yeah, I'm clear. And, for the record, Sam, I would have let you handle the prelim anyway. You're doing a good job."

An unqualified compliment at the District Attorney's Office? For me? Either Frist was a different kind of supervisor or I was becoming a real jerk.

I picked up the phone to call Roger but couldn't bring myself to ignore the message light on my phone.

It was Chuck. "Hey, babe. Good news back from the crime lab. Give me a call."

I hate those messages that keep you hanging. Either tell me what you need to tell me or ask me to return the call. I was eager for the lab reports but felt obliged to get the call to Roger over with.

I dialed the first six digits of his number before tapping on the handset for a new dial tone. A call to Susan Kerr would allow me to procrastinate a little longer. I still needed to talk to her about Tara's suspicions that Clarissa was seeing someone else, not to mention her little visit this afternoon from Townsend.

When I identified myself, she jumped right in.

"I'm so happy you called. I was going to see if there's anything I can do after Townsend's press conference last night. I was in bed by then and couldn't believe what I saw in the paper this morning. I didn't even know he had a lawyer."

"Neither did we."

"Would it help if I called someone at the mayor's office to support the bureau? I know I was a bit critical of how the police handled the situation with Townsend Monday night, but I think you're all doing a great job."

I assured her that I appreciated the offer, but there was no need for her to pull strings. "But, since you brought it up, do you have any idea why Townsend would rail against us like that?"

"No, and it shocks me."

"He didn't mention it when he was at your house this afternoon?"

Wow. I hadn't planned on blurting it out that way. Very Perry Mason.

Unfortunately, it didn't have a Perry-Masonian effect. Instead of breaking down and sharing a lifetime of secrets with me, Susan Kerr made me feel like shit.

"Are you actually having Townsend followed or something? My God, are you watching my home? Maybe Townsend was right to rail against you, as you put it."

I immediately launched into a back pedal, explaining that I had passed her house on my regular run and happened to notice his car.

"If you had simply asked like a regular person instead of ambushing me, I would have told you all of this anyway. What I was about to say was that I can only chalk up the press conference to the fact that Townsend just hasn't been himself since— well, since, Clarissa was found. He's been drinking more, and sometimes he'll start rambling incoherently. My best guess is that someone from work might have suggested it, because I know it didn't come from me or Clarissa's family.

"As for his visit this afternoon, if you must know, I initially suggested it, hoping to pull out some of the old Townsend. When he's in work mode—well, everything else sort of fades away. I've been helping him with some fund-raising for the hospital's pediatric wing and thought it might help him to put his mind back into that for the afternoon. But of course he told me about the arrest, and one thing led to another. I wound up crying away another afternoon, while he sat like a zombie on the sofa. So, no, we did not talk about the press conference."

I didn't know what to say. I floundered around for an appropriate apology, finally lamely offering that I was sorry for her loss.

She sighed. "I know. I can tell you care, and I do appreciate it. My God, I thought it was hard when I lost Herbie, but to have a loss like this—I don't know how Townsend will ever get over it. Quite honestly, I'm beginning to question his stability. He doesn't seem to be thinking straight."

Her worries about Townsend made it even harder to share what I'd heard from Tara. I omitted T. J. Caffrey's name for the time being.

"Boy, you are full of good news today, aren't you?" Her attempt at levity didn't change the fact that she wasn't having any of it. "I know I've already told you this," she said, "but Clarissa and Townsend had a perfectly normal marriage. Well, about as normal as it can be given how hard the guy works. But, trust me, if there was something wrong, Clarissa would have told me. And, my God, if she was cheating—" She laughed at the mere thought of it. "She'd definitely tell me before she'd say anything to Tara."

"I'm just trying to reconcile Tara's information with everything else we've heard," I explained. "Why would Tara make something like that up?"

"Perhaps she misinterpreted something Clarissa said. We all vent about our husbands now and then, don't we? And Tara can be very melodramatic."

"She seemed fairly certain about Clarissa's meaning," I said.

"Just because she was sure doesn't make her right. And even if Clarissa was fooling around—which I'm sure she wasn't— what use is there in bringing it up now? I understood from Townsend that you had a mountain of evidence against this Jackson guy."

"We do," I said, "but we still need to cover our bases. I don't want the defense springing something on us down the road because we were afraid to ask the tough questions."

"Well, you've asked them, and my answer hasn't changed. Clarissa wasn't like that, and I hope you'll leave it at that. If the police go to Townsend with this, it could send him right over the edge."

Tara had expressed the same concern. Townsend might be the one in charge at the hospital, but apparently, in other areas of his life, those closest to him felt the need to be strong on his behalf.

"I know you're worried about Townsend," I said, "but I hope you're not holding back information you think would hurt him. Tara already told me that's why she initially didn't say anything about this."

"I am most definitely not holding back with you. If anything, I feel a little guilty for mentioning Townsend's irrational behavior. But I don't want to hear anything else about Tara's little suspicions. This son of a bitch Jackson killed my best friend. You just told me a second ago that it was basically a sure thing. But instead of anyone asking me about her life or what she was like or how wonderful she was, you just want to make sure she was a good wife."

I did my best to explain how important the questions were to the case, and she did her best to say she understood. But I nevertheless hung up feeling like the worst kind of bottom feeder.

I probably should have waited before calling Roger, but I didn't.

"Roger Kirkpatrick." I could picture him in an office high above the Willamette, feet on his desk, answering the phone on speaker to avoid wasting his valuable time on extraneous hand movements.

"Roger, it's Samantha."

"I assume you're calling about Easterbrook?" He still hadn't picked up the receiver.

"Good guess, since I've never called you about anything else in the last three years. Now unless you've once again got your hands where they don't belong, pick up the damn phone and get me off speaker."

I heard a click and then his voice was directly in my ear. Perhaps I should have left well enough alone. "I had hoped you'd either squelch the hostilities, Samantha, or remove yourself from the case."

He had no idea how much I had squelched. There was a time when I wanted to rip his guts out in public—if not literally, then at least through well-placed billboards announcing that Mister Communitarian was a cheat and a liar. He liked to think his charitable donations and board memberships made him a good person, but Roger Kirkpatrick was a thief of the worst kind, no better than a con man. His grift began with the hours he spent with Nike's newest spokesperson, the aforementioned volleyball pro. It was only after weeks of inner debate that I had finally asked him if I needed to worry. Surely, he had noticed that she was seventy-two inches of legs, breasts, muscle, and tan. Negotiations, he assured me.

And, with that, I had given him my trust, not just in the general way a wife trusts her husband, and not even just in the way I trusted Roger. I had given him the trust I have in myself, in my own ability to judge a man who looks me in the eye and tells me he's for real.

Yes, Roger had gotten off easy. If I seemed a little brusque, he was going to have to deal.

"I wanted to make sure you knew that Jackson requested a prelim," I said. "It's Friday morning. I'll need Townsend there at eight-thirty, just in case."

"I know," he said. "I sent a paralegal over this morning for the arraignment. I told Townsend to expect to be there. If you don't mind, I'll be with him."

"Suit yourself. Easy billables, I suppose." Eventually, Townsend's retention of a defense attorney would look terrible in front of a jury, but it would be irrelevant to the judge who handled the prelim. "We also would like him to meet with us before we make a final decision about whether to seek the death penalty."

He assured me they'd both be at the meeting the next day.

"Is that everything?" he asked.

"Johnson needs to talk to Townsend. Some evidence might come out at the prelim that could be disturbing." I told Roger about the nonoxynol-9, my conversation with Tara, and Clarissa's phone records.

"That's a hell of a lot to dump on a guy, Samantha. Your cops didn't think to mention any of this to him earlier?"

"Don't blow this out of proportion. This is the usual way it's done. We guard the information, but in the end the family hears it first from us. The only thing that's making this hard is having to go through you to get to our victim's husband."

"When Johnson asked him the other night about barrier methods, Townsend assumed there must have been a sexual assault."

"We still don't know," I said. "Maybe the nonoxynol's Jackson's. Either way, Tara seems to think Clarissa was seeing someone else. Think what you want about the phone calls."

"I'll tell him myself," he said.

"I want to send someone over, Roger. You can pick whomever you're most comfortable with, and you can be there. But I want a cop to tell him." It was the first step to bridging the gap between Townsend and PPB, an accomplishment that would help the rest of the case run smoothly.

Roger wasn't having it. "I'm not trying to be an ass, Samantha, but don't tell yourself you're doing this for Townsend. There's not a man in the world who'd choose to hear something like that from a cop instead of someone he at least knows is on his side. You want the cop there to see his reaction, and it's totally unnecessary. Townsend's cleared. I'll tell him myself."

I had to admit it—with Townsend's alibi and poly, there was no compelling justification for having a detective present when he heard the news. "Fine," I said, "but some words of advice?" He was silent during the pause. "When you break the news to Townsend, try to be a little more subtle than you were with me."

I hung up, angry at myself for losing my cool. I wrote a memo for the file about my conversation with Tara and sent a duplicate and the phone records to the discovery desk. Now that Townsend would be getting the news, I could make the disclosure to Slip.

I needed a pick-me-up. Fortunately, I had saved the best call for last. Chuck answered at MCT.

"I was wondering when I'd hear from you," he said. "You find my note last night?"

"Pretty cute. I'm not sure Vinnie enjoyed being the messenger, though. Looked like he tried to chew it off of his collar."

"He was probably trying to eat the damn thing. Greedy mutt snarfs down anything within a three-foot radius."

"Takes after his mommy that way. Now, as much as I'm enjoying deconstructing my little man's eating habits, can you please share the good news? I didn't appreciate the cliff-hanger."

"I am pleased to announce that Heidi Chung, famed PPB crime lab specialist, will testify that blood on the hammer Johnson took from Jackson's apartment belonged to Clarissa Easterbrook. The ME says it's consistent with her injuries."

"Yes! I knew we'd get it." Even so, I felt relieved to have the news officially in. Establishing probable cause against Jackson would be a breeze.

"Ah, but there's more," he said. "A little surprise to end your day with."

I kicked my door shut with my foot and dropped my voice low. "It's not exactly a surprise if you tell me about it ahead of time."

"Get your mind out of the gutter, Kincaid. This surprise is from Chung. She got Jackson's prints from his booking. Matched his right index and middle to two of the unidentified latents on the Easterbrooks' door knocker."

I let out a small scream. It always felt good when a case came together, but it was particularly satisfying to have my first murder case wrapped up with a tidy little bow on top. I told him to ask the crime lab to get the reports to me ASAP so I could include them in Slip's discovery package.

"Now," he said, "if you want to get back to that conversation you started a second ago, I'm up for it. But I charge two ninety-nine for the first minute and one ninety-nine thereafter."

"As tempting as that sounds," I said, "I think I'm in the mood for something a little more personal."

"I could probably handle that. Maybe come up with a surprise or two of my own."

"You're on. Seven o'clock, my house. Bring your toothbrush. This one might be an overnight."

8

WITH THE EVIDENCE in against Jackson and the charges formally filed, I finally got a taste of a regular MCU morning on Thursday. It was just like a morning in DVD, but instead of grinding out morning drug custodies, I was churning through the night's assault arrests.

As required, I finished the misdemeanor screening cases first. I held back only one to issue as a felony. Robert Jenkins, a thirty-seven-year-old man with a prior trespass conviction at an elementary school, was tackled by the father of a four-year-old girl after the father found Jenkins taking pictures of his daughter at the park. The girl remained clothed the entire time, but Jenkins had manipulated her into various poses that revealed his Chester the Molester ways. When the responding police officer perused the other shots in the guy's digital camera, he found forty photographs of eight different kids. Bent over, legs spread, fingers in their open mouths; the details varied, but the gist was always the same. Jenkins admitted to the officer that he used the pictures to pleasure himself sexually and did not consider them to be art.

A single line at the end of the police report hinted at the problem with the case: "I decided to arrest the suspect for harassment, since he touched the vic to achieve the desired pose, and such touching was offensive under the circumstances." It wasn't obvious what to charge the defendant with, but I wasn't about to let a guy like Jenkins off the hook with the misdemeanor of harassment.

I flipped through the penal code to confirm my recollection, but the child sex abuse laws all required physical contact or at least nudity. I reread the victim's statement. For the photograph of her straddling the slide, she said Jenkins told her to climb up the ladder, then pulled her feet on either side of the slide before she went down. She said the slide hurt her skin and she didn't know why she couldn't keep her dress beneath her legs. The officer noted some redness on the backs of her thighs. Good enough for me. An assault on a four-year-old is a felony, and I had an appellate case saying a red mark is enough to get an assault charge before a jury, which I'd pack full of parents. Jenkins could make all the arguments he wanted about strict statutory definitions, but the charge would stick.

I sent a follow-up request to a detective I knew in the child sex abuse unit asking him to run Jenkins's other photographs by the DARE officers who worked the schools near the park. Even if finding the other kids didn't lead to more charges, telling the parents seemed like the right thing to do. They were probably convinced that the "don't talk to strangers" talk had been enough to protect their kids. It never is.

Thanks to a grand jury appearance and an overdue response to a motion to suppress, I didn't finish reviewing the rest of the custodies until nearly noon. I apologized to Alice as I put them on her desk. For her to finalize the paperwork in time for arraignments, she'd have to work through lunch.

"The least I can do is bring you something," I offered. She told me it wasn't necessary. If the attorneys here paid for lunch every time they screwed over the staff, we'd all be broke, and they'd all be fat. But, after the polite amount of argument, she accepted.

Alice estimated she had another hour of work, so I decided to take in a quick run. Jessica Walters was also in the locker room and asked if I wanted to join her for a loop around the waterfront.

Whenever I run with someone new, I let them set the pace. We were clocking about an eight-minute mile, which was comfortable for me, but I couldn't tell if she was holding back.

We crossed the Willamette over the Morrison Bridge, saving the prettiest, downtown side of the loop for last. Once the noise of the bridge was past us and we had dropped down to the river's edge, she asked me if I had ever tried to run with the office's Hood-to-Coast team.

The Hood-to-Coast is Oregon's annual relay race from Mount Hood to the Pacific coast. At one time, there had been an official District Attorney team. When Duncan found out that the members wore T-shirts bearing electric chairs, one for each defendant the runner had placed on death row, he pulled the plug.

I reminded Jessica that the group was no longer the official office team, making no effort to hide my sarcasm.

"Whatever. Have you ever run with them?"

"I didn't think I was eligible." My impression was that a team member needed to have a reliable eight-minute mile, the ability and willingness to drink mass quantities of alcohol, and a penis. Two out of three didn't cut it. "In any event, I figure you choose your battles." If I was going to become the office's rabble-rouser, it wasn't going to be for the privilege of running with a group that likes to polish off the day by watching each other light their gas.

We had started a subtle incline but hadn't dropped the pace. Jessica didn't say anything until the path flattened out again.

"How's the evidence against Jackson looking?" she asked. She was winded but could still get the words out.

I gave her the abbreviated version. "I know the case is strong, but ever since I issued it, I've been finding myself getting worried. Frist thinks I might regret telling the defense about the affair."

"It's your first murder case," she said, "so you're worrying more than you need to. It's normal. You'll feel great by the day of trial."

She was right. A case is always strongest at the beginning, when all you've got is what the police have given you. As you move toward trial, your job—and the defense's—is to pick, poke, and prod at every last thread, any possible wrinkle that might turn out to be the glove that won't stretch over the defendant's hand. But by the first day of trial, you've tucked in the loose strings and ironed out the wrinkles, and the case is clearer than ever.

"I also still wonder why she was calling you," I said, "and if it had anything to do with the murder. Maybe because of the gang unit? Do you work with public housing at all?" It wasn't unusual for us to work with other agencies on long-term crime reduction plans.

She shook her head. "The community prosecution unit will call HAP sometimes if they know of a problem in the projects, but we stay out of that stuff in the trial unit. Hard enough to get cooperation on cases without getting people worried about losing their apartment."

When I didn't respond, she looked over at me and laughed.

"You need to chill out, Kincaid. It's just a phone call. I called twenty people this morning, and if someone chops me up in little pieces tonight, I guarantee you it won't have anything to do with any of them."

"It just seems weird to call someone you don't know, leave a message, and not say what you're calling about," I said. "And that number she left you was her cell, by the way."

"It was?" Jessica's tone told me she found that unusual too.

They say murder cases are like any other criminal case, but with one important difference: Your most important witness, the victim, is gone forever. The reason for Clarissa's phone call was lost with her death, along with all the other information she took with her.

We picked up the pace as we passed the courtyard at the north end of the waterfront, then began the slow jog through downtown back to the courthouse. She stopped at the Plaza Blocks to stretch, and I put in about thirty seconds with her before I grew impatient. My doctor says I've got the heart of a healthy horse but the bones of a ninety-year-old man. Regardless of his warnings, I still spend every exercise minute I can spare going after every calorie I can burn.

"I stuck Alice Gerstein with some last-minute custodies and told her I'd bring her back some lunch, so I better get a move on," I said, explaining my abrupt departure.

"Don't let Frist know you're being so considerate," she said. "Makes everyone else in the unit look even worse."

I was happy to find the Mexican food cart parked outside the courthouse. I got fish tacos on corn tortillas for me and a chicken burrito for Alice, then climbed the stairs to the eighth floor to polish off my workout.

Alice accepted the bag with the burrito in it and thanked me. "Sorry to break this to you, but you've got another visitor."

Still out of breath and in my sticky running gear, I was in no condition to have a meeting. "Who is it?" I asked.

"Melvin Jackson's mother. She's been here about twenty minutes."

"Can you tell her to schedule an appointment? I'm a mess, and I have some work I need to do before the death penalty meeting on that case."

"I'll do it if you want me to," Alice said, "but I can tell you right now it won't be pretty. She threw a fit when I told her no one was here to talk to her. We finally calmed her down by telling her you were on your way back."

"We don't usually meet with a defendant's family members. Maybe she should call the defense attorney."

Alice was patient, but the look on her face reminded me of that plumber I'd hired when I told him to try adjusting the flushy chain doohickey. "I tried that," Alice said, "but I believe her response was, 'I don't need to talk to some lazy-ass public defender. I need to talk to the lady who's buying all this bullshit about my son.'"

Given Walker's description from the night of Jackson's arrest, it sounded like the last two days had actually done wonders for Mrs. Jackson's forbearance.

"Fine. I'll be ready in a few minutes."

When I'm not distracted by the television, the refrigerator, or singing in the shower, I can get ready in seven minutes flat. It's one of the advantages of never learning how to put on makeup or do my hair. A shower, a hair clip, and a change of clothes are all I need to transform back into my regular every-day self.

Martha Jackson was in the reception area, shifting in her seat and tsk-ing every time someone walked by for a reason other than to see her. She was short for her weight, a trait that was only accentuated by the hot pink lilies on her dress that appeared to bloom from her generous bosom and broad hips.

I managed to get my name out, but she was off and running before I had a chance to offer her some water and a seat in the conference room. "You got a hundred lawyers in this office. How come I got to wait half an hour to talk to someone about a case that's been on the news every day of the week?"

I tried to explain that not all the lawyers work on each individual case, but she was looking for a fight.

"You trying to tell me you'd leave someone waiting here if they ready to say they seen Melvin Jackson do it?"

"Is that what you're here to say?" I asked.

That did the trick. "Hell, no. No way Melvin could kill that woman." It was exactly what I expected to hear, and I herded her into a conference room while she repeated it every way she could think to say it. I hoped the closed door would at least buffer the outburst that was sure to greet the bad news: I wasn't going to drop the charges and send Melvin home with her.

When she was done saying her piece, I did my best to say mine sympathetically. For all I knew, she had nothing to do with her son turning out to be the kind of man he was.

"I can't pretend that I understand how difficult this must be for you, Mrs. Jackson, but the police have compelling evidence suggesting that your son, as hard as it must be for you to accept, was responsible for Clarissa Easterbrook's death. I would not be doing my job if I ignored that evidence simply because a loving mother told me her son was innocent. If he claims he's innocent, he has his own attorney to help him defend against the charges. You might want to call his lawyer and see how you can help."

In a capital case, the bulk of the defense work often goes into the penalty phase. If Slip could calm Martha Jackson down long enough to put her on the stand, a mother's plea for mercy can sway a jury to spare a son's life.

"Oh, trust me, I'll be talking to that man too, but I know there's only so much he can do. Only you people can shut off this assembly line of a court system once it gets to going. You say you wouldn't be doing your job to ignore evidence, but let me ask you this, Ms. Kincaid. Isn't part of your job to pay attention to evidence that's looking you right in the face?"

Given the circumstances her son was in and my role in that process, I showed her more patience that I normally would. "Of course it is, and I'm doing that."

"You probably went to some fancy law school, didn't you?" she asked.

"I'm not sure what you want me to say, Mrs. Jackson."

"I'm pointing out that you a smart woman, but you only looking at what you want to see."

I was getting frustrated. She was going to have to come to terms with this eventually, so it may as well be now. "I'm very sorry for your situation, but, ma'am, you know where the police found the murder weapon, and your son's fingerprints were on the victim's front door."

"C'mon now, my boy was just trying to get the woman to talk to him. He wanted to sit down, look her in the eye, and ask how in the world someone can lose his home and children because of something his cousin did."

"And maybe he finally found a way to do that." I immediately regretted saying something so mean-spirited, but it seemed to be exactly what Martha Jackson expected.

The fire in her voice was gone. She clicked her tongue against her teeth and shook her head. "I don't know why I bothered. Y'all just ain't usin' the heads God gave you. How that poor lady's death gonna help my grandchildren? You see a colored man and assume he ain't got sense, just an animal lashing out at the world."

I was angry at the accusation, but knew that nothing I said would change either her perception of the criminal justice system or the many events in her lifetime that were responsible for it. "I'm sorry, Mrs. Jackson, but I can't help you." I opened the door to show her out.

She had one more thing to say before she left. "Melvin's living in Section Eight—one step above begging on the streets— for a reason. Why's he all the sudden got regular work at some fancy office development? And wouldn't you know that's where your poor missing judge turns up. Believe what you will about my son, but y'alls the ones ain't thinkin.'"

She walked past me through the doorway and headed for the elevator. I assumed she didn't need an escort.

Russ Frist was standing outside the conference room.

"Melvin Jackson's mother," I explained.

"Alice told me about her when I got back, but I didn't want to walk in. Sounded like you had everything under control."

"Sure, if you consider being an insensitive prick having things under control," I said. "It's not her fault her son's in a jam."

"More hers than yours, Kincaid. Let it go."

Letting things go never was my forte.

At two o'clock, the members of the death penalty committee gathered to decide whether Melvin Jackson should live or die if convicted. Even the boss himself showed up, joining Russ Frist, Jessica Walters, Rocco Kessler, and me.

Rocco Kessler spoke first. His real name is Richard, but somehow the macho nickname grew out of his initials. Knowing him, I suspected he engineered the transition himself.

I hadn't seen him since leaving DVD, where he was most memorable as the supervisor who wanted me fired. He must not have missed me much, since he took his chair in the conference room without so much as a hello.

"Let's get this show on the road. Duncan wants to keep things moving, and I plan to stick to the format we've always used." The dearly departed Tim O'Donnell had previously chaired these meetings. "The husband's coming in at three, Kincaid?" he asked.

I nodded. "He's the only one. The trip downtown's too hard for the parents, and the sister just called—her kids are having a meltdown and she couldn't pawn them off on her folks. For what it's worth, my gut tells me they'll go either way on the sentence. They know nothing's going to bring Clarissa back."

"Okay, then. Take as long as you need to tell us about the case and the defendant, this"—he looked down at his notes—"Melvin Jackson. What we usually do is just go around the room and give our initial impressions, then go from there."

I finished in twenty minutes, spending only half of that on the evidence itself. What made this meeting a difficult one wasn't the question of Melvin Jackson's guilt but the balancing of two seemingly irreconcilable images of the man. I tried to give it to them straight, covering both the aggravated nature of the crime and the sympathetic story of a father with no prior criminal history beating a lifelong addiction to keep his children.

Rocco asked Jessica to speak first.

"I think this is one of the hardest cases we've seen. At first blush, it's got death penalty written all over it. The guy snatches a woman off the street, for Christ's sake. But when you think about it, the reason those cases give you such a visceral reaction is that you think of a sex offender. You think of the Polly Klaas or Dru Sjodin cases. Melvin Jackson's not one of those guys. He's not a predator. And we also don't have any prior acts of violence; I'd be inclined to seek life."

Rocco looked to Russ.

"I'd go death penalty but accept a plea to life. We might not know exactly what Jackson did to her, but the ME says the vic's shirt was off when she was beaten. We also know he stalked her. I see where you're coming from, Walters, but to me this isn't just some guy who snapped. Think of what it must have been like for the victim in those final moments, taking her clothes off for him. That's more than garden-variety murder."

Rocco jumped in next. I was getting the impression he forgot I was there. "I'm with Frist," Rocco said. "The guy might not have any priors, but that just means no one caught him before. Even by his own sad story, he's a doper who thinks he deserves a medal for choosing his kids over heroin."

Jessica shook her head. "Forget for a second that Melvin Jackson's a black man who lives in public housing and Clarissa Easterbrook's an attractive, wealthy judge."

Rocco accused her of playing the race card, and the room broke out in a cacophony rivaling *Crossfire*. Duncan made a time-out sign with his hands and told everyone to let Jessica finish speaking, but Jessica held up her hand. "Never mind."

I, however, minded. She had a valid point, and they should at least take it into consideration. If this was going to be my case, I couldn't be afraid to speak up.

"Jessica's right," I said. "When a defendant looks like Melvin Jackson and the victim looks like Clarissa Easterbrook, that alone pushes buttons we might not even know we have."

Rocco didn't want to hear it. "That's a PC load of crock, Kincaid." Aah, sweet memories of my former boss. "Jackson's race has got nothing to do with this, and I don't want to hear another word about it."

"Well, that's all you're going to hear about if Jackson's not comparable to other capital defendants. You tell me: Have we ever asked for a death sentence against a white defendant with no prior violence?"

The immediate silence at the table was answer enough, but it wasn't the right one for Russ and Rocco, who began walking through individual cases, struggling to compare them to Jackson's. Duncan chose to stare at the ceiling. I couldn't tell if he was seeking spiritual guidance or picturing himself under fire by civil rights protesters on future campaign stops.

We were still debating the case when Alice Gerstein rapped on the door and peeked in. "Dr. Easterbrook and his lawyer are here whenever you're ready."

From what I'd heard, the usual goal of these meetings was to make the decision before the family arrived, then use the rest of the time to get the family on board. But Duncan wasn't going to make Townsend wait while we continued to argue.

"For now, we'll hear what he's got to say. If I make a final decision, I'll let everyone know. We may just have to meet again."

I moved to the empty chair between Rocco and Russ. It might have seemed like a thoughtful gesture so Townsend could sit next to his own attorney. In truth, it was to ensure that Roger didn't sit next to me. I wasn't sure I could resist the temptation to kick him in the shins if he irritated me.

With constituents in the room, Duncan ran the floor. He got about as far as any government lawyer short of the solicitor general would have before my ex took over. Roger Kirkpatrick is and always has been a power lawyer.

"We appreciate your having Dr. Easterbrook here so he can communicate his views in person. I'm sure you understand that this is not an easy thing for him to talk about."

As much as Tara and Susan had emphasized Townsend's deterioration, they had nevertheless understated it. His eyes were puffy, his skin pale; he looked at the table when he spoke, barely registering our presence. He mumbled something about being against the death penalty, hating Melvin Jackson, and being a doctor, before Roger spared him—and us—further embarrassment.

Roger placed his hand on Townsend's shoulder. "It's OK. Let me see if I can explain what you told me earlier." He shifted his attention to the rest of us. "Townsend has struggled this week with a new emotion—a hatred of Melvin Jackson that is more intense than anything I'm sure any of us has felt before. When he first heard Monday about the evidence found in Jackson's apartment, his instinct, and I'm being frank here, was to kill Jackson himself."

Townsend didn't currently look capable of—let alone driven to—revenge, but maybe the change was further proof of what this week had been like for him.

"I spent a lot of time calming him that night, talking to him about the court system and convincing him that the case was strong enough that I was confident your office could convict. I left his house Monday night certain that he would be lobbying you to pursue this prosecution as a capital case. But when we talked the next day, Townsend told me he'd been up all night, trying to picture what the rest of his life would be like if Jackson were dead or if Jackson were in prison. And, he's convinced the right outcome is a life sentence—not just to spare Jackson but to spare himself. He's a doctor in the business of saving lives and was quite frightened, I think, of the emotions that

Clarissa's death triggered in him. I don't think he could live with himself if another human being—even one as despicable as Jackson—were put to death, even in part to console him. Townsend, do you have anything you want to add?"

From appearances, I wouldn't have thought that Townsend was even listening, but he responded to the question. Sort of. "Clarissa's gone. She's not coming back."

I had heard of similar cases, even stories of the families of murder victims going to bat to save the defendant. But I couldn't begin to understand it. I wondered if they ever saw the videotape of that guy who killed all those nurses in Chicago. After his capital sentence was reversed by the Supreme Court, an investigative reporter caught him on camera in prison, taking drugs, talking up the joys of prison sex, and boasting to his fellow inmates about the ways his victims begged for mercy before he strangled them. The death penalty might not be a deterrent and might cost a hell of a lot more than a life sentence, but it meant that a victim's parents never had to go to sleep at night wondering what their kid's murderer was up to. Townsend was telling us to ignore the only factor that made me hedge on the death penalty—a survivor's need for what's lamely referred to as closure.

Duncan had launched into "the speech," the one every prosecutor gets used to giving, the one where we promise to take into account the person's feelings about the disposition of a case but explain that the ultimate decision needs to be on behalf of the entire citizenry. Roger cut him off.

"I've explained all that to Dr. Easterbrook already, Duncan."

Griffith gave me a look across the table at the use of his first name. No one ever said my ex-husband lacked balls.

"Townsend, why don't you wait for me in the lobby?" When the door was closed, Roger continued. "I've also explained to

Townsend that you shouldn't have a problem sticking with this as a noncapital case. You're in a liberal county where most people feel the same way he does about the death penalty. In fact, according to our research, your office seeks the death penalty in only a third of your agg murder cases. Let me be blunt here; I'm not real impressed with what I've seen so far in your office."

I shouldn't have changed seats. Talking me down to my boss was bad enough. But doing it in front of my coworkers was definitely shin-kick-deserving behavior.

"Until we essentially served Jackson to them on a platter, the police were content to sit back and assume this was a textbook case of 'the husband must have done it.' I'm sure you have fine lawyers if given the appropriate resources, but I also know what can happen when people are overworked. Maybe to save resources, you go for the death penalty hoping to plead it out to a life sentence. Given how this case started, I would hope you would defer to Dr. Easterbrook's wishes. If anyone has a right to dictate what happens to Melvin Jackson, he does. If I feel like you've continued to ignore him, I'll follow up again with the media."

When I was with him, I had actually been attracted to Roger's confidence. I understood now why everyone else had called it arrogance, and I felt responsible that he was unleashing it on my office. I couldn't stand another minute of it.

"Even for you, Roger, you are totally out of control."

The table went silent. Roger looked smug, Duncan looked embarrassed, every one else looked shocked, and I couldn't stop myself. "What kind of person can take Townsend Easterbrook's pain and parlay it into billable hours and a chance for a few minutes in front of the cameras? Stop thinking about yourself for one minute and you'd realize that the screwup you keep rubbing in our faces had as much to do with the owners of the office park—who happen to be your clients—as with the police."

"Samantha, you're embarrassing yourself," he said.

"No, she's not." It was Russ. "What's embarrassing is your attempt to bully this office. You assume that because we're prosecutors, we're a bunch of bloodthirsty rednecks. As for the bureau's delay homing in on Jackson, your client wasn't exactly forthcoming. The cops had to get their information from the workers on the site, and—funny—they seemed to be under the impression that it was union work."

Talking about the Glenville development project brought Mrs. Jackson's words back to me.

"Who is your client anyway, Roger?" I asked.

"I told you," he said. "Dr. Easterbrook came to us through OHSU."

He knew exactly what I was talking about. "Who's in charge of the construction in Glenville?"

"I wasn't aware that the DA's office had taken over the operations of the National Labor Relations Board. For what it's worth, the nonunion work on the site was permissible."

"So tell me who the client is. I want to know how they came to hire Melvin Jackson. From what I've heard of him, I'm not sure I'd want him to mow my backyard, let alone hire him on a major development project."

But Roger was done talking to me. He stood up and offered Duncan his hand. "Duncan, unless you have any more questions, we'll be on our way. Please let me know your decision once you've made it."

Then I got a glimpse of how Duncan Griffith had earned his political reputation. When he took Roger's hand, I could tell his grip was firm. "The decision was made before you interrupted me with the theatrics, son. We'll be asking for life without parole. You might want to consider knocking the last twelve minutes off Dr. Easterbrook's bill. Now, if it's all right with you, I'll walk you out so I can thank your client for coming in."

We were still rehashing the events of the meeting when Duncan returned. "Anyone got a problem with that?"

No problems. "Very good then," he said, knocking on the table as he walked out. "Oh, and by the way, Samantha, your ex-husband's a major asshole."

I don't think Duncan realized he was dropping a bombshell. I hightailed it out of the room while my coworkers were still begging for the tawdry details of my short-lived marriage.

A few minutes later, Russ came into my office.

"I hope you didn't mind me sticking up for you back there. I know you had everything under control, but, Jesus, what a prick."

"And they say chivalry is dead," I said.

"Yeah, well don't let the word out. I've got a reputation to protect."

"Don't worry. One act of semidecency won't make a dent," I said, smiling. "So I was surprised Duncan made a decision. You think it was because of the racial politics or to appease the husband?"

"Christ, Kincaid, you're almost as bad as your limousine-liberal ex. Duncan might have done it because he thought it was the right thing to do."

I suppose with politicians it's the decisions that count, not their reasons for making them.

"So how long were you guys married?" Russ asked.

I felt like I owed him at least the party line. "Not long. Things were all right for a few years in New York, but they fell apart when we moved to Portland." Then I surprised myself by not stopping in the usual place. "We seemed to have a disagreement over the appropriate use of his penis."

Russ almost spit out the coffee he had just sipped.

"Sorry," I said sheepishly. "A little too much information?"

"No, just a—well, it was a funny way of putting it. You're not one of those girls, are you?"

"I don't know what you're talking about, but I know I haven't been any kind of *girl* since I was seventeen years old."

"Excuse me, Gloria Steinem. You're not one of those crazy *women* who always goes after the bad boy, are you? First it's that guy, now it's Forbes. You know something none of the other women around here know, or do you just like to flirt with disaster?"

"I've known Chuck Forbes since I was fifteen years old, and he's nothing like Roger Kirkpatrick."

The silence was not just uncomfortable. It made me wonder what everyone in the office must be thinking. And saying.

"Sorry," he said, "it's none of my business. You ready for the prelim tomorrow?"

I was grateful for the change of subject. "Piece of cake," I said. "Was it just me, or did Roger seem reluctant to give us anything about the owner of the Glenville property?"

Russ shrugged his shoulders. "He's probably no different from the rest of those private-firm fucks. Acts like the big man, but when push comes to shove he's scared shitless of his clients. You don't need it, but if you're really curious, call one of the paralegals in the child-support enforcement unit. They're pros at running down property-owner records."

Maybe I would.

"If I don't see you, good luck tomorrow," he said. "Do you know who the judge is yet?"

"Prescott."

"Got news for you, Kincaid. You could be looking at a long day."

Kate Prescott is the slowest judge in the courthouse. A big fund-raiser for the Democratic Party, she came to the bench a year ago from a large corporate firm. She tries to make up for her lack of litigation experience by being thorough. I had a plea fall apart once in her courtroom when a transexual prostitute who'd been through the system a hundred times finally gave up on the process. In her words, "Honey, if I knew it was gonna take this long, I'd have asked for my trial. If I'm losing time on the street, it might as well be interesting."

If Prescott didn't move things along, Jackson's prelim could be painful.

"Page me if you need anything," Russ offered. "And, Kincaid, for what it's worth, any guy who'd even think of stepping out on you is clearly out of his mind."

Now *that* might ruin Russell Frist's tough-guy reputation.

Roger's show was not the only power play I'd have to contend with that day. As I was getting ready to leave, Duncan called. Before he got to the point, he had to dress me down for my outburst in the meeting.

"Don't get me wrong," he said, "it wasn't what you said that was the problem. He deserved every word of it. But when I'm in the room, you've got to trust that I'll handle it."

"Does this mean I'm fired?"

"I'll give you a Get Out of Jail Free card for that particular outburst. Your reward for being married to the jerk. But, seriously, over time I hope you'll stop trying to carry the load all on your own."

"I'm independent, sir."

"Tell me about it. So don't freak out that I'm calling to give you a heads-up. T. J. Caffrey just called. He's rabid. Seems your defense attorney has subpoenaed him to the prelim."

I couldn't say I was surprised. Slip knew he stood little chance of getting the case kicked at a prelim. He was trying to give us a preview of the mess he'd create for us at trial. Fortunately, Duncan's own trial experience wasn't too far in the past for him to recognize it was inevitable too.

"I told him there was nothing I could do," he said, "but his attorney wants a courtesy sit-down with you tomorrow morning. I told him you'd oblige."

It gave me something to look forward to.

9

GRACE HAD LEFT a voice mail while I was in Duncan's office. "Hey, Sammikins. Want to grab some dinner tonight? And before you say you're busy, I'm just warning you; you're turning into one of those women who dump their girlfriends when they're getting laid. I'm thinking cocktails and truffle fries."

That could only mean one place: 750 ml, a cool but cozy Pearl District wine bar. Even though we were the only déclassé martini drinkers in the joint, the main attraction was the french fries tossed in white truffle oil.

Grace likes her drinks the color of Maybelline nail polish, and this week's preference was a ginger-infused something or another. Beach vacations aside, I usually stick with the standards, switching periodically between my favorite gin and my favorite vodka. Tonight, Bombay Sapphire beat out Grey Goose.

I tried to fight Grace when she told the bartender to jazz it up for me, but Grace just couldn't help herself. When a guy's that gorgeous, she'll find any excuse to talk to him.

He turned away to muck up a perfectly good olive by stuffing it with bleu cheese, and Grace's eyes were anywhere but on me. "Ahem, my dear, but I do believe you accused me today of ignoring my girlfriend in favor of the boy du jour."

"Well, in your case, that'd be the boy du decade."

It dawned on me that her jab was accurate. *Literally.* Truly pathetic.

"Now does this mean we're going to have an evening without the boy talk?" she asked.

"Unless you've got something."

She eyed the bartender again. "Not yet," she said, smiling and taking another sip of her pink drink. In truth, Grace has a fairly routine dating life, but she enjoys hamming up the sex goddess persona. "So why didn't I hear from you last night? Another evening with Chuck?"

"I'm afraid so. We're moving toward boring domesticity remarkably quickly."

I thought about mentioning the weirdness with my father, but talking about it would only upset me more. The truth was, I knew I'd been keeping myself busy to avoid calling him. Part of me was afraid he might actually tell me whatever he was holding back. From the look on his face the other night, it seemed pretty disturbing.

Instead, I talked about work, confessing my guilt over the accusatory tone I'd used the previous day with Susan Kerr.

"Susan Kerr with sort of wild brown hair? A little older than us?"

"Wild to you, maybe, but take a look at who you're talking to. Actually, she had it pulled back when I saw her."

"That's because her hair's completely uncontrollable. She's a client."

"What do you think of her?"

"She's awesome—my kind of chick. Did you really accuse

her of sleeping with her dead friend's husband? I don't even want to *think* about how she handled that."

"No, luckily I kept that suspicion to myself and found out the visit was perfectly innocuous. But I did ask whether she thought it was possible *Clarissa* was having an affair."

"I suspect even that was enough to set her off."

"It was."

Grace shrugged her shoulders. "She always speaks her mind. She started coming in probably a year before her husband died, right around the time I opened. When word started to leak he was losing it, she was ferociously protective. I remember her telling me about this one woman who was the source of most of the gossip. Susan found out the cow had a nasty little coke habit, cornered her in the gym, and threatened to out her unless she started singing another tune."

"I didn't realize the two of you were so close."

"We're not," she said with a laugh. "But that's what Susan's like—an open book. Hell, she seemed proud of it, and why shouldn't she be? She was sticking up for her husband. The sad part is, I heard later that the husband got wind of what she'd done and had the nerve to take her to task for it. Rumor is, Susan got so pissed at the ungrateful fuck she flung his humidor of Cubans into the fireplace."

"I guess I'll try not to make her mad," I said. "She's worried that the trial's going to turn into an attack on Clarissa's character."

"And, of course, there's no chance of that, right?" Grace asked facetiously.

"Let's just say between Susan Kerr and you the other day at Greek Cusina, I've gotten the message."

She touched my forearm and smiled. "I'm just giving you a hard time, sweetie. I know you do what you can. What else has been going on? Oh my God, I almost forgot to ask—any run-ins with Shoe Boy?"

I gave her a blow-by-blow of Roger's visit to the office.

"You had quite the busy day today, didn't you? Have another martini."

A second wouldn't kill me. "He's screwing up my judgment. I feel total confidence in my case against Jackson. Then he pisses me off, and I find myself wanting to complicate things, just so we're not on the same side."

"Sorry, hon, but it doesn't sound like there's much to complicate. I believe this one's what your buddies call a slam dunk."

I told her what Mrs. Jackson said about her son's sudden employment at a well-funded suburban construction site.

Grace shook her head. "That's probably not unusual. Development out there has gotten so out of control it's attracting some pretty low-rent people. I wouldn't be surprised if some little outfit got in over its head and tried to trim the budget by hiring the cheapest labor it could find."

"Well, I'll tell you what complicates things. One of Griffith's political cronies has been subpoenaed by the defense and is going to raise a stink tomorrow."

"Holy shit, Samantha. If this case gets any hotter, you're going to wind up on *Court TV*."

"No, Grace, you can't give me a new haircut." She was disappointed that I'd seen right through her. It takes more than a martini or two before I let her get too creative.

"So who's the crony?"

"I really can't say, Grace."

"Oh, yes, you will. You can't tell me a little, then not disclose. Against the rules."

It was pretty sensitive information, but, hell, this was Grace. We told each other everything. I even told her about my most embarrassing trial story, the time I reached into my suit jacket for my Sharpie pen and pulled out a Tampax instead. She never told a soul.

I leaned in so close to her ear that I almost fell off my bar stool. She was shocked.

"Oh ... my ... God. And he's supposed to be such a do-gooder."

"Maybe they're all pigs."

"Don't be bitter," she said, throwing her maraschino cherry stem at me. Chewing on another french fry, she said, "Now if you're looking for coincidences, he'd be what you're looking for."

"Maybe I should have passed up that second drink, because I'm not following."

"You know. The thing with the Metro Council."

I didn't know.

"A second ago, you said it was a coincidence that a fringy guy like Jackson was working on the Glenville site. But the real coincidence is that your defendant dumped the victim on a property that's smack dab in the middle of a Metro controversy."

"What's that office park got to do with Metro?"

"I told you all about this at Greek Cusina. Remember? The second Lockworks I was going to open? Not to be rude, Sam, but sometimes I could swear that you can't chew and listen at the same time. And given the way we eat, that could be a major problem."

"Hey! I was listening. You weren't sure if the growth was going to continue, but prices were already high, so you backed off."

"Right," she said, "and the reason prices are so high is that everyone thinks Metro's going to expand the urban growth boundary right in that area. Hell, if Metro *doesn't* expand the boundary, I wouldn't be surprised if prices actually fell out there."

"You didn't say anything about Metro before. They're not really going to change the urban growth boundary, are they?" I asked.

"Do you pay any attention whatsoever to the local news?" she asked. I'd gotten spoiled during the few years that my local paper was *The New York Times,* so I haven't given it up. In theory, I'm extremely well informed because I subscribe to it as well as the *Oregonian.* Grace, however, knew my habit of getting absorbed in the *Times* crossword puzzle before ever hitting the local paper's metro page.

"Of course I do," I said. "I know I was featured prominently in several stories about a month ago. And Monday I watched Gloria Flick's report on the Easterbrook case, not to mention Shoe Boy's press conference."

"Man, Gloria Flick's annoying."

"Damn straight. It's the price I pay for being so impressively well informed."

"So you *must* know that Metro is talking about expanding the urban growth boundary."

Anywhere else in the country, that statement would sound a little like *You must know that Spock's Starfleet service number was S179–276.* But to people who live in my city, the urban growth boundary is the secret ingredient in Portland's warm gooey cinnamon bun. The city's strong neighborhood feel is what makes this place special, and those neighborhoods would be gone by now if not for Metro.

I had read about proposals to expand the boundary by more than two thousand acres but assumed it would never happen. Grace informed me otherwise.

"The assumption is that it *will* happen. The population has exploded. It will be a close vote, but everyone thinks the time is ripe for expansion, and the place where it's most likely to happen is in Glenville. The land outside the boundary there is nothing special, so the theory is that Metro can hand it over to developers without pissing off the greens too much. Unfortunately, the rest of the market shares that same theory. For the last couple of years, buyers have been gobbling up land in the area on the gamble that the growth's going to spread. And from what you told me about your office park, it's right at the line. I wouldn't be surprised if the same owner bought the adjacent rural land."

"So if the line moves," I said, "the owner cleans up. And T. J. Caffrey's one of eleven votes."

"Not only that, he's one of the swing votes. He's good on the environment, but he's pro-business. In exchange for his vote, he can probably set the terms about where the line gets moved."

That was definitely a coincidence. I was suddenly looking forward to my morning meeting—pardon me, my "courtesy sit-down."

I called it a relatively early night so I could get some work done at home and rescue Vinnie from boredom.

The only message on the machine was from Chuck. "If it's not too late when you get back, give me a call if you want me to come over. Otherwise, have a good night, and I'll talk to you tomorrow."

Apparently, Grace wasn't the only one resenting the time I'd been devoting to Chuck. Vinnie seemed pleased when I stayed put and continued scratching him ferociously behind his goofy bat ears. When he finally started in with his familiar snorting sounds, I knew I was back in his good graces. I'd been so neglectful lately that I let him stay on my lap with his Gumby while I prepped the Jackson prelim. If only my father were so easy to assuage.

Maybe it was the second martini, but my thoughts kept wandering to one of the seemingly inconsequential questions I would ask Ray Johnson as background. "Where was Clarissa Easterbrook's body located?"

I fished my office phone directory out of my briefcase and

left a message for Jenna Markson, a paralegal in the child support enforcement unit who was known for her dedication and investigative skills. Maybe she could satisfy my curiosity.

Seven thirty A.M. was the time Duncan had promised, so there I stood on Friday morning in the office's front lobby, waiting for T. J. Caffrey and his lawyer. They finally arrived twenty minutes late, wholly unapologetic for the delay.

I recognized Caffrey from the local paper, but I'd never seen him in person. Probably around fifty, he was known for his casual garb, but today he'd chosen a suit and tie that looked good with his salt-and-pepper hair. He was a bit of a chubster, but I could see the attraction.

The man running the show, though, was Ronald Fish. A high-priced, high-power trial attorney, Fish was the guy CEOs called in a pinch, whether it was for corporate mismanagement or a sixteen-year-old girl in the backseat. He didn't even bother introducing himself. He was big enough in the civil litigation world that he assumed every lawyer in the city already knew who he was—and maybe he was right.

I checked my posture while I led them into the conference room. In my sling backs, I edged out the notoriously napoleonic powerbroker by a full inch. He straightened his trademark bow tie. I chose to interpret the nervous gesture as a very small leveling of the playing field.

Make that a very, very small leveling. Fish was ready to go the second I shut the door.

"I won't take up your time, Ms. Kincaid, because I know you've got a court appearance to prepare for. I was hoping I could convince you to support Mr. Caffrey's motion to quash the subpoena. Duncan sounded amenable to it when I spoke with him yesterday."

I noticed that the spineless Mr. Caffrey had no problem letting his attorney handle the talking.

"I believe what Duncan was amenable to was a meeting this morning at seven thirty," I said, glancing at my watch, "as a courtesy to your client. As you know, the decision whether to grant your motion is entirely in the trial court's discretion."

I had spent the early morning researching the issue. There was no clear correct legal answer to Caffrey's motion. Most important from my perspective, there was no risk the court's ruling on the motion could lead to a reversal of Jackson's conviction down the road.

"It seems patently obvious to me, Ms. Kincaid, that it would be in the government's interest to prevent this Mr. Sillipcow—"

"Szlipkowski," I corrected.

"Yes, this public defender, from deflecting the court's attention from the very strong evidence against the defendant."

"That's one way to look at it, but I plan on staying out of it."

"I'm not certain how else one could possibly look at it."

"Well," I began, "one might look at the defense's subpoena as an opportunity to make certain the state's not missing something we should know about prior to trial. If, for example, your client was having an affair with the victim—and I'm not saying that he was—then one might believe it better to get that news out in court during the prelim, rather than having a desperate defense attorney leak it to the media in the middle of trial."

I watched Caffrey glance at his attorney. Clearly he could tell this sit-down was going nowhere.

"Or perhaps," I continued, "one might see this as an opportunity to make certain, outside of the presence of the jury, that the state isn't missing some off-the-wall defense theory that might take off at trial. Something like a connection between the victim being found in Glenville and Mr. Caffrey's power to shape the future of suburban development out there. I don't know, something like that. But, again, maybe it's better heard now rather than later."

I didn't take my eyes off Caffrey's face. Nothing.

I had no idea what his wooden affect said about his knowledge of the case or any possible connection between Clarissa and development in Glenville. But I knew one thing: I'd never vote for T. J. Caffrey, whatever his politics. There was no doubt in my mind that this man had some kind of relationship with Clarissa. I had spent the week watching Tara, Townsend, and Susan struggle with their profound grief. But here sat Caffrey observing this discussion like a Wimbledon match.

I excused myself to prepare for court and walked them to the exit.

News crews from all four local stations were waiting in front of the Justice Center. Fortunately, they weren't allowed in the courtrooms, so they only polluted what the attorneys said before and after the main event.

Slip and Roger were giving competing statements. Slip was accusing the police and prosecutors (I guess that would be me) of rushing to judgment to comfort a nervous public that was demanding a quick arrest. Roger, on the other hand, was grateful that the police had finally gotten around to catching the right man.

When the cameras rushed over to me, I gave them the standard prosecutorial line. We're confident about the evidence, wouldn't be going forward if we weren't, blah blah blah. Because of the ethical rules that govern the public statements of prosecutors, we never get to say the good stuff.

Once we were in JC-3 before Judge Prescott, it was a whole other story. In a prelim, the prosecutor runs the show, since the only relevant question is whether the state's evidence, if believed in its entirety by a jury, could support a conviction. Slip most likely would try to get some free discovery by squeezing in as much cross-examination as Prescott would tolerate, but he'd know there was little to gain by grandstanding this early in the process. Roger was completely irrelevant, sitting next to Townsend with the other observers. I couldn't help but wonder how much he was charging.

I wheeled my chair toward Slip. "You subpoenaed Caffrey, huh? I assume you know that he'll move to quash."

"His lawyer wants to wait until I actually call Caffrey to the stand. He's probably making sure it's not a bluff. I told him I'd call him when you were done presenting your evidence, so they wouldn't have to wait."

"Hate to break it to you, Slip, but I doubt your courtesy's going to be enough to win Ronald Fish over."

"I'm a good guy. What can I say?"

Prescott took the bench and called the case. Every other judge in the county lets the prosecutor call the case, and we do it in about five seconds flat, the words so routine that the court reporter has no problems keeping up with the pace. But Prescott treated even this routine function like a constitutional moment.

When she was finally done, it was my turn for a quick opening statement.

"Thank you, your honor. Deputy District Attorney Samantha Kincaid for the state. As your honor is well aware, the only question here is whether the state has sufficient evidence to hold the defendant over for trial on the pending Aggravated Murder charge. The ultimate decision regarding the defendant's guilt must be made by the jury at trial, and the jury is entitled to make its own determinations about credibility. Accordingly, the standard for today's hearing requires the court to credit as true all testimony that benefits the state, and to discredit any contradictory evidence from the defense, even if that would not be your own assessment of the evidence were you to sit in this case as a juror."

I went ahead and cited the controlling cases for good measure. I would never spell out the governing law as thoroughly for a more experienced judge, but Prescott was still learning the basics of criminal law. The last thing I needed was for her to substitute her own opinion for the jury's because I forgot to cover Criminal Procedure 101.

I gave a brief outline of the critical evidence and then called Ray Johnson to the stand.

Ray looked dapper, as usual, in a lavender dress shirt and black three-button suit. Half that man's salary must go to the Saks men's department. He had removed the diamond stud from his ear for his testimony. Good call, given Prescott's transition from a corporate culture.

We covered the evidence quickly despite our judicial assignment. I wasn't asking any questions that were objectionable, so there was no reason for Prescott to get involved.

In straightforward question and answer format, Johnson and I covered the critical points: Jackson's pending case, the letters he'd written to Clarissa, the paint on Griffey and in Jackson's van, his employment at the site where the body had been located, his statements, and the weapon. My criminologist would cover the fingerprint and blood evidence. It was more than enough.

I had decided to keep it simple. Since we weren't alleging a sexual assault as part of the charges, getting into the nonoxynol-9 and the ME's opinion that Clarissa had been undressed when she was killed would only muck it up. If Slip chose to get into those complications, he ran the risk of making his client look like a rapist and not just a murderer. Down the road, I'd have to worry about a jury thinking that Clarissa's nudity was inconsistent with Jackson's motivation of revenge. But even a judge as inexperienced as Prescott knew that rape was about exercising power over the victim, not sex.

I wasn't surprised when Slip chose to cross. One of the only benefits to the defense of a prelim is the chance to test the state's case and its witnesses in advance of trial. Here, Slip could risk asking Johnson questions that might backfire if asked for the first time at trial in front of the jury. Some judges would cut off a prelim fishing expedition at the start, but I knew Prescott would give Slip some line.

"Good afternoon, Detective Johnson. My name is Graham Szlipkowsky, and I represent Mr. Jackson."

It sounded funny to hear Slip pronounce his full name. It had been a couple of years since we'd had a formal hearing together.

"You arrested my client late on Tuesday night, is that right?"

"That's correct. Technically, it was Wednesday morning."

"When you woke up on Tuesday morning, did you believe that my client killed Clarissa Easterbrook?"

"I believed it was a possibility, yes."

Johnson was wasting his witness skills. He's a master of spin, which helps in front of a jury. In a bench hearing, it was better to cut through the crap.

"But you didn't believe you had probable cause, did you? Or surely you would have arrested him."

No doubt about it. Slip was good.

"Prior to Tuesday evening, we had not yet made a determination of probable cause, against Mr. Jackson or anyone else."

"You said you thought it was possible on Tuesday morning that Mr. Jackson killed Clarissa Easterbrook. Who else would you say that about?"

"Any number of people," Johnson said. "We had not yet

identified a suspect, so at that point anyone was a possible suspect."

"How about the president of the United States. Was he a suspect?"

"Not a likely one," Johnson said. He threw me a look to let me know he thought I should have objected, but he was going to have to sit through it. Judges are insulted by objections during a bench hearing. If the question's absurd, they believe they should be trusted to disregard it on their own. Slip's rhetorical question definitely fell within that camp.

"What about the victim's husband, Townsend Easterbrook? Isn't it true that he was still a possible suspect?"

"I wouldn't call him a suspect."

Johnson was falling into the pattern that a lot of cops get into on the stand. They're so suspicious of defense attorneys that they fight every point, even those that aren't damaging.

"But it's true, isn't it, that you were looking at him as a possibility?" Slip asked.

"We were interested in him, as we are always interested in anyone close to a murder victim. But, in this case, we were interested in excluding Dr. Easterbrook beyond any doubt, so we could focus the investigation on more likely subjects. Once he took the poly—"

I wasn't surprised when Slip cut him off with the objection. Johnson knew better than that. Polygraph results are inadmissible, whether it's at trial or in a preliminary hearing. It was an easy call, even for Prescott. "Sustained. Do that in front of a jury, Detective Johnson, and it's a mistrial. Mr. Szlipkowsky, you can be assured that I will disregard the witness's mention of any polygraph examination that may have taken place."

"OK," Slip said, getting back on track. "So the husband was

someone you were 'interested in,' in your words. What about Terrence Caffrey? Were you looking at him?"

"I was in the process of trying to contact Mr. Caffrey when the evidence started to snowball against your client."

Johnson was giving Slip a preview of what he could expect at trial if he pushed too hard on the stand. A defense attorney's worst nightmare is a cop who can turn any question into an opportunity to prejudice the defendant.

"Your honor, please instruct witness to answer the questions presented to him without editorializing."

Prescott flipped through the large binder she keeps with her on the bench, then told Johnson, "Please refrain from providing nonresponsive information."

See, that thing about the truth, the whole truth, and nothing but the truth isn't quite right. Witnesses are only allowed to provide the truth when it's been specifically requested.

"Isn't it true that you were trying to contact Mr. Caffrey to determine if he was involved in Ms. Easterbrook's murder?"

"No, I wouldn't put it like that."

"Since semantics seem so important to you this morning, Detective Johnson, why don't you tell us why you were trying to talk to Mr. Caffrey?"

"To determine whether he had relevant information."

"Isn't it true that you found Mr. Caffrey's name in Ms. Easterbrook's phone records?"

"No, that is not true."

"Excuse me. Isn't it true that you located a telephone number in Ms. Easterbrook's phone records that you subsequently determined to be associated with Mr. Caffrey?"

"That's correct," Johnson conceded. He was having a little too much fun. I'd need to talk to him about playing lawyer on the stand.

"And isn't it true that those records showed multiple calls between Mr. Caffrey's telephone number and Ms. Easterbrook's cellular phone?"

"Yes."

"And isn't it also true that you have evidence that Ms. Easterbrook had sexual relations with someone other than her husband?"

"If one considers rape sexual relations, then one could draw that inference, yes."

"I'm sorry, Detective Johnson, are you saying that you are certain beyond doubt that Ms. Easterbrook was raped?"

"No, but that is one possibility, and I was uncomfortable describing that possibility as one involving what you called sexual relations."

"Let's talk a little bit about what that evidence is," Slip said. "In the autopsy of Ms. Easterbrook, the medical examiner found an antispermicide gel within her vaginal canal. Correct?"

"That's correct."

"A gel that's often associated with condoms?"

"Yes."

"And, according to Ms. Easterbrook's husband, the two of them did not use condoms or any such gel in the course of their own marital relations, is that right?"

The question clearly called for hearsay. Under the rules, if Slip wanted to introduce something Townsend said as true, he had to get it from Townsend. But I'd been hoping to spare him from testifying. I let it slide without objection, and Johnson conceded the point.

"Is it fair to say, Detective Johnson, that you at least wondered whether Ms. Easterbrook and Mr. Caffrey were engaged in an extramarital affair?"

"I considered it a possibility."

"In light of what was at least the possible connection between Mr. Caffrey and the victim, did you ever question him to determine whether he had relevant evidence?"

"No, I did not," Johnson said.

"Did you try to?" Slip asked.

"Yes."

"How so?"

"I left a message on Tuesday afternoon with his scheduling assistant."

I hadn't realized that Johnson had gotten around to making that call. He must have seen to it right after the MCT meeting, before he learned that Jackson worked in Glenville.

"Did you tell the assistant that you were calling about Ms. Easterbrook?" Slip asked.

"No, I did not."

"Did you tell the assistant anything about the nature of the call?"

"I believe I told him that I was calling about a pending criminal investigation."

"A murder investigation?"

"No, I would not have said that. Just a criminal investigation."

"Is that a fairly standard message that you leave when you're trying to reach a potential witness?"

"Yes."

"And is there a reason why you say the call relates to a pending criminal investigation, rather than just leave your name and number?"

"Sure. Lets them know I'm not just fund-raising for the PBA. Makes it more likely I get a prompt callback."

"And, in this case, did you get your prompt callback?"

"I have not spoken with Mr. Caffrey."

So the respectable T. J. Caffrey was a total slime. What does it say about a man's character when he'd hide from his lover's murder investigation just to cover his own ass? It did not, however, make him a murderer.

"So if I understand you correctly," Slip said, "a man who may have been having a special relationship with the victim on a murder case did not call you back, even though he knew you were trying to contact him about a pending criminal investigation. Is that right?"

"That's correct. But I have no way of knowing he got the message."

"Maybe we'll find that out later," Slip said. "After Mr. Caffrey failed to get in touch with you after you left this message with his assistant, did you continue your efforts to reach him?"

"No, I did not."

"To be clear," Slip said, "Terrence Caffrey is a member of the elected Metro Council, correct?"

"That's correct."

"Did that have anything to do with your decision not to continue your efforts to contact him about this case?"

"No, it did not."

Slip looked and sounded incredulous. "If it wasn't because of this man's power and political influence, why then did you not want to speak with him, given what is at least the appearance of a close and unexplained relationship between him and the victim?"

A tip to defense attorneys: Don't ever ask a cop a question that begins with *why*. It's an invitation for a subjective opinion and a quick way to sink your client. Johnson batted it out of the park. "I stopped trying to reach Caffrey when it became clear to me that your client murdered Clarissa Easterbrook. To question him at that point about the nature of his association with her would have been exploitative, more like daytime television than a legitimate investigation. Or maybe a defense attorney."

Slip was on his feet immediately, but even Prescott knew that Johnson's answer was, just as Slip had requested, responsive.

My next witness was Heidi Chung from the crime lab. Heidi must be pushing forty but could be mistaken for a teenager. In trial, I always spend some time on her impressive credentials to be certain that the jurors understand that she's a pro. Prescott, however, had seen Chung enough to know she knew her stuff.

By the time Heidi was done, there could be no doubt about it. The hammer Johnson pulled from Jackson's closet had been the one that killed Clarissa, and two of the unidentified latent prints pulled from the Easterbrooks' door knocker had been left by Jackson's right index and middle fingers.

Slip couldn't do much to Heidi on cross. Sure, there were no prints on the hammer, but wiping down a weapon is easy and a lot more obvious than remembering to clean the door knocker.

When he was done, I rested. Given my low standard of proof, there was no point giving him a look at my entire case in chief and a chance to test all my witnesses for weak spots. And, thankfully, there was no need to call Townsend to the stand. I'd managed to cover all the important stuff with my two pros.

Even though he had told me about his intentions all along, part of me was still surprised when Slip told Prescott he'd be calling witnesses before we moved to arguments. I half thought he was bluffing, since he had absolutely nothing to gain from the move. The judge was essentially required to disregard any testimony that helped the defense, since at trial it was possible that the jurors would not find it credible.

Maybe Slip was using the prelim as a formal version of the usual posturing that goes on between the prosecution and the defense: trying to make his case look good in the hope of getting me to give Jackson a plea. Or maybe he hoped Prescott was inexperienced enough to make the call herself.

"Call your first witness, Mr. Szlipkowsky."

"There's one complication, your honor. One of my witnesses is moving to quash the subpoena I served on him yesterday. If I may make a suggestion, perhaps I could call just one witness now, and we could take up the motion to quash after a lunch recess."

"That would be fine. Please proceed." That simple plan would have taken Prescott fifteen minutes to conjure on her own.

"The defense calls Nelly Giacoma."

Unlike Ray, Nelly hadn't toned down the fashion statements for the courtroom. I watched Judge Prescott eye her from head to toe, pausing extra long for the ankle tattoo. I couldn't wait until Prescott learned that this funky chick with a nose ring and hot-pink pixie cut was a law school graduate. And I couldn't wait to hear what Nelly could possibly offer to the case.

Slip's initial questions established Nelly's working relationship with Clarissa and her job responsibilities. Bo-ring.

Then he pulled out a document, a move that never fails to get my attention.

"Do you recognize this document, Ms. Giacoma?"

"Yes. It's a letter to Judge Easterbrook that I received at the office on Wednesday."

Slip gave me a copy and had the original marked as evidence. I recognized the scrawl from the other letters he'd written. This one was comparatively brief:

> Dear Judge,
>   What does it take to get your attension? I am making good money and have proof to show you. I will do ALL I can do to save my family. PLEASE understand that.

"The letter is signed *Melvin Jackson,* is that correct?" Slip asked.

"Yes."

"And it relates to a pending case about his eviction from public housing."

"It's a *threat* relating to his pending case, yes."

Nelly was growing on me. I have an affinity for women who talk back. The letter was indeed a threat, very much like the ones Jackson had been sending for weeks.

"And is this the envelope that the letter arrived in?" Slip asked.

I restrained myself from objecting to the dangling preposition and waited while Slip marked the envelope as evidence.

"Yes."

"Could you please identify the date on the envelope's postmark?"

Nelly did. The date was the previous Monday, the morning after Clarissa died.

The panic was momentary. After a few seconds, Slip's cheap trick was apparent. I used my cross to make sure the judge saw it too.

"Hi, Nelly. Samantha Kincaid. We met earlier this week."

"I remember."

"You've used the mail before, right?"

"Of course."

"And in your experience, are post offices open on Saturday nights and Sundays?"

"No, they're not."

"So a letter mailed on Saturday evening would be post-marked—"

"On Monday."

A lunch hour from a court hearing isn't much of a break. In an office where we're each entirely on our own, each precious minute of recess must be spent on the research and follow-up that supporting attorneys would do in a large law firm. Every time I go to trial, I lose a few pounds from the combination of adrenaline and starvation.

I stopped at the mini-mart on my way into the courthouse and grabbed a Diet Coke, yogurt, and banana. I wolfed down the food in the elevator and sneaked the Diet Coke into the law library. I spent half an hour in the stacks, confirming the research I had done on Caffrey's motion to quash. This would be a fight between Caffrey and Slip. If Prescott asked for my opinion, I'd cite the cases I found, making it clear that it was entirely in her discretion.

Before I left again for the Justice Center, I ran up to my office to check messages.

The first was from Susan Kerr. "Hi, Samantha. Susan Kerr. I'm sorry to bother you again. I know you're busy, but I didn't know who else to talk to. Can you call me if you have a chance? Thanks." I hit the nine button to save the message, then went to the next one. It was from Jenna Markson, the child-support paralegal I had called last night.

"Hi, Samantha. It's Jenna. I had a chance to run that property you asked about when I was doing some other record searches. The owner's a corporation called Gunderson Development, Incorporated. I checked with the corporate registry division of the Secretary of State, and the registered officer is a guy named Larry Gunderson."

I scribbled his name and the name of his company on a Post-it note while I listened to the rest of Jenna's message.

"I went ahead and ran his financials. It looks like he was a bit of a wheeler-dealer until he went Chapter Eleven about ten years ago. My guess is that Gunderson Development is little more than Mr. Gunderson himself. Let me know if you need anything else. Oh, and Samantha, don't tell anyone else I ran the financials. We only have access to that database for child-support investigations."

Now I understood why the attorneys all rave about Jenna. She'd probably been running defendants for everyone in the office, telling each of them it was an exception.

I looked at my watch. I only had three minutes to get my butt out of the courthouse, across the street, and into the Justice Center, but Grace's comments about the Glenville property last night were still bothering me.

I hit six to respond to Jenna's message. At the beep, I said, "Hey, Jenna. Samantha Kincaid in Major Crimes. Thanks for the information on Gunderson. Could you do me one more favor? Can you see who owns the adjacent parcels? Sorry for the extra work, but I forgot to bring it up earlier."

I hit the pound key twice to send the message, hung up, and grabbed what I needed for court, making a vow to myself as I ran out the door. If Gunderson didn't own the rural property beyond the urban growth boundary, I'd let it drop.

10

WORD MUST HAVE spread about T. J. Caffrey, because the TV crews were back. Asked to comment on the anticipated motion to quash, I said I was not going to address matters that had not yet been brought to court. It sounded more civilized than, "You mean that coward's motion to squirm out of testifying? No comment."

Back in the courtroom, I noticed that Roger had returned without his client. Under the circumstances, I couldn't blame Townsend for wanting to avoid sitting in the same room with Caffrey.

When the motion was argued, I stayed out of it as planned, but I found myself rooting for Slip. As much as I hated the idea of letting the defense use Caffrey as a distraction, I deplored even more the idea of Caffrey invoking the legal process to protect his ass politically. Fish's polka-dotted bow tie wasn't helping matters.

I watched Caffrey occasionally catch himself chewing his lower lip while his attorney argued the motion. When Fish had finished his presentation, he summarized his principal point. "Your honor, Mr. Szlipkowski's subpoena would add nothing to this case other than an opportunity to question a high-profile public figure under oath about private matters, a spectacle that should be permitted only if there is a clear showing of the need for the information. Mr. Szlipkowski has made no showing at all, let alone a clear one. Put simply, even if he were to establish what he alleges—a contention that we are not conceding—it would have no bearing whatsoever on the question of Mr. Jackson's guilt."

Put simply, Fish was insinuating that the subpoena was setting up a political perjury trap. He couldn't have spun it any better, especially for a big party Democrat like Prescott. There wasn't a soul among the party faithful who wasn't wary about demanding answers about sex under oath.

Slip did his best, but in the end, it was all a big so-what? So what if Clarissa and Caffrey talked? So what if they were even boffing each other? There was no other reason to believe that Caffrey knew anything about Clarissa's murder.

Except, of course, that nagging coincidence that she was found and Jackson worked at a property whose value would be determined by T. J. Caffrey's vote.

Prescott being Prescott, she had to take a break in chambers before issuing her ruling. When she finally retook the bench, it was clear that Fish's spin had taken. She quashed the subpoena, thanked Caffrey for being present in the event she had decided otherwise, and told him he was free to leave.

Hopefully, the news crews would be waiting for him outside, yelling the questions on the street that he'd bullied his way out of in the courtroom.

Slip had played his last card. He did his best to gnaw away at the medical examiner's report, arguing that the state should be barred from proceeding until they reconciled their theory of the case with the fact that Clarissa had been dressed *after* she was killed. But, in the end, we all knew that wasn't the law. He'd have to do that kind of gnawing in front of the jury.

"Does the defense have any more witnesses?" Prescott asked.

"Not for this afternoon, your honor," Slip replied, "but we had assumed that the hearing would continue until Monday. I would like to have the weekend to reconsider. As your honor knows, the parties were given only a day to prepare by Judge Levinson."

Any other judge in the courthouse would have ripped Slip a new one for assuming anything about the length of the hearing. To judges who have forgotten what it's like to practice, the lack of time to prepare is never an excuse for a lack of preparation.

Prescott, however, had no problem with it. "I was planning on taking the weekend to consider my decision, so here's what we'll do: Reconvene here Monday morning at nine. If either party wishes to submit additional evidence, the record remains open. Otherwise, I will announce my decision then. And, in the event that it makes a difference to the lawyers, I have formed a tentative opinion based on what I've heard today."

She was sending a message to Slip. He was going down in flames, but she was going to give him a reprieve before pulling the trigger.

Slip caught up with me on the staircase. "What'd you think about Caffrey?"

"He's a skunk, Slip, but he's not your murderer. For your sake, you might want to reconsider your Plan B before trial."

"Maybe Plan B is for the two of us to sit down and talk. Got time for a drink after work?"

"Sure. Right at five?" I'd been up late enough the night before working on the prelim. I wasn't about to spend my entire Friday night talking about the case.

"Meet you at Higgin's. You still drinking martinis straight up?"

"Damn straight."

"You're my kind of woman, Kincaid."

"Let's see what you've got to say after we have our little chat."

Whatever Slip's plan had been for the prelim, it had clearly failed. Prescott may have thrown him a line, but we both knew he was in no position to grab it. I was sure the meeting at Higgin's would be a fish for a plea.

I had three new voice mails back at the office. The first was from Jenna Markson. "It's Jenna again about your question on the property adjacent to your crime scene. You were right. Gunderson Development owns another hundred and twenty acres west of the property he's building on. Gunderson purchased all the land at once as four separate parcels. You probably already know this, but the other parcels are mandatory rural. That's probably why he's not building on them."

At least, not until they were redesignated as ripe for development.

"I'm sending my printouts about this to you interoffice mail," she said. "Let me know if you need anything else."

The next message was from Nelly. "This is Nelly Giacoma. Judge Easterbrook's clerk? I testified today in the hearing you had on Jackson?"

I've noticed that the people I remember assume I don't know them, while the people I've forgotten think we're best pals.

"I overheard something after the hearing and think I should talk to you about it. I'm at City Hall right now, but I'm leaving in a few minutes." She had left her home telephone number and asked me to call over the weekend. I noted the time of her message, only fifteen minutes ago. Maybe I could still catch her.

The third call was from Russell Frist. "I just got done with my grand jury. Looks like you're still out, so I'm assuming you're still in your prelim. Jesus, with Prescott running the show, she might hold you over until Monday. Anyway, I was calling to see if you were up to having a drink after work. Let me know how it went."

As much as I was warming to my new boss, fifty-plus hours a week at the courthouse is enough time for me to talk with my coworkers. I'd update him on the case, but we'd do it on the clock.

First, I was calling Nelly. The voice that answered sounded flustered. "Oh, I'm glad you caught me. I was just about to leave, and I was worried you'd call while I was out running around."

"Well, it sounded important."

"I don't know whether it is or not, but I really can't talk about it here. Can you meet me somewhere?"

I looked at my watch. If I was going to make my meeting with Slip, it was going to have to be quick. "Can you leave right now? The SBC behind the courthouse?"

Seattle's Best Coffee isn't my usual choice, but it was only steps away.

"Meet on the other side of the elevators in the building lobby," she said. "It's less likely someone will see us there."

I dialed the general number for MCT. Nelly might want to sneak around like the Spy Kids, but I'd need a witness for whatever was about to go down. It was probably nothing, but attorneys can't testify in their own cases. With my luck, Nelly would show up and confess.

"Forbes."

"Chuck, it's Samantha. Is Ray around?"

"That's all I get? I never heard from you last night."

"Sorry. When I got back from dinner, I still had a bunch of work to do. And right now I really need to talk to Ray. Is he around?"

"Nope. Might've left already." Their usual shift, which they rarely could stick to, ended at four.

"Is anyone else there?"

"You mean someone other than me? Sure, there's bodies here."

"Anyone on the Jackson case? Walker or Calabrese?"

"Sorry, babe, just me. I'm getting the feeling that's not the answer you're looking for."

Damn. I had tried to minimize Chuck's involvement on the case, but now I didn't have much of a choice. I told him I didn't have time to explain anything but needed him to meet me and Nelly.

"Far as the department's concerned, the case is cleared, Sam. The lieutenant will look at any OT we put in on it, and that might ripple back to your office. You sure?"

See, this is why it's not wise for us to work together. His heart was in the right place, but Chuck was questioning my judgment when any other cop would be happy at the chance for easy time-and-a-half. "You don't need to tell me how it works. Just meet me over there."

When he got to the corner where I was waiting, he tried to give me a peck on the lips, but I held a hand up.

I led the way up the escalator to the main lobby. Nelly was already waiting.

She was visibly alarmed that I wasn't alone, and seemed even more uncomfortable when I told her Chuck was a cop. For a second, I thought I was going to have to give her the "I'm not your lawyer, so there's no privilege" speech, but Nelly had obviously been paying attention during her ethics classes. "I guess even if I talked just to you, you could turn around and tell him everything anyway."

"And I would. Now why don't you go ahead and tell me what's going on. You sounded pretty worked up on the phone."

She looked around the lobby to confirm that no city hall types were around. "I don't know whether to be worked up over it or not. But when I got back to the office after I testified, Dennis Coakley was in Judge Loutrell's office. He's the chief administrative judge."

I nodded.

"I've been helping him out, now that I'm down to one judge. Anyway, they were talking about Judge Easterbrook and were saying something about privileged information. I don't think they heard me come in at first, but then when the phone rang and I answered, they closed the judge's door."

"Could you tell what kind of information they were talking about?"

"No, but it sounded like the judge thought they should tell you about it, and Coakley was saying they couldn't because it was privileged."

"They were talking about me specifically?'

"Well, I don't know if Judge Loutrell knew your name, but he said something about telling the DA, and then Coakley said something like, 'We can't tell her anything that's privileged.'"

"And you don't have any idea what they could have been referring to?"

"No. I knew Coakley had reviewed Judge Easterbrook's files for privileged materials, but he said he didn't have to remove anything."

Nelly stopped talking, but I could tell from the way she ended the sentence that she had cut herself off.

"But?"

"I went back to the chambers and searched Judge Easterbrook's office. I didn't find any files other than the ones you already saw, but I did find a key."

"To what?"

She reached into her jacket pocket and removed a tiny silver key. "I don't know, but it looks like it could fit a safe deposit box.

I found it in the drawer she keeps her personal junk in. She used to throw her purse in there during the day with some makeup and a hairbrush, that kind of thing.

"It's probably nothing," she said, "but I was still getting over my nerves from testifying, and when I heard them talking about the case and then shutting the door, I got majorly paranoid. I was in her office searching like crazy. I opened her compact, and this was in the bottom with the puff. At the time, it felt important but now I guess it sounds a little stupid."

It was definitely worth looking into. Given its location, the key had clearly been important to Clarissa. I took it, gave Nelly my home number, and asked her to call if she overheard anything else about the case.

"For what it's worth," she said before turning away, "you were great in court today. I think Judge Easterbrook would have really trusted you to handle this case."

Chuck gave me a look but knew me well enough not to comment on the compliment. When we were leaving the building, he said, "You'd look kind of cute with a haircut like that. Maybe purple instead of the hot pink."

"You're into that kind of thing, are you?"

"Nope. Can I have my kiss now?" he asked.

"Not a chance. You know my views on PDA." There is a reason for every rule, and the reason for this one is that the only adults I ever see making out in public are ugly. I doubt there's a cause-and-effect relationship, but I'd rather not risk it.

He mock-sighed, then turned his attention to the key I was rotating between my fingers. "You want me to tag that and put it in the property room?"

"That's OK. I'm going to hold on to it."

"Why do I get the feeling that you're about to make some mischief? After that run-in you had with Johnson the other day, he's not going to like it if you do anything to mess up what's standing as a perfectly good case."

So Johnson had told the rest of them about the dress-down. "And why do I get the feeling that if Russell Frist made the same call you'd keep any doubts you had to yourself?"

He looked away for a few seconds. When he turned back toward me, he pushed my hair behind my ear and said, "Sorry, Kincaid, but you're so much cuter than he is. I'll try to get used to it."

"About that PDA you wanted?" I said, leaning into him.

"Uh-huh?"

"Come over around nine. We'll order a pizza, and I'll display some affection in private."

I had just enough time to touch base with Russell before meeting Slip. I found him chatting in his office with the other MCU boys.

"Sorry, I'll come back."

"No, that's all right," he said, waving me in. "Sorry, guys, but we need to talk about a case real quick."

They all filed out without saying a word to me, clearly disappointed that they'd have to move the socializing to a smaller office.

"How'd it go today?"

I filled him in on the preliminary hearing and Slip's request to meet with me at the end of the day.

"He's probably hoping for a quick plea," he said. "If he offers to take a life sentence to avoid the death penalty, you're going to find yourself in a bind. You want me to come along?"

Duncan hadn't formally announced his decision not to seek a death sentence, but I knew his mind was made up. Letting

Jackson enter a plea without that information might not violate the ethics rules, but it still seemed sleazy.

"That's all right. It's just talk for now. I won't make a deal without running it by you and Duncan."

"Anything else?" he asked.

I decided not to hold back on him. I told him about my conversation with Nelly and the key she'd given me. "I might ask Johnson to track it down for me, find out what she was hiding."

"Don't even think about it, Sam. How many times do I have to tell you? The case is cleared. You eat up bureau overtime chasing down what's probably a stupid luggage key, and there's going to be pressure to rein you in. Save us both the headache."

I pulled the key from my pocket and showed it to him. "It's not a luggage key. It looks like it's for a safe deposit box."

"Jesus Christ, Kincaid. Why isn't that in the police property room? You can't go lugging evidence around in your pocket. Get it through your head: You're the prosecutor, not Jackson's defense attorney. You put that in the property room, make sure Slip gets a copy of the receipt in discovery, and forget about it."

In the spirit of cooperating with my new, relatively decent supervisor, I would put the key away as instructed, but I wasn't about to forget about it.

It took the guy in the precinct property room less than five minutes to add the key to the other evidence seized in the Jackson case and complete a supplemental report to document the addition. I pocketed two photocopies of the supplemental, one for the file and one for some mischief-making.

Slip was waiting at the bar at Higgin's, looking at his watch.

"You starting to think I was standing you up?"

"There are a couple of people in your office who find that sort of thing humorous," he said.

"And do I strike you as one of them?"

"Nope. That's why I waited."

We ordered our drinks at the bar and found a quiet table in the corner. Higgin's looks exactly like the kind of bar where you'd expect lawyers to meet after work to talk cases. Dark wood, brass fixtures, the works.

"So how've you been, Sam? I haven't seen you much since you handed my ass to me in trial about a year ago."

I wrinkled my nose. "I don't remember it being quite that bad."

"So tell me the truth. How many times have you pulled that 'Don't take it out on my case that I'm young' shit?"

"Only with you, Slip. Had to do something to level the playing field against your cords and tennies."

I have this thing I do to counteract the shtick that some of the older attorneys have developed over the years. In my final closing, I give the jury my best doe-eyed look, even turning slightly pigeon-toed if I can get away with it. Then I say something like, "I might not have as much trial experience as the defense attorney, but don't take it out on this case. The evidence is there, etc. etc." It gets the jury back on track, and is a lot more subtle than saying, "I'm not as slimy as the rest of these guys."

In my last trial with Slip, he'd gone after my cops on a reverse drug buy. I suppose it's the only tack for a defense attorney to take when his client insists on putting his word against an undercover officer's. When little innocent me got done with the jury, they saw things the way they really were.

"Well, it's a cute trick, Kincaid. I wanted to haul out your power résumé and hold it up against my University of Oregon degree."

"As much as I enjoy your company, Slip, I assume we're not here to reminisce. What's up?"

"The Jackson case, of course."

"What about it?"

No attorney ever wants to be the first to say *plea*. It's a sign you don't have faith in your case. I'd sit here all night if I had to, but Slip was the one who'd asked for this meeting.

"It's fishy."

Now that was not what I was expecting.

I plucked a ten from my wallet and put it on the table as I stood to leave. I had planned on giving Slip the report from the property room to make sure Clarissa's secret key didn't get lost among the discovery, but now that I knew his agenda, it was time to go. That old saying about family describes how I feel about my cases: Only I can bad-mouth them. I got enough argument from defense attorneys during the workday; I wasn't about to spend my Friday night on this.

"Please stay, Sam. I thought you knew me well enough, but ask around the courthouse if you have to; I don't bullshit. Posture one too many times, and you can never get a prosecutor to listen to you again."

That was his reputation.

"Hear me out," he said. "I know it rarely happens, but I really am starting to think this guy's being set up. And it's a good set-up. He's poor, and he's black, and your victim is incredibly sympathetic."

I was still standing with my briefcase, but I hadn't walked away.

"Honestly, I'm scared shitless I'm going to lose this case and never be able to sleep again."

I think I had been fearing the same thing. I sat down again, and he started his pitch.

"What's bothering me most is how neatly it all adds up. What's a guy who lives hand-to-mouth doing getting a phone call one day on a fancy new development job?"

"Easy," I said. "Developers are greedy and will try to save

money wherever they can. What do they care who does the landscaping?"

There was too much evidence against Jackson for that one nagging point to prove a setup, especially since Grace had explained it wasn't particularly unusual for developers to use day labor. I told Slip he'd need to explain away the most incriminating pieces before I could take him seriously.

"Without waiving privilege?" he asked.

I gave him my word.

"First of all, we've got that thing your cops keep calling an admission."

"It's a classic admission, Slip. The police kick the door, and your guy blurts out, 'I know what you're looking for.' Leads them right to the paint."

"Right. He leads them to the paint. If he's giving himself up, why doesn't he point them to the hammer? Because he didn't know it was there."

"But what made him think they were there for the paint? Because he saw the early news stories about paint being on the dog," I said, answering my own question.

"No, Sam, because he stole it. He's been keeping his nose so clean he thought the police were barging in over a couple of cans of paint he took from the building site. He was going to paint his mom's house."

"Isn't that sweet?"

"You're starting to sound as insensitive as the rest of your office."

"Sorry, Slip, but I'm not buying it. A judge he's threatening turns up dead, and when the police look at him, he thinks it's for petty theft?"

"He didn't know the woman was dead. This is not a man who keeps up with the news. I'm telling you, I believe him. You've got to understand, the only thing that drives this guy is keeping his kids. He thought if he got caught with the paint, he'd lose the Glenville job and it would hurt him with everything else that's going on. I guess one of the other workers at the site saw him take it, so when the police showed up, he assumed the guy had ratted."

Now that was interesting. It would tie whatever Slip was talking about back to the property. "What do you mean someone saw him?"

"He noticed that some workers had left a couple buckets of paint outside on Friday, so he went back with his truck to pick them up. He says another worker was still there and saw him. Melvin started to make up a story, but the guy told him to go ahead; he wouldn't tell anyone."

"Does he know who the man was?"

"Since we're being so honest with each other, all he could tell me was 'some white guy.' But, c'mon, there are lawyers in your office who've given a witness a lineup with worse initial statements. Get me some pictures and I'll see what I can do."

I shook my head. "There's a ton of people working down there. And it doesn't do you any good anyway. So what if he stole the paint? It's still on the victim's dog, so he's still tied to the victim's disappearance."

Unless, of course, the mystery man who spotted him with the paint had something to do with it.

"Let me ask you something," I said, "what does Jackson say about how he got the job?"

Slip pulled a file from his briefcase. "I was getting there. Melvin runs an ad in the Penny Power classifieds. Two lines only costs a few bucks, and he occasionally gets a home maintenance job, that sort of thing. Well, last Monday, he gets a phone call from a Billy Minkins. Melvin's pretty sure about the name, but he never actually met him. He hired Melvin as an independent contractor for twenty bucks an hour, more than Melvin's ever made."

I scribbled down the name on a cocktail napkin.

"The check he got is from a company called Gunderson Development."

I didn't need to write that one down.

"I didn't find a listing for either Minkins or the company," Slip said, "but you're probably in a better position to track someone down. Maybe you can get a picture of Minkins, see if he's the one who told Melvin to take the paint."

"You're pushing your luck, Slip. I'm here to listen. Don't tell me how to do my job. Tell me about the fingerprint on the door."

If Slip was convinced Melvin was innocent, he must have an explanation for the print.

"Melvin went to the house Wednesday night. He was so excited about the new job, he thought it might help if he talked to her in person."

That's what Melvin's mother had said.

"How'd he know where she lived?" I asked.

Slip looked down then looked back to me. "Let's just say that part doesn't help me so much."

"I'm going to assume he did something stalkerish, like follow her home at some point."

Slip's silence was enough.

"So what happened when he knocked?" I asked.

"Nothing. No one was home. After he left, he realized that showing up on her front door was probably not the wisest litigation strategy."

"But threatening letters are?"

"I never said Melvin was rational," he said, "just innocent. By the way, he tells me he mailed that last letter Monday morning, and I believe him. And, I know you can explain it away if you need to, but you've got to admit that Melvin as a sex offender doesn't ring true. That leaves you having to explain how your vic got dressed after she died. Come on, Samantha, part of you has a hinky feeling about this."

I let the comment go. I didn't need him telling a judge down the road that I had supposedly expressed doubt about the prosecution. "How come I haven't heard anything about an alibi?"

"That part doesn't help either," he said.

"Slip, that's usually shorthand for sitting alone by himself, with no one to verify it."

"The kids go to church with Grandma on Sundays. You know those Baptists; it's an all-day thing."

"And I assume under your theory, someone planted the hammer," I said.

"There are no prints on it. And you heard Johnson. He tried to call Caffrey before he homed in on Melvin. If Caffrey was doing your victim, he'd know about Melvin. That's plenty of time to dump the hammer. And, hell, Caffrey's powerful enough to have someone do it for him. Melvin was at the mall with the kids from six to nine that night."

Now that I heard Slip's attempt to explain the things that had been nagging at me, it sounded ridiculous.

"How does someone get inside the apartment? My cops didn't see any sign of a break-in."

"Melvin doesn't bolt the door, and you should see the locks on public housing. It took my investigator about four seconds to slip it with a credit card."

It still didn't sound right. The framing of a defendant is rare enough, but the way Slip spelled it out, this one involved not only someone from the property site but also an elected official. It didn't fly without a connection between the two.

Maybe Slip would find one. I fished the property receipt out of my bag and scribbled my home phone number on the back.

"Here's a present," I said. "Don't say I never did anything for you."

I had some work to do this weekend too, but first I needed to track down the envelope that Jenna Markson had sent interoffice.

Searching for it in my office, I remembered that I still hadn't returned Susan Kerr's call from the morning. Better to do it now than to call her over the weekend or let it sit until Monday.

She thanked me for calling. "I feel stupid bothering you when you're in the middle of the hearing, but I—"

"Don't worry about it, Susan. What's up?"

"I was just wondering how Townsend was at the hearing today."

"He was there with his lawyer, but as it turned out he didn't need to testify."

"Is that good?"

"Sure. Court proceedings are always difficult for victims."

"But when you first said he didn't need to testify, you said it in a way that suggested you were particularly appreciative. Was there a reason for that?"

I wouldn't normally run down my victim's husband, but Susan and Tara had already expressed concern about Townsend's recent appearance, so it wasn't like I was saying something new. "Well, quite honestly, he didn't look like he was up to it."

"So you can see it too." Susan sounded relieved. "I was wondering if it was just my imagination. I'm really starting to worry about him. When I was with the family last night, he was totally out of it, but I only saw him have one drink."

I thought about it. Townsend had seemed almost drunk at the death penalty meeting, but I hadn't smelled any alcohol on him, either then or today in court.

"Maybe it's just lack of sleep," I offered. "And he might still be suffering from shock."

"You're probably right. Well, it's the end of a long day, and I'm sure you want to go home. I was really only calling to see if you could try to protect Townsend in court today, but as it turned out it wasn't necessary."

"Sorry I didn't get back to you sooner."

"Not a problem. I'm just glad you think what he's going through is normal. You've probably seen a lot more of this than I have, fortunately."

Actually, I hadn't. I had no idea what normal behavior was from a man whose wife had been murdered. And Townsend was a man with access to his own personal prescription pad.

"Still, Susan, you should probably keep an eye out for him and ask Clarissa's family to do the same. He could be prescribing himself medication."

"I was wondering the same thing but didn't want to say it. He could lose his license for that, couldn't he?"

"Maybe not under the circumstances, but let's not get ahead of ourselves. Just keep your eyes open, maybe check the medicine cabinets, that kind of thing." Then I remembered I wasn't just a sympathetic human being; I was a prosecutor. "Look around if you choose to as a private party, I mean, not as an agent of the government."

I could almost hear a small smile. "I get what you're saying. And, Samantha, thanks a lot."

"No problem."

I hung up pleased that I had earned Susan's trust. Even though prosecutors aren't victims' attorneys, they should in most cases be their advocates. If I could handle a busy caseload and still find time and compassion for the people in that case-load, I'd be proud of my job.

I went back to searching for the envelope from Jenna Markson, working backward from my office, starting with the mail slots on the sixth floor. It could have been worse. The envelope hadn't made it into the slot for MCU, but I found it when I pawed through a bin of mail left in front of the boxes. The mail guy had probably checked out at precisely 5 P.M.

Inside I found the printouts Jenna had run on Gunderson. They contained exactly what I was looking for: a list of the properties Gunderson had owned when he had filed for Chapter 11.

It was too late to get into the public library's archives to do the research I was planning, so I headed home for a long run before Chuck was scheduled to show up. By the time I finished, I had mustered up the energy to call my father, but all I got was his machine. I hung up without leaving a message.

When Chuck showed up twenty minutes late with beer on his breath, I was good and didn't ask him where he'd been. Then he was better and apologized for being late, explaining how he'd gotten trapped at a sit-down with Calabrese. Apparently Mike and his wife were having a hard time adjusting to life with a new baby.

We were total gluttons and ordered a large pie from Pizzacata—half pepperoni for him, half goat cheese and artichoke for me. An hour and a bottle of chianti later, we were starting to fool around on the sofa while Chris Matthews and his guests played hardball. Some folks might have a problem getting turned on with talking heads going at each other in the background, but with Chuck and me, anything could lead to foreplay, even those icky surgery shows. One minute I'm trying to grab the remote from him, and the next, we've got our own doctor show going on my coffee table.

Around the time Chuck had flung my bra into the empty pizza box and I was beyond caring, the phone rang. I started to wiggle out from beneath him, but his warm breath in my ear stopped me. "Don't even try it."

I heard my own voice on the machine. "You've reached Sam and Vinnie. Maybe we're home, maybe not. At the tone, proceed at your own risk."

"Hi—uh, sorry to call so late. I'm going to assume that's a joke so I can hold on to my remaining self-esteem in the event no one picks up. This is a message for Samantha Kincaid."

See? It works. Ever since Roger moved out and Vinnie moved in, my Frenchie had been my other half on the all-important outgoing message. No reason to advertise your woman-alone status to every creep out there dialing random numbers for kicks.

"This is Graham Szlipkowski."

My wiggling resumed. In fact, it escalated to an outright scramble. When Chuck realized I was serious about getting to the phone, he sat up, clearly frustrated.

By the time I picked up, I heard Slip say, "I'm sorry to bother you on the weekend, but I need you to contact—"

"Slip, it's Samantha."

"You mean I made the cut? I've earned some honors in my career, but—"

"Slip, it's eleven o'clock on a Friday night. Get to the point."

"I looked at the present you dropped on me this afternoon. Needless to say, I want to check it out, the sooner the better."

"So check it out," I said, "and tell me if you find anything."

"That's why I'm calling so late. I want to track it down with the banks tomorrow, but the bureau won't release the key to my investigator without your OK."

"That's fine. Whom do I need to call?"

"I'm sorry about this, but they need a fax."

What a pain in the ass. I jotted down the fax number for the property room and assured him I'd figure out something.

When I hung up, Chuck threw me a skeptical look. "Why do I have a feeling that I don't want to know why a defense attorney's calling you at home?"

"Because you probably don't."

"Most guys, their girlfriend gets a phone call from another man late at night, it means one thing. If only I had it so good. Just promise me you're not doing anything dangerous."

"Hardly, unless you consider clerical work dangerous." I tried to hide my glee that he'd used the *girlfriend* word. Down the road, he'd need to settle on more mature verbiage. For now, though, I reveled in the general sentiment.

"Get back over here, then," he said.

"Sorry. I've got one more thing to do. I can either drive to Kinko's or figure out how to send a fax on my computer."

"You have no idea how to use your computer, do you?"

"Sure. It's a giant typewriter with a button that puts me on the Internet."

"I'll make a deal with you. I'll send your fax and you turn off Matthews and get your ass in bed. And no sleeping."

It was a win-win situation.

11

I KICKED CHUCK out the next morning so I could get to work, but not before convincing him to pull DMV photos of Larry Gunderson and Billy Minkins for me.

At first he balked. "My lieutenant will be all over me about Saturday OT on Jackson," he said, "unless, of course, I can tell him why it was essential."

When that didn't get an explanation out of me about who Gunderson and Minkins were and why I wanted their pictures, he finally relented. I was ready to go by noon.

I'd get the pictures to Slip soon enough, but my first priority was the downtown public library.

No doubt about it, the library crowd's an interesting one: Birkenstock moms, amateur academics, and burnt-out hippie homeless people, all in one quiet beautiful place.

I pulled the volumes I was looking for and searched for an empty table. Finding a work spot was not an easy task, given my criteria: no children, schizoids, or stinky people.

I finally dumped the books on a corner table, retrieved a

county map and the envelope from Jenna Markson from my briefcase, and settled in for what I thought would be the first day in a full weekend of research. As it turned out, the task at hand—tracking down Gunderson's stake in the urban growth boundary over the years—was easier than I had imagined.

First, I marked all of Gunderson's seven properties on the map. Without exception, the properties would have been considered the boonies when I was a kid, but they had been developed by the time I was out of college. The next step was to figure out where the properties fell along the growth boundary.

Fortunately, the library maintained a series of maps depicting the original boundary line and all the changes made in the twenty-five years since. The trend became obvious immediately. Six of Gunderson's seven properties fell just inside the original boundary line. The land would have been rural at the time, then made valuable by the sudden restriction against future growth. The seventh was brought within the urban area after the first boundary expansion.

Either Larry Gunderson was the luckiest landowner in Portland or I was on to something.

I found a records librarian and asked her if she could pull the legislative history for the Smart Growth Act, which had established the original growth boundary in the summer of 1980. She looked at me like I had to be kidding, then sighed heavily and walked away when she realized I wasn't.

A good hour later, she reemerged with a handcart stacked with ragged and dusty binders. "I can't tell you exactly where it is in here, but each binder has an index by bill number. Do you need help finding the number too?"

"No, I've got it. Thank you so much. I really appreciate it."

I gathered from her look of confusion that she rarely heard those words.

The rest of the afternoon was spent wading through hundreds

of pages of legislative findings, debates, floor speeches, and other forms of word combinations that hardly deserve to be called part of the English language. Most of the talk was about whether to limit urban growth and how. What captured my attention, however, were the pages detailing the debates about where to draw the boundary line itself. I couldn't make sense of it all, so I fell back on my handy dandy anticonfusion treatment, list-making.

Using a legal pad, I listed the various property areas in dispute, then located each on my map. Four of the six Gunderson properties within the eventual boundary had not been included for development under the original proposal.

Next I turned to the legislators involved in the debates, noting their names and where they stood on permitting development within each disputed geographic area. For the most part, predictable pro-development and pro-environment patterns emerged, with the act's opponents favoring open development across the board while proponents favored restrictions. But one legislator was clearly pushing the expansions that favored Gunderson more than he was pushing others: Representative Clifford Brigg.

I went back to the records librarian and asked for anything she could give me on Brigg within six months of August 1980.

"Unfortunately," she said, "the articles from back then aren't computerized, so you're going to have to do it by hand." She led me to a table in another corner that contained the old microfilm machines, pulled a couple of notebooks from a nearby shelf, and explained they were the indexes of *Oregonian* articles from 1980 through 1981. If I made a list of the ones I wanted to see, she'd pull the rolls of microfilm I needed.

If it involved making a list, I could handle it.

Brigg was no stranger to the press. Some of the articles appeared to concern the growth legislation, but most seemed campaign-related. It must have been a reelection year.

I requested all the articles that looked like they might relate to the growth boundary and a handful of the ones about the campaign.

My new best friend had the rolls of film in just a few minutes. After a quick refresher course on how to use the machine, I jumped in, turning first to the stories on the growth legislation.

Most of the articles were brief, containing competing sound bites from developers and environmentalists, with a few remarks from legislators thrown in for flavor. But a longer feature offered a good overview of the debate and Brigg's role in it.

The first section of the article described the rapid growth that was swallowing rural land along the I-5 corridor from Salem to Seattle. Although the last decade had seen only an 8 percent increase in the population of the Willamette Valley, the geography of the urban area had sprawled 22 percent.

The article explained the Smart Growth Act and the general policy arguments on each side of the debate. Planned growth versus the free market, environmental preservation versus human use of land, the collective good versus individual choice, open space versus affordable housing, blah blah blah.

Then the writer got to Brigg:

> The future of the Smart Growth Act is likely to be deter-mined by a handful of moderate legislators who appear to favor the theory of an urban growth boundary but who are focusing upon the particularities of how that boundary will be drawn. Key among these detail-oriented legislators is Rep. Clifford Brigg. Staff members to several other legislators report that Brigg has been active behind the scenes, working to ensure that the line is drawn to his satisfaction before he lends his support. In a statement issued in response to inquiries from the *Oregonian* about these reports, Brigg stated, "If we publicly debated every bit of minutia about every piece of legislation, we'd never get any work done as a body. So, yes, I have been talking to my colleagues about

what I'd like to see in this legislation for me to support it. I'm in favor of the idea, but we need to do it right. My eventual vote will be public and open to scrutiny."

As Brigg put it, all he was trying to do was to make sure that the line was drawn properly, so the prettiest, most sacred land wasn't turned into a Kmart. It sounded perfectly logical, but was it coincidence that Clifford Brigg's notion of smart growth just happened to deliver a windfall to Gunderson?

Once I finished plodding through the Smart Growth articles, I had just enough time to take a quick look at the reelection stories before the library closed. The campaign pieces were quaint compared to today's politics: Brigg eats ice cream at a strawberry social, Brigg feeds ducks at the Rhododendron Gardens, Brigg is in favor of a new fire station.

Then, in the background of the next photograph, I saw a familiar face in an unfamiliar uniform. The shot was a closeup of Brigg shaking hands with a former secretary of state who had come to town for a commencement speech. The face in the background was my father's.

When I picture my father in his work gear, I see him in his standard green forest-ranger togs. Not that I'd remember it, but I didn't think I'd ever seen him in the Oregon State Police dress blues he wore in the photograph. Those would have been the exception even when he was a state trooper.

For just a second, I enjoyed the chance to see my father as he was then. His light brown hair was silver now, and his face was thinner, but he was still just as handsome. I looked at the date of the article. Dad left the state for the forest service just two months later.

Then, for reasons I didn't fully understand, I found myself wishing I hadn't stumbled onto this picture at all. What was my father doing with a man like Clifford Brigg?

I looked up to give my eyes a rest and to stretch my neck. When I had reached into a full extension on my right, I noticed a man standing by the table where my books of legislative history were still open. Did he want my table, the books, or maybe just to stand there being weird?

Before I made it across the room he had disappeared behind a bookshelf next to the table. I took a quick tour of the floor, but he was nowhere to be found. Damn. There had been something familiar about him, but there was no way I was going to place him without a second look.

I put an end to the search when the friendly librarian started making the rounds to tell everyone that the doors would be closing in ten minutes. I noticed that she looked directly at me when she mentioned our ability to support our local library by cleaning up after ourselves.

I stole a final look at the photograph of my father. I felt foolish. My occasionally overactive imagination was at it again. No mystery men were following me, and my father wasn't wrapped up in anything nefarious with Clifford Brigg. Surely he was there as security for the event.

I pushed PRINT on the machine before tucking away the film. Dad would get a kick out of the picture, and he might even have some background to share on Brigg. In the meantime, I had earned a night off.

One advantage to being a woman alone should be the occasional luxury of coming home and falling straight to sleep. By the time I finished my night out with Grace—three Nordstrom shopping bags, two martinis, and a slice of lemon cheesecake later—I was exhausted.

But I had the usual crap to attend to. My phone was ringing as I walked in the door, and Vinnie had left a little message of his own for me, right inside his doggie door to make sure I knew it was intentional.

"It's after midnight," I said to my caller, "way past any reasonable notion of call cutoffs."

"It's Graham Szlipkowsky."

"And how's my favorite defense attorney doing on this very late evening?" I held the phone between my ear and shoulder while I began scooping, scrubbing, and disinfecting my tile, Vinnie watching contentedly from the nearby wicker chair.

"He's very sorry to be calling you."

"Not a problem. What's up?"

"I wanted to make sure you're going to be around tomorrow. We need to talk."

"We are talking."

"No, I need to show you something. Can you come to my office?"

I was too tired to try to pry the information out of him. If he was going to insist on meeting, better to get it over with. "Fine," I said, "but let's make it early. I'll meet you at seven."

"A.M.? When do you sleep, Kincaid?"

"Who says I sleep?" I said, hanging up.

So much for a full Sunday off.

We met at his office at seven sharp. I noticed that in his khakis and navy pullover, he dressed better on the weekend than he did at the courthouse.

"It better be good, Slip."

"I don't know if it's good, but it's definitely notable."

My usual Sunday routine of reading the *New York Times* over dim sum at Fong Chong was notable. This had better top it.

Slip led me into a small library that appeared to double as a lunchroom, coffee bar, and chat area. There was a tiny television on the countertop. Four men in jellybean colored T-shirts were wiggling up a storm with a room full of toddlers.

"You better have something better for me than a show that transforms perfectly cute kids into annoying little freaks."

"Very funny," he said, hitting a button that turned the screen to an even blue. "I think this is big, Samantha."

"Enough with the dramatics. Just show me why you brought me here."

He pulled a plastic Gap bag from a nearby chair and set it on the card table in the center of the room.

"My investigator found a safe deposit box at First Coast Bank rented by Clarissa Easterbrook. The key was a match."

"And that's what he found?" I asked, looking at the bag.

He nodded.

"And how exactly did your investigator convince the bank to turn over the contents of a safe deposit box that didn't belong to him?"

"Do you really need to know?"

The truth was, I didn't. If there was any legal violation, it was probably only civil. Anyway, courts don't care if evidence is obtained illegally, as long as the government's hands were clean.

He pulled out a manila folder, a videotape, and a computer disc.

He handed me the folder first. Inside were photocopies of what appeared to be a case file for *Gunderson Development v. City of Portland*.

Slip must have seen a flash of recognition cross my face. "Does that mean something to you?"

"I'm not sure yet," I said, flipping through it. This little joint venture definitely fell outside the lines of normal procedure. I wasn't about to tell him everything until I figured out for myself how the pieces fit together.

From what I could gather in my quick review, the city had

denied Gunderson's request for a variance to convert an historically significant building into condominiums. Gunderson appealed, arguing that the city employee who denied the request had been untrained, filling in for the usual specialist who was on maternity leave. Gunderson argued that the employee had failed to consider whether his redevelopment plan preserved the original architecture to a significant degree, which was required to obtain a variance.

I didn't know squat about administrative law, but Gunderson's appeal looked like a major loser. No judge—administrative or not—wants to be in the business of second-guessing the discretionary decisions made by front-line bureaucratic implementers.

But Clarissa had agreed with Gunderson. Result? Gunderson threw some plumbing and a few walls into a run-down old church and ended up with condominiums that probably sold for four hundred dollars a square foot.

The case sounded familiar. Had I seen it when I reviewed Clarissa's files at City Hall? I looked at the dates. Clarissa had ruled in favor of Gunderson almost four months ago, and I had only seen the cases that were currently pending.

At the end of the file I found a page of handwritten notes. They were dated a week before Clarissa's death and were in the same slanted scrawl I'd seen in Clarissa's files.

Tt/ DC about Gunderson appeal. He advd me city would not reopen. We agreed re Grice.

Something about the file was still tugging at a corner of a memory. Each time I thought I was close to plucking out the thought, I'd lose hold of it entirely. "What else?"

He held up the floppy disc. "I've got to give this back to my investigator. It's password protected."

"And the video?"

"That's the doozie."

Slip popped the videotape into the built-in VCR beneath the small television screen. The blue screen turned to static, then to a shaky image of a couple walking out a door.

It was Clarissa Easterbrook and T. J. Caffrey. Caffrey looked around but apparently didn't see whoever was holding the camera. He held Clarissa's face and then kissed her. It was long but gentle. I felt my eyes shift away instinctively from their private moment, but I forced myself to focus.

Their faces still close, they spoke a few words to each other. Then the camera followed as Caffrey walked Clarissa to her car, giving her one last kiss before she got in. He hopped into his car, and the two drove away. The camera panned outward to show the backdrop, a two-story motel with doors that edged the parking lot. A sign at the road declared it to be the Village Motor Inn.

When the screen went to static and then back to blue, I looked at Slip. "It's a motel north of Vancouver," he explained, "about thirty miles out."

They'd gone all the way to Washington to avoid being spotted. Obviously, they hadn't been careful enough.

"I guess that confirms the affair," I said. "You think someone was blackmailing her? I hate to break it to you, Slip, but it might've been Jackson." If sympathy and threatening letters didn't do the trick, a videotape like this one might. He had followed Clarissa at least once before.

"If it's blackmail," he said, "what do you make of this?" Slip handed me a brown padded envelope addressed to Mr. and Mrs. Terrence J. Caffrey on a street in Eastmoreland. "The video was inside that envelope."

There was no postmark.

"Maybe it was hand-delivered, and Caffrey showed it to Clarissa?"

"Possible. Or maybe Clarissa was going to mail it and never got around to it."

I thought about it. Tara had gotten the impression that Clarissa's mystery man was reluctant to live happily ever after with her. Maybe Clarissa was playing hardball? I had seen obsession inspire crazier actions against a supposed loved one.

The only thing I knew for sure was that I didn't know everything yet, a state of knowledge I was never good at accepting.

Before I left, I gave Slip the photographs of Gunderson and Minkins that Chuck had pulled for me. I kept their PPDS reports for myself. Gunderson was sixty-five with a clean record. Minkins was thirty, on probation for a forged check.

My eyes stayed on Minkins's picture. When Chuck gave it to me yesterday morning, I hadn't given it a second glance. But now he looked familiar. The guy by my table in the library. With shorter hair and a closer shave, he could've been Minkins. On the other hand, he could've been yet another lanky guy with dark hair and a mustache. I might have to arrange an in-person look-see.

For now, I wanted to know what Jackson could tell me. "Have your guy take a look at these. See if he recognizes them from the site."

Slip glanced at the photographs. "Are you going to tell me who they are?"

"Nope."

When I left Slip's office, I called my father to make sure he was home. I wasn't sure I could make it over for dinner, I told him, but I needed to talk to him now, if he didn't mind.

Five minutes later, he was pouring me a glass of iced tea as we sat together at the breakfast nook. We both had finally adjusted to the clean tabletop. When my mother was still living, this was the place where she stacked her books, mail, and bills. Now that my father was in charge of running the house, those things piled up in the den.

"Look what I found." I handed him a copy of the newspaper article, showing him in the background at the college commencement. "You look very handsome."

Something dark crossed my father's face. "Where'd you find that old thing?"

"I came across it when I was going through some old newspaper articles at the library trying to tie up some loose ends."

"Well, thanks, Sammy. I'll hold on to it. I forgot what I looked like back then. Not too shabby in my day, was I?"

"I think it's safe to say you were a full-blown hottie, Dad. I was actually hoping to talk to you about it. Were you doing security for the commencement?"

Dad shook his head. "I was driving one of the bigwigs. We did a lot of that in OSP."

"Who were you driving?"

"Oh, who can even remember? That was so long ago. What's this about, hon?"

"I'm not sure yet. A couple of names keep coming up on something I'm looking into, and one of them is Clifford Brigg. What do you remember about him?"

Dad put the article face down on the table. "Not a lot. I left OSP when you were just a little kid, and I never looked back. I remember reading that Brigg died—oh, that must have been more than fifteen years ago."

"But what was he like back then? What was his reputation?"

"I'm sorry, Samantha, but I told you before, I don't want to talk about this. What's past is past."

No, he told me he didn't want to talk about his reasons for leaving OSP. The knot I'd felt when I first found the article began to settle its way back into my stomach. "Dad, does this have something to do with why you moved over to the forest service? Because *that's* what you told me before that you didn't want to talk about."

He was silent for a moment, as if he were mulling something over in his head before speaking. "I didn't say anything other than I don't want to talk about it. End of discussion."

End of discussion? I hadn't heard him say that since I was in junior high school and he forbade me from taking the Greyhound with Grace for a Duran Duran concert in Seattle. Grace's mother had nixed the idea too, so we caved.

This time I wouldn't quit so easily. "Dad, I hope you know there's nothing you can't tell me. Obviously this picture is upsetting to you, and it's got something to do with our conversation the other day about Mom—"

"It's got nothing to do with your mother."

"OK, whatever, but something about this upsets you. I wish you'd talk to me about it." I couldn't believe I even had to say that to him. As long as I could remember, his favorite pastime was to tell me things. Anything. When I was a kid, it took all he could handle not to divulge where Mom had hidden the Christmas presents.

Now he wouldn't talk to me about a legislator who had died when I was in high school.

"Dad, I came across these articles doing research on the Easterbrook investigation. If you know something, you have to tell me. It could be important. Melvin Jackson might be innocent."

"If anyone's innocent, it's you, and you're the one I'm worried about. It's these people, Sam. These people. They'll eat you alive to advance their agenda."

"What people? Dad, don't leave me in the dark."

He stood up, walked to the kitchen sink, and stared out the window for a minute, and then another, without saying a word to me. Then he sat across from me again.

"I did security for Clifford Brigg. The man was—well, he was a son of a bitch. Pardon my language. He's dead and gone, but if anyone associated with him is injecting himself into your investigation—please, Sam, just walk away."

"Why, Dad? The least you can do is tell me why."

"I can't, Sam. I just can't."

"And I just can't walk away."

I left my father with whatever secrets he was holding on to and drove to my office, feeling incredibly lonely. Part of me wanted to lie on my couch, watch TV, and cry, but I knew I needed to work.

I made a list of everything I knew about Clarissa, Gunderson, the Glenville property, Caffrey, Townsend, and Jackson. Then I used lines to connect facts that might be related, like Clarissa's ruling on the Gunderson case, Gunderson's stake in the urban growth boundary, and Clarissa's affair with Cafferty.

Before I knew it, my legal pad was so filled with overlapping lines that I couldn't read anything. Frustrated, I finally circled my pen around the entire list over and over again until I popped a hole in the paper. *What the hell were you up to, Clarissa?*

Making sense of everything I'd learned over the weekend was going to take some legwork. I paged Johnson.

I tried to keep it simple, telling him about Clarissa's safe deposit box. "I was hoping you'd have another go at Caffrey since you never got in touch with him the first time. We need to find out what Clarissa was doing with that videotape."

Johnson obviously didn't share my enthusiasm. "Sorry, Sam, but I'm working other cases now. I can't pull off to put in more time on Jackson."

"Do you know if Walker can do it? I've got the rest of the prelim tomorrow." I had a hard time hiding my frustration. The

Major Crimes Team owed its existence to the District Attorney's insistence on sufficient investigative support for cases carrying mandatory minimum sentences.

"That's going to be a problem too. Look, since it's you, I'll give it to you straight. When we saw the lieutenant this morning, he told us that any overtime on Jackson needed to go through him."

"Did he say why?" The bureau could be stingy on overtime, but I'd never heard of an order to run each minute through the supervisor.

"I got the impression someone had put some extra time into the case after it was cleared. But I know it wasn't me, and it also wasn't Jack. You know anything about that?"

"Chuck went with me to pick up the key from Clarissa's assistant, but it only took a few minutes."

"And why didn't you call me or Walker? We're the leads."

"I did call you, but you weren't in." He didn't respond. "Look, do we have a problem here?"

"Just remember how you felt when I went around you for the polygraph. You've got my pager number."

"I didn't *go around* you, Ray. It was a quick walk across the street, and Chuck happened to be in." Again with the silence. "If you want to say something, just say it."

"I just think it's funny how you say your old buddy just happened to be in when you wanted something done on a cleared case. Maybe part of you knew I wouldn't be too happy about doing work that's going to bite me in the ass down the road."

"And how's that?"

"When you tell me three months from now that you're pleading the case down because of something the defense attorney's twisting around. You know, it's always those little extra details—stupid things like a safe deposit key or the occasional extramarital roll in the sheets. Stuff that we both know—or at least *I* know—doesn't change the fact that Melvin Jackson's guilty."

"I don't know what to say, Ray. I wasn't trying to hide anything from you, or I wouldn't have called you just now. And I wouldn't ask you to do something if I didn't think it was important."

"If you want to call the LT, that's fine with me," Ray said. "But for now, we're not supposed to be working a cleared case. I don't want to get stuck between my boss and your office."

Neither did I, I thought, as I hung up. One thing was for sure: I wouldn't be getting any more help from the bureau.

The notes that Clarissa stashed in her safe deposit box mentioned a case she referred to as Grice. It still felt familiar.

I found my own notes from the review of Clarissa's files. It didn't take long to realize where I'd seen Grice's name before. It was in the list of cases from which Clarissa had recused herself. According to my notes, Grice Construction was the company that had complained that the city had unfairly denied its request to rehabilitate some Pearl Street buildings. The date of Clarissa's recusal was the same day she had apparently talked to DC about both the Grice case and the case involving Gunderson's own rehabilitation program. If DC was Coakley, that might explain what Nelly overheard at City Hall.

I didn't know the details yet, but it was becoming clear that Gunderson had some kind of connection to Clarissa.

Good thing I knew who his lawyer was. I even had his home number.

I was surprised when a woman answered. When I asked to speak to Roger, she asked who was calling. I was tempted to tell her she was right to be suspicious, but I gave her the boring answer instead.

"It's for you," she hollered. "Someone named Samantha Kincaid."

I wasn't sure which was worse, to be known as the evil ex-wife or not to be known at all.

"Hello?"

"Is that company, Roger, or a roommate?"

"Something in between, actually, but I assume the point of the question was more in the asking than the answering. If you're calling about Townsend, yes, we plan on being there tomorrow."

"Nice to know, but that's not why I called. I want to talk to Larry Gunderson."

It always feels good to show another attorney you know more than he thought you did. But this time it was especially rewarding.

"Why would you be calling me about that?"

There were lots of bad things to be said about Roger, but lawyering skills were not among them. His question was perfect in its ambiguity, neither denying nor confirming knowledge of Gunderson.

"Because you said Dunn Simon represented him. Remember? That's how you got Melvin Jackson's name? If you're saying you're not Gunderson's lawyer, that's fine. I'll contact him directly." I read Gunderson's street address from my PPDS printout.

"I'm not actually Gunderson's lawyer. One of my partners is, Jim Thorpe."

I remembered seeing his name on Gunderson's appeal. "Fine. I'll call him. What's his home number?"

"Jesus, Samantha. What's your problem? Can't this wait until tomorrow?"

"Nope."

Roger might have come into the firm as a partner, but he was still junior to a corner office guy like Thorpe. Junior partners who hand out home phone numbers to government lawyers stay in the middle of the hallway.

"Fine. Tell me what you want to know, and I'll talk to Jim and get back to you."

I could hear his house guest slash live-in beginning to whine in the background. Apparently Roger had found what he never had in me—someone who needed his undivided attention to be happy.

I didn't show him all my cards, just enough to ensure I'd get Gunderson's attention. "It turns out that in addition to being Melvin Jackson's employer and the owner of the property where Clarissa's body was found, Gunderson also had a case in front of Clarissa a few months ago. In light of that, I think we should at least talk to him about how Jackson happened to find himself on Gunderson's radar."

"I'll get back to you, but don't hold your breath. Given the insinuation, he's more likely to be insulted."

It had to have been one of the fastest decisions ever made by a lawyer who gets paid by the hour. Eleven minutes later, my phone rang.

"It's Jim's call, and he advised Gunderson to enjoy the rest of his weekend. If you want to work something out for this week, get in touch with Jim at the office tomorrow."

"Unbelievable, Roger. I've got the rest of the preliminary hearing tomorrow, and you guys think it's a good idea to tell your client to be uncooperative. Does Thorpe know enough about criminal practice to understand how suspicious it makes Gunderson look?"

"To you, maybe. Quite frankly, I don't see the problem."

"Well, since I'm handling the case, I guess my opinion has to matter to you on this one."

"Sam, if you're doing this because you're pissed off at me, I'm sorry I said some harsh things about your office at the meeting, but they weren't directed at you personally. I was only trying to get Duncan's attention. Hell, you're the one who told me at one time all he cared about was politics." He laughed, but I didn't see what was funny. "Can't you just be happy that you finally got the promotion you wanted and that your first big case came together? I realize I'm not the best messenger for this, but you're not acting like yourself on this one."

"You're a piss-poor messenger, Roger. You don't even know me anymore."

"Well, you're not acting like the person I used to know. Look at the evidence: You've got a fingerprint, the weapon, motive, something approaching a confession. Prescott all but told you on Friday she'd hold Jackson over. And you're spending your Sunday night chasing down figments of your imagination. Gunderson's just some guy who gave Jackson a job."

"And who happened to have an appeal in front of the victim."

"And how long ago was that, Samantha? And how many cases did Easterbrook hear on a monthly basis? It's like you're trying to make your job harder than it is—I don't know—maybe to recapture some of the glory days back in New York."

It was a telephonic slap in the face. Before Roger took the job at Nike, I had been an up-and-comer in the busiest federal prosecutor's office in the country, on my way to handling complex high-stakes conspiracies. We both knew that in the world of lawyers who never stop measuring themselves against one another, I had suffered a serious slip down the ladder when we moved to Portland.

He was already trying to apologize, telling me he didn't mean it the way it sounded. But, to me at that moment, there was only one possible meaning.

"The only slumming I ever did, Roger, was when I married you."

I wanted the satisfaction of slamming the phone into a cradle, but all I had was my thumb against the disconnect button of my cordless.

I tried not to let his comment get to me. Not that Roger's opinion mattered, but I knew I wouldn't even be a prosecutor if it weren't for him. I graduated from law school planning on selling out as necessary to pay off my mountainous debt. But when I was offered a position as a federal prosecutor in New York, Roger was the one who told me I had to take it. And when he moved us to Portland for his Nike job and I couldn't transfer into the U.S. Attorney's Office here, he was the one who encouraged me to remain a prosecutor, even though the choice required a 50-percent pay cut and a serious hit in the prestige department. He paid off my loans in full, using the bundle we'd made selling the New York apartment his parents had given us. Then, when I kicked him out of the house and insisted on a quick divorce, he nearly floored me when he told my attorney to forget about the money. He wouldn't be able to live with himself if I had to represent corporate clients because of him.

I knew I'd been a bigger jerk than I should have been, but I didn't know what to think about his criticism. It was easy to imagine the lawyer in Roger trying to psych me out so I wouldn't subpoena Gunderson and disturb Jim Thorpe. On the other hand, Roger wasn't the only person telling me I was wildly off the mark on this one.

The train was about to run right over Melvin Jackson, and I could do nothing to stop it. I wasn't even sure I wanted to; I just wanted to make sure that we were heading in the right direction. But the bureau had essentially washed its hands of this case, and if I tried to haul Gunderson into the prelim, a quick call from Dunn Simon to the boss would get me overruled and probably fired. And, if Jackson really did it—which he most likely did—it would all be for nothing.

Luckily, I'd been doing this long enough to know that one of the best ways to wield power is to do it subtly.

I left a message for Graham Szlipkowsky to call me right away.

I had been home from a run for thirty minutes, my stomach was growling, and I was getting ready to cave in to take-out cravings when the phone rang.

"Hey, babe. At the risk of sounding pathetic, I'm beginning to miss you. If you're willing to chance my cooking, how does a quiet dinner at your place sound?"

There's something to be said about a man with good timing. Unfortunately, in this man's case, that something was that he couldn't cook. So we compromised. After a quick run to Fred Meyer, he was washing and chopping, and I was doing the stuff that mattered.

When we finally sat down at the table, he could tell I was exhausted.

"What's up with you? Big party last night?"

"You bet. The orgy didn't end till four; then I had to deal with the bikers. Between the meth and the Jack—"

"Seriously, Sam, what's going on?"

"Nothing. I've been working my ass off, and I'm tired."

"Is this still on the Jackson case?" I nodded since I had a mouth full of sea bass. "What have you been digging around in? I thought that case was locked up."

Add another to the list of people reminding me the case was cleared. "I'm just double-checking."

"Here's an idea. Why don't you tell me what you're unsure

about. I have some experience dealing with these kinds of things, you know."

It would be nice to have his take on the case, but I didn't want him to be in a position where he was torn between me and the department. When we eventually decided whether we could handle working on the same cases, I'd have to add that to my reasons for believing it was a bad idea.

For now, I was keeping it vague. "I've been looking into some things Clarissa might have been involved in, making sure they're not related to the murder."

"Does this have something to do with the conversation we had with Pink and the fax I sent to the property room on Friday?"

"Maybe. I haven't quite figured it out yet."

"I see. Let me be more specific. What exactly did that key open, and what was located inside?"

"Don't interrogate me, Chuck."

"You're not giving me any choice, Sam. Getting information out of a perp is a cakewalk compared to a conversation with you these days."

"Here's an idea. You let me do my job, and I'll talk to you as much as you want about anything else you choose."

"I'm not trying to be a jerk, Sam. There are two separate issues here. One is the bureau being pissed off that you appear to have second thoughts on the case. I don't give a shit about that. But the last time you left me in the dark about the poking around you were doing, you almost got killed. I'm worried about you. Please just tell me enough so I know you're not playing cowboy again."

"If you're going to worry about me every time I'm dealing with bad people, this is never going to work."

"Sam, this isn't about you going after bad guys. Don't you get it? I love it that you do what you do. You could be making half a million bucks a year by now as some corporate drone, but that's not who you are, and that's great. But you have a tendency to want to go it alone, no matter how wacky the plan. I don't want you to get hurt again."

"Look, it's fine. What happened before was different. I went in blind knowing someone was out of custody and angry at me, to say the least. Right now, the worst that's going to happen to me is that I ruffle a few political feathers." I left out the part about the mystery man at the library, since I wasn't actually sure that it was Billy Minkins or that he had been watching me. "I'm taking enough crap from my father about this. I don't need it from you too."

For the next few minutes, the only sounds were our forks against the plates and Vinnie breathing under the table.

"Ever since I got this case, he's been on a trip about so-called powerful people and the way they can take away everything from me if I get in their way. He's always been suspicious of authority—"

Chuck was laughing, and I looked at him to see if he was going to continue listening to me. "Sorry," he explained, "but that sounded funny, coming from you."

"Well, I guess we know where I get it. Anyway, I assumed he was worried that someone as influential as Townsend would be calling for my head if I screwed things up. But then this morning I asked him about some work he did when I was a kid, and he got all quiet and weird. I've never seen him like this before."

"What did you ask him?"

"Nothing, really. When I was doing that research at the library, I came across an old newspaper clipping of him when he was with OSP. I asked him about this legislator he used to drive, and he clammed up."

"Who was the legislator?"

"A guy named Clifford Brigg."

"Never heard of him." Chuck was familiar with political circles through his father, but Brigg's time was long ago. He didn't offer to ask about him, and I didn't ask. Chuck and his father weren't exactly close; the former governor, Charles London Forbes, Sr., made little effort to conceal his disappointment with Chuck's career choice. "Did you try to talk to him about it?"

"Of course."

He looked at me skeptically. "For more than a couple of minutes?"

"A few." Having been on the other side of my impatience before, Chuck knew I had a tendency to give up when I was frustrated. "The more I pushed him to talk to me, the more he pushed me to lay off him and get off this case. Then we both realized we weren't getting anywhere."

"You Kincaids are a stubborn people. What did someone put in the water supply at that house?"

"Whatever the hospital put in your baby formula."

"You should try to talk to him about it again. But in the end, Sam, if he wants to keep something private, you need to respect that."

"I know. Honestly? I think the reason I haven't talked to him since then is that I don't want to see that look on his face again. It's like he was ashamed of something. Seeing that was absolutely horrible. I thought I was going to lose it."

The phone rang, saving me from having to talk anymore about my father. I kissed Chuck on the cheek on my way to the kitchen to answer it.

It was Slip.

"Sorry it took me awhile to get back to you. I spent my entire day down at Inverness trying to see Melvin. And people wonder why defense attorneys hardly speak to their clients."

"So, what'd you find out?"

"Well, I showed him the two pictures you gave me. He's never seen the old guy, but the younger one might be the worker who saw him take the paint."

"How good was the ID? And no puffing. You know I'm out on a limb."

"The truth? It could've been stronger. But it was probably just as good as any cross-racial ID your cops get before they firm it up for the courtroom."

Jackson hadn't ruled Minkins out. If he was high up enough with Gunderson to have hired Jackson, he could also be in on the setup. If, of course, there was a setup.

"Anything else?"

"My investigator's got some computer whiz working on the floppy disc. I'm going to feel like a total idiot if I wind up paying this guy out of my own pocket, and the disc turns out to be the family grocery list. And speaking of total idiots, that's what I felt like when Jackson asked me why I was showing him those pictures and I couldn't say anything. Now that I spent my Sunday with the other jailhouse groupies, why don't you let me in on the secret."

"Hold on a second." I made it look like I needed something from my desk and went upstairs so Chuck wouldn't overhear. "Got anything up your sleeve for court tomorrow?"

He laughed. "Yeah, my piece of shit watch. Prescott's obviously inclined to find PC, and I don't have squat. The best I can hope for is to buy more time."

More time was what we both needed. Getting anyone to take a second look at the case against Jackson was hard enough as things stood. If Prescott found probable cause without at least a bend in the road, it would be impossible.

"I'll tell you who the men in the pictures are if you'll do something for me. I've got an idea that might help both of us."

12

I WAS FINISHING some last minute prep in my office Monday morning when Jessica Walters walked in.

"Hey, there. Thought I'd stop in and see how you're holding up after a week in here with the boys."

"Crazier by the day, but I'm sticking it out."

"Good for you. You want to grab some coffee?"

I held up my Starbucks commuter cup. "Already went, but definitely some other time. I'm getting ready to go back in on the Jackson prelim."

The legal pad I'd been using on Sunday was at the edge of my desk, the top page barely legible from all the black ink. Walters saw it and laughed. "A woman after my own heart. Do those notes actually mean anything to you?"

I laughed too. "No. But maybe if you scribble enough, it's like a giant Rorschach." I held the pad up to her. "Tell me, Ms. Walters, what do you see in this one?"

She squinted at it, exaggeratedy furrowing her brow. "Let

me see." But then her expression turned serious. "Grice? You have a case on someone named Grice?"

"No, just a name that came up in an investigation."

"It's not Max Grice, is it?"

"Actually, I don't know the first name." I hadn't written it in my notes, and I hadn't called Nelly yet to try to get another look at the file.

"Oh-kay?" She said it slowly, inviting an explanation for why I wouldn't know the first name of someone involved in one of my cases.

"Why? Who's Max Grice?"

"A major pain in my ass is who Max Grice is. Some schlepper contractor who's been bitching to anyone who will listen about his business problems. I wanted to blow him off, but you know the boss. Any allegation of official misconduct gets a thorough vetting. I'm probably going to wind up letting the guy have a say in front of the grand jury, then I'll tell them to no-bill it."

"What kind of misconduct?"

"The guy's paranoid. I guess there's this process they have to go through to get permission to make certain changes to histor-ically significant properties, which includes just about every old building in the central corridor. His company's request got declined, and he's claiming that someone at City Hall's on the take, since other companies don't seem to have any problems."

"Why would that come to you?"

"It shouldn't. There's a city process the guy's using, and the police could potentially investigate the allegation as a crime if there were any meat there. But this guy called Duncan person-ally, so now I'm stuck trying to find a palatable way to dump it. Technically Gangs is the white-collar unit."

The reality, of course, was that this office had never prose-cuted a significant white-collar criminal. Those cases went to the feds, and the small-time embezzlers simply got away with it, the victims brushed off with an explanation that the theft was "a civil matter" or an "employment issue."

But now wasn't the time to hash out office filing decisions. I wanted to know more about Grice.

"So if someone called the switchboard and asked for whoever dealt with white-collar crime or government corruption or something like that, Liz would connect them to you?"

"She *should*."

"Then I think I know why Clarissa Easterbrook called you. Is Max Grice's company called Grice Construction?"

"I'd have to double-check, but that sounds right."

"Clarissa recused herself from a case where Grice Construction appealed an adverse decision relating to a remodel of a Pearl District warehouse."

"That'd be my guy."

And the guy was complaining about the very program that had been at issue in Gunderson's case in front of Clarissa. A case where Gunderson had won because of Clarissa's decision.

I looked at my watch. "I've got to go over to the Justice Center. But can you get me a copy of whatever you have on Grice?"

"No problem."

Roger was already waiting in the courtroom with Townsend. In the row in front of them, two men I recognized as Gunderson and Minkins sat with a lawyer type I assumed was Jim Thorpe. I should get a kickback for all the fees I was bringing in to Dunn Simon.

I noticed that four of the five of them watched me as I passed. Men tend to do that when there's nothing else going on. Although they all looked unhappy, Roger looked particularly pissed. At a formal level, I'd hidden my role in what brought them here, but Roger knew me well enough to suspect something.

The fifth guy, Minkins, was still wearing his hat and turned his head the *other* way when I walked by. That's what we lawyers call consciousness of guilt. Like a suspect who flees, Minkins was hiding something. I was pretty certain that the something was his snooping around at the library.

Judge Prescott walked out of her chambers promptly at ten. She noticed Gunderson et al. in the front row. "I see we've got some newcomers, but where, pray tell, is Mr. Szlipkowsky?"

"I haven't heard anything, your honor," I said, "but I'm sure he'll be here. He left me a message last night saying he had subpoenaed some additional witnesses."

I heard someone huff behind me and guessed it was probably Gunderson.

Prescott ordered her clerk to tell her as soon as Slip arrived and then headed back to her chambers. Some judges enjoy the chitchat that goes on with the lawyers before proceedings commence. Not Prescott.

Her departure left the courtroom awkwardly silent. Since I was supposedly an innocent, I figured I'd better play the role of cooperative prosecutor. When I walked back toward Roger and Townsend, I noticed that, once again, Minkins looked away.

"Hi, Townsend. How are you holding up?"

"Fine," he mumbled, "under the circumstances. Thanks." Then he went back to staring at the bench in front of him.

"Well, I don't think you'll have to testify today. The defense attorney said he served some subpoenas last night, but his message didn't say anything about calling you."

He just nodded. I was beginning to think he might actually be on something. Roger rolled his eyes at me. "I went ahead and told Townsend about the subpoenas. As you can imagine, Jim Thorpe called me right away when they were served."

"So I assume the two of you have talked about the possible

conflicts of interest involved. I mean, Dunn Simon is now representing multiple witnesses in the same case."

Big surprise. According to Roger, they'd already discussed the matter, and the whole lot were snug as bugs with the current situation. That's the problem with a rule that lets the conflicted lawyer be the one who discusses the conflict with the clients; I seriously doubted if Townsend had gotten the big picture. If he was in a position to understand how wrapped up Gunderson was in his wife's life, he wouldn't feel so comfortable about sharing a lawyer with him.

Before Roger got a chance to grill me about the coincidence of Slip's eve-of-hearing decision, I heard tennis shoes squeaking outside the courtroom. The door wrenched open, and in walked Slip, out of breath, using one hand to hold all his belongings while his other hand fumbled to fasten his belt buckle.

A nice person would have rushed over to help him. I bent over laughing.

"I'm sorry, but that looks really bad."

"And they say men have dirty minds. I was already running late, and then I got stuck at security. It's getting as bad as the airport down there."

He shoved his briefcase in my arms so he could finish the belt, then started to steer me into the hallway. We never made it to the door.

"Nice of you to join us this morning, Mr. Szlipkowsky." Prescott was out of her chambers and ready to go.

"My apologies, your honor. I was delayed at security."

"And yet everyone else managed to be here on time. Amazing. Don't let it happen again." As she was telling the sheriff's deputy to bring Jackson in from the holding cell, Slip continued to throw me eager looks. He definitely wanted to talk.

"I'm sorry, counselors, is there a problem?"

We both shook our heads like kids who've been caught roughhousing in the classroom. Whatever Slip had to say to me, it was going to have to wait.

Jackson took his place at the defense table, looking the worse for wear after nearly a week in jail.

Prescott called the case and put us back on the record. "OK, when we left on Friday, it was unclear whether the parties intended to call additional witnesses before I ruled. Where do things stand now? I see Jim Thorpe is with us this morning from Dunn Simon."

Thorpe started to rise, but Slip beat him to the punch. When a court's viewing a dispute cold, it's always better to get your side out first.

"Your honor, last night my investigator delivered subpoenas to Larry Gunderson and William Minkins. Larry Gunderson is president of Gunderson Development, which owns the property where Ms. Easterbrook's body was found and where my client was employed as a landscaper. Mr. Minkins is an employee at Gunderson and hired my client to work at the site. As I have investigated this case, it has become clear to me that both Mr. Gunderson and Mr. Minkins hold relevant evidence that casts serious doubt on the guilt of my client. Just to give you one example—"

Prescott cut him off. "Wait a second. No need to get into your proffer before there's been an objection. Mr. Thorpe, why don't you go ahead and approach? Your clients may remain seated."

"Good morning, your honor. Jim Thorpe from Dunn Simon, representing Gunderson Construction, its principal officer Larry Gunderson, and its employee William Minkins. I understand that your honor quashed a subpoena on Friday in this case after Mr. Szlipkowsky tried to haul in a member of the Metro Council for a fishing expedition. This morning, he's at it again with my clients. They know nothing about this case, have been pulled away from business on absolutely no notice, and wish to be relieved from this court's jurisdiction forthwith."

Forthwith? That's why big-firm lawyers often get their asses handed to them in jury trials. Who the hell says forthwith?

Prescott sighed and gave Slip a look to kill. I wasn't sure how she'd done it, but somehow it seemed as if her bun had been pulled back even more tightly during Thorpe's statement. "Now, Mr. Szlipkowsky, why don't you proceed with your proffer—"

"Excuse me, your honor," I interrupted. "I just wanted to make sure all the parties realized that the media are present in the courtroom."

I gestured toward Dan Manning from the *Oregonian* at the back of the room, sitting with a few others who presumably were also reporters. Cameras aren't permitted in Oregon courtrooms, and lawyers who don't spend a lot of time around the courthouse don't always recognize the media. Just me, trying to be helpful.

It got the response from Thorpe that I wanted. "In that case, your honor, we request that the proffer be delivered in chambers. Whatever Mr. Szlipkowsky is about to say is groundless speculation, and the damage to my client would be further aggravated if it were repeated in the media."

Thorpe, Gunderson, Minkins, Slip, and I followed Prescott through the door behind the bench. I got a better look at Minkins when he passed me. He could definitely be the guy from the library, but I still wasn't positive.

Since Roger was there as Townsend's attorney, he had to stay outside. All to the good, since he knew better than Thorpe how devious I could be. Jackson stayed put too. I'd long gotten used to the criminal justice system's practice of leaving the defendant at the counsel table, just in case he was beginning to think his presence was relevant.

Slip and I were at the back of the pack, and no one seemed to be paying attention to us. He scribbled something on the corner of his legal pad, ripped it off, and passed it to me as I walked through the door behind him. By then, Prescott was sitting at her desk, so I slipped the page into a folder. If the teacher caught us passing notes, we'd get the grown-up equivalent of detention, and whatever was on that piece of paper would be public information.

"Let's hear it, Mr. Szlipkowsky."

"Melvin Jackson is presumed innocent. So presume just for a moment, your honor, that someone *other* than Melvin Jackson killed Clarissa Easterbrook. If that's true, as I believe it is, then—let's be honest—that someone did a pretty good job setting up my client. My client was upset with the victim, he worked where the body was found, paint from his van was found on her dog, and then, of course, the weapon's the icing on the cake. As I delved into the question of who might be in a position to accomplish such a setup, I kept coming back to the construction site in Glenville."

Slip continued to spell out the coincidences for her. Jackson, his landscaping business a fly-by-night operation in the penny newspapers, suddenly gets a call from Minkins asking him to work on a multimillion-dollar project by Gunderson Development. Minkins sees him take paint from the property, and later that paint turns up on Clarissa's dog. When Clarissa's body is found at the property, it's Gunderson Development that makes sure the police get Melvin's name. And then it turns out that Jackson's not the only person with business in front of Clarissa Easterbrook; a case in which Easterbrook ruled on behalf of Gunderson had her troubled enough that she kept a copy of the case file under lock and key.

Prescott raised her eyebrows, clearly surprised by the amount of detail in the proffer. The problem was that the proffer was enough to raise eyebrows, but Slip still didn't have enough to tie everything together. It was, in Thorpe's words, pure speculation. Prescott's ruling could go either way. Convincing her to pull the trigger and put the witnesses in the chair would be a matter of strategy.

First, we had to sit through Thorpe's diatribe. "To suggest that my clients had anything whatsoever to do with Ms. Easterbrook's murder is outrageous. Mr. Szlipkowsky should be grateful that Mr. Gunderson hasn't sued him for slander." Thorpe handed the judge, Slip, and me copies of an affidavit signed by a Lee Block. I had to admit, I was impressed by the work Dunn Simon had done in the hours that had passed since the subpoenas were served. "As you can see," Thorpe explained, "Mr. Gunderson was in Bend, Oregon, looking at a property all day on the Sunday when Ms. Easterbrook disappeared. Mr. Minkins was in the casino at Chinook Winds until four P.M. that day. We are working on locating a videotape to substantiate that, and I'm confident we will have it by the end of the day."

The plan was working. Without even getting a ruling on the subpoenas, the attorney who refused to let me talk to Gunderson and Minkins informally had just locked them into alibis for the time of Clarissa's death. Go figure.

Having set up the facts he wanted to rely on, Thorpe launched into his argument. He took the predictable route, borrowing many of the same points made by Bow Tie on Friday.

I opened the folder on my lap to sneak a glance at the note that Slip had passed me. The man's handwriting was as sloppy as his attire, but I made it out: *Disc = finances of OHSU pediatric wing.*

I tried to pull my concentration back to Thorpe, who was using words like *ludicrous, preposterous,* and *farcical.* If Dunn Simon was charging by the word, he should have checked his thesaurus and added *cockamamy* and *wacky* while he was at it.

Why had Clarissa kept the financial records from Townsend's hospital wing in her safe deposit box? Maybe they were his backup records and she was keeping them for him, but would she really tell him about a safe deposit box that contained a video of Caffrey and her at a motel? If she wasn't holding them for Townsend, why was she holding them at all? It didn't make any sense.

"Ms. Kincaid. Does your office have a position on this?"

"I'm sorry, your honor. On what?"

Slip looked at me like I'd lost my mind.

"Well, as I understand it," the judge said, "Mr. Thorpe's principal argument is that the defense's argument is one big paranoid delusion and that, in any event, Mr. Szlipkowsky has failed to draw any kind of nexus between the folks at Gunderson and this supposed frame-up. Correct me if I'm misstating it, Mr. Thorpe, but he's essentially arguing that the starting point for the alleged conspiracy would have to be knowledge of Mr. Jackson's animus toward Ms. Easterbrook. And I haven't heard the defense articulate any reason to believe that the Gunderson company would have that knowledge. It happened to have a case decided by her, but so do hundreds of other companies doing business in the city. Before I rule, I'd like to hear where you stand on the motion."

Something about what she said was bothering me, but I needed to get the plan back on track. "Obviously, this is a matter for the court's discretion, your honor, but it strikes me that the issue we're looking at is different from the one your honor ruled on last Friday. The previous subpoena struck me as an attempt to introduce inflammatory information about possible activities in the victim's personal life, without ever tying those activities concretely to the victim's murder or to Mr. Szlipkowsky's client.

"Here, in contrast, Mr. Szlipkowsky has provided specific information that appears to raise questions that I would be inclined to pursue at least in some form prior to trial. Let me be clear: I am still confident of our case against Mr. Jackson. But what I don't want to see is a situation where we'll be dealing with these same issues down the road at trial in front of a jury who might be misled or confused. Quite frankly, if the court were to grant Mr. Thorpe's motion, my office might be inclined to serve grand jury subpoenas instead. In the event that possibility affects the court's exercise of its discretion, I thought I should be forthright about my intentions."

"Well, thank you, Ms. Kincaid, for your candor. It certainly wouldn't make sense to have the witnesses leave, just to return tomorrow for a grand jury session."

While I was getting brownie points for my honesty, Thorpe was working his way into the doghouse.

"That doesn't make any sense at all, your honor. If you decide to quash these subpoenas, you should quash any subpoenas that Ms. Kincaid might order in the future."

Prescott, Slip, and I just looked at him. In addition to being rude, Thorpe's statement was simply wrong. Courts live with the fiction that grand juries are independent of the judicial and prosecutorial systems. Convincing a judge to quash a subpoena to appear in court was one thing; convincing her to mess with the grand jury was quite another.

While Prescott corrected Thorpe's misunderstanding, I thought more about what was bothering me. Prescott was right. If Gunderson was behind this setup, he had to have known about Jackson's letters.

My immediate attention, though, was on the subpoenas. Thorpe hadn't thrown in the towel yet, and we were moving into part two of the plan, the good part.

"With all due respect, your honor"—lawyers should never say this, since what they're essentially saying is *I have no respect for you, your honor*—"I don't see how the court's decision about this hearing should be affected by something that the district attorney may or may not do in a separate grand jury proceeding. And if we're going ahead and playing that game, the reality is I can always instruct my clients to invoke their Fifth Amendment rights either today or at a subsequent grand jury hearing."

Oh, yeah. As I'd hoped, Thorpe had been the first to mention the Fifth Amendment. It was time for my move.

"Actually, your honor, on that point: I don't want to get too far ahead of ourselves here, but in the event Mr. Gunderson and Mr. Minkins are ordered to testify—either today or at a subsequent grand jury hearing—it strikes me that it may not be appropriate for the two of them to share counsel." I looked down at a PPDS printout. "I see here that Mr. Minkins is on probation for forging a check. His probation officer might not be happy about a failure to cooperate with a murder investigation—or gambling, for that matter, since Mr. Thorpe has said his client was in a casino just eight days ago. As a matter of fair process, Mr. Minkins should at least have an attorney who is thinking solely about Mr. Minkins's best interests."

They had good poker faces, but I could've sworn that Gunderson looked afraid, and Minkins looked mad. And they both looked nervous.

Prescott must have seen it too, because she suddenly displayed a decisiveness I'd never before witnessed in her. "I am not going to quash the subpoenas. Although I granted a similar motion filed by a different witness last Friday, I believe that the defense's desire to question Mr. Gunderson and Mr. Minkins is distinguishable. The questioning does not raise the same issues of privacy implicated by the earlier subpoena, and the defense has articulated a plausible nexus between these witnesses and this offense. Although it is not a nexus that has in any way been proven, I believe the defense should be entitled to at least question these witnesses further to determine whether they possess relevant exculpatory evidence. As for potential harm to the witnesses, Mr. Thorpe, you said so yourself: They can always invoke if they believe the questioning is likely to incriminate them."

Thorpe was clearly stunned, but he did his best to cover. "I'd like a moment to confer with my clients, your honor, to determine how they would like to proceed."

"Of course. We'll reconvene here in ninety minutes. And, with respect to Ms. Kincaid's observations about the appropriateness of joint representation, if either of your clients wishes to speak to me in chambers about that matter, I will be available and can assist in obtaining substitute counsel if necessary. Ms. Kincaid, you might want to stay nearby, in the event you're needed."

Prescott had gone one step further than I expected. If Minkins had missed the point of my earlier comments, Prescott's certainly set the stage for Minkins to jump ship.

As we left chambers, Thorpe said something to Roger, who then excused himself from Townsend, no doubt so he could accompany his partner and Slip's next witnesses back to some conference room at Dunn Simon.

"Roger, I was hoping we could talk before you leave," I said. "I need to speak to Townsend about something."

"Now's not exactly a good time, Samantha. Jim told me about the stunt you pulled back there. I don't know what you're up to, but don't say a word to Dr. Easterbrook while I'm gone, or I'll have your bar ticket. On my instructions, he's going home."

I stood by the door and watched them head down the hall. By the time they got to the elevator, Jim and Roger were already playing referees between Gunderson and Minkins.

I turned to my favorite flannel-and-cords guy. "Hey, Slip. You gamble?"

13

I WON THE bet. Minkins called Judge Prescott just forty minutes later from a pay phone in the lobby of the Dunn Simon building. Slip had guessed it would take an hour.

I spent some of the time talking to Slip. He gave me a copy of the spreadsheets he'd printed out from Clarissa's mystery disc. Based on a quick scan, I had to agree that nothing interesting popped out, except, of course, the fact that the data had been password-protected in a safe deposit box.

I thought about the security system on the Easterbrook house. Maybe they were cautious enough to keep something as innocuous as a backup file under lock and key. But would Clarissa really stow a copy of her husband's file alongside a video of a tryst with her boyfriend?

I spent the remaining half hour thinking about everything I had learned about Clarissa this week. Based on what I'd heard, it was hard to imagine that she'd sell her office to someone like Gunderson. But ultimately I could picture it. After all, there had been times when I wondered whether the cops and lawyers

I knew were always squeaky clean. You never know how a person's circumstances might affect their decisions. A few years of pushing through the morass of boredom I saw in Clarissa's files, and your average person might not see the harm if a couple of arbitrary, meaningless decisions went the wrong way.

So what had been Clarissa's circumstances? Maybe she felt guilty about her affair and wanted the money—if in fact there had been any money—to make it up to Townsend. Or maybe the money was to help her leave Townsend and start a life with T. J. Caffrey.

Judge Prescott's clerk finally saved me from my aimless speculation when she told me about the call from Minkins.

Prescott handled the stress well. She made a quick call to Thorpe to confirm that he was aware of Minkins's decision, then found the nearest defense attorney in the hallway to stand in as counsel. The short straw went to Lisa Lopez, one of the most liberal cop-haters in the PD's office. If you need a defense attorney who can cut through the crap and pull a recalcitrant defendant to the plea table, Lopez is a pain in the ass. But here, we'd paint the picture of a down-on-his-luck chump-change cheat, eager to flip the switch on the big bad white-collar criminals in exchange for a walk. Lisa'd be all over it.

Prescott gave Lisa a chance to talk to Minkins alone. I called Minkins's probation officer to make sure I wasn't missing anything. The PO had never heard of him and told me to do what I needed to do.

A half hour later, I was sitting with Lopez and Minkins in a jury room. Lisa cut to the chase. "Before he says anything, I want full transactional immunity," she said.

She knew that was impossible. Transactional immunity is the brass ring of plea deals, and no one ever receives it. Hand that over to a defendant, and he can boast of every bad thing he ever did, and you can never touch him for any of it.

"First of all, you know that's not going to happen," I told her. "More important, you know that what I'm willing to give him depends on what he's got to say."

"Are you in a position to give him a walk?"

I was nervous about making a deal without talking to Russell. But if I called him now, not only would I look weak, but he might screw things up and stop the flow of information. I steeled my courage. This was no different than what I'd done hundreds of times before with drug informants.

"Again, it depends on what he's got to say. Can he give me PC for murder?" With probable cause for someone other than Jackson, I'd have enough to make arrests and obtain search warrants.

"No," she said without hesitation, apparently surprised that I had even entertained that as a possibility. Minkins eyed her suspiciously, and I got the feeling that he would've offered to say whatever was necessary to save his ass.

"No promises," I said. "You've got to take your chances or take the stand. Up to you."

Lisa nodded at Minkins, and he said what he had to say.

"First off, I got nothing to do with anyone dying. Swear to God, to this day I still don't know what the fuck's going on. But far as I can tell, you think someone set up this Jackson for a fall. As to that point, what I can add is that Larry handed me the dude's number a couple weeks ago and told me to hire him. Didn't matter what the terms were. Gunderson owed a friend a favor, and that meant I had to get Jackson on-site. Turned out not to be a problem. The guy jumped at it."

"Did he say who the friend was?" I asked.

"No clue."

Most likely a cover story Gunderson gave Minkins just to get Jackson on the property.

"Anyway," he continued, "Jackson gave his information to a

girl we use for personnel-related stuff, and that's about all I had to do with him. Then Friday I'm working at the site late, checking out the status of things, and I see Jackson packing away some paint into his van. I didn't recognize him, so I asked the guy his name. I remembered it from when Larry told me to hire him, so I told him, Go ahead and take it. Then I called Larry."

"What was his reaction?"

"Nothing special. Just thanked me for telling him about it. Next thing I know, we got a body on our hands Monday and Jackson's getting arrested for it."

"Why didn't you call the police?"

"So I'm not a good Samaritan. Sue me."

I wasn't buying it. If his decisions today said anything about his behavior generally, Minkins was self-interested. No way did he sit there silently while Gunderson dragged him into the middle of this.

"You're leaving something out. How'd you wind up at the library?"

He pursed his lips and looked at the ceiling. "So you did make me. I was beginning to wonder."

Sucker.

"When I saw the news about Jackson, I asked Larry what the fuck was going on. All he said was—and I remember this—'Take a lesson from it, Billy, and keep your mouth shut.' Scared the shit out of me. So I started doing some snooping around of my own. Figured if I got the goods on whoever pulled that shit on Jackson and the lady judge, they couldn't pull anything on me."

"And what did you find out?"

"Not a lot. I know Larry's leveraged up the ass trying to keep the bills paid. And I know you were doing some serious research into the urban growth boundary."

"You're still not telling me why you were following me, Billy."

"It was stupid, OK? I watched the news Friday about the hearing, and they said something about there being a shooting at your house last month. I was thinking about trying to work something out with you, so I went by Saturday morning, just because I wasn't doing nothing else. Then I saw you driving away. Next thing I know, I'm following you around the library. When I saw what you was working on, I realized I didn't have a fucking clue about what was going on, and I was like to get myself in more trouble than be able to help myself."

"But now you're coming clean anyway."

"Well, when you said what you said earlier, I figured it was about the only choice I had. Larry sure as hell ain't gonna take care of me."

It sounded credible. I could see a guy like Billy Minkins feeling desperate enough to follow me around while he tried to figure out what to do. Thanks to the local news, anyone who was curious could find out what block I lived on from a search of the Internet.

"Did you tell Gunderson about the library?" I asked.

"No way. I hightailed it out of there and laid low. I ain't saying I'm perfect. Hell, it's not like I'm blind—it's not every businessman who's gonna let a guy like me take care of an operation. But no way did I sign up to be in the middle of a murder trial and whatever crap led up to it."

"You certainly don't sound like someone who trusts Larry Gunderson. How'd you hook up with him anyway?"

Minkins let out a chuckle. "AA. Court-ordered after my check-writing scheme went awry. I couldn't get work after that, and Larry'd been in the program for years. Fucking ironic, ain't it?"

There's a reason guys like Minkins wind up in the system. Instead of taking some responsibility for the decision that led him to this room, he had found a way to blame it on the only chance a court had given him to get his life under control. But Minkins seemed to think I liked him, so I kept my mouth shut.

"Do you know of any connection between Gunderson and Clarissa Easterbrook?"

"Other than her body being found there? Nope."

"Do you know anything about Gunderson paying bribes or kickbacks to her or any other public officials?"

"Nope, but I wouldn't put it past him."

"Are you going to bother telling me what you're fishing for, Kincaid?" Leave it to Lisa Lopez to think she's not doing her job unless she butts in every once in a while.

"Me telling you what I think isn't part of this deal," I said. "What matters is your client telling me what he knows, and I'm trying to make sure he's done that."

I asked a few more questions, but I couldn't get anything more out of him.

Lopez could tell the debriefing was coming to a close. "There you go, Kincaid. Billy never even broke the law, so I want assurances that he doesn't face potential prosecution. And his PO better not jam him up, either."

"But he hasn't given me anything, Lisa. He said it himself. He doesn't know what happened."

"You've got more than you had before. And he might not know all the details, but that's because he doesn't have anything to do with it."

She was right. That's the problem with our system of flipping. Those who have the most to trade are the ones least deserving of a break. If Minkins was telling the truth, he had some serious moral shortcomings but he wasn't a murderer.

"Fine, but only after he passes a poly."

Billy Minkins had his own priorities. "And I want some protection."

"Explain it to him, Lisa. I'm not exactly running a witness protection program here."

"Fuck that noise," Minkins said. "I get the impression you don't know any more about what's going on than I do. You turn me loose after Gunderson knows I cut a deal, and I might wind up like that judge of yours."

Shoot. Why didn't I think of that?

There was only one way to swing this, and it all depended on how badly Billy wanted protection. As it turned out, he was more scared than I thought.

Lisa and I told Prescott's clerk that we were ready and returned to the courtroom. Thorpe and Gunderson were already there, presumably waiting for Slip to call Gunderson to the stand pursuant to the subpoena.

"We're back on the record," Judge Prescott made clear. "Mr. Minkins has chosen to proceed with separate counsel, and he is now present and represented by Lisa Lopez. The motion to quash the subpoenas served upon Larry Gunderson and William Minkins is quashed. Mr. Szlipkowsky, you may proceed to question your witnesses."

This had happened too quickly. I hadn't had a chance to talk to Slip. I crossed my fingers and hoped that the fifty-fifty odds would fall my way.

"The defense calls Larry Gunderson to the stand."

I exhaled a sigh of relief, and Jim Thorpe rose. "Excuse me, your honor. It was my understanding that the purpose of the prosecutor's conference with Ms. Lopez was to determine whether Mr. Minkins was offering testimony that would warrant an offer of immunity to him. As your honor is well aware, such conferences often invite fabrications, especially where—as in Mr. Minkins's situation—the person being questioned is on probation and therefore subject to the whim of law enforcement. It only seems fair that my client should know what occurred in that conference before being questioned."

Somewhere along the road, when I wasn't looking, Prescott had truly come into her own. Without asking any guidance from the other attorneys, she reached the right conclusion. "Mr. Gunderson is merely a witness in these proceedings, not the accused. He has no standing to request information about other witness's potential testimony. Please instruct your client to take the witness seat."

Thorpe whispered some last minute advice in his ear and Gunderson took the stand. Short, round, and balding, he might have appeared jolly under happier circumstances. But here, his expression was stern but concerned as he repeated the same response to each of Slip's questions: "On the advice of counsel, I decline to answer pursuant to my Fifth Amendment rights."

Although typically the bane of my existence, today the words were music to my ears. Larry Gunderson, the supposedly disinterested landowner, was invoking his rights. It was better than anything I could have hoped for.

When Slip had finished his list of questions, he called Minkins to the stand. To everyone's surprise (well, maybe not everyone's), Minkins also invoked his Fifth Amendment rights. When the questioning was done, I rose.

"Your honor, at this point, I would request that the sheriff's deputy place Mr. Minkins in custody on a probation detainer pursuant to the request of his probation officer."

"This is ludicrous, your honor." I wasn't surprised at Lisa's acting skills. Having seen her profess her faith in her clients time and time again in court, I knew she could pull it off. "Ms. Kincaid is obviously penalizing my client for invoking his Fifth Amendment rights."

"Ms. Lopez is forgetting, your honor, that Mr. Minkins was a defense witness, not a suspect. The State is continuing to pursue its case against the defendant, Melvin Jackson, and is simply informing the court of a decision by the probation department. The probation officer has already faxed a formal detainer to the sheriff's department. He is concerned about Mr. Thorpe's earlier representation about Mr. Minkins's whereabouts at the time of the offense. The witness is on supervision for a forgery that arose from an alcohol and gambling addiction."

Moments later, Minkins was led away in cuffs, where he'd be safe and sound in a relatively clean and comfortable county holding cell until I told his PO it was time for a hearing. It wasn't the Four Seasons, but it provided the protection Minkins was after.

Larry Gunderson's head looked like it was about to explode. My guess was that he had been tempted to perjure his way through the questioning, but was smart enough to play it safe once he assumed that Minkins had given him up. It's nearly impossible to make your way through an interrogation when you don't know what cards the questioner has already drawn. Any screwups would be under oath and on the record, preventing him from wiggling around at a trial down the road.

Lisa threw me a glance before leaving the courtroom. Other lawyers might have worried about the long-term repercussions of crossing another attorney, especially one as powerful as Jim Thorpe. But Lisa Lopez, ever the true believer, did what was best for Minkins.

"Unless someone has further need of Mr. Thorpe and his client," Prescott said, "the two of you are free to leave as well." They almost looked surprised when no one spoke up.

With the witnesses gone, Prescott asked Slip if he had any additional witnesses.

"No, your honor."

"Rebuttal, Ms. Kincaid."

"None."

Slip and I went through the motions on argument. He wove the strongest conspiracy story he could given the information he had. I stood by my case against Jackson, emphasizing that any questions about possible conspiracies must be decided by the jury. If anyone from the office called Prescott to check up on me, it would look like I'd played my proper role in the system. I wasn't looking for a dismissal against Jackson, just enough of a reaction from the court to get my office's attention.

When we were done arguing, Judge Prescott gave me what I needed.

"All right, I don't know what exactly happened in here today, but I'm ready to rule."

When I got back to my office, I was greeted by a note on my chair. *See me ASAP. And, no, that doesn't mean after a quick run.—Russ.*

I didn't go for a run, but I did take a second to check my voice mail: two defense attorneys, a victim, and my father. Since I had changed my outgoing message to say I'd be in court all day, the callbacks could wait.

In Russell's office, I did my best to look worn out from my crazy morning. "Hey, there. I'm finally out of the Jackson prelim." I held up the note he'd left for me.

"What the hell's going on over there? Your gem of an ex-husband called Duncan a couple of hours ago claiming you were sabotaging your own case. Something about you telling the defense attorney to subpoena some clients you called him about over the weekend?"

Russell had been good to me so far, so I almost felt bad

about lying to him. Almost. "Roger's got his head up his ass. The defense subpoenaed the same witnesses I asked him about, because anyone giving a second thought about this case would be asking the same questions. If anyone should be in trouble, it's him. He's thinking more about the other clients than he is about Townsend."

"Sounds like a conflict," he said.

"I thought so too, but apparently all the clients signed off on it."

"So what was the end result?" he asked.

"Prescott found probable cause, but not without a fight. She said on the record that the defense had raised serious questions about whether we had the entire story, and that we skated through only because the standard of proof's so low. Oh, yeah, and the media were in the courtroom."

"You're fucking shitting me."

"I shit you not. After the morning I've had, I am in a strictly nonshitting mode of communication." I did my best to sound upset, but now I had the office right where I needed it. No way would Duncan permit the bureau to continue ignoring the evidence pointing to Gunderson.

"I'm almost afraid to ask: Who are these witnesses?"

"Larry Gunderson, who owns the Glenville construction site, and Billy Minkins, who works for him."

"For the love of God, Kincaid. Not this again. The defendant's mom says one thing to you—'my boy ain't never had a job so good'—and ever since then you can't let it drop."

His Mrs. Jackson impersonation wasn't half bad.

"It's more than that, Russ." But before I got a chance to explain it all to him, his phone rang. Checking the caller ID, he decided to answer it.

"Hi, Duncan . . . Yeah, she's right here. . . . No, Prescott found probable cause, but it's a little more complicated than that. . . . OK, yeah, we'll be right down." Russ hopped out of his chair as he hung up. "I'll do what I can for you, Samantha, but if I were you I'd hold my nose and pucker up, because you've got some serious ass-kissing in front of you."

In the couple of minutes it took to run down the back stairs to Duncan's office, I managed to give Russ at least the big picture. I left out the part about my role in steering Slip's action, but I did tell him about the contents of Clarissa's safe deposit box and Gunderson's stake in the urban growth boundary.

"So what's your theory?"

"I'm not done telling you everything yet."

"*Reader's Digest* version, Kincaid. Duncan's waiting for us."

"I think Clarissa had some kind of deal with Gunderson where she agreed to rule in his favor on his appeal. I also think that Gunderson has a lot to lose if the urban growth boundary doesn't expand in Glenville, and that Clarissa's affair with Caffrey had something to do with that. For whatever reason, though, Clarissa was thinking about blowing the whistle—"

A voice cut me off. "Where the hell are they?" Shit. It was Duncan standing in the hallway, apparently counting the seconds to make sure we weren't dillydallying.

"I think that's for us, kid," Russ said. "Let's do this."

My pulse started to accelerate the minute I sat on Duncan Griffith's leather sofa. If what they say about state-dependent learning is true, his office would eventually begin to trigger an automatic gag reflex in me.

He wasn't helping to calm my nerves. "Sounds like you've had a busy morning, Samantha."

"Yes, although not nearly as chaotic as Roger Kirkpatrick apparently led you to believe. Russ told me that Roger called you."

"Well, he called me, but the bigger problem is Jim Thorpe, who called the chief of police, the mayor, and everyone else who was willing to listen. The way I understand it, Kirkpatrick's pissed on behalf of Townsend, because he doesn't want to see the prosecution of his wife's murderer derailed. And Thorpe's pissed because his client's being dragged through a three-ring circus. Do you want to explain to me why you're sabotaging your own case?"

"I did nothing of the sort. The defense threw us some curve balls today, and I still managed to swing the probable cause finding." It was hard to keep a straight face with the sports metaphor.

"According to Kirkpatrick, you called him Sunday afternoon asking to talk to this Gunderson fellow. Then, when he said no, lo and behold, the defense attorney ups and subpoenas the guy. You want to explain that to me?"

I gave him the same version I gave Frist—the one where Slip and I are equally savvy and wind up on the same track. I also gave him a rundown on what Minkins had confirmed about Gunderson and what I still suspected.

By the time I was finished, Duncan's eyes were pressed shut, his right palm pressed against his temple. "That's one a hell of mess, all right," he said, his eyes still shut. Then, opening them to look at me, he said, "We'll talk about your role in this in a second, but first things first. Russ, the last time I checked, you were working this case too. What do you think?"

"I don't like it," Russ said. "But I think the defense has dug up enough that we have to look into it. If we ignore it, Szlipkowsky will haul it all out in front of a jury, and we'll look like we're steamrolling a poor black guy to cover up some white-collar dirty laundry."

For a second, I thought I'd stroked out and was having delusions. I looked down. Nope, I was still wearing panty hose and my calves were still puffy. This was definitely not heaven. But my supervisor was actually defending me to our boss.

"You guys can't possibly be telling me that you buy this conspiracy theory shit," Duncan said. "Planted evidence, for Christ's sake?"

"I don't know what to think," I said, "but I agree with Russ. We can't ignore it. How many times have I heard in this office that only the guilty lawyer up? You should have seen Gunderson in there. He invoked to every question. He's definitely hiding something, and if he takes the Fifth in front of a jury, we're toast. Jackson will walk, and so will any hope we have of trying someone else for the same crime."

Duncan thought about it, his prosecutorial instincts kicking in. Prosecutors share a belief system resembling a kind of secular faith, and a central tenet of that system is that a witness who invokes is hiding something. Maybe not the thing you're looking for, but something. In our church of prosecutors, it's the equivalent of *the truth shall set you free.*

"Help me think this thing through," he said. "If it's all connected, the victim and Gunderson had some kind of arrangement, and Gunderson killed her because she was planning to talk?"

"Right," I said. "I think it went beyond that one appeal Clarissa heard. I think her affair with Caffrey fits in somehow. He's a swing vote on whether to expand suburban development, an issue Gunderson stands to profit from. A lot. It would explain the videotape Clarissa had of her and Caffrey coming out of the motel. Maybe she was blackmailing him but couldn't go through with it."

"And they set up Melvin Jackson as the bad guy?" Russ asked.

"It certainly wouldn't be the first time a white criminal took advantage of stereotypes." We'd all seen the stories before. When that woman sunk her kids in the river, the first thing she said was that some black guy took them—and everyone immediately believed her.

Duncan did not look happy. "Well, I guess we're going to need to look into this guy's business dealings, but the police aren't going to like it if it means trashing the case against Jackson. Any possibility the guy had a deal with the victim but *didn't* set up Jackson?"

"I don't see it," I said. "If Gunderson was bribing Clarissa, it's too much of a coincidence that Jackson winds up working for Gunderson and putting Clarissa's body there."

Russ was shaking his head. "No, there is a way. You told me early on, Sam, that you thought Clarissa felt sorry for Jackson, at least initially, right?"

"Right. She had notes in her file showing she'd done some legal research trying to find a theory she could use to rule for him."

"OK," Frist continued. "So what if you're right, and she's on the take with Gunderson? Maybe she calls in a marker of her own and gets Jackson the job."

Minkins did, after all, say that Gunderson had told him he was hiring Jackson as a favor to a friend. I followed Frist's theory. "But Jackson didn't know that, of course, and is still pissed off about his eviction."

"He kills her, dumps her at the site, and everything else falls into place."

"Except the part where Gunderson tells Minkins to keep his mouth shut when Clarissa's body turned up," I said.

"But think about it. Gunderson knows he's crooked on the bribery scheme, and all of the sudden the other half of the equation winds up dead on his property. Maybe he used it to scare Minkins into staying quiet about the Jackson hire, which might have shown a connection between the victim and the company."

I completed the thought. "Which might've revealed whatever quid pro quo they had."

"Or maybe Minkins made that part up," he added. "It wouldn't be the first time an informant threw in a little extra to help the case."

Man. First Russ defends me, then he outsmarts me. It's a crazy world, this one we live in. A world where Clarissa Easterbrook might have used her position with Gunderson to help out Jackson, only to have him kidnap and murder her.

I was frustrated that I hadn't seen it earlier. I had been so focused on figuring out the connection between Gunderson and Clarissa that I had just assumed that it was related to Clarissa's death. But I had never been able to figure out how Gunderson knew about Jackson in order to frame him.

Russ's scenario gave our office a reason to send the cops back out to work: We still think Jackson did it, we could say, but we need to find out what Gunderson was up to so the defense doesn't blindside the jury.

The truth was, my gut was telling me that I'd been wrong about Jackson. He did it. I'd never forgive myself if Slip actually got Jackson off using information I'd hand-delivered.

"The way things stand now," I said, "I think we need to get MCT back on this right away." I told Duncan about Prescott's comments in the courtroom and the near certainty that the news would be breaking imminently.

"That's just great. She had to make sure that my day was fully fucked. All right, here's the deal. Thorpe's got everyone's attention on this thing. I'm supposed to meet at City Hall this afternoon with the MCT lieutenant, the mayor, and the city attorney to determine how to proceed."

Noting our looks of disbelief, he said, "I know, it's overkill. But the bureau already took an embarrassing hit on this case and doesn't want it going down the drain, the city attorney's worried about getting sued, and the mayor—well, the mayor's probably going to make sure we don't all kill each other. If I had to guess, with so many offices involved, it could take a couple days before anything happens, but Jackson's not going anywhere, right?"

I shook my head.

"The defense attorney's not going to make any noise?"

I shook my head again. "But are you going to make MCT follow up on the Gunderson angle?" I asked.

"Like I said, Kincaid, I doubt anything's going to happen for a couple of days."

"But, in a couple of days, that's what you're expecting, right?"

"Not that I owe you an explanation, Samantha, but no, I wasn't planning on asking MCT to look at a possible corruption case, because that's not MCT's jurisdiction. We'll get the bureau on it, and we'll get some answers by the time of trial, but that's good enough for now."

Now I saw Duncan's take on the situation. If the corruption involving Gunderson wasn't related to the Jackson murder case, there was no reason to start a beef with MCT about opening a closed case. The problem was, the bureau wouldn't be under the gun to see the Gunderson investigation through.

"Duncan, I think it *is* appropriate to ask MCT to do the work. It's Jackson's defense attorney who's trying to set up Gunderson as the killer, so it's the detectives on that case who are going to be motivated to get to the bottom of it. If they find out that Gunderson was bribing Clarissa and blackmailing Caffrey but didn't set up Jackson, everyone will be happy."

"You don't get it, Samantha," he said. "MCT's not going to be happy about anything that makes this case any more complicated than it needs to be. And if we ask them to look into Gunderson Development, it looks like we believe there's actually a

connection between Gunderson and the murder. And we don't."
His point was a good one, but I wanted the work done well, and
I wanted it done soon. "And, for the record, Sam: slight problem claiming Szlipkowsky came up with these witnesses on his
own. How'd he know to serve the subpoenas on Jim Thorpe?"

Crap. I thought Slip had served Gunderson and Minkins
directly. Apparently, he was willing to flirt with unconventional-
ity, but wasn't about to bypass retained counsel. The problem,
of course, was that it looked like his knowledge of the representation came from me.

I couldn't remember saying anything to Slip last night about
Thorpe. But I did remember something else.

"Probably because Jim Thorpe represented Gunderson
Development on the appeal in front of Clarissa. His name was
in the file Slip found in her safe deposit box."

Duncan didn't like it, but he knew he couldn't prove I had
done anything wrong.

"Anything else?" he asked.

The last thing I wanted to do was set him off. But I couldn't
let him go into that meeting without telling him about Minkins's immunity deal and the OHSU financial records in the
safe deposit box. If those facts eventually came out later, he'd
look foolish in front of the bureau and the mayor, and whoever
put him in that position—namely, *moi*—would pay the price.

"Well, there's a few other details you should probably know
about," I said.

"Details? Why do I have a feeling that, coming from you,
Samantha, those details are going to be something like a pin
that fell out of the grenade?"

I told him about my secret immunity deal with Minkins.

"Did you know about this, Frist?"

"No, sir, I didn't."

I couldn't bear to look at him.

"Big surprise," Duncan said, shaking his head. "Before I lose it, let me get this straight: You let a witness invoke on the stand, knowing you had given him immunity, without telling the defense attorney? No, forget about the defense attorney, without telling the *judge*?"

I never thought about it that way. I knew I was keeping something from Gunderson, but I didn't owe him any information unless and until he was a criminal defendant. I had thought about Slip at the time, but figured I'd explain it all to him later, and he wouldn't mind under the circumstances.

But, from a technical perspective, I had misled the court. Once a witness has immunity, he's got no Fifth Amendment rights, so technically Minkins should have answered all of Slip's questions. Even if Slip didn't mind the lost opportunity, Judge Prescott wouldn't be pleased that I used her courtroom to dupe Gunderson.

"It seemed like a good idea at the time."

"See, that proves we've got a problem, Samantha. You're better than that. I know you've got a tendency to go your own way, but this is something different. I don't know if it's the new caseload, the ex-husband, the mess that went down last month— but for whatever reason, you've lost your judgment on this one."

I couldn't hold my tongue any longer. "No, I haven't, and this is no different from what goes on around here every day. We can do whatever we want on our cases as long as no one's paying attention, but the minute someone raises an eyebrow, we're second-guessed at every turn. And if you're not part of the club, you're third- and fourth-guessed. And now it's even worse, Duncan, because you've personalized it. Maybe I've made some mistakes, but don't suggest there's something wrong with my motives."

"You're the one choosing to make it personal, Samantha. You need to take emotion out of this."

If I had a dollar for every time a pissed-off man told me *I* was being emotional, I wouldn't have to deal with angry men any more. Apparently rage is only an emotion when combined with estrogen.

"I'll call Judge Prescott and take my licks, but I don't hear anyone suggesting what I should have done as an alternative. If Gunderson *was* involved in Clarissa's death, telling him that Minkins flipped wouldn't just jeopardize our investigation, it would've put our informant at risk."

Duncan was no longer in the mood to argue. He didn't need to; he was the boss. "I'll give some thought to all this, Samantha, but right now we both need to cool our heels. Until you hear further: Russ, you handle anything having to do with Clarissa Easterbrook. And call Prescott. It's better she hear about this from you as the MCU supervisor."

I had expected Duncan to kick me off the case. Maybe it was even the right thing to do, given some of the calls I'd made. But having Frist apologize to a judge for something I'd done? I started to interrupt, but Duncan signalled for me to keep quiet.

"No, Samantha, I'm not risking it. If you're not apologetic enough, she's just going to pick up the phone and complain to me. If you're lucky, she'll figure you're in enough trouble at home not to report you to the bar."

I shook my head.

"I know what you're thinking. If you want to resign, that's up to you. Alternatively, you could turn your attention and your talent to the many other cases assigned to you. Your decision."

All the earlier huffing and puffing aside, it had come down to this—the ultimate trump card. Unfortunately, Duncan had seen me in action enough these past weeks to know that, when push came to shove, I'd rather put up with the crap I take here than fight over corporate money with attorneys like Roger and Jim Thorpe. Maybe Grace would give me a job sweeping up hair at Lockworks.

"I'll let you know." Then I walked out of his office, leaving him there with Melvin Jackson's new prosecutor.

I had hoped to be out of the building before Russ made it up to the eighth floor, but he managed to catch me while I was still getting my things together. One more reason not to keep such a messy office.

"Don't worry about the call to Prescott," he said. "I won't make you look like a jerk."

"I think Duncan already took care of that," I said, throwing my pumps in my gym bag. One of them didn't quite make it in and hit Frist in the leg.

"Easy now. For what it's worth, it would've been a lot worse if Duncan didn't actually like you."

"If you didn't notice, I just got kicked off my first murder trial," I said, pulling the pictures of Vinnie and my family from my corkboard and tucking them safely away in my briefcase, just in case.

"Yes, but you walked out with your job and the case on track, and with very minimal ass-kissing. I know you'd rather hang on to it, but I won't bungle it."

"Better not," I said, laughing, while I pulled my rain slicker on.

"You're obviously going somewhere, but before you leave, why don't you let me in on the parts you edited out for Duncan."

I did my best to look confused.

"Cut the shit, Samantha. I can tell you're leaving something out. If you need me to go into cross-examination mode, I'll point out that you told Duncan there were some details you left out. As in plural. And you clearly had more to say to me before we got pulled into Duncan's, but I don't think it was the secret immunity deal, because you obviously didn't realize it was going to be so explosive. So spill it: What were you saving up for last?"

What the hell. He'd stuck by me so far.

"Earlier, I thought it was a big deal, but now that you've convinced me I had my head up my ass"—he laughed too—"anyway, it's probably nothing, but the safe deposit box that had the videotape and the Gunderson file?"

He nodded.

"Well, the one other item in the box was a password-protected floppy disc containing the budget information for Townsend's new hospital wing."

"And how does that fit in with everything we just talked about downstairs?"

"It doesn't. If you're right, it just so happens that Clarissa stored a backup of her husband's data in the same place as the other things. But, earlier, it made me wonder if maybe Townsend had something to do with it. Maybe Gunderson coughs up money for the hospital in exchange for Clarissa's help, something like that."

"And he lets her sleep with Caffrey so she can deliver his vote for Gunderson? I don't see it."

Me neither. On the other hand, according to everyone who knew him, the pathetic guy we'd been talking to the past week wasn't the same man Clarissa Easterbrook had married.

We talked it through but kept going around in circles.

When I finally retrieved my gym bag from under the desk, Russ handed me my briefcase. "So where *are* you going, if you don't mind me asking?"

I wasn't ready to answer that question yet. "Sounded like Duncan was going to steer the meeting toward a holding pattern. Let the news sink in and the personalities calm down."

"I know," he said. "I was there, remember?"

"It may have been a mistake to drag Gunderson into the murder case, but now he knows we're looking at him on the bribery. Not the best situation for the preservation of inculpatory evidence."

"You mean Slip's mistake," he said.

"Right."

"Well, you heard the boss: Nothing's happening until decisions get made at the highest level," he said, like we were still shooting the breeze.

"But maybe someone could poke around a little on the side. Just to see what falls loose," I said.

"Maybe."

"You mind if I take the rest of the day as personal time?"

"Not if you need it," he said. "Just tell me what you find out."

14

By the time I got to Metro Council headquarters, Terrence Caffrey's office was already locked down. Metro was probably only a part-time legislative gig.

I took a chance and drove past the address I had copied from the mailing envelope Slip had found in Clarissa's safe deposit box. T. J. Caffrey and his family lived in a brick colonial just a couple of houses south of Reed College. A woman—probably Caffrey's wife—was planting bulbs along the front walk. A minivan and a Toyota Avalon were parked in the driveway.

Two cars hopefully meant two drivers.

I wanted to talk to Caffrey alone, but I was willing to do it the hard way if necessary. I parked my Jetta around the corner on Woodstock Boulevard, confident that it blended in among the students' cars across from the library.

I looked at my watch. I'd give it an hour before I knocked on the front door.

Fifty-five minutes later, the front yard was empty, my stomach was in knots, and my self-imposed boldness deadline was preparing to bend. Chuck had been paging me, and I hadn't called him back out of fear that he'd convince me to take the night off and abandon my stakeout. Then I got lucky.

The gardener walked out the front door holding a toddler and a Meier & Frank shopping bag, yelling back to someone inside. A little boy—probably four years old—followed her. She strapped them both into the minivan, threw the bags in front, and drove off.

I didn't know how many kids Caffrey had, but most folks stop at two nowadays. Then it dawned on me he might not even be there. What woman in her right mind takes her children on a mall run when she could leave them at home with their dad?

There was only one way to find out. I mustered my courage, got out of the car, marched to the front door, and panicked.

Just when I was about to bail, Caffrey opened the door. "I thought I saw someone. Can I help?—Oh, Ms. Kincaid. It's you."

He looked down the street, no doubt to make sure the missus had left.

"I'm not trying to cause you any problems."

"As I know you're aware, my lawyer quashed that subpoena."

"Well, that's just it. The subpoena was served by the defense to require you to testify under oath at the preliminary hearing. I just want to talk to you, but I need to know if you're still represented."

"Ronald Fish is my lawyer. I'm sure you remember the very uncomfortable meeting we had Friday morning."

Of course I did, but that wasn't what I was getting at.

"I guess what I'm asking you, Mr. Caffrey, is whether you hired an attorney specifically because of the subpoena, or are you telling me that you've retained counsel to defend you in all matters involving Clarissa Easterbrook?"

Caffrey was savvy enough to know that, as I had worded it, the latter sounded bad. It sounded—well, guilty. By now, he may even have heard the news about witnesses taking the Fifth at the prelim. In the news, they always make that sound like a confession.

I was taking advantage of a loophole in the rule against contacting a represented party, but I was squarely on legal ground. And I had no respect for a guy who was more worried about his own political future than the murder of a woman he'd been sleeping with.

"No," he said, without hesitation. "I thought I should have a lawyer for the courtroom proceedings, but I've got no problem speaking to you informally. Within limits, that is. I've only got about ten minutes."

He was giving me a warning signal. I needed to be gone before the wife came home. Press too far, and I'd be out of here. With the rules of the game defined, he asked me in.

"Since time is short, I'm not going to waste it pushing you to answer a question I think we both know is pointless." As I spoke, he folded his hands in his lap and looked down at them. At least he seemed to have some shame about his cowardice. "I think Clarissa got herself in trouble on one of her cases at work, something to do with Gunderson Development. And I also think she talked to the City Attorney about it."

"Gunderson Development had a case in front of Clarissa?"

I told him about the file, including the note about Clarissa's conversation with *DC*. The skin on his hands creased as he tightened the resistance in his fingers. I was on to something, and he was surprised by it.

I went for broke. "Clarissa also had a videotape of the two of you leaving the Village Motor Inn, and it was in an envelope addressed to this house. She was blackmailing you, wasn't she?

Was it so you'd leave your wife, or was she trying to pressure your vote for Gunderson?"

He was no longer surprised. He was downright flabbergasted. He was looking at me like I had just invited him to a fund-raiser for Satan.

"No?" I sounded pitiful.

He shook his head, then said what his expression had already made obvious. "Clarissa was *not* blackmailing me."

"But you do know something that might be related to her death." I could state the obvious too.

When a few moments passed and he realized that I wasn't going to interrupt the silence, he finally spoke up. "Clarissa wasn't perfect. No one is."

"Is that why you haven't said anything? With all due respect, making sure we get the guy who killed Clarissa is a hell of a lot more important than preserving her reputation."

"I've been tearing myself apart. When she first disappeared, I didn't know what to do. But then it sounded like the evidence against Jackson was so strong, I felt I'd be dragging Clarissa through the dirt for no reason."

The fact that he got to keep his own name clean may have factored in as well.

"Look, the case against Jackson is strong, but the defense is arguing that someone set him up. I started to believe it myself, but it looks like whatever Clarissa had going with Gunderson wasn't involved in her death. But I think it did have something to do with your upcoming vote on the urban growth boundary."

"If it's not related to her death, why does it even matter at this point?"

"I hope I don't need to explain to you, of all people, that if Gunderson was blackmailing or bribing a public official, he should be punished." The argument seemed to fall on deaf ears.

"And if we don't find out for ourselves what was going on between Clarissa and Gunderson, then the defense attorney can use innuendo and speculation to confuse the jury at trial. I don't want Jackson to walk."

The possibility of Clarissa's murderer going unpunished seemed to be more persuasive. "It doesn't have anything to do with my vote." He was clearly insulted at what he perceived as the insinuation. "Clarissa never talked to me about that. Just like I never tried to tell her what to do on her cases. But I think she did have a connection to this Gunderson you're talking about."

He stopped, but I did nothing to disturb the silence.

"A few weeks ago, she told me she rigged an appeal for someone. I don't know the details of the case, but I know she ruled in his favor when she shouldn't have. I was shocked when she told me. It was totally unlike her."

"Did she tell you why she did it?"

"No. I think she only told me because she was worried about something else, some newer problem. She said the arrangement was supposed to be the one case, but it hadn't ended at that. They wanted something else, but she wouldn't say what. I begged her to talk to me about what was going on, but she wouldn't. She said she was going to handle it herself."

"How was she handling it?"

"I'm not sure. I know she went to Dennis Coakley so she could clear herself from any other cases where she might be pressured, but I don't know if she told him the full extent of what she did. The next thing I knew, she said she had figured out a way to get out of the position she was in, but that there was a risk that people would learn about—well, about our friendship."

"Did she talk to anyone else about it?" I asked.

"Not that I know of. I doubt it. She was incredibly embarrassed. Ashamed. She was trying to find a way to get herself back on the right track without losing everything. God, in retrospect, it explained why she'd been so damn . . . *good* those last couple of weeks. You know she actually felt sorry for that monster?"

"For Gunderson?"

"No, for Melvin Jackson. Well, she never told me his name, but she did tell me his whole sad story. She called HAP to see if zero tolerance really meant zero tolerance. She called SCF to see if he was really going to lose his kids. Hell, she was even talking about finding the man a job to make sure he'd be on his feet when he was evicted. At the time, I asked her why she didn't just rule in his favor. But that was before I knew she'd already gone down that road before. I guess she wasn't willing to bend the law again, even for what she thought was a good cause."

Despite what Clarissa had done for Gunderson, I respected her even more now that I knew what she'd gone through. She died doing everything she could to turn her life around, looking for redemption by helping a man like Melvin Jackson, a man who showed his gratitude by bashing her head in with a hammer.

"How long had you been . . . close?" I asked.

"Almost seven months." It was clearly painful for him to talk about this, and I had allowed the conversation to get off track. Just then, my pager vibrated. Chuck again. I turned the thing off.

"When she said people might find out about your friendship, I imagine that must have alarmed you a great deal."

"Perhaps not as much as you might think. I had very real feelings for Clarissa. Think what you want about me, but she was truly a decent person. She was under so much stress—the guilt over what we were doing, combined with whatever she was involved in—I could tell it was tearing her apart. Obviously,

I pressed her to tell me what our relationship had to do with her problem, but she refused. In the end, I told her to do what she had to do."

"When was that?"

"The Friday night before she disappeared."

I tried to think of any other information I needed from him while he was being so cooperative. I had a newfound respect for cops. This off-the-cuff stuff was much harder than the questioning I was used to with a legal pad and the artificial setting of a courthouse on my side.

"I know I gave you my assurances that I wasn't going to push on certain topics, but there's one other thing I need to know." I explained the ME's report of nonoxynol-9 in Clarissa's vaginal canal. "It's very intrusive, I know, but is it possible that was due to her relationship with you?"

He bumbled around awkwardly trying to find the right words, but he finally got the point across. He and Clarissa had used a condom on Friday night.

"We met—well, let's be frank—we met at the hotel you mentioned on the videotape you found. Her husband was at the hospital late." I noticed he didn't use Townsend's name. "She was in good spirits, although a little nervous. She said that on Saturday she was finally going to clear herself from this problem she was having. I braced myself all weekend for some news, wondering if I needed to sit down with my own family. But then I woke up Monday to the news she was missing. I still can't believe I'll never see her again."

"I can't believe you didn't come forward." The words must have leaped from the most spiteful part of my brain, straight out the mouth, no filter. I regretted saying them aloud immediately, but I didn't want to feel sorry for this man. Whatever he said, he had betrayed not only his wife and children but also Clarissa.

Instead of throwing me out of his house, Caffrey made me feel even worse. "I suppose it's understandable that you judge me. Certainly it's nothing I haven't done myself."

I got into the car trying to find some satisfaction in the facts I'd confirmed: Clarissa was on the take, the nonoxynol was Caffrey's, and it looked like Clarissa had gotten Melvin the job with Gunderson.

But then I realized that Caffrey had raised as many questions as he'd answered. If the spermicide was from Friday, why was Clarissa's sweater off when she was attacked? And if Clarissa was tired of being tangled up with Gunderson, what was she planning to do on Saturday to sever the ties?

Clarissa had gotten home from shopping around seven, but we'd been so focused on Clarissa's whereabouts on Sunday, we'd never pressed Townsend about whether anything had happened Saturday night. And I couldn't talk to Townsend without going through Roger.

But I wasn't totally out of the game yet. Roger may have told me to stay away from his client, but there might still be a way to find out what he had to say.

Raymond Johnson picked up on the first ring.

"Hey, Raymond. Samantha Kincaid."

"Your ears burning?"

"No. What's up?"

"You've been quite the topic of conversation around here today. The lieutenant's at City Hall now for the big powwow. I assume you know about it."

Johnson must not have heard I was off the case yet. There was no point telling him now, since it would only put him in a difficult situation. "I think everything's under control."

"News to me," he said. "Last I heard, you were floating conspiracy theories about Jackson being innocent."

"No, the defense did that. I helped convince Prescott to hold Jackson over for trial. We need to make sure we can counter everything the defense is saying, that's all. Duncan will work it out with your lieutenant."

"I hope that's it, Kincaid, because we believe in this case, you know."

"I realize that. We're on the same side here, Johnson. It's just a matter of cleaning up some details."

"Just making sure. Now, you were actually calling me about something, weren't you?"

"Yeah. The defense attorney was making noise this morning about Townsend, but while everything's up in the air, his lawyer's not letting us talk to him. Do you have a copy of his polygraph examination?"

"Sure. We always get those if they're willing to turn it over. The guy he used is top-notch. Retired FBI."

"I want to see what he asked. See if there's anything there about what Clarissa did on Saturday, maybe in the background questions."

"Not that I remember," he said. "She went to Nordstrom with her girlfriend."

"I know that. I just want to see the questions and answers, OK? I'll be there in about fifteen minutes."

The polygrapher had included eleven items: eight dummies and the three money questions. Just as Roger said, the three critical questions put Townsend in the clear: Were you at OHSU on Sunday? Did you kill your wife, Clarissa Easterbrook? Did you hire, solicit, order, or ask anyone to kill your wife, Clarissa Easterbrook? Yes, no, no. Truthful on all three.

For current purposes, I was interested in the dummies, hoping to find something about whether Clarissa had left the house Saturday night or whether they'd had visitors. Unfortunately, the questions weren't helpful: name, birthday, address, the basics. Nothing detailed a timeline.

If Townsend knew what Clarissa was up to with Gunderson, I wasn't finding that out with this polygraph. If he weren't represented, I could probably shake him up with the little I already knew, but I wasn't anywhere close to having the goods it would take to rattle Roger. I suppose that's why people hire lawyers.

I was going to have to live with the fact that I might not be able to wrap this one up by myself. There were other people who could handle the wrapping just fine. Russ Frist was at least as capable as I was, and he'd make sure that my stunts with Szlipkowsky wouldn't ruin the Jackson prosecution. I didn't have complete confidence that the bureau would make the Gunderson investigation a priority, but Russ knew some questions needed to be answered before the Jackson trial. Once those answers started rolling in, I had to believe that someone would pay attention—Jessica Walters, or maybe the Attorney General's Office. Maybe Duncan would even let me get involved again.

But for now, I thought as I pulled out of the Justice Center parking lot, I was tired of beating my head against the wall. I had lingering issues in my personal life to deal with, too.

Tension with my father was foreign to me, and I still hadn't figured out a way to move past it. But he had extended the olive branch by calling me this morning, and I owed it to him to return the gesture.

I don't know why I did it, but, perhaps for the first time in my life, I knocked on the front door of the house I grew up in.

"Hey, look at you. What a surprise. Come on in. Did you lose your key?"

"I couldn't find . . . I just wasn't sure . . . well, you know."

He gave me a sad smile, and my eyes welled up looking into his. Then he got teary-eyed too, and that did it. I burst out crying in front of my father for the first time since I had walked in on Roger and then driven straight to my parents' house.

Just as he had then, he sat me on his couch, put his arm around me, and rocked me, telling me everything would be OK before I'd even told him what was wrong. When I finally quieted down to the point of quiet sniffles and deep breaths, he asked me what happened and why I wasn't at work.

"Nothing," I said, wiping my cheeks with my sleeves, "it'll be fine. I just want to be here right now if that's OK."

"It's more than OK. It's a treat. You hungry? I could make something."

I still hadn't eaten lunch, but it wasn't even four o'clock. If I ate dinner now, I'd be hungry again before bed, then I'd be up all night. "That's all right," I said. "Can you stomach a couple hands of cribbage?"

My mother had been the cribbage player, passing the habit down to me so she'd have someone to play with other than my father, who never hid the fact that he played only to make her happy.

After I soundly trounced him, he insisted that I begin to shuffle more thoroughly. I was on my sixth waterfall when I finally brought up my reason for being out of the office in the middle of the afternoon. I didn't bog him down in the legal details, but I gave him the gist: I'd persuaded the defense attorney to raise a stink about a bribe the victim was taking, and now I'd been tossed off the case.

To his surprise, though, when he started in on Duncan, I

actually defended the decision. "I don't know, Dad. It might've been for the best. For a first homicide case, it was probably a little too much for me to handle on my own."

"You were doing the right thing, but it happened to lead you to the doorstep of some people who don't want a hard-working prosecutor looking into their business deals. Who knows? Duncan may have pulled you off because he's in the pocket of this guy—what did you say his name was?"

"Gunderson, Dad. And Duncan can be political, but he's not on the take."

"You'd be surprised, Samantha. The people who get into a position like Duncan's—most of them would sell their own mothers to get an advantage. This is exactly what I was worried about. You challenged the wrong people, and now they won't be happy until your credibility is run into the ground."

Just then, my pager buzzed. I didn't recognize the number, so I ignored it.

"No one's trying to ruin my credibility, Dad," I said, shutting off the signal. "I got removed from *one* case, and it was because I blew it. I got so wrapped up in the Gunderson angle that I forgot who the bad guy was. I used Jackson's defense attorney to prove my hunch was right, but in the process I handed him a defense theory that might get his client acquitted."

Dad nodded to appease me, but I could see that he disagreed.

"I can tell something's on your mind, Dad. Go ahead and say it."

He chose his words carefully. "You said you forgot who the bad guy was, but I don't see what's good about this Gunderson fellow. Even if you're right and he didn't set up Jackson, that doesn't make him a good guy."

Now it was my turn to sigh with exasperation. "All I meant was that he wasn't as bad as Jackson." He looked at me skeptically.

"Oh, come on, Dad. Gunderson slipped a low-level city judge a few bucks so he could develop some old building. Jackson *killed* a woman. There's no comparison."

"But that's how these people get away with things, Sammy. There's always someone out there who's scarier, who's more threatening. And every time someone whose heart is in the right place—someone like you—finally starts to go after the white-collar types, out comes a bogeyman to prey on the public's darkest fears. As long as the world's afraid to walk in their neighborhood at night because of Melvin Jackson, guys like Gunderson can always say, 'Hey, I'm not so bad. The police should be going after that guy over there.'"

"But Jackson *is* worse. If my probing around Gunderson means Jackson gets off, it wasn't worth it."

Dad shook his head.

"What?"

"I just don't buy into the assumption that there has to be a trade-off. That sounds like something Griffith came up with so he could sweep his pal Gunderson out of the mess you were about to create for him."

"It doesn't have to be a trade-off, Dad. He said he'd make sure the bureau looked into it."

"But who in the bureau's going to do that? I mean, you're always talking about how good Chuck is at his job. Will *he* be the one to work on it?"

"No," I conceded, "because it's not under MCT's jurisdiction."

"Right," he said. "It'll go to some overburdened detective who's got his hands full of burgs and car thefts and whatever other property crimes have been thrown at him. You won't stand a chance of making a case stick against Gunderson."

This conversation was echoing some of the broader debates we'd had about the allocation of law enforcement resources.

I knew how frustrated Dad was, for example, that some of the highest-profile white-collar perps remained unindicted years after their scandals erupted. And I knew he saw a link between corporate practices that thwart the American dreams of every-day workers and the desperation that causes people to rob, sell drugs, or even kill, like Melvin Jackson. To Dad, economic crimes and street crimes were inseparable, each feeding the continuation of the other.

"I don't get it, Dad. You originally begged me to stay away from this case because I might wind up stepping on the toes of someone with influence. But now it sounds like you want me to go after Gunderson."

"The only reason I was worried was that I knew something like this would happen if you started scrutinizing the wrong people. And, sure enough—"

"You told me so?" I said, with a small laugh.

"No," he said, also laughing. "I was worried that if some-thing like that were to happen, your office wouldn't back you. That's what I meant when I said 'sure enough.' So, yeah, some-one needs to go after Gunderson, but it should be someone who's not going to get hung out to dry."

My pager buzzed again, the same number as before. Some-one was being terribly pushy, considering I didn't know them well enough to recognize their phone number.

"Duncan said he'll get the bureau to look into it," I said. For an attorney who makes her living persuading people I'm right, it was lame. Even I didn't sound convinced, and, from Dad's expression, he clearly wasn't either. "OK, so maybe it's going to fall through the cracks," I conceded. "At this point, I can live with that."

For only the second time in my life, my father looked disap-pointed in me. The expression had been there for just a moment, but it was enough to bring me back to that day in second grade, when the principal called him after I teased the poorest girl in school for wearing the same jeans three days in a row.

"What, Dad? What do you expect me to do?"

"I want you to take care of yourself, Samantha. But, in the process, don't tell yourself something you know isn't true."

"So you want me to be self-interested but mad about it? That's totally messed up," I said, laughing.

He smiled, but his eyes were still serious. "You've always had a way of putting things."

And he had always had a way of forcing me to acknowledge the truth. I knew in my heart that Gunderson wouldn't be indicted, and I had tried to comfort myself that an ending with Gunderson walking away would still be just. It wouldn't.

I rose from the couch, kissing the top of his head.

"You're heading out?" he asked, surprised. "I thought you'd stay for dinner."

"Not tonight. But don't worry. I'm good."

Before I could even take out my cell phone to call the impatient pager, the device hummed again, this time to the number we used to dial into the office voice mail system, followed by my extension. Apparently someone wanted me to check my messages.

It was Russ Frist. "Don't ignore your pager again, Kincaid. Next time it might be a murder call-out. I know you're officially off the case, but I wanted to let you know that Duncan called me. He met with the bigwigs all afternoon and laid out where we stand. The agreement is to ask the defense to stipulate to a continuance while the Attorney General's corporate affairs department investigates Gunderson. I'll let you know if I hear anything else."

He left his home number in case I needed anything. "Oh . . . and I'm assuming you're coming back to work tomorrow. I noticed you took the pictures from your corkboard, but maybe you're out buying new frames for them with your time off."

I would indeed be in tomorrow, but I wasn't going to wait for the AG's office to do something. I may have gotten kicked off of the Jackson case, but I wasn't going to stand by while Duncan and the bureau found a way to ignore whatever Gunderson and Clarissa had been up to. I hit the 9 button on my keypad to save Russ's message, just in case I needed him later.

15

IF I WAS going to get any answers, I needed more information so I could ask the right questions. I drove straight to City Hall.

I had just missed closing time, and security wouldn't let me in. But I got lucky. Clarence Loutrell actually answered when I called his office.

"Judge Loutrell, it's Samantha Kincaid from the District Attorney's Office."

"Oh, sure, from the other day. Yes, well, would you mind calling tomorrow morning? My secretary left for the day. I picked up because I was expecting my wife."

"I'm sorry, sir, but I'm afraid it can't wait."

"Unless it's a real emergency, I'm afraid it's going to have to. I was just about to head home for the evening. Promised to help at the house with some things. You know."

Actually, I didn't, since I did just about everything myself. But Loutrell didn't need to hear about my domestic issues.

"That's fine. I'll call tomorrow," I said. Too bad for him, he didn't know I'd already checked with security. After five, all employees had to exit through the Fourth Avenue doors. I planted myself on a bench across the street in the park, hoping he meant it when he said he was leaving soon.

As it turned out, he must have walked out right after we hung up. I jaywalked across traffic to catch up with him at the corner, pulling out a copy of Clarissa's memo from my briefcase while I walked. He didn't hide his dismay when he saw me.

"I'm sorry, but I really do need to speak to you. I'll talk as you walk to the car if I have to." I handed him the copy of the memo. "Apparently Clarissa had a discussion with Dennis Coakley about an appeal filed by Gunderson Development. She cared about it enough to lock a copy of the file and this memo in a safe deposit box. I need to know why she took such a special interest in the case, and I thought, as chief administrative judge, you might have some idea."

I left out the fact that Nelly overheard him with Coakley arguing over whether to tell me about it. Nelly said that Loutrell sounded like he wanted to talk to me, so I hoped I could get what I needed without diming Nelly up.

"I'm sorry, but if Clarissa had such a discussion with Dennis— and I'm neither confirming nor denying that she did—the conversation would clearly be privileged." He was walking so quickly I had to alter my stride to a slow jog.

"And, I'm sorry, Judge Loutrell, but now Clarissa's dead."

"Attorney/client privilege survives the client's death." I got the impression he was parroting back the words he'd heard from Coakley.

"It does, but unlike the City Attorney, you never represented Clarissa Easterbrook. You're just her coworker. Even if her conversations with Coakley were privileged, what you know is fair game if she came to you about her concerns first."

He knew I was right about the law. On the other hand, he was still thinking through what Coakley might say in response. One more push would do it.

"If it makes a difference, I already know, but I need confirmation." That one always worked on my junkie drug informants, and it was enough at least to get him to stop walking. "Clarissa was biased on the appeal. She ruled for Gunderson as a favor of some kind. That's why she recused herself from a case filed by Grice Constuction. Grice was complaining about unfairness in the urban rehabilitation project, and Clarissa knew from personal experience that at least one company was getting preferential treatment."

Still nothing. If the push didn't do it, maybe a shove would.

"I can have a grand jury subpoena at your house this evening, but I really don't think that's going to be necessary."

I pictured him imagining the scene at home tonight if I followed through on my threat and his wife were to learn that it was preventable.

"All you need is confirmation?"

"Yep." I couldn't believe I was actually going to get it.

And, sure enough, I didn't. "Well, too bad," he said. "I can't confirm something so completely ridiculous. She may have talked to Coakley about the case, but you are entirely off base. My God, what you're suggesting is offensive."

See how that works? In the course of denying the part of my theory that surprised him, he had confirmed the rest of it.

"But she did talk to Coakley about the Gunderson case. Why?"

He looked at his watch, looked at me, then rolled his eyes. "Coakley can be nuts about privilege for reasons I don't always understand. But you're right. She came to me first. She said she had something she needed to talk to me about. She'd ruled on a case a few months earlier without realizing that the claimant had donated money to her husband's hospital wing. If she'd known about the potential conflict at the time the case was assigned to her, she should've recused herself. I told her to talk to Coakley to see if he wanted to reopen the case. I won't tell you that part of the conversation, since he thinks it's privileged, but, let's just say that the Gunderson case wasn't reopened, and Clarissa recused herself from the Grice matter because of the potential appearance of a conflict."

"I get the impression that you don't share Coakley's concerns about privilege."

Loutrell shrugged. "Dennis is Dennis. He sees potential city liability around every corner, but he's well-intentioned. I actually considered calling you last week about this. The media were insinuating that something was going on between Clarissa and T. J. Caffrey—which I know nothing about, by the way—and for some reason the conversation with Clarissa stuck in my mind."

"I'm missing the connection," I said.

He shook his head quickly as if to shake the suggestion away. "Not a connection, really. It was just that Clarissa seemed so serious about the matter when she raised it with us, particularly when she was talking about how important the hospital wing was to her husband. She seemed unreasonably upset by the situation, considering how innocuous it was. I think my imagination got the best of me, and I started wondering if maybe the entire situation had something to do with the state of her marriage. By the time Coakley spelled out his bogus privilege concerns, it just didn't seem like anything worth bothering you about."

People don't realize that a criminal case is rarely built on a single piece of evidence, relying instead on tens and hundreds of clues in context, each by itself insignificant. Too many helpful witnesses show up late in the game, because they didn't want to bother the police with insignificant information. In the meantime, the wackos flood the phone lines with visions and premonitions.

Clarissa may not have given Coakley and Loutrell a full-blown admission, but at least I was on the right track.

From City Hall, I made a stealth pop into my office to grab copies of the Gunderson case file, the information Jessica Walters had copied for me detailing Max Grice's complaints, and the financial records for the hospital wing. Within thirty minutes, I had gathered everything I needed for my research and was nestled back in my home office and ready to start filling in the missing pieces.

Based on Jessica's notes about Max Grice, he wasn't a happy camper. At the heart of his discontent was a woman named Jane Wessler, city licensing official for the Office of Landmarks Preservation at City Hall. Three years ago, as a nod to preservationists, the office had designated an area surrounding the train station an historic district, seeking to protect the small neighborhood from the warehouse-to-luxury-loft conversions that marked the nearby and rapidly expanding Pearl District. As a result of the designation, the Railroad District, located at the eastern edge of trendy northwest Portland, still remains an enclave for starving artists, aging hippies, and other eccentrics who are happier in the neighborhood's traditionally industrial atmosphere than with high-end yuppified retail, restaurant, and residential development.

One year after the designation, however, the preservation office created a licensing provision that permitted developers to obtain special-use licenses for approved "urban renewal" projects that were consistent with the architectural history of the Railroad District. For the first sixteen months of that program,

Jane Wessler was in charge of deciding which projects qualified as special uses. Grice's three proposals, in her view, did not.

Grice, however, was persistent. After seeing several similar projects in the neighborhood approved, Grice filed a request under the Oregon Public Information Act for the names of all companies who applied for special-use licenses and for Wessler's determination on each application. Using the data, Grice had tried to make the case to Jessica Walters that Wessler was on the take. I looked at the list he had compiled. Maybe there was a trend; a few companies were three for three while Grice had no luck at all. But I could see why Jessica had decided there was nothing criminal; with so few examples, it was impossible to tell if it was just coincidence.

According to Jessica's notes, Grice had resubmitted his applications after Wessler left for a yearlong maternity leave, but the city had refused to reconsider the original decisions. That must have been the appeal from which Clarissa had recused herself.

I took another look at Grice's list. No mention of Gunderson.

Next, I turned to Clarissa's copy of Gunderson's case file. I'd read through it when Slip had first shown it to me in his office, but I wanted to see how it fit together with Grice's complaint. Gunderson's Railroad District project had also been rejected by the city, but by a different licensing official, a month after Wessler went on leave. Unlike Grice, however, Gunderson had appealed, and Clarissa had reversed the decision.

Then I spread out the pages of financial information Slip's investigator had printed from Clarissa's password-protected disc. The text at the top of each page identified the spreadsheet as the budget for the Lucy Hilton Pediatric Center. Lots of money coming in, but no substantial expenditures yet. That made sense, given that the center was still in the planning process. From what I knew, the project had been dropped at

one point because of the bad economy, but Townsend had res-
urrected it as his baby.

Whatever he was doing, it seemed to be working. There were
pages of entries for donations, large and small, from individu-
als, corporations, and the major local foundations. But no
money from Larry Gunderson or Gunderson Development.

I took a break and grabbed a Diet Coke from the kitchen.
This time Vinnie followed me upstairs, sprawling himself
beneath the desk near my feet. When I stopped scratching him
behind his ears and returned to my documents, he looked up at
me and snorted. It was as close as he could come to saying,
"Snoozapalooza."

"Tell me about it, little man," I said, rubbing my eyes with
the palms of my hands. For some reason, Clarissa had kept a
copy of the Gunderson file, Townsend's financial records, and
the videotape of her and Caffrey together under lock and key. If
there was a connection, where was it?

I studied the list of the hospital donors again and finally saw
it: a name. The MTK Group had made a donation of $100,000
to Townsend's pet cause. I reopened Jessica's file on Grice.
There, on Grice's list of companies affected by the decisions of
Jane Wessler, was the MTK Group: three renewal projects in
the Railroad District, and every one of them approved. So what
the hell was the MTK Group?

I called the corporate filing division of the Secretary of
State's office, hoping to get the company's basic registration
information, but their business hours were long over. Then I
called information, but there were no listings under MTK. I
even tried an Internet search. Bupkes.

I cross-referenced Grice's list of development companies
with Townsend's list of donors but didn't find any additional
overlap.

More than ever, I missed the resources of the U.S. Attorney's

Office. What I needed was access to LEXIS/NEXIS. From what I could remember, NEXIS's public records database included corporate filing information from all fifty states. Unfortunately, Duncan never saw fit to include the service in the office's budget. If we needed legal research, we did it the old-fashioned way.

Out of desperation, I pulled up the LEXIS/NEXIS Web site on my computer and tried my old federal password. Part of me was relieved when it didn't work. Getting busted by the feds wouldn't exactly help my current professional standing.

Then I remembered that the computer research sites all give free passwords to law students and judicial clerks. It's the legal profession's equivalent to a dealer handing out drugs on the playground. Once the kids are hooked on an easy fix, they'll pay anything for more.

I found Nelly Giacoma's home number where I'd jotted it in the file.

"Nelly, hi, it's Samantha Kincaid from the District Attorney's Office."

"Oh, hey there. Congratulations on your PC determination. I heard about it on the news."

"Thanks. It was pretty much what we expected, though."

"Right," she said. "So did you ever figure out what the key was that I gave you?"

"We did, actually, and that's sort of why I'm calling. Clarissa had some documents in a safe deposit box. I'm trying to make sense of them, but I need to do some NEXIS research."

"Um, sure, I don't see why not. I'm not doing anything tonight anyway."

What a trooper. "No," I said, laughing. "I don't expect you to do it for me. I just need to get onto the system. Believe it or not, you lose all that fancy stuff if you join a prosecutor's office."

"You're kidding. How do you get anything done?"

"I usually manage, but I need to look at some public records that are hard to get after business hours. Do you think it would be OK if I used your password?"

She didn't need to think about it long. "What the hell? It's not like it costs the city anything, and I hardly use it anyway."

I jotted down the series of letters and numbers she gave me, thanking her profusely before I hung up.

First, I perused the Public Records library. This was perfect. I had access not only to the corporate registry information of all fifty states but to records of all civil court judgments and property liens filed.

I looked up the information that MTK had filed with the Oregon Secretary of State. According to the filings, the president of the corporation was Carl Matthews. The name didn't ring a bell. I searched next for Gunderson Development. Larry Gunderson was listed as both the president and secretary of the corporation, which usually signaled a one-man operation. The Gunderson listing also included an entry for a former corporate name of Gunderson Construction, Inc., as well as for Gunderson Construction's bankruptcy dissolution years earlier.

I switched to the database of recorded judgments. That's when my search got more interesting. Typing in GUNDERSON DEVELOPMENT had yielded nothing, but my search for the former GUNDERSON CONSTRUCTION turned up twenty-seven civil judgments, each one representing a judgment *against* the company. No wonder the guy had filed for bankruptcy. On the fourteenth hit I had a connection, a judgment of $126,000 against Gunderson Construction in favor of the MTK Group.

So ten years ago, Gunderson and MTK had enough business together that it led to a judgment against Gunderson. Now they were both doing business in the Railroad District. MTK had obtained Railroad District development licenses from Wessler and had given money to the hospital wing. Clarissa had helped

Gunderson get a license to build in the Railroad District and had kept a copy of his appeal in the same safe deposit box as the hospital wing records. But if there was a connection between donations to the hospital wing and licenses to develop the Railroad District, how did Gunderson manage to win his appeal without donating to the cause?

I turned back to the screen and accessed the news files. Then, starting at the top of the list of Townsend's donors, I ran search after search for any *Oregonian* articles containing the word GUNDERSON and the name of each donor. Somewhere there had to be a link.

The work was tedious, but it finally paid off. A couple named Thomas and Diane Curtin had made a generous donation of $50,000 to the hospital wing. According to the announcement of the Curtins' marriage two years ago, the generous wife was the daughter of Portland developer Larry Gunderson.

Having grown up in Portland, I know the place can be incestuous. People joke that it's more like a big room than a small city. But my head was beginning to hurt from the points of connection among Gunderson, MTK, the Railroad District project, the urban growth boundary, and Townsend's new hospital wing. I did my best to keep track of them, drawing lines and making notes until I finally gave up and threw my pen at the wall of my office.

After I apologized to Vinnie for the disturbance, I took another look at my list of players and the various lines between and among them. If Clarissa had sold her ruling on Gunderson's appeal in exchange for the donation, what, if anything, did she have to do with the MTK Group?

I jumped back to the corporate registrations to see if either Larry Gunderson or Carl Matthews, the president of MTK, was registered as an agent or officer for any other corporations. It wouldn't be unusual for a small businessman to be associated with more than one company over his lifetime.

My search for Gunderson's name turned up only the listings for Gunderson Development and Gunderson Construction, but Carl Matthews's name also yielded two results: one for the the MTK Group and one for a company called Columbia Holding Company. I clicked on the hypertext of the company name.

The first few lines of the entry showed that Columbia Holding Company was an inactive Oregon corporation, with a corporate filing date nearly twenty-five years ago. When I scrolled down farther, I had to reread the text twice to make sure my eyes weren't playing tricks on me. The secretary of the now defunct company was Carl Matthews, current president of the MTK Group. The president was none other than Herbert Kerr.

I had found my connection.

Susan Kerr's Mercedes was parked in her driveway. I had risked a complete waste of time by driving up without calling ahead, but I knew from experience that surprise confrontations were my best chance of getting information from the uncooperative. Susan was the link. She was Clarissa's best friend. She was connected to Carl Matthews and the MTK Group through her husband. And she had been helping Townsend raise money for the hospital wing. It couldn't be a coincidence. She had to know more than she was telling. But, once again, she was protecting her friends and maybe even herself.

I circled the block to steel my resolve. I wasn't going to accept any lame stories about shielding Townsend in his grief or defending Clarissa's memory. It was time for someone involved in whatever this scheme was to flip, and the someone was going to be Susan. If I had to haul her into a grand jury tomorrow, I'd find a way to do it, Duncan be damned.

I'd gotten myself good and pumped up and was ready to home in for the kill when I registered a faint buzzing sound. It stopped, then started again. My cell phone. I must have forgotten to turn the ringer on after I had silenced it during court.

It was Chuck.

"Hey, sweetie. Can't talk right now. I'm in the zone."

"The zone for what? Ignoring everyone close to you?"

I looked at my watch. How did it get so late? "I'm sorry. I completely lost track of time."

"I've been trying to call you all afternoon. I think I scared the bejesus out of your father. I called him freaking out about where you were, but I guess you'd just left there before I talked to him. You all right?"

I looked at the tiny screen on the face of my cell phone and, sure enough, saw a little envelope indicating unchecked messages.

"I'm fine. The day's just been a little crazy."

"More than a little crazy, babe. I was running around all day on a rape out in Rockwood, but when I got back the guys were in a tizzy about something that happened at the Jackson prelim."

"Really, it's fine. Roger got pissed about something that happened, Duncan took me off the case—"

"What? No one told me that. You're not fighting it?"

"No. Look, Chuck. I promise I'll explain everything to you later. Tonight, even, if you're willing to come over." I realized as I was extending the invitation how nice it would be to curl up with him and finally relax tonight. "I'll call as soon as I'm out of here. I promise."

"And where exactly is *here*?"

"Nothing important. Just an interview, something I've been meaning to take care of." I didn't have time for the riot act he'd surely read me if he knew my errand related to the Jackson case. I could tell him the full story after I saved the day.

"Fine," he conceded. "It'll give me time to call your father and apologize for getting so freaked out."

"One quick flip of a witness, and I'll be done in time for Mexican take out and margaritas?"

"Ooh, now that sounds good."

"It's a plan. I'll call you in probably thirty minutes."

I flipped the phone shut, turned the corner, and parked next to Susan's Mercedes, still in the zone.

I rang the doorbell, and Susan peeked out through a small window at the top of the door before opening up.

"Samantha," she said, looking at her watch, "what a nice surprise. Come on in." She stepped aside so I could enter.

I started to turn right toward the sitting area where we'd met last time, but once the door was shut she led me in the other direction, through the kitchen at the back of the house. "Have a seat," she said, gesturing toward the padded stools surrounding a generous island at the center of the room. "Can I get you something? I'm terrific with take-out leftovers."

"No, I'm fine. Thank you."

"You sure? Tuna niçoise salad from the Pasta Company. It's my favorite, and there's still half a salad left."

"No, I'm sure."

"Suit yourself," she said. "So what happened in court today? I tried talking to Townsend a few hours ago, but he wasn't saying much, and quite frankly what he had to say wasn't making much sense. The defense is arguing that Clarissa took a bribe?"

"More than just an argument. The Attorney General's Office is going to look into the possibility."

Her dismay appeared genuine. "Townsend didn't say anything like that. He said something about a continuance on Jackson's case because of what happened today in court, but nothing about an Attorney General investigation."

"Did Clarissa ever mention Larry Gunderson or Gunderson Development to you?"

She shook her head.

"It looks like Clarissa had some kind of arrangement with Gunderson on an appeal he had before her."

"I can't believe Townsend didn't tell me this. He probably knew I'd go ballistic at the mere suggestion of such a thing."

"I think you might know more about this than you've been willing to admit, Susan."

She looked at me as if I were kidding. Then, in case I missed the look, she said, "You're kidding me, right?"

"Nope. No more kidding, Susan, and no more protecting Townsend and Clarissa or even yourself. I know what's been going on, and it's time for people to start owning up. If you were involved somehow, we'll work something out. I can help you. But you'll be a lot better off telling me what you know before someone else beats you to the punch."

"Samantha, honestly, I have no idea what you're talking about."

"Well, I do. I know, for example, that a woman named Jane Wessler was helping developers get special-use permits for projects in the Railroad District. And I know that when Wessler left and Gunderson found himself without a permit, Clarissa made sure he got one. And I know that in exchange for all this help, developers were contributing to Townsend's hospital wing, the project you were helping him with."

"If Townsend convinced Clarissa to do something like that, he certainly didn't tell me about it."

"Come off it, Susan. I know how much you've helped him with the fund-raising. You told me you'd never heard of Larry Gunderson, but who's Diane Curtin? And what's the MTK Group?"

She clearly wasn't used to being confronted this way. I was reminded of days back in law school, when students would come under fire by a probing professor. But like any good student, Susan regained her composure and presented a rational, coherent response.

"That's what this is about? The MTK Group? That's a company run by some of Herbie's old business buddies. And, yes, I did hit them up on Townsend's behalf, and, yes, they responded generously. I'm good at fund-raising. That is, after all, why I was helping Townsend."

"And what about Diane Curtin? And what about the MTK Group's Railroad District projects?"

She laughed. "If you think I have any idea what Herbie's friends actually *do* to earn the money I help them spend, you are terribly mistaken. As for Diana Curtin—"

"Diane," I corrected.

"Whatever. It sounds familiar, but you're going to have to give me more information."

"You told me you hadn't heard of Gunderson—"

"And I hadn't—until just now, that is," she said.

"Diane Curtin's his daughter, and she and her husband, Thomas, are also among your generous contributors."

"Well, that explains where I've heard of her, then."

"So why don't you tell me why Gunderson's daughter just happens to write a fifty-thousand-dollar check to Townsend days before Clarissa rules in his favor?"

She looked at me incredulously. "I like you, Samantha, I really do. But you are seriously pissing me off right now."

I shook my head and had to laugh. It was hard not to like her back. "Not a nice feeling, is it?"

"No, it's not," she said, laughing as well. "I don't know what you think I know, but you're totally off base. And you're lucky I'm not easily offended."

"And you're lucky I'm not either. There are too many coincidences here. I think you knew Gunderson through Herbie and his friends, and that you might have thrown Clarissa and Townsend his way when Gunderson didn't get the license he needed. If we get this squared away, it doesn't need to be messy. But if it drags out, you can bet that Jackson's defense attorney will do everything he can to haul each and every one of you into court."

She looked at me, mulling over what I'd said. "There might be something, but it's not what you're suggesting, at least not my part of it. In fact, I didn't even realize the possibility of it until just now when you were talking about MTK."

"So explain it to me."

"What about Townsend? He'll lose everything. His hospital appointment, his reputation. He could even lose his license."

"And all that's still going to happen if this comes out at Jackson's trial. But if we take that road, Jackson might go free."

She swallowed before she spoke next. "Gunderson," she said. "You say there's some connection between him and MTK?"

I nodded.

"About a year ago, Carl Matthews—he's the president of MTK—"

I nodded again.

"You *have* done your research," she said. "Carl Matthews and Herbie were friends from way back, and when Carl and his wife had a party about a year ago, I took Townsend and Clarissa so Townsend and I could talk up the new hospital wing to Carl. There were a ton of guests there. Maybe Gunderson was one of them. Townsend could have met him then."

I pulled the photograph of Gunderson from my briefcase.

"Maybe he looks familiar," she said. "It was quite a while

ago, and I really wasn't paying attention, but he might have been there."

So much for a conclusive ID. "Was your husband involved in MTK?" I asked, tucking the photo away.

"Sure," she said, seeming to assume that I'd already known. "He was the K. Matthews, Tykeson, and Kerr. The boys made lots of money back in the day. Tykeson's retired, and Herbie's gone, of course, but the letters live on through Carl."

"So are you part of the company then?"

"Oh, God, no. The estate handled all that stuff, but Carl essentially bought Herbie's interest in the company after he died."

"Did you know that MTK had a judgment against Gunderson's old company 'back in the day,' as you say?"

That seemed to take her by surprise. "Like I said, I've never heard of Gunderson. But I can see why you said there were so many coincidences here. Maybe I was wrong about that dinner party, then. I can't imagine Gunderson would pal around with someone who sued him, right?"

"Not unless they've put the bad blood behind them. The judgment was taken right before Gunderson filed bankruptcy. I guess he's worked his way up since then."

"Well, that makes a little more sense. I mean, if a guy's going to file bankruptcy, it doesn't hurt if his partners are at the front of the line."

I hadn't thought about it from that perspective before. If someone knew he was about to go under, high-dollar civil judgments against him would help soften the blow for his business buddies by helping them recover at least some of the money through the bankruptcy court.

"I can give you Carl Matthews's phone number," Susan offered. "I'm sure he wouldn't mind talking to you about Gunderson."

"Susan, I just got done telling you Matthews might also be part of this."

"Or maybe he's not," she said. "You won't know until you ask him, will you?"

No longer on the defensive, Susan Kerr was back to taking care of everybody. She was jotting down a phone number from the Rolodex on her kitchen counter. "I can also print out a list of all of the donors I know about for the hospital project."

"Sure," I said. "I've got one already, but yours might be more up-to-date."

"And I've got a bunch of Herbie's old files and books and things downstairs if you've got any interest in them. Who knows, maybe he's got something on Gunderson, right?"

She started toward the basement, and as I trailed behind her down the stairs, I wondered when the tide had shifted. Talking to Chuck, I had been convinced that I would be leaving this house with a cooperating witness, armed with the substantiated facts I'd need to build a case against Gunderson and whoever else was involved. Now, I was tiptoeing through Susan's basement, trying not to lose one of my fancy new shoes in the construction chaos, on my way to leaving with nothing but yet another pile of documents. How did that happen?

I checked out the basement while Susan began dredging through some old file cabinets in the corner, pulling out piles of paper and stacking them next to her. From what I could tell, she was completely refinishing the place into a home gym and a walk-in wine cellar.

"Wow," I said, peeking in. "There must be room in here for a thousand bottles."

"Twelve hundred actually. Go ahead. Check it out."

I stepped into the room, stroking the smooth mahogany cubbies. "This is amazing," I said.

"Ridiculously overindulgent," she said, looking back at me. "But Herbie and I had always talked about it, and since I was redoing the basement anyway, I figured it was time to go nuts. Cute shoes, by the way."

I looked down at the pointy-toed mules Grace had convinced me to buy the other night. They weren't exactly practical, and I was still figuring out how to walk in them, but they were definitely cute.

"Thanks. Nordstrom anniversary sale," I said, still proud of my little purchase.

"Best sale of the year." She was stacking more and more documents next to her, and I was wondering how I'd ever carry them out, let alone read them. "Clarissa and I always went on the very first day. Annual tradition."

"So what happened this year?" I said, running my fingers up and down the mahogany stemware shelves.

"Nothing. We splurged just like always."

"Well, you must not have gotten enough, if you went back again last Saturday."

"Right," she said, after a second. "But we did that half the time anyway. You know, you exercise a little bit of willpower, but three days later you've just got to go back and buy everything you left behind."

It all sounded good, but I'd registered that telling pause. Susan was lying.

I quickly changed the subject. "So do these things really help keep the wine fresh, or is it just for show?"

"A little bit of both." I half listened to her explanation about air seals, ventilation systems, and temperature controls, but I was still trying to figure out why her pregnant pause about the Saturday afternoon trip to Nordstrom seemed so meaningful. Still playing with the smooth shelves, I realized what I'd been missing all along. I had assumed a lecture from Duncan was the worst thing that could happen to me by confronting Susan Kerr, but I'd been wrong. I needed to get out of here. Immediately.

But I was too late. The door swung shut behind me, and I heard a lock slip into place. "Sorry, Samantha, but you've got shitty timing. Ten minutes later, and I would've been on my way to the airport. But, as it turns out, I've got a flight to catch, so you're going to have to wait right here."

I banged the palm of my hand against the door. "Susan, don't do this. My God, you just told me this room was airtight."

"And it is. But you haven't given me a lot of choices here. And don't try to tell me that if I open the door you'll let me go."

"You're scaring the shit out of me!" I yelled into the door. "I promise, I *will* let you go. I'll wait two hours before I tell anyone. You're talking about my *life*."

"Forget it, Sam. We both know that's not in your nature. Hell, if you were that easy, I could have just paid you off and I wouldn't have to run."

"Don't run, Susan. We can work out a cooperation agreement. You can start over."

"Yeah, right," she scoffed. "That's how all this shit began. Those last few years with Herbie, I took care of everything, and I did it my own way. Starting over, as you say. I distanced myself from his old friends and all of the wheels they grease to get ahead, and guess what?" She was no longer talking to me, so I didn't bother answering. "That's right, by the time Herbie died, we were flat busted. I couldn't go broke; everyone would know. A few calls to Gunderson and Matthews, and I was back in the black. It was so easy, but then everything fell apart."

"I understand, Susan. I know how much Clarissa meant to you, and you've got information to trade. Just let me out of here."

The sound of my voice seemed to knock away any remorse she had started to feel.

"If I were you, Sam, I'd try breaking off some of those wood strips. Maybe you can wedge them through the seal at the bottom of the door and buy yourself some time. Otherwise, I'm told you've only got about fifteen minutes."

Bizarre. Even at this moment, there was Susan Kerr, trying to be helpful. Without any other options, I followed her advice. I tried pulling on the thin strips of wood that made up the stemware holders but couldn't get enough torque to break them. Then I adopted a different strategy, hooking the heel of my shoe on a rail of wood running along the floor and stepping on it with all my weight. After a few tries, my body weight won, making me grateful for those eight pounds I can never quite drop.

I crammed the jagged edge of the broken wood beneath the cellar door, wiggling and pushing the rail until I felt the tight rubber seal around the door begin to give about it. Outside, I could hear Susan making trips up and down the stairs, probably removing from the house whatever documents she had taken from the files.

"Oh, hey, there you go, Sam. Looks like it's working. You keep at it. Get your head down by the floor if you need to." This woman was the Martha Stewart of murderous lunatics. I had an image of her as an aerobics instructor at the Mac Club, cheering clients on in the same way.

I broke another piece of wood and wedged it a few inches from the other one, trying to create a large enough gap to get some air in. I tried to convince myself that I was only out of breath from the physical exertion, but I was beginning to panic.

I lay flat on the floor, getting my nose and mouth as close as I could to the small crack I had made beneath the door. I started to relax when I was sure that I could feel air coming in from the basement. I took a few deep breaths and felt my pulse slow from pounding to a moderate race.

I told myself I was going to be OK. I had air, and I was

patient. But then I wondered just how patient I would need to be. The footsteps on the stairs had stopped. If Susan had left for her flight, when would anyone find me? Chuck was expecting my call, but he had no idea where I'd been heading. If he went to bed assuming I'd blown him off, would anyone come in the morning? For all I knew, Susan had told her housekeeper and contractors to take the week off.

I needed to find a way out of here.

I kicked my shoes off and climbed on top of a shelf, holding on to the bottle slots for balance. I knocked on the wood panels on the ceiling, listening for any hollow space above, but I never did have an ear for such things. Explains why I can never buy a good melon. I raised both hands above me and pushed as hard as I could. The panel didn't give, but I couldn't tell if it was because the wine room ceiling was built against the ceiling of the original basement, or simply because I hadn't pushed hard enough to pop the panel up.

I tried again but felt light-headed after the push. It might have been my imagination, but I could have sworn I was running out of air.

I jumped back down to the floor, taking another series of long, deep breaths. It definitely helped. I'd rest a little more, then try the ceiling again.

Just when I'd regained my balance on the shelf again, I heard more footsteps in the house. These sounded like they were on the floor right above me. Then I heard a voice. I couldn't make out what the person was saying, but from the low register, I was pretty sure it was a man. I pounded my fists against the ceiling, yelling at the top of my lungs. I hopped back down for a few more breaths, then climbed up and made some more noise.

As I heard movement on the basement stairs again, I began pounding on the cellar door.

"Samantha, baby. Is that you?"

This time the voice was right on the other side of the door, and tears welled in my eyes when I recognized it. Then I heard metal against metal, but I kept listening to my father's voice telling me not to worry, that everything would be OK. And I knew he was right.

My father's grip was so tight, I thought I had a better chance at oxygen in the wine room.

"I'm so glad I found you. I knew it. When Chuck told me you were out with a witness, I felt it in my gut. I got here as soon as I could, and I knew something was wrong when I saw her leaving."

"Dad, wait. I've got to stop her." I took the stairs two at a time and used the kitchen phone to call 911. "My name's Samantha Kincaid. I'm a deputy in the Major Crimes Unit at the DA's office, and I was just kidnapped by a woman named Susan Kerr." The dispatcher was trying to cut me off so she could do the usual Q and A format for these calls. I kept on talking right over her. "Kerr's a white female, shoulder-length dark brown hair, approximately forty years old. About five-seven, one hundred and twenty pounds. I'm calling from her house, but she left here for the airport about ten minutes ago to flee the jurisdiction. I don't know what airline. You need to get officers out there right away to stop her. MCT knows who she is, and I'll page them directly. Don't bother sending an officer to the house; I can file a report later."

I hung up, knowing that she could play back the tape if she missed any of the information.

My next call was to Chuck.

He was happy to hear my voice. "Thirty minutes on the dot. You ready for margaritas?"

If only. "Susan Kerr killed Clarissa Easterbrook. She locked me in her basement and is on her way to the airport. You've got to get out there right now. I'll call Johnson too and tell him to hook up with you." Chuck lived in northwest Portland and would be a few minutes behind Susan, but if Ray was at his house in north Portland, he might actually beat Susan to the airport.

"Whoa, back up, Sam. She locked you in the basement?"

"Yes, but I'm fine. I guess you told Dad where I might've gone, and he showed up"—I still didn't know why, I realized—"and let me out."

"Wait a second, I didn't tell your dad anything. And how do you know she killed Clarissa?"

"Please, Chuck. I'm begging you. Just go to the airport, find her, and hook her up for kidnapping me. I'll explain the rest later. Now go. Don't let her get away."

"All right, I'm going right now. Love you."

"You too," I said, hanging up before either of us had even realized what we'd just said to each other.

I didn't have time to savor the moment. I needed to call Johnson so he could back up the man I loved.

I gave him the same bare-bones explanation.

"Wait a second. She locked you in the basement?"

Chuck had asked the same question. Why did everyone find it so hard to believe?

"Yes, in a wine cellar her construction workers were putting together. The thing's airtight. I was lucky to get out alive."

"And she's on her way to the airport?"

"That's what she said. Maybe she meant to throw me off, but it's all we've got."

"I'm leaving right now. We'll hold her on the kidnap. And, Sam, don't worry about a thing. That crazy bitch had better hope patrol finds her before Chuck and I do."

When I hung up, I saw that my father was standing in the doorway waiting. "They're going after her?"

I nodded and exhaled.

"So, Dad, obviously I'm grateful," I said, smiling expectantly, "but what exactly are you doing here?"

"You ran off from the house so suddenly, and you had that glint in your eye. I was afraid of whatever you might try stirring up. Then Chuck called looking for you, and I assumed he'd catch you at your place. But then when he called again and said you'd gone out on a witness interview—I don't know, I felt like I needed to find you. It was just a hunch, but I thought I'd at least check."

"But how'd you know to come—"

"I'm going to get to that. I'm just telling you what I saw. When I turned the corner, I saw her carrying bags out to the car, even though your car was obviously still there. I knew right then that something was seriously wrong. If I'd been packing, I would have stopped her, but I was more worried about you."

"Well, thank God. The last thing we need is another Kincaid shoot-out." He smiled, but I could tell he was mad at himself for letting her get away. "Dad, you did the right thing. Chuck and Ray will get her."

"Yeah, you're probably right."

I looked at him, waiting for him to get to the rest of the explanation. "Dad, you still need to tell me what's going on. How did you know to come *here*? What do you know about Susan Kerr that you haven't told me?"

I could tell he was trying to find a way to say it to me. He was finally ready to talk.

16

IT WASN'T EASY for my father to get through his story; I had to prod him along occasionally like any reluctant witness. But as I finally understood it, my father's concern about my involvement in the Easterbrook case began the morning of the first press conference, which he had caught on the local news.

He recognized the woman standing near the podium, the one in the light blue suit. He never knew her personally, but the man she eventually married had changed the course of his life back when she was probably still a teenager. Given the connection, he couldn't help but notice their marriage announcement and the occasional reports about their many community activities that followed over the years. Yes, the woman in the blue suit on the television was definitely Mrs. Herbert Kerr.

As an Oregon State Police officer in 1979, he found himself pulling escort duty for Representative Clifford Brigg. Brigg would ride in the back of Dad's highway patrol car, using the time to read the paper, confer with other bigwigs, or occasionally sneak in a round of footsie with his large-breasted, short-skirted so-called legislative aide. He paid little attention to my father, but my father paid plenty of attention to Brigg. It was his job.

On a sunny afternoon in July 1980, my father drove Brigg to Salem from a press event in downtown Portland to announce the groundbreaking of a new office building. As usual, Brigg was multitasking, this time meeting with major campaign supporter Herbert Kerr during the ride. Watching the two discreetly in his rearview mirror, Dad saw Kerr slip an envelope to Brigg. From the way Brigg stuffed it into his coat pocket, my father concluded that the deal was rotten.

Others would have let it drop, convincing themselves that it was either none of their business or nothing to worry about. Or perhaps they'd seek cover before talking, reporting the observation to a supervisor or perhaps anonymously to the press, happy to let someone else steer the course. But not my father.

The next time he had Brigg in the car to himself, he made the mistake of confronting him. I don't know how my father expected Brigg to react. Maybe he was naive enough back then to believe he'd come clean and return the money. But, instead, Brigg denied any wrongdoing. He gave Dad a choice. He could let the matter slide, in which case Brigg and his cronies would make sure he worked his way straight up the OSP ladder. Or he could repeat the story, in which case Brigg's legislative aide was prepared to file a complaint that my father had groped her.

My father's face tightened at the memory, his palms working the edge of the kitchen table where we sat. "You should have seen his girlfriend when she told me later the things she was willing to say if it came down to it. These were truly ugly people, Sam." Herbert Kerr would back up Brigg's denial, and my father's career would be ruined.

The arguments he had with my mother were not, as I had inferred, about his hours or the physical dangers of police work. The truth was that they didn't see eye to eye about Clifford Brigg and his threats.

To my father, the choice he'd been given was no choice at all. He wanted to blow the whistle, career be damned. He'd work as a janitor if he had to.

"And Mom?" I asked.

One look at his face, and it all became clear to me. Mom was a good woman, about as good as they're made. But she and Dad didn't always approach the world from the same perspective. She loved my father, but part of her probably wished he'd earned more money or recognition. She was ecstatic when I announced my engagement to Roger, while my father feigned acceptance. And, although she never said as much, she no doubt wondered how different her life would have been if she could have quit teaching and pursued her passion for painting.

Dad didn't need to fill in the blanks. My mother must have wanted him to play the game and accept Brigg's deal.

But instead, my father hung up the state system and found a quiet, humble job with the federal forest service. He told my mother about his decision only after he had given notice at OSP. He hoped Brigg and Kerr were smart enough to see the move as a sign that he planned on going silently, and he had been right. He never heard another word about it.

"Not from him, at least," I had said.

He did his best to explain that my mother's concerns were for me. She didn't believe Dad could run away from the problem. And since he wouldn't be able to convince anyone that he'd seen something suspicious, he might as well get what he could out of Brigg and Kerr.

But for my father, the decision wasn't about pragmatism. Brigg was forcing a choice between the two most important components of his character—dedication to his family, and an unwavering commitment to good over evil.

My father had found a third way. He should have been proud. He had avoided accepting the favors of corrupt men like Brigg and Kerr, and he had refused to let martyrdom destroy his reputation and family. But to him, his departure from OSP felt cowardly—an easy way to tell himself that he'd rejected a deal with the devil, without actually confronting Brigg. It was the kind of moral equivocation he despised.

When he saw Susan Kerr on television that Monday morning, the unfairness of the choice Brigg had given him and the shame of his response came flooding back. His instinct was to save me. If someone was going to stumble onto the secrets of someone like Clarissa and her friends, Dad reasoned, let it be someone other than his daughter. His family had paid their dues.

I felt a wave of anger. I had suspected all along that someone was blackmailing Clarissa; if he'd shared his story about Brigg and Kerr earlier, I might have made the connection to Susan instead of spinning my wheels all week. Maybe I hadn't been particularly forthcoming with details of my own about the case, but it would have been easy enough for him to bring me into the loop.

I understood why he'd been struggling, though. From his perspective, the pit in his stomach had seemed irrational, a sour remnant of his own mistakes. Why, after all, should he have assumed that a woman who married Herbert Kerr years after his own encounter with the man was herself corrupt? Nevertheless, his instincts were what they were—and he'd been right.

My plan was to call information to find the closest Pasta Company, but then I had a better idea. I pulled the garbage can from beneath the kitchen sink. On top of the heap lay a take-out bag with the receipt still inside. Tuna niçoise salad, just as she'd said.

I used Susan's phone to call a sergeant I knew at central precinct. He agreed to send a patrol officer to meet me at the restaurant with the pictures I needed.

Pulling out of the driveway, I waved to Dad in my rearview mirror. He followed me to the bottom of the west hills, letting loose a final honk before going his own way.

At the light at Fourteenth and Salmon, I paged the medical examiner, Dr. Jeffrey Sandler. We'd never worked together before, so I had to explain who I was and what I was calling about before we got down to business. But then the business was quick.

"Just how sure are you on the time of death?" I asked.

"Time of death's never as certain as they make it sound on TV shows. You draw inferences from the forensic evidence, but in the end, it's exactly that—an inference. I often tell people that in my thirty-eight years of experience I've only seen one case where I could pinpoint the exact moment of death. And that was because the defendant unplugged a clock from the wall and used it to bash in the victim's skull."

For a disgusting story, it was actually pretty cute.

"So what about Easterbrook? You calculated time of death based upon her stomach contents?"

"Exactly. By the time she was found, her body temperature was already down to the ambient temperature at the crime scene, so her liver temperature was of no use. Rigor mortis had already come and gone, which would normally signal at least thirty hours postmortem, usually more like thirty-six."

"But she was found Monday afternoon, putting her death at Sunday morning, not Sunday afternoon."

"You're still assuming more precision than exists. I said it would normally be thirty-six hours or so, but change the facts and it could be entirely different. Say, for example, there was significant physical exertion immediately before death. Through the exertion, the victim's already depleting her body of the chemical that keeps her muscles relaxed. So the stiffness sets in sooner, quickening the entire process."

I could see why the DAs all said that Sandler was a pro on the witness stand. No jargon or scary science stuff.

"Here," he explained, "we got lucky. Once Johnson told me he knew what time the victim ate lunch, I went by that instead. Death stops digestion. Based on the state of her stomach contents, she died an hour or two after she ate."

"What if Johnson was wrong about the time?"

"It's just like any other system of inferences. Garbage in, garbage out."

"Is it possible she died Saturday night?" I asked.

"Sure. Like I said, this isn't down-to-the-minute stuff, especially once you're past the first twenty-four hours. To reconcile the physical state of the corpse with what Johnson told me about the victim's lunch on Sunday, I had to make certain assumptions, like the physical exertion before death that I mentioned early. I also assumed she was kept somewhere warm, which was consistent with what we knew about the body being moved. With the very same state of deterioration, sure, the death could have occurred on Saturday, especially if the body were kept in a relatively cool atmosphere."

I had a feeling I knew exactly where that cool spot was.

When I pulled into the Pasta Company parking lot, a young patrol officer was already waiting for me. I still had a quick call to make, though. I dialed into my voice mail box at work and jotted down Russ Frist's home telephone number.

I got lucky. Unlike most of the lawyers on the office homicide call-out list, Frist apparently didn't screen his evening calls.

"Russ, it's Samantha Kincaid."

"You better not be calling me to give notice."

"That depends on how you react to what I'm about to tell you." I spelled everything out for him. "Johnson and Forbes are on their way to the airport, but I need you to get together with Calabrese and Walker for a search warrant for Susan's house. Make sure the judge approves destruction if necessary. I've got a feeling the crime lab will find blood evidence beneath a wine cellar she's got going over there."

"And where are you off to?" he asked.

"To get you the rest of the evidence you're going to need for that warrant."

The dinner rush was over by now, so I was able to walk right up to the hostess desk. Unfortunately, when I got there, the two girls at the counter felt free to ignore me while they finished discussing the pressing issue of the day—whether the new waiter had been checking out Stacy, another hostess who was supposedly a "skank." Given that these two appeared to have all skank bases covered, that was saying a lot.

I waited patiently until the one with the hoop through her navel made eye contact with me, but they immediately resumed chatting. I resisted the temptation to grab the edge of the other girl's purposefully exposed thong underwear and deliver the mother of all wedgies. Instead, I got their attention by using my District Attorney badge.

"Hey. Girls. I need the two of you to plug back into the world that doesn't revolve around you and pay attention. Were either of you working a week ago Saturday night?"

They rolled their eyes at each other to be cute, but they at least seemed to be listening. "We both were," said Thong.

"Yeah, Saturday's like totally crazy around here." Belly

Button obviously thought I was like totally clueless for so not knowing that.

I showed them the DMV photographs of Clarissa and Susan that the officer from central precinct had run for me. "Do you remember seeing them in here together?"

The idea of doing something that might get someone else in trouble seemed to appeal to them and they actually took a close look at the photographs. Unfortunately, their facial expressions remained completely vapid. Nope, not the slightest bit of recognition. On the other hand, these girls probably paid little attention to women outside of their age range of competition.

I was reaching for the photographs when one of the waiters stopped by to complain that the hostesses had put too many screaming kids in his section. When he noticed the badge I was still holding, he leaned in to take a look at the pictures.

"Cool, man. You got some *Matlock* action going on here or what?" He pushed his long highlighted bangs from his forehead to get a closer peek.

"Are you even old enough to remember that show?" I asked.

"Syndication, señorita."

"And I apparently remind you of Andy Griffith?"

"Sure, if he was a little younger with a knockout fem bod."

I know, I'm a total hypocrite. You take all those characteristics that infuriate me in a teenage girl and bundle them together in a nice-looking boy package, and I'm done.

"I was hoping someone here might recognize these women from last weekend," I said, pointing to the pictures.

"Yeah, I remember those birds. That one was pretty well preserved for her age, if you know what I mean," he said, gesturing toward Clarissa.

This one definitely had a thing for mature women. God bless him.

"Do you remember what day that was?"

"Not exactly. But if it was last weekend, it was Saturday. Sunday's for wind surfing. Yeah, that definitely could have been Saturday. I remember it was the lunch menu, and I don't work days except Saturday."

"Do you remember what time?"

"Weekend lunch menu's good till four, and I don't come in until two. You do the math."

"Do you remember what they ordered?"

He laughed and pushed the hair back again. "I don't have nearly that many brain cells left."

When you looked like this guy, you probably didn't need them. "Is it possible the well-preserved one had linguine with browned butter?"

"Yeah, might have been something like that. 'Cause I remember the other one saying something bitchy about the pasta. She was one of those salad-with-the-dressing-on-the-side types. You chicks can be terrible to each other, you know?"

He had no idea.

It wasn't the perfect ID, but it was enough for probable cause. I called Russ as soon as I left the restaurant.

Before I even made it to the precinct, I got a call from Chuck. "We found her on a flight roster for American Airlines, outbound to JFK. She had a one-way ticket to Portugal."

"Otherwise known as one of the last few lovely retirement areas that puts up a fuss about extraditions. So you've got her?"

"It took a fight, but we finally convinced the airline to hold the flight. We're bringing her in now."

"Is she talking?"

"Not yet. Ray's putting her in the car. We figured we'd wait until we got her in the box downtown."

Once they had her in a holding room, Russ and I watched the questioning through a one-way mirror. Susan played it cool. According to her, she "might" have gotten tied up in a scheme Townsend had with Gunderson, but Chuck and Ray were nuts if they thought she'd do anything to hurt Clarissa.

Then Walker called my cell with some preliminary feedback from the search at her house.

"I don't know how you figured it out, Kincaid, but it's just like you said. We found a copy of the video of Clarissa and Caffrey. It was right there in the entertainment center with a bunch of yoga tapes. And the lab guys are saying there's some seepage in the concrete beneath that wine room. It could definitely be blood, but it's going to take awhile to confirm it."

"No sign of those documents I saw piled next to the file cabinet in the basement?"

"Nothing." Johnson didn't find them in Susan's car either. She must have dumped them somewhere on her way to the airport.

"Sorry you can't be here for the questioning," I said. "You might've gotten a second chance at catching the look."

"Yeah, right. That's OK, as long as I get to see a different kind of look—the look on Jackson's face when we release him. I feel like shit we had the wrong guy; every cop's worst nightmare, right?"

"Should be. But you didn't know, Jack. Susan Kerr sent us off track from the very beginning."

"Well, you did real good, Kincaid."

"Thanks," I said, flipping my phone shut so I could pass the word on to the rest of the team.

Russ and I watched Johnson and Chuck break the news to Susan. She'd already met the nice Ray at her house, so Chuck was playing the bad cop. If I hadn't been so nervous, it might have been fun to watch his performance.

The MCT guys were pros. They told her about the videotape first, reeling her in with questions about the bribery scheme before confronting her with the murder.

"It's not what you think," she said, changing to a resigned tone. "This was all Townsend and Gunderson. Townsend found out about Clarissa's affair and used it to guilt-trip Clarissa into ruling for Gunderson in exchange for the hospital donation."

Like all coconspirators, she was spinning a version that undoubtedly shifted the blame from herself but which nevertheless contained some undercurrent of truth.

"So what was the videotape for?" Chuck asked. "And what were you doing with it?"

"Clarissa brought it over here a couple of weeks ago to show me. She must have left it. Townsend initially had it made to get an upper hand in the divorce, but then he told her he'd mail it to Caffrey's wife unless she convinced Caffrey to vote in favor of development in Glenville. I guess Gunderson stood to make a lot of money, and Townsend would be rewarded in kind."

"Could that be it?" Russ asked me.

I shook my head. "If Gunderson and Townsend hooked up at a cocktail party and reached this one-time deal to help Gunderson's Railroad District project, how would Gunderson even know that Clarissa could get to Caffrey? Or if Townsend's the one who thought of this, how would he know that Gunderson had investments out in Glenville? It doesn't make any sense."

"So what's your theory?"

"Susan's the link. She pretends she's a trophy widow, but she learned everything she knows from Herbie. I think she, Gunderson, and MTK are all still in bed together. They were bribing Jane Wessler at the city for the Railroad District licenses. When

Wessler went on maternity leave without giving Gunderson his permit, Susan turned to Clarissa. I always thought it was weird that Clarissa hadn't told Susan about her relationship with Caffrey. I think she did, and that her best friend turned around and used it to convince her that she owed this to Townsend. Then even that wasn't enough. She got that videotape and told Clarissa she'd mail it to Caffrey's wife if Clarissa didn't deliver Caffrey's vote."

Back in the holding room, Susan's explanations continued to contain just enough truth to confirm at least part of what I suspected. Chuck and Ray had broken the news to her about the blood in the basement.

Her demeanor changed again, and this time she feigned sadness for the loss of her friend. She even managed to shed some tears. "It wasn't me. It was Townsend. Clarissa called me Saturday, completely hysterical. I guess she told him that morning that she wasn't going to go along with Gunderson anymore. If they were going to mail the videotape, she was willing to go to the police. She was over here telling me about it when Townsend showed up. They went down to the basement to have a private conversation, and the next thing I knew there was yelling. It sounded like a terrible struggle. I ran downstairs." Her voice cracked for effect. "Oh, my God, I couldn't believe it. Townsend told me I had to help him, or he'd tell everyone I'd been in on it. I realized how it would look. My house, my husband's old business partner—I panicked."

"You didn't panic." Chuck spoke quietly, but was convincingly disgusted. "You went shopping, Susan. You went and picked out an outfit to dress your dead friend in, so it would look like she died Sunday. You hired carpenters for a fucking remodel. Don't lay this all on Townsend."

I made a mental note to have a handwriting analyst check the charge receipt for Clarissa's purchases last Saturday at

Nordstrom. My guess is that the signature would be close, but not quite right. I was also pretty sure that, as much as Susan had joked about Clarissa being the reluctant shopper, we'd find out that Susan hadn't bought anything for herself that day.

"But it was his idea," Susan was insisting. "He's the doctor. He's the one who cooked up this whole thing about using the food in her stomach. You tell me, how could I come up with that myself? I still don't even understand it."

Russ poked me in the side with his elbow. "She's got a point there."

I nodded. "Sure. Townsend came up with the idea of throwing us off with the take-out container from Sunday, but she's still the doer. You met Townsend. It had to have been the other way around. Clarissa confronts Susan; Susan kills Clarissa and then tells Townsend he'd better help or she'll pin it all on him."

"It would certainly explain why the guy's been a walking corpse. But what about the poly?"

"He passed it because of the questions." I told him about the transcript of Townsend's interview. He was asked if he'd been at the hospital Sunday, if he killed Clarissa, and if he hired, solicited, ordered, or asked anyone to kill her. But they neglected to ask the money question: "Do you know who killed your wife?"

Chuck was asking Susan to walk them through the rest of the plan.

"Townsend called Gunderson to come over for Clarissa's . . . to get Clarissa," said Susan. "He came over and took Clarissa to the Glenville property, then stashed the hammer at Jackson's."

"And how would Gunderson know that Jackson had a grudge against Clarissa? Your story's not adding up." Chuck did a better bad cop routine than most. His tone struck the perfect balance between anger and dismissiveness.

"She's cooperating, OK?" Johnson said.

Susan looked at Johnson. She probably recognized the routine, but she played along anyway. "Townsend told him about Jackson."

"And Jackson just happened to work for Gunderson? Wrong again, Susan."

"Clarissa got Gunderson to give Jackson a job. I told you she felt sorry for the guy. I think she was probably trying to turn what she'd done into some kind of good deed. Karma and all."

"God, she's good," I said.

"Maybe," Russ said, "but I still can't believe she hasn't lawyered up."

I shook my head and smiled. "That's because you don't know Susan Kerr. She thinks she's way too smart for all of this. She's been manipulating people her whole life, getting away with it every time. And she probably figures, Hey, she's a woman, she's in here first; she'll be the one to get the deal. She's convinced Gunderson and Townsend will go down, and she'll waltz out with a few months of local jail."

"That's not going to happen, is it." It wasn't a question.

"No way," I said.

"Ready to call Duncan?"

"Let's do it."

It took a good forty-five minutes, but we finally laid it all out for the boss.

"And you think we've got PC for Townsend and Gunderson?"

"I do," Russ said. "We've got a coconspirator implicating Townsend directly in the murder, and at the very least she's implicating Gunderson in the cover-up. Add the circumstantial evidence of the various connections between everyone, and we've got enough for warrants."

"Start working on search warrants," Duncan said, "but call their lawyers and give them an hour to turn themselves in."

"What?" I screeched into the speakerphone. "You've got to be kidding. This is a murder case, Duncan."

"No shit, Samantha. But we're not dealing with a bunch of gangbangers here. You don't need a perp walk on this one. They'll turn themselves in."

"Right," I said. "Just like Susan Kerr did. In case you forgot, we pulled her off a plane after she tried to kill me."

"Don't be dramatic. She locked you in a room," Duncan argued.

I looked at Russ and shook my head. "Yeah, Duncan, without any *air*."

"Look, Samantha. You're new to this. We let guys TSI all the time, even in murder cases. Russ, if you're worried about it, call the airlines and make sure they know not to let these guys fly out. But giving them an hour's not going to kill anyone."

If only he'd been right.

When the deadline came, Gunderson was there with Thorpe, but Roger had been stood up. We dispatched cars immediately, but we were too late. Townsend Easterbrook was dead.

17

A WEEK LATER, I attended the funeral with Chuck and my father.

I don't know why I went or why I made anyone come with me. Maybe because death was still new to me. Or maybe part of me actually felt sorry for him.

Susan Kerr may have tried to put all the blame on Townsend, but in the end he had the last laugh. He had found one decent concluding act to his life. He left a note. He'd probably written it as the final dose of painkillers settled in, but I was confident it was reliable. Unlike most coconspirators, Townsend no longer had a reason to point the finger at others. He just wanted, finally, to tell the truth.

These are my words, not his, but the truth went something like this: Townsend Easterbrook had believed that building the pediatric wing was the most important accomplishment of his life. He knew he'd earned his position more for his administrative skills than his healing ones, and the new wing was his way of securing a legacy at the hospital. Several months earlier,

Susan Kerr had offered to help, and Townsend had happily accepted. The money came rolling in.

But then, on the Friday before Clarissa's death, he discovered the deal's strings. Clarissa sat him down and told him that, in exchange for Susan's generosity, she had rigged a decision in favor of a company in which Susan had an interest. She said she'd done it to help the hospital wing and out of loyalty to Susan, but now things had gone too far. Susan was asking her to do even more, and Clarissa planned to say no. The money would dry up.

Townsend told her to put her foot down. Screw Susan. They'd build the wing without her.

But that's not what happened. Clarissa left the house to meet Susan on Saturday for lunch. A couple of hours later, Townsend got a call. Something was wrong with Clarissa, Susan said. He needed to come over.

When he got there, Clarissa was dead, lying in a pool of blood in the basement. Susan claimed that Clarissa had tried to destroy some documents and attacked her when Susan put up a fight. According to Susan, it was self-defense.

While Townsend was still reeling, Susan said she'd blame it all on him if he told anyone Clarissa had been with her that day. The documents detailed the connection between Clarissa's thrown case and the donations to the hospital project. Townsend would lose everything. Then she told him something he'd never even suspected—Clarissa had been cheating on him. Guilt over the affair was the reason she'd been willing to fix Gunderson's case in the first place. Susan even had a videotape to back the story up.

Because Clarissa had died shortly after lunch, all they needed to do was make sure her body wasn't found for a day or so, and make it look as if she'd eaten her Saturday meal on Sunday. As a doctor, Townsend knew some of the rules about determining time of death—"garbage in, garbage out," as Dr. Sandler had put it.

Townsend ensured that the police found a fresh take-out container in the house by using a short break between surgeries to dash to the nearby Pasta Company. He'd also set up the initial call-out by leaving Clarissa's loafer to be found in the gutter, and dropping Griffey, on his leash, along Taylor's Ferry Drive. Susan had taken care of the rest. She'd shown up at the house Saturday night with an empty Nordstrom shopping bag to put in Clarissa's dressing room. She told Townsend she'd make sure the body wasn't found until Monday. He realized that the medical examiner would figure out her clothes had been switched, but it didn't seem to bother investigators. And when the evidence against Melvin Jackson came out, he assumed that Susan must have set up the plan ahead of time. By then, he was too out of his mind on OxyContin to figure a way out.

He'd been considering suicide for days, but Roger's call on Monday night had sealed the deal. He took the pills, wrote his letter, placed a plastic bag over his head, and let go of the situation. Whether we'd get the note in at trial remained to be seen, but I knew in my heart it held all the answers.

The services were modest, arranged as a courtesy by Dr. and Mrs. Jonathon Fletcher. Townsend's death had made headlines, as had Susan's arrest and Jackson's release, but so far the official explanation for his suicide and its relationship to those other events was under wraps.

Clarissa's family chose not to attend. From what Tara had told me, she and her parents were still coming to terms with the idea that Clarissa had been killed by people they'd treated as family. The only eulogists were Townsend's professional acquaintances. They remembered his commitment to patients and his love for Clarissa, careful to keep their comments general enough that they reflected a relationship that once *was*.

Roger found me in the lobby of the funeral home. I told Chuck and Dad I'd meet them in a second.

"I'm surprised you came," he said.

I shrugged.

"I hope you realize that I didn't know," he said. "If I had—"

"Don't worry about it. I know. I was fooled too, remember?"

"I should have sensed it, though. I could have talked him into coming forward."

"Really, Roger, you don't need to say anything. It's fine."

We stood there awkwardly while he searched for something else to say.

"So Jackson's out, huh?"

"Released last Wednesday," I said. "Took a couple days, but he couldn't be happier." He hadn't been the only one. Mrs. Jackson was waiting in the lobby with Melvin's kids. She burst into tears with the first look at her freed son, and before long we all lost it. Walker insisted the sniffle I overheard was from allergies, but I knew better.

"Is the poor guy still getting evicted?"

"Some people are working on it." Dennis Coakley of all people was intervening with HAP to hammer out an agreement for Melvin and the kids to stay in public housing.

"So how does your case look?" How strange that after our years together, this conversation would be like any typical one between lawyers.

"Not too bad," I said.

"Let me know if there's anything I can do to help you lay the foundation for Townsend's letter. I was the last one to talk to him, I guess."

"All right, thanks."

"You've probably got enough evidence without it. Jim Thorpe's been keeping me up to date," he said by way of explanation.

Gunderson had already cut a deal for three years on bribery and abuse of corpse for helping Susan move the body. It was a gift, but, in the end, we were never able to prove he'd been in on the murder. In exchange, he had delivered the goods. Gunderson had come to suspect that Susan wasn't quite as loyal as his old pal Herbie and recently began taping their conversations. The recordings of Susan telling Gunderson to hire Jackson a week before the murder and to come to her house the night Clarissa died would be gold at trial. Add the documents he had confirming Susan's investment in Gunderson Development, and we had motive to go with opportunity. As for means, we'd ask the jury to infer from the blood in the house that she had hit Clarissa in the head and then planted the hammer at Jackson's.

"We'll see, right?" Roger knew me too well not to sense the impatience in my voice.

"I'm holding you up. Just humor me on one more question: Was it premeditated?"

Gunderson had confirmed that Susan was the one who asked him to hire Jackson, but we knew Clarissa was trying to find a job for Melvin. Susan may very well have made the request on her behalf. And from what our shrinks were telling us about Susan, she was far more likely to kill in a rage triggered by what she saw as Clarissa's betrayal. The more closely we looked into her background, the more stories we were hearing like the one Grace had told me about Susan burning her husband's favorite humidor. My best guess was that, in Susan's screwed-up mind, she'd done Clarissa and Townsend a favor by hooking them up with Gunderson.

"I don't think we'll ever know," I said, "but my gut tells me it wasn't."

"Well, you've always had good instincts." More awkward silence. "So I'll see you later, I guess."

"Yeah, maybe."

He stopped me before I walked out. "I know it's not my business, but I couldn't help but notice that you came with Forbes."

I followed the direction of his glance to Chuck and my father in the parking lot. "You're right. On both counts."

He nodded. "I guess the two of you always were close."

"Uh-huh." It wasn't the most articulate response, but talking to my ex-husband about my boyfriend was awkward, to say the least.

"You know, Sam," he said, "it might not matter to you anymore, but I do feel bad about what happened between us."

So that's what he'd been hemming and hawing about. As if "what happened" had involved both of us?

"If it makes it any easier, she didn't even mean anything to me."

I looked at the floor while I summoned my patience. There was nothing to gain by fighting him. "I always knew that, Roger. And that's why I couldn't stay with you."

I left him then, wondering if I'd ever get over the fact that a man who loved me as much as he knew how to love another person had thrown it all away for someone who hadn't even mattered.

Outside, I was greeted by the sun for the first time in weeks. Dad put his arm around me. "You OK there?"

"I'm good," I said, walking to the car. "Less sad than I was a few hours ago. Maybe it's because the rain finally stopped."

"Maybe," he said. He gestured to the lobby. "What was that about?"

I paused, wondering the same thing. "Nothing that mattered. We talked about the case a little." I looked at Chuck and smiled.

"You mean the case where you're the star witness?" I could always count on Chuck to lighten the mood.

"That would be the one." I was still off the case—I couldn't testify and prosecute—but Russ had assured me I could help plan the trial. Looking Susan Kerr in the eye and giving evidence against her would be even more rewarding than sitting first chair.

If my first two weeks in MCU were any indication, my first major trial would come soon enough. In the meantime, I was happy to wait it out.

Author's Note

Striking the optimal balance between fact and fiction is a real writing challenge. Readers notice when a defendant gets off on inconceivable grounds or when the cops get a warrant with nothing approaching probable cause. And not only do they notice, they feel cheated. On the other hand, too much loyalty to reality makes for dry novels.

Samantha Kincaid's life is based on fact. Unless I mess it up, you won't find her making nonexistent objections or prosecuting laws that would never make the books. Along the way, I even ask for help to make sure I've got my facts straight. For the answers, I thank Larry Lewman, Deputy State Medical Examiner for the State of Oregon; Multnomah County Deputy District Attorneys Josh Lamborn, Jim McIntyre, and John Bradley; and Hofstra Law School professors Nora Demleitner and Matt Bodie. If I bungled something they told me, it's my fault, not theirs.

The smart growth plan at the heart of *Missing Justice* is also based on fact. When Samantha Kincaid describes Portland's urban growth boundary as the "secret ingredient in Portland's warm gooey cinnamon bun," she speaks from my heart. I did, however, exercise some artistic license. The legislation creating Portland's urban growth boundary is not called the Smart Growth Act; the Metro Council is not just a part-time gig; and there is neither an Oregon suburb called Glenville nor a Portland neighborhood called the Railroad District, let alone a development licensing program based in it. In other words, the book's still fiction.

And a better book it is thanks to the continued dedication and talent of Jennifer Barth, Maggie Richards, and John Sterling at Henry Holt. Their support, hard work, and creativity have made all the difference, and I'm forever grateful.

About the Author

A former deputy district attorney in Portland, Oregon, ALAFAIR BURKE now teaches criminal law at Hofstra Law School. The daughter of acclaimed crime writer James Lee Burke, she is a graduate of Stanford Law School and currently lives in New York City. Missing Justice is the second in the Samantha Kincaid series.